STRAVAGANZA
City of Flowers

Mary Hoffman

BLOOMSBURY

Published by Bloomsbury Publishing, New York, London, and Berlin
Distributed to the trade by Holtzbrinck Publishers

The Library of Congress has cataloged the hardcover edition as follows:
Hoffman, Mary.
Stravaganza: city of flowers / by Mary Hoffman. — 1st U.S. ed.
p. cm.
Sequel to: Stravaganza, city of stars.
Summary: Seventeen-year-old Sky joins Georgia and the other Stravaganti, "who travel
between worlds and do what is required," when he leaves London for Giglia, a city
similar to renaissance Florence, and becomes involved in ancient feuds and palace intrigue.
ISBN–10: 1-58234-887-1 • ISBN–13: 978-1-58234-887-2 (hardcover)
[1. Space and time—Fiction.] I. Title: City of flowers. II. Title.
PZ7.H67562Su 2005   [Fic]—dc22   2004055445

ISBN–10: 1-58234-749-2 • ISBN–13: 978-1-58234-749-3 (paperback)

Printed in the U.S.A. by Quebecor World Fairfield
1 3 5 7 9 10 8 6 4 2

Bloomsbury Publishing, Children's Books, U.S.A.
175 Fifth Avenue, New York, NY 10010

All papers used by Bloomsbury Publishing are natural, recyclable products made from
wood grown in well-managed forests. The manufacturing processes conform to
the environmental regulations of the country of origin.

Acknowledgements

Franco Cesati's book *La Grande Guida delle Strade di Firenze* and Franco Cardini's *Breve Storia di Firenze* were indispensable, as were Christopher Hibbert's *The Medici* and *Florence*. My thanks to Carla Poesio and, as always, Edgardo Zaghini, for reading the first draft, and other invaluable support. Ralph and Elizabeth Lovegrove advised on fencing and other matters. My long-suffering family endured a month of my absence in Florence, shouldering my share of the domestic load, particularly Stevie. Matteo Cristini told me wonderful things about the history of Florentine art. Santa Maria Novella and its Officina Profumo-Farmaceutica were as magical as always and an obvious destination for a Stravagante. Thanks to my editor, Emma Matthewson, who has always liked this book best, and to all the many fans who email me on the Stravaganza website, urging me to make things happen between Luciano and Arianna; I have done my best.

For Jessica, maker of potions and expert on Giglia

'Non v'è città al mondo che non senta, nel bene e nel male, il peso del suo passato.'
Franco Cardini, *Breve Storia di Firenze*, 1990

('There is no city in the world which does not feel, whether for good or ill, the weight of its past.')

'Non ha l'ottimo artista alcun concetto,
ch'un marmo solo in sè non circonscriva
col suo soverchio; e solo a quello arriva
la man che ubbidisce all'intelletto.'
Michelangelo Buonarotti

('The greatest artist does not have any concept which a single piece of marble does not contain within its excess, though only a hand that obeys the intellect can discover it.'
Poem 151 in Christopher Ryan's translation,
J. M. Dent, 1996)

'È necessario a uno principe, volendosi mantenere, imparare a potere essere non buono, e usarlo e non l'usare secondo la necessità.'
Niccolò Machiavelli, *Il Principe*, 1513

('For a ruler, it is necessary, if he wants to stay ruler, to learn how not to be good and to use this power, or not, according to need.')

Contents

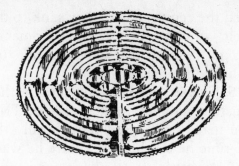

Prologue: *Walking the Maze*

In a black and white striped church in the north-west of the city, a friar in a black and white robe was waiting his turn to step on to a curious pattern set into the floor. It was a labyrinth made of strips of black and white marble contained roughly within a circle, and friars came and went along it, tracing the pattern with their footsteps. They walked in silence, but other friars were softly chanting plainsong from the choir stalls. It was early in the morning and the church was empty, save for the friars, weaving their silent patterns, moving past one another in the circle.

There were eleven circuits between the outside edge and the centre, but each was so folded into loops that the friars seemed to be thwarted in their goal the closer they got to it. Still, every few minutes one or two reached the centre, where they sank to their knees in heartfelt prayer for several moments before continuing on the path that led them out to the edge again and back into the world.

Brother Sulien was the last to step on to the maze. It was his custom and his right as Senior Friar. Sulien walked the maze even more thoughtfully than usual and by the time he reached the centre he was the only one left. The other friars had gone about their business, some to feed the fish in the cloister pool, some to dig carrots and others to tend vines. Even the members of the choir had dispersed, and Brother Sulien was left alone in the uncertain dawn light of the church's cool interior.

He knelt stiffly in the centre, on a circle surrounded by six lesser circles arranged like the petals of a flower. At the very heart was an inlaid figure that the friar's robe concealed. Indeed, an early morning visitor to Saint-Mary-among-the-Vines would scarcely have been able to see Sulien either, his hood cast over his face, kneeling in stillness at the centre of the maze.

After a long meditation, Brother Sulien rose, said 'Amen' and started the slow return out of the maze to his daily life. So began every day for Sulien, but there was something different about this one. At the end of the ritual, he pulled a threadbare carpet over the pattern, as usual, but instead of walking back through the Great Cloister to his work at the Farmacia, he sat in a pew, considering the future.

He thought about the threat to the city of Giglia and how there was trouble brewing. The great di Chimici family, on whose wealth the city floated, was busier than usual. The Duke had announced the forthcoming weddings of several younger members of the family, including his three remaining sons, all to their cousins. And no one doubted that there was more to these marriages than love.

It was common knowledge that the Duke had organised a spreading network of spies throughout the city, led by a ruthless agent of his known only as l'Anguilla, the Eel, because of his ability to get into and out of tight corners. The spies' purpose, both here and in other cities, was to sniff out all that could be known of a certain brotherhood or order of learned men and women – scientists, some people said, though others said magicians. Brother Sulien shifted on the hard wooden pew at the thought of this order, of which he was a member.

The di Chimici were resolutely opposed to the brotherhood and suspected that it was behind the resistance to their plans to expand their power throughout Talia. Duke Niccolò also believed that this brotherhood was responsible for the death of his youngest son, Prince Falco, less than a year ago. The young prince, horribly injured in a riding accident two years before, apparently committed suicide while staying at the di Chimici summer palace near Remora.

But everyone knew that the Duke believed it was murder – or perhaps something worse. Some said that the boy's ghost walked abroad, others that he was not really dead at all. When Duke Niccolò returned from Remora with his son's body, the whole city was shocked by the change in the Duke's appearance: he had aged by years and now bore a head of white hair and his beard was silver.

The funeral of Prince Falco had been a mournful if

splendid affair; the Duke had buried him in the chapel of his palazzo near the city's centre and the great Giuditta Miele herself had carved his memorial statue.

But Sulien knew that Giuditta's next commission was to come from Bellezza, the independent city-state in the Eastern lagoon. Its ruling Duchessa, the lovely young Arianna Rossi, was rumoured to be coming to Giglia for the di Chimici weddings. Despite her city's fierce resistance to all the di Chimici's attempts to overcome its independence, she was surprisingly friendly with the Duke's third son, Gaetano. He was one of the betrothed and so the Duchessa had accepted the invitation because of him.

Sulien was familiar with Bellezza, since he had only recently come from a religious house near the lagoon city to take over the friary at Saint-Mary-among-the-Vines. He saw the danger to the young Duchessa. The city of Giglia would be fuller than usual of strangers and visitors during the period of the weddings and it would be hard to afford the Duchessa the protection she needed. Indeed, he was a little surprised that her father and Regent, Senator Rodolfo, had agreed to it.

Now he gathered up the skirts of his robe and strode off to the Farmacia, as if he had come to a decision. He walked through the tranquil Lesser Cloister, with its series of chapels, and on to the Great Cloister, where a door opened into the first room, his laboratory.

As always as he climbed the two stone steps into his domain, Brother Sulien breathed its fragrant air with relief and joy. Things in the city might change but here, in Saint-Mary-among-the-Vines, certain things remained the same – the maze, which always brought calm, and the perfumes and medicines distilled here in the Farmacia now newly under his guardianship.

He passed through the laboratory, where two young apprentices, in the robes of novices, were bent over the distillery equipment. After the briefest of greetings, he took himself into his inner, private room, hardly more than a cell, and sat at his desk. He was writing a list of recipes for all the perfumes, creams, lotions and medicines made here in the monastery's church. Not forgetting its famous liqueur and the secret of making drinkable silver.

Now he pushed the parchment to one side and sat gazing at a small blue glass bottle with a silver stopper which he had taken from a shelf. Beside it he placed a silver cross, which he usually kept locked in a carved wooden box. He looked at the two thoughtfully. Then, 'It is time,' he said. 'I shall go there tonight.'

Chapter 1

A Blue Glass Bottle

Sky woke, as usual, to the smell of flowers. But it was stronger than usual, which meant that his mother was up and uncorking bottles. This was a good sign; perhaps she would work today.

Heaving Remedy, the cat, off his feet – another good sign because it meant he must have already been fed – Sky made his way to the kitchen and found his mother spooning coffee into the cáfetière. She looked bright, with a rather hectic flush on her cheeks.

'Hey, Mum. Morning,' he said, giving her a hug.

'Morning, lovely boy,' she said, smiling fondly at him.

'Why didn't you wake me? It's late.'

'It's only half past seven, Sky.'

'Well, that's late,' he said, yawning. 'There's a wash

to do before school.'

'Already on,' said his mother proudly, pouring the just-boiled water on to the coffee. Then her mood changed abruptly and she sat down at the table. 'It's not right that a boy your age should have to worry about housework,' she said, and Sky saw the telltale glitter of tears gathering in her eyes.

'Now, none of that,' he said, deliberately heading her off into a different mood. 'What's for breakfast? I'm starving.'

He didn't want one of those heavy 'We're all each other has got' scenes so early in the morning. His mother couldn't help her illness, which was so erratic that some days, like today, she would seem normal, and on others she couldn't even get out of bed to go to the bathroom, which meant he had to tend to her most private needs.

And Sky didn't mind looking after her; it was true that they were all-in-all to each other. Sky's father had never been around, except on CD covers and concert posters. Rainbow Warrior, the famous black rocker of the '80s, had been interested in fair, shy Rosalind Meadows for all of one night and that was all it took.

When Rosalind found she was pregnant, her best friend, Laura, who had dragged her to the Warrior's concert in the first place, wanted her to have an abortion, but Rosalind couldn't bear the thought. She dropped out of university and went home to brave her parents' wrath.

Although her parents were strict Plymouth Brethren they were surprisingly understanding, even when the baby turned out to be chestnut brown in colour (she hadn't said a word about his father). But when Sky was eighteen months old, they had suggested she might be happier in London, where a very pale-skinned blonde with a brown baby might attract less attention than in a sleepy Devon village. Not attracting unnecessary attention to oneself was something Rosalind's parents considered to have the force of an Eleventh Commandment.

So she had packed her bags and her baby and arrived in London with the deposit on a flat in Islington, a diploma in Aromatherapy and no other means of support. Her greatest consolation was that Laura was also in London, working as an MP's secretary, and she would often babysit while Rosalind built up some contacts in the evening with people who wanted aromatherapy.

'After all,' Laura would say, jiggling Sky inexpertly on her lap, 'he wouldn't be here at all if I hadn't taken you to that concert in Bristol.' Rosalind never mentioned that Sky wouldn't be there at all if she had followed Laura's other suggestion too.

When Sky was two, Rosalind wrote to Rainbow Warrior, feeling stupid about not knowing how to address him. In the end, she just wrote:

Dear Rainbow,
I don't suppose you remember me but I was at your concert in Bristol in '87. Your son, Sky, is two years old today. I don't want anything from you, only for you to know that he exists and to have this address, in case you ever want to get in touch with him. I enclose a photo taken a few weeks ago.

She hesitated. Should she put 'love from'? It was a

common enough empty phrase but she didn't want him to get the wrong idea, so she wrote 'Yours sincerely, Rosalind Meadows'. The letter was sent care of the Warrior's agent and marked Personal and Urgent, but the agent took no notice of that; women were always putting that sort of thing on letters to the Warrior. And it was definitely from a woman; the envelope smelt of flowers.

'Hey, Colin,' he said, waving the letter when he next saw his famous client. 'It seems you've been sowing some more of your wild oats.'

'Don't call me that,' said the singer irritably, snatching the envelope, 'and don't open my personal correspondence – how often do I have to tell you?'

Gus Robinson was one of the handful of people in the world who knew that the great Rainbow Warrior, famous across four continents, had been born Colin Peck on a council estate in Clapham Junction.

The Warrior sniffed the envelope, read the formal little letter, looked at the photo and smiled. That 'Yours sincerely' got to him the way no hysterical tear-stained diatribe would have done. Yes, he remembered Rosalind, so shy and so smitten. And the little boy was cute.

'You should get that letter framed,' said Gus. 'So you can prove she said she doesn't want any of your dosh.'

'Mind your own business,' said the singer, and that night he wrote a letter of his own, not very well-expressed and full of spelling mistakes but enclosing a huge cheque, which he could easily afford.

Rosalind had been stunned and wanted to send the money back but Laura convinced her otherwise.

'It took two, didn't it?' she demanded. 'And he should have been more careful. It must have been obvious that a goose like you wouldn't even have been on the pill.'

'But he says he doesn't want to see Sky,' said Rosalind, her tears spilling down her cheeks.

'So much the better,' said Laura firmly. 'Take the money and run.'

In the end Rosalind had used the money to pay off her mortgage and return her parents' loan; there was no denying how useful it was. She wrote to the singer again, saying that she would send a photo of their son every year, on his birthday. This time Gus Robinson didn't open the letter or all the other sweet-smelling envelopes that came from her once a year, but handed them to his richest client without a word.

Rainbow Warrior had been married three times and had fathered eight children, but no one knew about the brown-skinned laughing boy and his fair mother, except for the singer himself and his agent. And between them the subject was never mentioned.

Nor was it often mentioned between Sky and his mother. When he was old enough to understand, she showed him a picture of his father, in *Hello!* magazine. He was getting married to wife number four, a leggy Colombian model called Loretta. There were lots of children at Sky's primary school whose parents had split up, so he was not particularly disturbed by the photos of the tall dreadlocked singer and his new wife; they seemed to have nothing to do with him.

Rainbow Warrior felt much the same each year as he looked at the latest photo of his secret son. But he kept them all. Sky didn't know that his mother sent pictures of him to his father. There was a period of some months around his thirteenth birthday when he rowed with Rosalind almost every day and once threatened to find his father and go and live with him, but these violent feelings eventually went away and soon after that Rosalind fell ill.

It was the flu, and she stayed in bed for a week, with a fever and a cough that no amount of hot lemon and honey brought relief to. The week turned into months and that was when Sky began to learn how to look after himself and his mother.

ME, said the hospital doctor to Rosalind after months of visits to the GP and being told to pull herself together. No treatment – only time and rest. That had been nearly three years ago and sometimes Rosalind still couldn't get out of bed in the morning. After a year, Sky took his courage in both hands and wrote, without telling his mother, to the famous Rainbow Warrior:

Dear Mr Warrior,
I am your son and I am worried about my mum.
She has been ill for a year. Can you send her to see a
top doctor? By the way, what she has got is called
ME. She is NOT imagining it.
Yours sincerely,

Sky Meadows

He sent it to a venue where the Warrior was appearing and he never got a reply. We can manage without him, he thought bitterly. We always have done and we always will.

'When Papa dies, I shall be Duke Fabrizio the Second,' said the little prince to his tutor. He had been six years old at the time and had got a thorough spanking for it. That was how he first knew dying was a bad thing, though at the time he had only been repeating what his nurse had told him.

Now, as Prince Fabrizio walked along the gallery of his father's palace, a tall and handsome twenty-three-year-old, he felt he had learned the lesson all too well. The walls were hung with portraits of di Chimici, the living and the dead, among the latter his mother, Benedetta, and his youngest brother, Falco, taken from them so cruelly only a matter of months ago. Fabrizio stood in front of this picture for a long time.

The likeness had been made before Falco's accident and showed him standing straight and proud, very conscious of his lace collar and holding a sword that scraped slightly on the ground; he had been about eleven then.

Fabrizio was in no doubt that his brother's death would hasten his father's, though he was no longer in a hurry to become Duke Fabrizio di Chimici the Second. He felt much too young to be both head of the family and in charge of all the schemes his father had put in place. Now he wished he had been one of the younger sons and without such a weight of responsibility to look forward to.

But he squared his shoulders and resumed his walk. At least he could accede happily to one of his father's plans. Fabrizio was to be married soon to his cousin

Caterina. And she was his favourite of all the cousins, from the time they had played games together as children at the summer palace in Santa Fina. A smile played round Fabrizio's fine mouth as he thought of Caterina.

That was the one good thing to come out of poor Falco's death – he refused to think of it as suicide – all the di Chemici weddings. His two remaining brothers were to be married at the same time and his cousin Alfonso, Duke of Volana, too. There would be hardly any unmarried di Chimici left – apart from fussy little cousin Rinaldo – and it was clear that his father Duke Niccolò wanted them all to get on with breeding his descendants as fast as possible. Well, Fabrizio was willing; Caterina was a pretty and lively girl and he had no doubt she would produce a superior crop of heirs.

Sky passed a day at school that felt almost normal. He was used to being in the sixth form now, but he had never quite felt part of the school and had no close friends there.

The trouble was, he looked the part of someone cool and trendy and he knew that lots of girls were initially attracted to him. He was tall for his age and he wore his gold-brown hair in dreadlocks. But he didn't listen to any kind of rock music. It reminded him too much of his father. Rosalind sometimes played the Warrior's CDs, which were the only ones she had that weren't classical or folk, and it made Sky almost literally sick.

He used not to care about his father but, ever since the singer had ignored Sky's letter, written from the heart of despair, he had begun to hate the very idea of him. He knew that the Warrior's music was having a fashionable revival at the time, because it had featured in a film that broke box office records, but Sky didn't see the film and he never told anyone of his connection with the singer.

If he could have been interested in football, he might have felt less of a fish out of water at school. He had the physique for it but just couldn't raise the enthusiasm. He supposed it was because he had more important things to think about. He probably wasn't the only student at his school looking after a sick parent; he'd read an article once about how many carers there were under the age of sixteen – really small kids like nine-year-olds, looking after parents in wheelchairs.

Well, he was better off than they were; he was seventeen, and his mother wasn't ill all the time. But he didn't know anyone else in his position and he felt set apart, somehow marked. And it showed. Gradually, the friendly overtures had tailed off and the girls wrote him off as useless too.

There was just one girl, though, quiet and fair, whom he really liked, and if she had ever shown any interest in him, things might have been different. But she was inseparable from her fierce friend with the dyed red hair and tattoo, so Sky never got up the courage to talk to her. Still, they were all doing English AS, so at least they were in some of the same classes.

It didn't take Sky long to reach home, since his flat was in a house right next to the school. He dawdled, wondering what he would find there, whether his mother would still be feeling OK or back in bed unable to move. But he was quite unprepared for what he did find. On the doorstep to their flats stood a small blue glass bottle, with a silver stopper in the shape of a fleur-de-lys. It was empty and incredibly fragile, just sitting there on the step, where anyone might knock it over.

Instinctively, Sky picked it up and took out the stopper; a heavenly smell wafted out of it, more delicious than anything in his mother's store of oils and essences. Was it meant for her? There was no message attached to it.

He let himself in through the front door and then into their ground-floor flat. Rosalind had sold the one that the Warrior had paid for and bought this smaller one less than a year ago because she couldn't manage stairs any more. The newly converted house still smelt of fresh paint and plaster. That and the smell of flower essences greeted Sky's return.

'Mum,' he called, though she would have heard his key in the lock. 'I'm home!'

She wasn't in the living room or the tiny kitchen, and he knocked on her bedroom door with a sick feeling that something terrible had happened to her. But she wasn't there and when he went back to the kitchen, he found her note:

Gone to supermarket; there won't be any biscuits till I get back.

Sky smiled with relief; when had she last been well enough to go shopping on her own? That was usually his job, every Wednesday afternoon after school, lugging plastic carrier bags on to the bus and then putting everything away. His mother must have taken the car, though; she couldn't have managed on the bus.

Sky took the damp wash out of the machine, put it in the tumble-dryer, washed up the breakfast things from the morning and looked in the cupboards to see what he could make for dinner. Normally, he would make a start on peeling potatoes or chopping onions, but he thought he'd better wait and see what his mother brought back with her; maybe she had planned something.

He fed Remedy, because the tabby rescue cat was in danger of tripping him up by twining round his legs, then made himself a cup of tea and sat down at the table, where the little blue glass bottle stood looking innocent and at the same time significant. Remedy leapt on to the chair beside him and started washing. Sky sighed and got out his school books and read a short story for French.

Sandro was delighted with his new master. Everyone knew about the Eel; he was becoming a figure to be reckoned with in Giglia. He now had dozens of spies working for him and bringing information back to the di Chimici palace from all over the city and beyond. It was just the kind of work Sandro enjoyed, following people and hanging about eavesdropping on their private conversations. He would have been happy to do it for nothing.

Sandro was small and quick-witted and completely inconspicuous, one of those many young boys, none too clean and a bit ragged, who hung about the busy places of the city, hoping for a few cents in return for running errands. But actually he had silver in his pockets, expenses paid to him by the Eel, because he might need to buy a drink for an informant or offer a small bribe for information.

Now Sandro was tailing one of the Nucci clan and it couldn't have been easier. Camillo Nucci was so obviously on his way to an assignation that Sandro had to stifle a chuckle; the young bravo in the red cap kept looking over his shoulder as he walked past the di Chimici's grand new building of Guild offices off the main piazza and across the stone structure that was still called the Ponte Nuovo, even though it had been built two hundred years before.

A lesser spy might have lost the Nucci on the bridge, with its crush of people, its butchers' shops and fishmongers and chandlers. But not Sandro. He had guessed where his quarry was headed, anyway – the half-built palazzo on the other side of the river. The Nucci family, the only one anywhere near close enough in wealth to rival the di Chimici, had started building their grand palazzo five years before and it was still not finished.

But, if it ever was, it would be much bigger than the Ducal palazzo on this side of the river, and that bothered Sandro; he was a di Chimici man through and through. It stood to reason that his masters must have the best, the biggest and the grandest of everything. Take the coming weddings; weren't the young princes and their cousins to be married in the great cathedral by the Pope himself, their uncle Ferdinando, who was coming specially from Remora to conduct the most lavish ceremony the city had ever seen?

Camillo Nucci had reached the walls of his father's palazzo-to-be and was talking to his father and brothers. Sandro saw to his surprise that the second storey was nearly complete; it wouldn't be long before the Nucci palace was finished after all. But why was young Camillo making such a mystery of his evening stroll, since he was joined only by other members of his family? Nothing remarkable about that. But Sandro followed them into a nearby tavern anyway.

And was rewarded by seeing them joined by a couple of very disreputable-looking men. He couldn't get near enough to hear their talk, unfortunately, but he memorised every detail of their appearance to tell the Eel. His master was sure to be interested.

*

'Do you think this was left for you?' Sky asked his mother when he had unpacked the shopping for her.

Rosalind was looking tired again now and had flopped down on the sofa, kicking her shoes off as soon as she had got in. She looked at the little bottle in his hand.

'No idea,' she said. 'It's pretty though, isn't it?'

'But empty,' said Sky, still puzzled. 'Shall I put it with your other bottles?'

'No, it would outclass all my plastic refillables,' said Rosalind. 'Just put it on the mantelpiece – unless you want it?'

Sky hesitated. It seemed a girly thing to want a blue perfume bottle in his room, but the little phial seemed to speak to him in some way he didn't understand.

'OK,' he said, putting it temporarily on the living-room mantelpiece. 'What shall I cook tonight?'

'How about spag bol?' suggested his mother. 'That's nice and easy and we can eat it on our laps. It's *ER* tonight.'

Sky grinned. His mother loved hospital dramas but always closed her eyes during the gory scenes and operations. You would have thought she'd have had enough of doctors and nurses, but she lapped it all up.

He went away to chop onions and peppers. Later, after they had eaten and Rosalind had seen even less of *ER* than usual, because it had involved a multiple road traffic accident, Sky carried her to bed. She was very light, he realised, and she had fallen asleep before he had time to help her into her nightdress or to clean her teeth.

But Sky didn't have the heart to wake her; he left her on the bed and went to do the rest of his homework. Then he washed up, put out the wheelie bin, folded the dry washing for ironing the next day, changed the cat litter, hung his damp jeans in the airing cupboard, locked up and eventually got into bed at half past eleven.

He was exhausted. How long can I carry on like this? he wondered. True, his mother had been much better that day but he knew from experience that she would be even more wiped out than usual the next day. He started to calculate the ratio of good to bad days she had had recently. Time, the doctor had said, but how long was enough time to make her well again?

If he looked ahead to the next few years, Sky could see nothing but difficulties. His mother wanted passionately for him to go to university and have the chances she had thrown away for herself, and he was just as keen. But how could he leave her, knowing that some days she wouldn't eat or be able to shower or even feed the cat? He envied other boys his age who could leave home in a year or two and go to Kathmandu if they wanted without worrying about their mothers. He'd probably have to settle for a college in London and living at home.

Remedy climbed on to Sky's chest to purr happily. He ruffled the cat's ears. 'Easy being you, isn't it?' he said. Then he remembered the bottle. Despite Remedy's protests, he got up again and fetched it from the living room. He lay in the dark, sniffing the wonderful scent that came from it and feeling strangely comforted. The cat had stalked off in protest; these were not the kind of smells he liked and there were far too many of them in the flat as it was – give him kipper any day.

I wonder where it can have come from? was Sky's last thought before drifting off into a deep sleep, the bottle in his hand.

When Sky woke, he was not in his bedroom but in somewhere that looked like a monk's cell. There was a cross on the whitewashed wall and a wooden prayer desk and he was lying on a sort of hard cot. The bottle was still in Sky's hand and the room was filled with the wonderful smell of flowers, but he knew it wasn't coming from the bottle.

He got up and cautiously opened the door. He found himself in a dark, wood-panelled room like a laboratory, filled with glass vessels like those used in chemistry lessons. But it didn't smell like a lab; it smelled like his mother's collection of essences, only much stronger. Light was coming from a door at the side of the room and Sky could see into an enclosed garden. People in robes were digging in the beds and tending plants. What a peculiar dream, he thought. There was a lovely atmosphere of calm and freedom from pressure.

He stepped out into the sunshine, blinking, still holding the bottle, and a black man, robed like the others, took him by the arm and whispered, 'God be praised, it has found you!'

This is where I wake up, thought Sky, but he didn't.

Instead the man pushed him back into the laboratory and hurried into his cell, bending over a wooden chest.

'Put this on,' he said to Sky. 'You must look like the other novices. Then you can tell me who you are.'

Chapter 2

The Hounds of God

Sky felt as if he were sleepwalking, as he let the monk, or whoever he was, throw a coarse white robe over his head and then a black cloak with a hood. Underneath he was wearing the T-shirt and shorts he had gone to bed in, an odd detail for a dream to include, he thought.

'That's better,' said the monk. 'Now you can walk with me round the cloisters and we can talk without anyone thinking it unusual. They'll just take you for a new novice.'

Sky said nothing, but followed his companion back out into the sunshine. They were in the enclosed garden he had seen from the open door. It was a square shape, surrounded by a sort of covered walk, like the ones you get in cathedrals and abbeys in England.

'I am Brother Sulien,' said the monk. 'And you are?'

'Sky.' He hesitated. 'Sky Meadows.'

It had always been an issue for him, his hippy-dippy name, as he thought of it. And it was even worse combined with his mother's surname; it made him sound like a kind of air freshener or fabric softener.

'Sky? That isn't a name we use here,' said Sulien, after considering it. 'The closest would be Celestino. You can be Celestino Pascoli.'

Can I really? thought Sky. What sort of game are we playing? But still he said nothing.

'You have the talisman?' asked Sulien, and Sky realised he was still holding the little glass bottle. He opened his fist. A strange feeling was beginning to creep over him that this was not exactly a dream, after all.

'Who are you?' Sky asked finally. 'I don't just mean your name.'

The monk nodded. 'I know what you mean. I am a Stravagante – we both are.'

'You and me?' Sky asked disbelievingly. He couldn't see how he and this mad monk, as he was beginning to think of him, could both be anything the same at all, except human beings and black.

'Yes, we are both part of a Brotherhood of scientists in Talia.' The friar stepped out into the garden, gesturing Sky to follow. 'Look behind you.'

Sky turned and saw nothing.

'What?' he asked, confused.

Sulien gestured to the ground and Sky saw with a shock that, although the friar's shadow stretched out behind him, black as his robe, at Sky's feet there was nothing.

'The talisman has brought you here from your

world, because there is something you can help us with,' continued Sulien.

'What, exactly?' asked Sky.

'Exactly what, we don't know,' said Sulien. 'But it will be dangerous.'

*

The night before, Sandro had stayed with his quarry until he was sure there was nothing more to be gained, then strolled back to his side of the river. A short walk through the great Piazza Ducale, where the government buildings were, brought him to the left flank of the cathedral. He felt more comfortable when he could see Santa Maria del Giglio; her bulk was reassuring and the little streets and piazzas snuggled up to her like kittens seeking the warmth of a mother cat.

Sandro felt himself to be one of those kittens; he was an orphan, who had grown up in the orphanage that stood in the lee of the cathedral. Clever as he was, and resourceful too, Sandro had never learned his letters or expected to enter any profession, so he had been delighted to be recruited by the Eel.

Now he could afford to throw a few small coins to the ragamuffins who played in the street outside the orphanage even at this late hour. He had been one of them not so long ago and it made his heart swell to think how far he had come.

He stopped in the little square where people played bowls; he had a ghoulish interest in it because of the horrible murder that had happened there a generation ago. One of the di Chimici had stabbed one of the

Nucci to death; that was all the boy knew, but it fascinated him. He imagined the blood staining the paving-stones and the cries of 'Help!' as the young nobleman bled to death under the flickering torches of the piazza. Santa Maria had not been able to protect him. Sandro shuddered enjoyably.

He walked on past shops and taverns selling all kinds of delicious-smelling food and drink, feeling secure in the knowledge that he would get supper. He cut up the Via Larga, the broad street leading away from the cathedral towards the di Chimici palace. The Eel didn't live there, of course; Duke Niccolò was too canny for that. But he wasn't far away, either. He lodged close enough to the Duke to be with him in minutes if sent for.

*

'Why don't I have a shadow if we are both Strav . . . what you said?' asked Sky. 'You seem to have one.'

'I have a shadow because I am in my home world,' said Brother Sulien. 'When I stravagate to yours, as I did to bring the talisman, I am without one, just as you are here.'

Sky was beginning to understand that he had travelled in space, and almost certainly in time, but he still couldn't quite believe it. Brother Sulien explained that they were in a great city called Giglia, in the country of Talia, but it looked to Sky as he imagined Italy to be. He couldn't speak Italian, yet he understood what Sulien was saying to him – at least he understood the words; the meaning was still impenetrable.

'What do you mean by helping you?' he asked, trying another tack. 'What can I do?'

They had walked, slowly, all the way round the square cloisters, back to where they had begun, and stopped by the door into the laboratory. Again Sky felt overwhelmed by the scent coming from the room.

'What is this place?' he asked. 'Some sort of church, or what?'

Brother Sulien gestured to him to resume their walk. 'It is a friary – Saint-Mary-among-the-Vines. We have a church, certainly, a most beautiful one, which is reached through the Lesser Cloister, but also an infirmary and a pharmacy, of which I am the friar in charge.'

'Is that the same as a monk?' asked Sky. He felt very ignorant about all this. He had only ever been in churches with his mother, as a sightseer.

Sulien shrugged. 'More or less,' he said. 'It depends what order you belong to. We are Dominicans. "The Hounds of God", they call us. "Domini canes" is Talic for God's hounds.'

'And that laboratory?'

'Is where I prepare the medicines,' said Sulien. 'And the perfumes, of course.'

'Of course,' said Sky, ironically.

Brother Sulien gave him a quizzical look, but just then a bell started clanging in the tower above them and all the other friars, as Sky supposed they were, downed tools and set off towards an archway in the corner.

'Time for prayers,' said the friar. 'The Office of Terce, but today I shall miss it and take you out into the city. I want to show you something.'

The Eel was feeling pleased with himself. He had comfortable lodgings, ample pay and the best of everything to eat and drink. Most satisfactory of all, he had power. As the Duke's right-hand man, he felt himself to be only a heartbeat away from the very seat of government. And it could so easily have gone the other way; he had at one time feared that Duke Niccolò would dispose of him by having his throat cut, after that business in Remora. Instead he now wore velvet, in his favourite blue, and carried a hat with a curling plume in it, and kept a horse of his own in the Duke's stables.

In fact, the Eel did not cut as impressive a figure as he thought, being short and a bit skinny. But he was well pleased with his new life, especially his little crew of spies. He liked Giglia better even than Remora, and much better than Bellezza. In a very short time, he had memorised its streets and squares and alleys, particularly the alleys – the Eel was an alley kind of fellow, even if he aspired to boulevards and avenues. You couldn't skulk in an avenue and skulking was his forte.

*

Brother Sulien led Sky through an archway in the corner of the Great Cloister into a smaller one and then in through a door into the church. Up at the far end Sky could see quite a number of black-robed friars on their knees and could hear the low murmur of voices. His eyes scarcely had time to adapt to the gloom inside the church before they were out in the sunshine again, under a clear blue sky.

Sky inhaled deeply and looked around him. The church fronted on to a large square, at either end of which stood a strange wooden post in the shape of an elongated pyramid. There were no cars or buses or motorbikes, but across the square there was a jumble of poor-looking houses and shops and then, every block or two, a noble building standing impressive among its surroundings like a racehorse in a field of knackered nags. Definitely the past, thought Sky. Then there was the dazzling sunshine which brought a warmth unknown in an English March, sunny though they could be. Definitely Italy, he thought.

They walked briskly along a street whose gutters were overflowing with debris, and Sky couldn't help noticing an unhealthy smell of rotten vegetables and worse. Two young men rode past; they were evidently noblemen, since everyone got out of their way and they paid no attention to their route but chatted to one another oblivious of the people scattering before their horses' hoofs. Sky saw they both wore long shining swords dangling from their belts and remembered what Sulien had said about danger.

A short walk brought them to a halt in front of what was the biggest building Sky had ever seen. It was familiar to him though, from art lessons at school.

'This is Florence, isn't it?' he said, pleased to have recognised where he was.

'I believe you do call it something like that, but for us it is Giglia,' corrected Sulien patiently. 'The City of Flowers, we call her, because of the meadows around that bring her such wealth. Her and the di Chimici,' he added, lowering his voice. Then, more naturally, he continued, 'It could as easily be called the City of Wool, since almost as much of her wealth comes from sheep, but that's much less pretty, don't you think?'

This is like *Alice in Wonderland*, thought Sky. There seems to be logic in it but it doesn't quite hang together.

'And this is the best flower of all,' said Sulien, gazing up at the bulk of the cathedral. 'Even if my heart lies among the vines, I must admire Santa Maria del Giglio – Saint-Mary-of-the-Lily.'

The walls of the cathedral were clad in white marble, with strips of green and pink marble in geometric patterns; Sky thought it looked like Neapolitan ice cream but sensed it would be unwise to say so. Though he noticed that the front was unfinished, just rough stone. A slender bell-tower in the same colours rose beside it, and the whole was dominated by a vast terracotta dome, encircled by smaller ones.

'In this cathedral in eight weeks' time,' Sulien continued, 'three di Chimici princes and a duke will marry their cousins. Now let me show you something else.'

He walked Sky round to a little piazza where people were playing bowls. 'In that square,' said Sulien, 'twenty-five years ago, a member of the di Chimici clan stabbed to death a young noble of the Nucci family.'

'Why?' asked Sky.

'Because of an insult to the di Chimici over a marriage arranged between the two families. Donato

Nucci was to marry Princess Eleanora di Chimici – a fine match for him, but he was twenty and she was thirty-one. And perhaps not one of the most beautiful of her kin, though intelligent, pious and accomplished. On the day of the wedding young Donato sent a messenger to say he was indisposed. Indisposed to marry Eleanora, as it turned out, for he was also in negotiations with another family and another, younger, bride.'

'Poor Eleanora,' said Sky.

'And poor Donato,' said Sulien grimly. 'He had the gall to show himself at a game of bowls the next evening and Eleanora's younger brother, Jacopo, stabbed him in the heart.'

'What happened to Jacopo?'

'He left the city. He had only come to Giglia for the wedding; his family lived in Fortezza, another great city of Tuschia, where his father Falco was Prince. The next year old Prince Falco died and Jacopo inherited the title. Some say the old Prince was poisoned by the Nucci, but he was a good age.'

'And what happened to Eleanora – and Donato's other girl?'

'No one knows what happened to the other girl. Eleanora di Chimici took the veil and so did her younger sister. Jacopo himself married – and had two daughters, one of whom is going to marry Prince Carlo di Chimici here in a few weeks. The other will marry her cousin Alfonso di Chimici, Duke of Volana.'

Sky was beginning to see, among this muddle of names and titles, a pattern emerging.

'Is this Jacopo still alive?' he asked.

Sulien nodded. 'He will give his daughter away to the second son of this city's Duke.'

'And the Nucci lot?'

'Will be invited, of course. They are still one of the great families of Giglia.'

'Phew,' said Sky. 'Could be pretty explosive. But I really don't see why you are telling me all this.'

'Come,' said Sulien, 'a little further.'

They skirted the back of the cathedral. Among the buildings behind it was a busy, noisy workshop, ringing with the sound of chisel on stone. Sulien stopped and looked both ways.

'This is the bottega of Giuditta Miele, the sculptor,' he said. 'She is another one of us Stravaganti. And her next commission is to make a statue of the beautiful Duchessa of Bellezza, who is coming here for the di Chimici weddings.'

'Sorry,' said Sky. 'I still don't see . . .'

'The Duchessa was supposed to marry Gaetano di Chimici, the third prince. Supposed by Duke Niccolò, that is. She refused him, some think because she was too attached to a young man who was her father's apprentice. Her father is Rodolfo Rossi, the Regent of Bellezza, one of the most powerful Stravaganti in Talia. And the young man, his apprentice, did her mother, the late Duchessa, great service, and is now an honoured citizen of Bellezza, but it wasn't always so.'

'No?' asked Sky, because it seemed expected.

'No,' said Sulien. 'He was once from your world, and I think you probably know of him.'

*

Gaetano di Chimici stood in the loggia of the Piazza Ducale and everywhere he looked he saw evidence of his family's influence on the city he loved. They had built the palace that housed the seat of government, with its tower that dominated the square, they had placed the statues commemorating victories of the weak over the strong, and they had built the Guild offices, with their workshops underneath, where silversmiths and workers in semi-precious stones plied their crafts along with the less important goldsmiths.

All over the city, poor housing was being pulled down and replaced with grand buildings, columns, squares and statues. And all this was the work of his father, carrying on the tradition of his ancestors, and part of Gaetano could not help feeling proud. But he also knew how much blood stained the family's omnipresent crest of the perfume bottle and the lily, in pursuit of acquiring land and showing themselves superior to the Nucci and other feuding families of the city. And what he didn't know, he could guess.

Why, even old Jacopo, the kindest and sweetest of Niccolò's cousins, had committed a murder only a few streets away from here! Uncle Jacopo, as they called him, who had fed all the little princes sweetmeats with his own fingers and wept like a baby when his favourite hound died. Not for the first time, Gaetano wished he had been born into a family of shepherds or gardeners.

Then he and Francesca could have got up early one morning and made their vows in a country church, decorated with rosebuds. He smiled at the thought of his beautiful cousin, the love of his life, clad in a homespun dress with flowers in her hair. How different from their forthcoming marriage in the vast cathedral, which would be followed by a grand procession and surrounded by dangers in spite of all the finery of silks and brocades and silver and diamonds.

Gaetano decided to walk towards Saint-Mary-among-the-Vines and look up the friar who his friend Luciano had told him was a Stravagante, like Luciano himself and his master, Rodolfo. Unlike his own father, Gaetano was not an enemy of the Stravaganti; in fact he thought they were probably the only people who could stave off the disaster he could feel brewing.

*

'Lucien Mulholland?' said Sky, disbelievingly. 'But he died – about two and a half years ago. He can't be here in your city.'

'Not yet,' said Sulien. 'He lives in Bellezza. But he will accompany the Duchessa to the weddings. You will meet him. And find he is very much alive, in Talia.'

Sky sat down on a low wall. He remembered Lucien – a slim boy with black curls, two years above him at school. He vaguely remembered that Lucien was good at swimming and was also musical, but that was about it. He hadn't known him well, and when the head teacher had told the whole school in assembly one morning that Lucien had died, Sky had felt only that shock that everyone feels when death comes to someone young and familiar.

But now he was being asked to believe that this person was not dead at all but living in another world, somewhere in the past, and that he, Sky, was going to meet him. It was too far-fetched for words.

Looking around him, he noticed that he and Sulien were not the only black inhabitants of Giglia. There were not many others but there were some, which struck him as odd, if this was a sort of Italy, goodness knows how long ago. Although Sky was taking history AS, he realised that he had only the vaguest of ideas about life in Renaissance Italy. And then had to remind himself that this wasn't Italy at all. But he was glad not to attract any strange looks, except from a rather scruffy boy lounging apparently aimlessly round the food stalls.

The boy caught his eye and made his way towards Sky and Sulien.

'Hello, Brothers,' he said.

Sky knew it was because of his robes that the boy called him that, but it made him jump all the same.

'Sandro,' said the boy, nodding at Sulien and sticking out his hand towards Sky.

'Celestino,' said Sky, remembering his new name.

'Brother Celestino,' said Sandro, with a sideways glance at Sulien. 'You're new here, aren't you?'

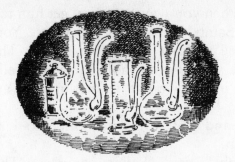

Chapter 3

Brothers

Sulien knew the Eel's boy and he hesitated about letting his new visitor spend time with him. But the friar couldn't continue to neglect his work at the Farmacia and it was essential for Sky to learn his way about the city.

'Brother Celestino is newly arrived from Anglia,' he told the younger boy. 'He is a stranger to Giglia – indeed he has never been to Talia before. Perhaps you would like to show him around?' He pulled Sky to one side and whispered, 'I have to get back. Let Sandro teach you about the city – no one knows it better than him, but tell him nothing of what I have said to you, particularly about the Stravaganti – he works for the di Chimici. And keep out of the full sun – you can always say it's too hot for you after chilly

Anglia. When you want to leave, get him to direct you back to Saint-Mary-among-the-Vines. You must go back home without fail before sunset. The talisman will take you if you hold it while falling asleep anywhere in the city, but it's best to come and go from my cell.'

'Come and go?' whispered Sky. 'So I am coming back again?'

'Certainly,' said Sulien quietly. 'That's what Stravaganti do – travel between worlds and do what is required of them in both.'

Sky had the strangest feeling that this friar was not so mad after all and that he knew all about his life in the other world. Brother Sulien slipped off round the side of the cathedral, waving to the two boys, and Sandro, who had been cleaning his nails with an alarming-looking dagger, gave Sky a big grin.

'Ready, Brother?' he asked. 'There's plenty to see.'

And so Sky found himself being shown round Giglia by Sandro. The boy had asked no questions, except for Sky's name and if he was attached to Sulien's friary. And those Sky could just about manage to answer, though it was odd to think of himself as Celestino – or Brother Tino, as Sandro began to call him, a novice from Saint-Mary-among-the-Vines. It was like taking a part in a play or a role-playing game.

Sandro was much more interested in telling than asking. He loved explaining his city to someone so ignorant, especially someone older than him.

'This is one of the grandest streets in Giglia,' he said at the end of their wanderings, taking Sky up the Via Larga some hours later. 'The Duke has his palace just up here and my master lodges not far away.'

'What do you do?' asked Sky, amazed that someone so young could have a job; perhaps he was an apprentice of some kind? Or perhaps boys in this time – he still had no idea when it was and only the haziest idea about where – went to work much younger? He had assumed that Sandro was only about fourteen.

But Sandro just tapped the side of his nose mysteriously and said, 'What you don't know can't hurt you. Maybe I'll tell you one day when we know each other better.'

He insisted on treating Sky like a big simpleton, more naïve than himself. Sky felt his mouth curving in a smile; it was how he imagined having a little brother might be.

'Here it is,' said Sandro proudly. 'The Palazzo di Chimici. Where Duke Niccolò lives when he is in Giglia.'

Sky saw a magnificent building, much bigger than the others around it, taking up an entire block of the street. A grand pair of iron gates inside an arch allowed the two boys to look into the huge courtyard beyond. A fountain played in the middle of geometrically arranged flower beds, separated by what looked like patterned marble slabs.

'Hey there, young Sparrow,' said a voice from behind them, and an absurdly overdressed little man attempted to put his arms across both their shoulders. It was easy enough to manage with Sandro but Sky was a head taller than him and the man had to stretch to reach.

He was wearing a blue velvet suit with a lace collar and a hat with a curling feather, and Sky couldn't help noticing a powerful smell of stale sweat.

*

Prince Gaetano entered the gate to the Lesser Cloister of Saint-Mary-among-the-Vines; he had always liked this Dominican friary. It was here that his family's great fortune had begun, when they backed the researches into distilling perfume from flowers and gained their surname of di Chimici, meaning Chemists. But he hadn't been here recently, not since the arrival of Brother Sulien as Pharmacist and Senior Friar.

Gaetano recognised Sulien from Luciano's description. He was supervising the delivery of cartloads of hothouse irises at the back door of the Great Cloister. But he stopped and came over as soon as he saw the young prince.

'Welcome, your Highness,' he said. 'I have been expecting you.'

*

The guard at the gates of the di Chimici palace knew the Eel well and let him in with his two companions, even though a scruffy boy and a young novice were hardly likely visitors for the Duke. But the Eel was not on his way to see the Duke – not yet. He wanted to show off in front of his young apprentice and his new friend.

'Come along, Sparrow,' he said, leading the two boys into another, larger courtyard, where a bronze statue of a naked Mercury with a sword stood guard over some very elaborate flower beds. 'Who is your friend?'

'Brother Tino,' said Sandro. 'He's new. He lives up at Saint-Mary-among-the-Vines.

'Really?' said the Eel, with an unctuous grin. He was genuinely interested. That Dominican friary was one of the few places where he didn't have a spy planted and he wondered if this rather simple-seeming novice might be useful as a source of information. 'Let me introduce myself,' he said, extending a none too clean hand from his blue velvet sleeve. 'Enrico Poggi, confidential agent of Duke Niccolò di Chimici, ruler of the city of Giglia, at your service!'

Sky accepted the handshake but felt wary; this employer of Sandro's didn't seem like the sort of person a duke would have much to do with and Sky instinctively didn't trust him. But things might be different in this other world he found himself in and he was still learning the ropes.

As if summoned up by his name, a richly dressed old man walked out from under an arch, into the courtyard, deep in conversation with a less aristocratic person carrying an armful of what looked like plans. A closer look showed Sky that the nobleman wasn't as old as he first thought; he had completely white hair but his face wasn't lined. In fact he was rather handsome in a slightly spooky way.

The Duke, for it was obviously him, stopped when he saw the three intruders. He dismissed the man he had been talking to, with, 'Come back tomorrow morning with the revised drawings,' and beckoned Enrico to him.

The Eel slithered across the courtyard, bowing and smiling. Sky could see at once that the Duke regarded the man with contempt. He might be content to use him but Sky doubted very much that Enrico had more of Duke Niccolò's confidence than he thought fit to show him. Sandro had made himself invisible, in the way he had of blending in with the background. He now slouched against a column, half-concealed in the shadows.

Suddenly Sky knew exactly what Sandro did for his unprepossessing master: he was a spy!

The Duke was looking straight at Sky now, who felt very exposed and wished he had as good a gift of disguise as his new friend. He was glad that he was standing in the shade. Enrico beckoned him over. And a small cloud drifted across the sun.

'Brother Tino, my Lord,' said Enrico, presenting Sky to the Duke, like a dog offering his master a share in a particularly precious and revolting bone. 'As I said, he is based over in your Grace's old family church among the vines.'

The Duke extended a long-fingered hand, ringed with silver and rubies, and Sky went to take it, as he had Enrico's a minute before. But a small gesture from the spymaster indicated he must kiss it not shake it.

'Indeed,' said Duke Niccolò. 'It is some time since I visited there. Perhaps you, Tino – short for Celestino, is it? – would convey my respects to your Senior Friar. Who is it nowadays?'

Sky got the feeling that this vagueness was put on and that the Duke was well aware who was in charge of every institution of the city. Which was more than Sky himself was.

'I-I work with Brother Sulien, in . . . in the pharmacy,' he stammered, glad that his colouring was not susceptible to blushing.

Duke Niccolò looked hard into his face. 'Mmm. I have heard something of that friar. Perhaps I shall pay him a visit myself soon. The pharmacy of course I am familiar with. It supplies me with perfume and pomades . . . among other things.' The Duke smiled slightly, as if remembering past triumphs. Then, 'Do make your acquaintance with my palace. We have some rather fine frescoes in the chapel that would interest one of your calling. Now, if you'll excuse us, I have some business with Poggi here.'

He waved an elegant hand in a gesture that was obviously dismissal, taking in Sandro as well – so he had noticed him, Sky realised – and moved off with Enrico.

'What a piece of luck!' said the boy softly as Duke and spymaster walked into the palace in deep conference. Sky couldn't help noticing that the nobleman kept widening the distance between himself and the man in the blue velvet suit, while Enrico kept sidling up closer again.

'Luck?'

'Yes. We've more or less got his Grace's permission to snoop about his palace! He wouldn't have said that if I'd been here on my own.' Sandro was thinking how useful it was to have such a respectable companion as a novice friar. 'He's wonderful, isn't he?' he added.

'The Duke?'

'No, the Eel,' said Sandro impatiently. The Duke was so far out of his sphere that he registered him only like a piece of fine architecture; he was much better equipped to appreciate a man like Enrico. Sandro hoped that his father had been a man like that. 'Let's go,' he said now, eager to take advantage of this unusual opportunity.

The boys walked through the courtyard and Sky noticed that the paving-stones between the flower beds all carried the symbol of the lily, in its elaborate fleur-de-lys form, like the stopper to his bottle. He asked Sandro about it.

'It's the symbol of the city,' he answered. 'Giglia means City of the Lily. And the di Chimici have it on their family crest too, with the shape of a perfume bottle.'

The palazzo had what looked like its own little cemetery, dominated by a recent white marble tomb. It was topped by the statue of a young boy and his dog. Sky stopped to look at it; there was something familiar about the boy.

'That's Prince Falco,' said Sandro. 'The Duke's youngest.'

'What happened to him?' asked Sky.

'Poisoned himself,' said Sandro dramatically. 'Couldn't bear the pain any longer. He was all smashed up after an accident with a horse.'

They were both silent for a moment while Sky thought about being in so much pain you would want to kill yourself and Sandro planned how to use their permission to roam the palazzo.

On the far side of the courtyard was a broad flight of stone steps, which the boys climbed. At the top was a heavy dark wooden door, which Sandro pushed cautiously open. They found themselves in a small chapel, where two tall candles burned in even taller candlesticks on the altar. But what made both boys gasp was the paintings which covered three walls.

They were rich with silver and, looking closely, Sky

could see that some of the figures had real jewels embedded in their elaborate hats. The paintings showed a long winding procession of men, horses and dogs against a background of, he supposed, Talian countryside. Deer and rabbits and other small animals were pursued through bushes by some of the hunting dogs, and birds perched on branches, oblivious of whatever the humans were doing. At the head of the procession were three figures even more grandly dressed than the rest, with crowns instead of hats.

Something bothered Sky about it; it was familiar but somehow different. Then he realised; the painting it reminded him of had gold wherever these frescoes had silver. Sandro was up close and Sky saw to his horror that he was trying to prise a small ruby from the hat of one of the minor figures in the procession.

'Stop that at once,' he said sharply and the boy looked up, startled.

'You can't go nicking bits off a great work of art,' Sky explained.

Sandro was surprised; he didn't see it as a work of art, just a collection of coloured paints and valuable jewels, some of which would never be missed. But he realised that Tino, as a friar, might see things differently. He sheathed his dagger and shrugged. 'If you say so.'

'I do,' said Sky. 'Look how beautiful it is. But why is it silver?'

Sandro really thought Sky must be a bit touched in the head.

'Because silver's the most precious metal,' he explained patiently, as if to a child.

'More than gold?' asked Sky.

'Course,' said Sandro. 'Gold goes black – gets the *morte d'oro*. Silver just keeps on shining.' He gave one of the candlesticks on the altar a bit of a rub with his cuff. 'Nah, you keep gold for a knick-knack to give your lady love if you're not really serious about her. Silver's only for the likes of the di Chimici.'

Sandro's words made Sky think about the quiet fair-haired girl at his school. What would Alice Greaves say to a gold bracelet brought back from Talia? He didn't think she'd see it as a trinket. Then he remembered he didn't have any money here and didn't even know what currency they used. He shook his head. The small dark chapel, with its lingering scent of incense, was beginning to feel stuffy. He wanted to get out into the fresh air again. Suddenly he panicked. How long had he been roaming the city with Sandro? A gnawing feeling in his stomach told him it must be getting late. He didn't want to miss the sunset.

Sky looked at his wrist but of course his watch was on his bedside table at home. He looked up and saw Sandro regarding him with his head on one side. With his bright, alert eyes, he did look a bit like a sparrow.

'What time is it?' Sky asked, feeling really alarmed. 'I must be getting back to the friary.'

'Oh yeah, you brothers have to say your prayers every few hours, don't you?' said Sandro. 'You've probably missed some already. Do you want me to take you back?'

*

Gaetano had spent several happy hours helping Sulien in his laboratory. The young di Chimici prince was attending the university in Giglia and was interested in all new branches of learning. But he hadn't been in a laboratory for a long time and was fascinated to see how the friars distilled perfume from flowers. It would take many cartloads of irises to produce a tiny phial of the flower's intense yet delicate perfume. And Sulien was easy to work with, calm and authoritative. Gaetano fell into the rhythm of the laboratory without even noticing.

He looked at tall glass bottles containing cologne, with labels like frangipani, pomegranate, silver musk, vetiver and orange blossom. Then there were pure essences like amber and jasmine, lily-of-the-valley and violet. There was almond paste for the hands, Vinegar of the Seven Thieves for ladies' fainting fits, Russian cologne for men's beards and almond soap. There was tincture of white birch and hawkweed, infusions of fennel and mallow and lime blossom, liqueurs and compounds of willow and hawthorn.

Cupboard after cupboard full of jars of lotions and glass bottles of jewel-like coloured liquids. No wonder the place smelt like heaven! But Gaetano knew that somewhere in the friary was another, secret, laboratory, where herbs were brewed that were not so healthy – his family's source of poisons.

But for now he tried to forget about that and to lend a hand stirring and measuring and mixing and adjusting flames under glass alembics like any other apprentice. Gaetano was the only one helping Sulien; the usual novice helpers had been dismissed so that the two of them could discuss the real reason for the prince's visit.

'Luciano told me where to find you,' he said,

steadily pouring a clear green liquid from one container to another.

'And how is he?' asked Sulien. He had brought his recipe manuscript into the laboratory and was carefully recording what they were doing to make infusion of mint. 'I know Rodolfo is worried about his coming anywhere near your father the Duke.'

Gaetano sighed, concentrating hard on his task. 'My father has his reasons for not trusting Luciano too. Do you know what really happened to my brother Falco?' he asked.

Sulien nodded. 'Doctor Dethridge told me,' he said. 'He was translated, like him, but to the other world.'

'Where he lives and thrives, as far as we know,' said Gaetano. 'I miss him terribly, but it was his decision. He wanted passionately to be healed by their medicine and be whole again.'

The two of them were silent over their tasks for a while, Gaetano remembering the last time he had seen his youngest brother, miraculously grown tall and straight again, riding a flying horse in Remora. His father had sat beside him, white and rigid at what other spectators took for an apparition of the dead prince. Duke Niccolò, in his ceremonial armour, had vowed vengeance on the Stravaganti but he had not moved quickly. Gaetano wondered whether the wedding invitation to Arianna was partly a ruse to bring Luciano to Giglia.

Sulien had been thoughtful too. He knew this young sprig of the Duke's family only by reputation, but he seemed quite unlike his father and his proud brothers. He was aware that Gaetano knew about the Stravaganti, had been on friendly terms with several of them, and would not betray their secrets to the Duke. And he was handy with tongs and glass vessels, something that made a good impression on the friar.

Brother Sulien came to a decision. 'I must tell you,' he said, 'that I have today been visited by a new Stravagante from the other world.'

Gaetano put down the vessel he was holding very carefully on the wooden bench. 'But that is fantastic!' he said, trying hard to contain his excitement. 'Where is he now? Has he gone back?'

'No,' said Sulien, getting up from his stool and walking over to the door into the cloister, to assess the quality of the light. 'He should be here soon. I told him he must go back before sunset.'

As if on cue, a flustered young man in a novice's robes burst into the room from the inner door. Gaetano thought him remarkable-looking with his skin like chestnuts and his long hair like golden-brown catkins.

'I hope I'm not too late,' said Sky, casting an anxious look in the direction of Sulien's visitor. 'I lost track of time in the Duke's chapel.'

'Ah, that is easily done,' said Gaetano, smiling. 'It has happened to me often.'

Sky looked at him properly. He was clearly a noble, dressed in fine clothes and wearing silver rings. But, if it had not been for his clothes, he would have seemed rather plain. He had a big nose and a very big crooked mouth. He reminded Sky of someone he had seen recently. And then he remembered. One of the kings with a silver crown in the chapel fresco had looked like that.

'Let me present myself,' said the young man. 'I am

Prince Gaetano di Chimici, youngest surviving son of Duke Niccolò. And if you have been looking at the frescoes in my father's chapel, you have seen a likeness of my grandfather, Alfonso. I am supposed to look rather like him.' And he made Sky a deep bow.

Handsome he might not be, but he seemed so warm and friendly, and not a bit conceited, that Sky liked him immediately. He glanced towards Sulien as he replied, 'And I am Tino – Celestino Pascoli. I come from Anglia.' And he tried to copy the prince's graceful bow.

'It's all right, Sky,' said Sulien. 'Prince Gaetano knows you are from a lot further away than that. In spite of his father, he is a good friend to us Stravaganti.'

'Indeed,' said Gaetano eagerly. 'Do you come from the same place as Luciano? Or Georgia? Perhaps you know my brother, Falco?'

A strange feeling was creeping over Sky. 'Georgia who?' he asked.

Gaetano thought for a bit. 'When she was here – well, not here in this city, but in Remora – she acted as a boy and was known as Giorgio Gredi. I don't know what her real surname was.'

'I think I do,' said Sky slowly. 'You must mean Georgia O'Grady. She goes to the same school as me.'

His head was spinning. Georgia O'Grady was Alice's fierce friend, the girl with the red hair and tattoo.

'But if you know Georgia then you must know Falco!' said Gaetano, his eyes shining. He came round the bench to grasp Sky by both arms. 'A beautiful boy, not like me. A boy with curly black hair, a fine horseman and fencer . . .' His voice broke. 'He is my little brother,' he went on, 'and I shall probably never see him again. Please, if you know anything of him, tell me.'

It had been the talk of the school at one time, Sky remembered, the friendship between Georgia and the boy who fitted that description. There had been all sorts of rumours, because Georgia was in the sixth form and the boy was only in Year 10, two years younger than her. Such things were not unheard of, but it was still unusual. Still, both of them had shrugged off all comment and remained friends.

Now Sky said, 'There is a boy like that, Georgia's close friend, but he isn't called what you said. His name is Nicholas Duke.'

The image of the marble boy with the dog floated into Sky's mind, even as he said it, and he felt the world turning upside down. It was like trying to walk up an Escher staircase and finding you were going downwards, and it gave him vertigo. But Sky knew that the boy he thought of as Nicholas could be this nice, ugly prince's lost brother. But if he was, what on earth was he doing at Barnsbury Comprehensive? Then he remembered something else he knew about Nicholas. He lived with the parents of the Lucien who had died – or who was now living in Talia.

Sky felt two pairs of strong arms catch him as his knees gave way and he sank on to the bench.

'Time to go home, I think,' said Sulien. 'That's quite enough for one visit.'

Chapter 4

Secrets

Rosalind had to shake Sky to wake him up the next morning. Normally he was first up, leaping out of bed as soon as the alarm went off and heading straight for the shower before he was really awake. But today he looked at her as if he had no idea who she was, sleep still fuzzing his brain.

'Come on, lovely boy,' she said. 'I know we live right next door to school, but you'll still have to hurry. It's quarter past eight already!'

'Mum!' said Sky, finally dragging his mind away from Giglia in the past and back to the present of his life in Islington.

'Who else?' said Rosalind, smiling. He registered that she was looking well again. That was two days in a row.

'You should have woken me sooner,' he said reproachfully, though it was himself he was cross with. 'I can't just go off to school and leave you with all the chores.'

'What chores?' said his mother. 'There's nothing urgent. Breakfast is made – you just have a quick shower and then come and eat. Everything's under control.'

Under the hot jet of the shower, Sky thought about this. It seemed to him that everything he had taken for granted about his daily life was spiralling wildly out of control. If what Sulien and Gaetano told him was true, he was a traveller in time and space, not an ordinary twenty-first-century boy with a sick mother.

The girl he fancied – yes, he acknowledged it now – was best friends with another such sci-fi traveller, whose other closest friend was a dead prince from centuries ago. And that prince seemed to have changed places with another school student who now lived in a world of magicians and duchesses, silver and treason.

He shook the water off his thick locks. He was going to have to go to school knowing that neither Georgia nor Nicholas was what they seemed. This was a much bigger secret than having a rock star for a father. But Sky had already promised to take messages between Gaetano and Nicholas; he hadn't been able to say no when he saw how moved the Giglian prince had been by the loss of his brother.

It was what everyone who had ever lost anyone to death wanted, Sky supposed. To believe that they were in a better world – and that it might still be possible to communicate with them.

Sandro was well pleased with his new friendship. A friar, even a novice one, was a perfect cover for nefarious deeds and Sandro had seen straightaway how useful Sky could be. But it was more than that; he liked the tall brown boy, so interested in everything he was told and so innocent about how things worked in Giglia. Sandro loved knowing more than someone else and telling them about it. The new friar was like a newborn lamb when wolves were about in a place like the City of Flowers. And then, secretly, he had the added satisfaction that, as a friar, Sky must know all sorts of things that he, Sandro, didn't – like all that book-learning clerics had to have.

Sandro had never had a brother, as far as he knew, but he had imagined lots of family for himself – a father like the Eel, a mother like the Madonna, a big brother to protect him and a little one to boss about. Now he felt he had found both brothers in Sky.

'Never thought he'd be a Moor, though,' Sandro said to himself. 'I wonder what the real story is there? The Eel is interested in Sulien. Maybe this Tino is the result of some secret scandal of his?'

He resolved to look into it. But not necessarily to tell his master. After all, he had always been well treated by Brother Sulien, who had more than once taken him into the kitchens at Saint-Mary-among-the-Vines and fed him, in the days before he was the Eel's man. And as for Tino, Sandro felt protective of any secret that might concern him. Even after one meeting, the strange Anglian was definitely his friend. And

Sandro had never had a friend before.

Nicholas Duke was the school fencing champion. He was legendary in Barnsbury Comprehensive, having arrived at the beginning of Year 9 with a twisted leg and able to walk only with crutches. Several operations, months of physiotherapy and a punishing training programme in the gym had resulted in a growth spurt, an athletic frame and a grace of movement that would have been unbelievable a year and a half ago.

Nicholas had been a bit of a mystery. He had been found abandoned, apparently having lost his memory. But he was clever and was soon in the top group for maths, French and English literature. Science and ICT were not his forte but he was picking them up well enough. And he was good at art and music. But the real surprise was that, as soon as he could balance and walk without crutches, he joined the fencing club and proved to be as skilled as a professional.

'You must have done this before,' Mr Lovegrove, their fencing teacher, had said.

And Nicholas had grinned, delighted. 'I suppose I must,' was all he would say.

Nick Duke had almost single-handedly made fencing fashionable at Barnsbury. He was popular with girls because of his dreamy good looks, especially now he had added height to his lithe slim figure, angelic smile and black curly hair. They were pretty annoyed that he was so obviously smitten with a girl two years above him that none of them got a look-in.

He was popular with boys too; even those who might have bullied him because of his girlish looks were impressed by his rigorous fitness training and a bit alarmed by his skills with a foil. And Nicholas was beginning to put on muscle too – he was a fine horseman and went riding every weekend. By the time he was a sixth former he was going to be a dangerous person to tangle with, even when unarmed.

The fencing club had never had so many members, male and female. Soon the school had been able to enter a team, first in the local championships, and then in the regional ones, which they won. National achievement was the next aim, and Mr Lovegrove and Nicholas Duke were training the team almost equally between them.

Now Nicholas was in the school gym, before lunch, doing a hundred press-ups. In a rare lapse of concentration, he glanced towards the door and saw a brown face encircled with chestnut locks, looking through the glass panel. And then it was gone.

'I shall move to the Palazzo Ducale as soon as the wedding ceremonies have been performed,' said Duke Niccolò. He was addressing his three sons and his daughter in the magnificent salon of his family's palace on the Via Larga. 'And I shall take Beatrice with me, of course.'

His daughter made a little curtsey. She had not been allocated a husband in the recent spate of di Chimici engagements and she did not mind. She was still young, not yet twenty-one, and she knew her father needed her. Beatrice had felt even more tenderly towards him since the death of her little brother Falco the year before. So she smiled in acceptance of the Duke's plans for her.

'I have ordered the changes necessary to give Fabrizio and Caterina a wing of the Palazzo Ducale,' continued the Duke, nodding to the architect Gabassi, who was clutching his usual armful of plans.

'I trust that meets with your approval?' Niccolò said to Fabrizio, but it was a formality. No one in the room dreamt of raising any objection to their father's plans. The only di Chimici prince to defy him now lived in another world, though only his brother Gaetano knew that.

'Carlo and Gaetano will live here in the Palazzo di Chimici, of course,' said the Duke, inclining his head towards his second and third sons, 'with their wives Lucia and Francesca. It is a large enough palace in which to raise children, I think.'

The Duke was looking forward to his grandchildren, lots of them. He believed with all his heart that it was the destiny of his family to rule all Talia, and he wanted all twelve city-states secured by having their titles in family hands. Preferably in his lifetime, but if not, he wanted to know before he died that there was a good supply of di Chimici princelings and dukelets in waiting.

Fabrizio was content. To live in the Palazzo Ducale was fitting for a prince of his family and future. And he would have more opportunity to study his father's ways of doing things, feel more like the Duke-in-waiting. The palazzo in the Piazza Ducale had been commissioned and paid for by the di Chimici, but no member of the family had ever lived in it. It was the seat of Giglian politics, where the city Council met, but a very grand building and quite large enough to house a Duke and his heir. And it would help with achieving his father's political plans to be living right above the place where the laws were passed.

If Fabrizio was heir to Duke Niccolò's title and political ambition, Prince Carlo was his natural successor in financial acumen. The di Chimici had made their fortune initially from perfecting the art of distilling perfume, but over the years it had grown through their role as bankers to the great families of Talia and the crowned heads of Europe.

'And our business meetings, Father?' Carlo now asked.

'Will continue as normal,' said Niccolò. 'It does not matter whether here or in the Palazzo Ducale.'

Gaetano said nothing. There was, as far as he knew, no part for him in his father's plans. He had feared once that he would be forced into the Church and groomed to be the next Pope when his uncle Ferdinando died. But then Niccolò had ordered him to propose to the beautiful Duchessa of Bellezza. Arianna had turned him down but encouraged him to ask the woman he really loved, his cousin Francesca. Gaetano's father had raised no objections to their marriage, so presumably he had given up the idea of his third son as a celibate priest, but doubtless he had something in mind for the young prince; Niccolò had a plan for everyone.

Sky waited until quite late to go into lunch, once he had checked that Nicholas was in the gym. He knew that Alice always had lunch with Georgia and most days Nicholas joined them. Sky timed his entry into the cafeteria so that he was about three people behind the two girls and could see where they chose to sit. There was no sign of Nicholas yet, but he guessed they'd choose a table with room for at least a third person.

And he was in luck. When Georgia and Alice had settled on an empty table for four, Sky moved swiftly in and asked to sit with them. It didn't escape his notice that Alice coloured up as soon as he approached, but he had a different quarry today; it was Georgia he had to speak to. And he had to get her on her own.

Georgia was regarding him with hostility; she had noticed Alice's blush too. But she wasn't actually rude – just someone with no small talk, Sky realised. Overcome with shyness, Alice got up.

'I forgot I meant to pick up some fruit,' she said, escaping for the counter.

This was Sky's chance, now that he and Georgia were alone, but he had no idea how to begin. Should he say, 'I know you're a Stravagante. I'm one too'? Somehow in the very ordinary surroundings of Barnsbury Comp cafeteria, with people munching chips and slurping Coke, it seemed absurd.

And as he hesitated, they were joined by Nicholas Duke.

'Who's your friend?' Nicholas asked Georgia, pleasantly enough but with a confidence that irritated the older boy.

'Sky Meadows,' said Georgia tersely.

'Sky?' said Nicholas. 'Unusual name, isn't it?'

This was Sky's chance. 'Almost as rare as Falco,' he said quietly.

The effect on the other two was absolutely electrifying. Georgia's fork crashed on to her plate and Nicholas dropped his drink, splashing orange juice over the table.

Alice arrived with her apple to find them all mopping up the mess with paper napkins and thought immediately that there had been some sort of row. She sighed. She really liked Sky, and they were both so shy that this was the first time he had made any sort of approach to her. She had left him and Georgia on their own so that they would have to make some sort of conversation. Alice was never going to get anywhere with Sky unless Georgia could be made to accept him. But it looked as if Alice had made the wrong decision.

'What on earth did you say to him?' she whispered to Georgia.

'Nothing,' said Georgia, white-faced and tight-lipped. She had never thought to hear Falco's name again unless she or Nicholas uttered it in one of their many conversations about the past, so it had come at her like a bolt of lightning. Now all she could think of was how to get rid of dear, sweet Alice and find out what Sky knew.

In the Ducal palace of Bellezza, a much better feast than chips and Coke had been consumed. It was the last night of Carnival in that great city and the guests all wore their best clothes. Even outside in the square, the revellers, who had eaten their own feast, were brushing crumbs and wine splashes from dresses gorgeous with lace and velvet or cloaks and doublets of slashed silk. Both sets of partygoers wore masks, the men as well as the women, and all restraint was thrown aside for this last night of the week-long celebrations.

Inside the palazzo, the Duchessa and her court were preparing for the ball. The Duchessa herself, being still only seventeen, wore ivory silk and got away with it. Her mask of white peacock feathers was echoed by the same design on her skirt and bodice, with every eye of the bird's brilliant display embroidered in silver and sewn with diamonds.

She started the dancing with Senator Rodolfo, her father, in his usual black velvet. His black mask was in the shape of a hawk's head and beak and carried blue-black feathers of its own.

'You are very lovely tonight, my dear,' he said, expertly guiding her round the dance floor as more and more couples joined the whirling throng.

'Thank you,' she said, smiling. Arianna loved to dance, as she loved to run or shout or swim or scull a mandola through the water of the Bellezzan canals, but all the other occupations were almost memories. Only on grand occasions like the Carnival ball could she lose herself for a while in the sheer joy of physical action.

'I must soon give you up to a younger partner,' said Rodolfo, smiling too. 'You are too energetic for an old man like me.'

'Will you choose a staid old woman to dance with

instead?' asked Arianna, teasingly. She had already spotted her mother, in her midnight-blue dress, masked like a silver leopard, and knew where Rodolfo's feet would lead him next. Arianna was now used to the risks her supposedly dead mother took every time she exposed herself to recognition on occasions like this; she knew how incapable her parents were of staying apart for long, even though one lived as Regent in Bellezza and the other kept up an alias as a rich widow in Padavia.

Arianna's mother Silvia took the floor now with a slim young man, whose long black curls were tied back with a purple ribbon. He was a good dancer, almost as good as his partner, and she was quite out of breath by the time they moved near to Rodolfo and Arianna.

'Time for my staid old woman,' murmured Rodolfo, taking his secret wife in his arms and whirling her away.

They did not break the rhythm of the music for a moment, Luciano and Arianna, but danced together smoothly and effortlessly, as if used to holding one another.

'You last wore a mask like that in Remora,' Luciano said. 'When Georgia won the Stellata.'

'I'm surprised you remember,' said Arianna. 'You had eyes only for her at that time.'

'You were at the window of the Papal palace,' said Luciano, 'looking down into the Campo. But even a glimpse of you remains in my mind always.'

'You are becoming quite poetical,' she said, laughing.

She always does this, thought Luciano. Just when I

try to say something serious about how I feel, she always turns it aside with a joke. How can I ever get her to understand? But he was used to Arianna's moods and always took his tone from hers.

'I wonder what Georgia is doing now?' he said now, skilfully guiding the Duchessa through the dancing throng.

But Arianna was not jealous of the girl Stravagante tonight.

'I hope she's having as nice a time as we are,' was all she said.

'Meet you both outside the school gate at half past three,' hissed Georgia to Sky and Nicholas.

Somehow she was going to have to give Alice the slip; she couldn't wait any longer to find out what Sky knew about Nicholas and how he had come by the name of Falco.

Chapter 5

Marble for a Duchess

Rosalind Meadows was pleased and surprised when Sky let himself in with two friends in tow; she often worried that he didn't seem close to anyone in school. After making them all tea, she made an excuse and took herself out, leaving them the flat to themselves.

Georgia was looking round the living room and sniffing. 'This flat is brand new, isn't it?' she asked. 'It still smells of paint.'

'Yes,' said Sky. 'We moved in a few months ago.'

'Who lived here before?' she pursued. 'Was it all one house?'

Sky shrugged. 'Yes, but I don't know who lived here – some old lady who died, I think my mum said.'

'That's it!' said Georgia, turning to Nicholas. 'This

must be the house my horse came from! Mr Goldsmith said it came from the great-niece of an old lady who died in a house near the school.'

'And Luciano said his notebook came from there too,' said Nicholas.

Georgia looked at Sky for a long time, as if deciding just how much to trust him. 'Our school is on the site of William Dethridge's Elizabethan laboratory,' she said eventually. 'Or a part of the school and perhaps a part of this house. Whenever a Stravagante comes to England in our time, they seem to end up here. We think that's why two of us were found by the talismans.'

'Three,' said Sky quietly.

'I knew it!' exclaimed Nicholas, jumping up and pacing the small living room. 'Where do you go? And what is your talisman?'

Sky went into his room and came back with the perfume bottle. Georgia smiled when she saw the bubble-wrap. It brought back memories of her own stravagations. But Nicholas was beside himself when he saw the blue glass bottle.

'That's Giglian!' he said. 'You go to Giglia, don't you?'

'Well, I've only been once,' said Sky. 'Last night.'

'Who did you see? Who told you about me?' asked Nicholas eagerly. 'Was it Gaetano?'

The two brothers, so different physically, were very alike in one thing, thought Sky. They were equally devoted to each other and eager for news.

'Yes,' he said to Nicholas. 'I saw him. He asked me to seek you out and give you messages. I think he wants to use me as a go-between.'

Nicholas looked as if he wanted to climb into Sky's mind and grab everything in it relating to his old life, but Georgia stopped him. Sky was impressed by the influence she had over the younger boy.

'Do you know why you've been chosen?' she asked Sky now.

'No, not exactly. I found myself in a sort of a monastery, with a pharmacy attached to it.'

'I bet it was Saint-Mary-among-the-Vines!' cried Nicholas.

Sky nodded. 'That's where I met your brother,' he said. 'But not at first. The first person I met was Brother Sulien. He . . . he told me we were both Stravaganti and that I was needed to help the city. He said there was danger coming from all sides. I think it's linked with the weddings in your family, Nick.'

'Oh, who is getting married?' he asked in an agony of curiosity. 'Gaetano, I know, is to marry our cousin Francesca, but who else?'

Sky saw that Georgia had gone quite pale.

'It's your other two brothers,' he said. 'Marrying some more cousins. I'm afraid I don't remember their names. And your cousin Alfonso, the Duke of Volana, is marrying yet another relative. You have a big family.'

He saw Georgia relaxing and heard her breathe out.

'And the Duchessa of Bellezza is coming to Giglia for the weddings and the Nucci clan could be plotting something, but that's pretty much all I know so far.'

'Arianna,' said Georgia, and Sky saw to his amazement that there were tears in this tough girl's eyes. 'And where Arianna is, there Luciano will be too. You know about Luciano?'

'Sulien told me. But what he said seemed too fantastic to be true. It wasn't until Gaetano told me about you two that I began to believe it.'

'And is Gaetano well? Is he happy?' burst out Nicholas.

'He seemed well,' said Sky. 'And happy, apart from missing you. He said to tell you that he has a new horse, a grey stallion called Apollo.'

He felt a bit silly passing on this message but both Nicholas and Georgia were listening intently, clearly horse-mad.

'Will you tell him about the fencing championships?' said Nicholas. 'I think he'd like to know I am still good with a sword.'

A bullock cart was delivering a piece of marble to Giuditta Miele's bottega. She had chosen it herself in the quarry at Pietrabianca, running her hands over the white stone as if sensing something locked within it. Now she was supervising the unloading, while the white bullocks sweated and shivered.

With her broad shoulders and muscular arms, she looked as if she could heave the marble off the cart herself, but she left it to the team of workmen. A space had been cleared in the middle of the sculptor's workshop, where soon the piece of quarried marble stood upright. Giuditta was slicing the ropes off the sacking that covered it before the workmen were out of the door.

Then she walked slowly round and round the

revealed white stone, getting to know it all over again. Her apprentices watched in silence, used to her methods; it would be days before she took a chisel to the block of marble.

Giuditta was remembering her visit to Bellezza, when she had met the young Duchessa. Titles and honours were of no significance to the sculptor; she saw all people as shapes and volumes, curves and relations between lines. Young and beautiful subjects rarely held much interest for her, since she had left her own youth behind and was now more interested in character and the way it stamped its mark on features and bearing.

Her last portrait statue had been of young Prince Falco and for that she had had no model. But she had seen the boy on several State occasions and been struck by his delicate beauty. And something underneath that – a kind of steel that made him interesting to her in spite of his youth. The funeral statue of Prince Falco was already attracting visitors to the palace in Giglia, as its fame spread. A slight boy with his hand resting on the head of a favourite hound, his gaze attracted by something in the distance. It was intimate, informal, domestic, as different as possible from the classical statues that lined the loggia in the Piazza Ducale.

And now the Duchessa. Giuditta grunted, looking at the copious sketches she had made. It was hard, this business of works of art commissioned by nobles. You had to show them still and dignified. She would have liked to sculpt Arianna in full flight, running forwards with arms raised and one foot off the ground, her hair tumbling loose down her back, like an Amazon or a nymph. But that would never do for the ruler of a great city.

My next statue, thought Giuditta, will be of a peasant in his eighties.

*

In Bellezza, a formal ceremony was taking place in the Senate. The Regent, Rodolfo, and his daughter the Duchessa were conferring an honour and title upon a young man.

'I wish to announce to the Senate,' said Rodolfo, 'that my late wife, the previous Duchessa of our great city, was subjected to an earlier assassination attempt, on the night of the Maddalena Feast two years ago. It was kept quiet at the time because it failed and the Duchessa wanted to find out more about who was responsible. Alas, the second attempt was successful, as you know, and we have concluded our investigations without finding definite proof of the identity of those who wished to rob us of her gracious presence.'

He paused to let the other twenty-three Senators take in the new information.

'In the need to keep our investigations secret, it was also necessary to keep from public knowledge the name of the person who prevented the first attempt on the Duchessa's life.'

He motioned Luciano forwards.

'But it is now possible to identify him as my apprentice, Luciano Crinamorte.'

There was enthusiastic applause from the Senate.

'In token of the great service he did to our city, I

hereby release him from his apprenticeship. And the Duchessa, honouring the memory of her late mother, bestows upon him the title of Cavaliere of Bellezza.'

Luciano knelt at Arianna's feet and she put over his head a purple satin ribbon with a large silver seal with the city's emblem of a mask embossed on it.

'Arise, Cavaliere Luciano Crinamorte,' she said in her clear, musical voice. 'Serve your city well and it will always serve you.'

The three teenagers sat in Sky's flat, quite exhausted. They had talked themselves to a standstill. Each was now wrapped in private thoughts.

For Sky it was still all too fantastic to take in. Yesterday he had been an ordinary Barnsbury student, living next to the school in a little flat with his sick mother. Today he was a time and space traveller, living over an alchemist's lab from more than four centuries ago. And his mother seemed to be getting better; could these two things possibly be linked?

They had pooled information and Georgia had told him that Luciano had always felt well in Talia. And Falco had taken the enormous step of becoming Nicholas in order to be healed. Yesterday Sky had arrived in a place of healing, which also produced perfumes. What did that mean and why had he been chosen? Only more visits to Giglia would tell.

Georgia was in a whirl of emotions. She hadn't been back to Talia since the previous September, nearly six months ago, when she and Nicholas had made a dramatic stravagation to Remora together and he, as Falco, had ridden the flying horse around and above the Campo. She hadn't seen Luciano on that occasion, hadn't seen him for over a year and a half in fact, because Falco's death in his old life and his new identity as Nicholas had caused the gateway between the two worlds to destabilise, so that more than a year had passed for her but not for her friends in Talia.

And she and Nicholas could travel only to Remora, while Sky had been chosen to stravagate to Giglia, Nicholas's home town. But if Luciano was coming to that great city, then that was the only place she wanted to be. She shook her head. This was madness. She had taught herself to do without Luciano after they had said goodbye in the Campo of Remora so long ago. He lived in a world she couldn't inhabit, only visit, and then in the wrong city. And he did not love her, except as a friend. His heart was given to the young Duchessa of Bellezza, beautiful, clever and brave, who was going to Giglia in spite of all the dangers that awaited her there.

Nicholas, too, was deeply unsettled. Like Georgia, he had learned to give up what he loved – his family, his city, all his old life. And he had adapted well. His physical health was the great prize he had surrendered everything else for and the sacrifice had been worth it. He had a comfortable home with Luciano's parents, lots of friends, and Georgia.

He was completely in thrall to her. Not just because of her bravery and daring, although that had been the initial attraction. It was her otherness, her coming from the magical world of the twenty-first century, which had not diminished now that he knew other people from the same time. And she had rescued him, had brought him here to the world and time that had cured him, so that he could ride and fence and, best of all, walk again without help. She had given him back his life and he would always adore her for it.

But it didn't alter the fact that she was nearly seventeen and he fifteen and such relationships were frowned on in their school, although there would have been no objections in Talia to his being engaged to a woman much older than Georgia. All he could do was settle for a close friendship and hope that things would change in time. He was ashamed at feeling secretly glad that Luciano was safely trapped in the other world of centuries ago.

And now everything had changed; Talia had thrust itself back into the foreground the minute he had heard his old name. Just thinking that Sky might see his brother again in Giglia that night made this new world of school and cafeteria and gym seem thin and insubstantial.

'Goodness, you're all quiet!' said Rosalind when she got back in. 'I thought there was no one here.'

'Sorry, Mrs Meadows,' said Georgia, snapping out of her thoughts. 'We've been . . . talking about the fencing championships.'

'Call me Rosalind, please. I didn't know you were interested in fencing, Sky.'

'I am,' he said quickly. 'Nicholas here is the captain of our team. I wondered if I could learn.'

Nicholas played along straightaway. It was instinctive the way they all wanted to protect both Sky's mother and themselves. Their strange bond was as vulnerable as a newborn infant and they jumped at a chance to defend it and prolong its life.

'I think Sky could be good,' he said now. 'We've been arranging for me to give him some lessons.'

And if Rosalind wondered why that made them all so solemn, she said nothing.

Sulien was expecting Sky when he arrived in Giglia the next morning. It was early, because the boy had gone to bed early in his own world, eager to visit Talia again. He woke already dressed in his black and white novice's robes.

They were both in Sulien's cell, but the door was open into the laboratory and through that Sky could see the other door, open to the cloister. The early morning sun steamed through and he stepped out into its light, without greeting the friar. He turned and checked: no shadow.

And then he spoke to Sulien. 'Tell me about William Dethridge,' he said.

*

Duke Niccolò had spent a busy morning with his architect in the Palazzo Ducale. The plans for the conversion of the private apartments were developing well. Now he turned into the neighbouring piazza, to visit the workshops under the Guild offices. His new quarters and Fabrizio's must have furnishings and ornaments worthy of princes.

In the bottega of Arnolfo Battista, he stopped to order tables inlaid with marble chips and semi-precious stones. From the silversmith's next door, he ordered an epergne in the shape of a dragon with wings spread. And then in the jeweller's, four thick ropes of rubies and pearls for his two nieces and two young girl cousins, as wedding gifts.

Well pleased with his arrangements, the Duke strolled through the cathedral piazza on the way to his old palace. And stopped outside Giuditta Miele's bottega. It brought back painful memories, faintly tinged with pleasure. She had sculpted a lifelike statue of his boy, Falco, that was at once touchingly familiar and a great work of art. The Duke respected art and he respected Miele, though his opinion of her would have been far different if he'd known she was a Stravagante.

Now he decided to call in on the sculptor. He found her apparently doing nothing, gazing at a block of white marble. It took her a few minutes to register her illustrious guest. One of the apprentices, who were all busy bowing and doffing their caps, tugged at her sleeve to rouse her out of her reverie.

'Your Grace,' she said in her deep voice, making a curtsey, although her rough work clothes hardly lent themselves to the action.

'Maestra,' he said, raising her graciously to her feet. 'I was just passing.'

An apprentice had been busy brushing stone dust off a stool and rushed forwards to proffer it to the Duke.

'I do not keep much in the workshop,' said Giuditta. 'But I can offer your Grace a cup of wine.'

'Thank you, most kind,' said Niccolò, repressing his fastidiousness to sit on the stool and accept the pewter mug. He sipped cautiously and had to disguise his surprise at the quality of the drink.

'Mmm,' he said. 'Bellezzan red. And a fine vintage too. You have a good wine merchant.'

'It was a gift,' said Giuditta. 'From the Duchessa.' She couldn't help her eyes moving to the block of marble. All the time she was exchanging pleasantries with the Duke, she could be spending time with it, getting to know the figure trapped inside.

Duke Niccolò's quick mind made the connection straightaway.

'Ah,' he said pleasantly. 'You are perhaps commissioned to sculpt her?'

Giuditta nodded. 'I have travelled to Bellezza to make my sketches and the Duchessa will grant me several sittings while she is here in Giglia.'

'Would that be before or after the weddings?'

'Before, your Grace.'

'So she is expected soon? I must hasten to send her appropriate gifts as an honoured guest to Giglia,' mused Niccolò. 'I should like her statue to show her holding in her hand a scroll of the treaty I hope she will make with my family.'

It irked him that this artist knew more about the Duchessa's movements than he did. What was the Eel's spy network up to?

But he didn't show his irritation. Instead he finished his wine and stood up, resisting all temptation to brush the seat of his velvet breeches, and walked over to the piece of marble. He hadn't seen the young Duchessa since the death of Falco and her rapid departure from Remora, but he thought about her often.

Arianna Rossi was unfinished business. She had

defied his wishes when she refused his son, just as her mother had always defied him in her resistance to any alliance with the di Chimici, and he must find a way of dealing with her. The white marble reminded him of the Duchessa's creamy unblemished skin, and he left the sculptor's workshop musing on youth and innocence and how little it could do in the long run against age and experience.

*

Sulien took Sky to walk the maze with him. At first the twenty-first-century boy was sceptical. It seemed a bit New Age-y to him, all this chanting and meditating and pacing slowly in silence. But it worked. He had stepped on to the black and white stone labyrinth with his mind all a-jangle.

Sulien had first explained to him about William Dethridge. 'He was the first Stravagante, an Elizabethan alchemist who was trying to make gold and instead, after an explosion in his laboratory, found the secret of travel in time and space.'

'And his laboratory was where my school and my house are now?'

'So it would appear,' said Sulien. 'When I brought your talisman, on the advice of both Doctor Dethridge and Rodolfo, I left it on the doorstep of what must be your home.'

Sky smiled at the thought of the friar in Islington. But monks and nuns and people like that still wore robes in Sky's time, so he probably wouldn't have attracted that much attention.

'You say that Dethridge and Rodolfo advised you,

but how did you speak to them? You said they both live in Bellezza now, and you don't have telephones yet.'

Sulien had then shown him a plain oval hand-mirror in which Sky saw not his own brown face reflected but a dark panelled room with a lot of strange instruments in it. Sulien passed his hand over its surface and closed his eyes, concentrating. And then there was a face, thin and bony, with hawk-like eyes and silvered black hair.

'Maestro,' said Sulien. 'Let me show you our new brother.'

He had encouraged Sky to look full in the mirror and he found himself face to face with Rodolfo. It had been an unsettling experience. Apart from his actual travelling between the two worlds, Sky had not encountered anything in Talia that could be described as magic until that moment.

Rodolfo was nothing but warm and welcoming, but Sky knew that he was talking to a powerful Stravagante – and doing it through an enchanted mirror. When he had stepped on to the maze a few minutes afterwards, his thoughts were a jagged and swirling mess.

When he left it twenty minutes later, he was quite calm. Sulien was five minutes behind him.

'Incredible,' said Sky.

'It was here when I arrived,' said Sulien. 'I found it under the carpet one day but the other friars didn't know how to use it. You don't have to believe it – just do it. I walk the maze every morning and evening, just so that I can find the centre whenever I need it.'

Sky looked alarmed.

'Don't worry,' said the friar. 'I don't expect you to do it that often. Only when you feel the need. I just wanted to show it to you.'

Sky was relieved. But a part of him knew he did want that experience again.

*

The Eel was waiting for his master outside the gates of the Palazzo di Chimici in the Via Larga. There was a new guard on duty that day who didn't know him. But he knew the Duke all right, and was apologetic when Niccolò arrived and waved the unprepossessing little man in after him.

'I wanted to talk to you about your contacts in Bellezza,' said Niccolò.

'That's a coincidence, your Grace,' said Enrico. 'That's what I've come to tell you. I've had a report from my man Beppe that the Duchessa will soon be in the city.'

'Buzz, buzz,' said Niccolò irritably. 'I learned that myself today. The point is I should have heard of it sooner.'

'And she is going to have her likeness made,' continued Enrico, unabashed.

'By Giuditta Miele, yes, yes,' said the Duke. 'Tell me something that I do not already know.'

'That her young paramour will accompany her?' hazarded Enrico.

'Paramour? You mean the old wizard's apprentice?'

'Yes, her father's favourite – and hers too, if rumours are true.' Enrico dared a familiar leer.

Everywhere he turned his thoughts or laid his plans,

Duke Niccolò seemed to come up against Rodolfo or his mysterious apprentice. He knew they were in some way connected with the death of his youngest son, which he believed was not a true death, even though he had held the lifeless body in his own arms and seen it laid in coffin and tomb. It was why he needed to persecute the Stravaganti. The very thought of the one young man alive while the other lay in a marble vault crowned by Giuditta Miele's statue, filled him with a wild rage that threatened to overturn his reason every time he entertained it.

Enrico read the signs; he wouldn't have mentioned the Bellezzan boy if the Duke hadn't known all his other information. Now he saw that he must try to direct his patron's thoughts to happier subjects.

'If I might ask, your Grace,' he said, 'how are the preparations going for the weddings?'

A long silence from Niccolò, then, 'Well. They are going well. I spent this morning ordering furniture and jewels for the young couples.'

Enrico decided to take a big risk. 'I wonder that your Grace doesn't think of taking a second wife yourself. Why should the young ones have all the fun? The princess Beatrice will one day need a husband herself, and a fine lord like your Grace needs the companionship of a good woman in his declining years.'

The gaze the Duke turned on him was terrifying.

'Not that your Grace is anywhere near declining yet,' spluttered Enrico, realising he had miscalculated. The Duke waved him aside, clutching at his throat, as if having trouble breathing. Then he regained control and looked at his spymaster with a new expression.

'You may leave,' he said. But after the Eel had gone, he said to himself in a ghastly voice, 'He is quite right. I shall take a wife. And I know just the woman.'

Chapter 6

Wedding Dresses

'Now we need to get out of the city,' said Sulien, when he and Sky had left the maze. He led the boy through the two cloisters to where a cart stood harnessed to two patient old horses in the cobbled yard.

'Where are we going?' asked Sky, surprised when Sulien motioned him up on to the seat and prepared to drive himself.

'To visit some more brothers up on the hill in Colle Vernale,' said Sulien, flicking the reins. 'We have plants to collect.'

It was an hour's ride, on the flat at first, but harder as they climbed the winding road round a steep hill to the north-east of Giglia. The views were fantastic from the city side of the hill, the whole of Giglia dominated by the great Cathedral of the Lily and its huge dome.

The air was a lot fresher than in the valley too and Sky breathed in the scent of flowers from the fields around.

He had never made a journey pulled by horses before; it made the whole pace of life seem slower and, as the cart moved steadily up the hill, Sky had the strangest feeling that his heart rate was slowing too, as it had in the maze. Sulien gave him a quizzical sideways look.

'How are you finding life in the sixteenth century?' he asked. 'We do things very differently from in your world, if the glimpses I've had of it recently are anything to go by.'

'It's weird,' admitted Sky. 'I'd have expected to find it a bit tame, but there seems to be so much going on. Tell me more about the dangers.'

'We take a long time to learn,' said Sulien, shaking his head. 'Family vendettas like that between the Nucci and the di Chimici go on for generations, sometimes bubbling underground, sometimes bursting out into violence and murder. At the moment the whole city feels like a cauldron, heating up to boiling point. These weddings provide the perfect opportunity for crime. The city will be full of strangers, the bridal procession will be through streets thronged with spectators, well-wishers and citizens, and no amount of city-guards could possibly keep an eye on all the crowds. It will mean that a single man armed with a dagger would be able to settle old scores.'

'And where do the Stravaganti come in?' asked Sky.

'There will be at least six in the city,' said Sulien. 'You, me and Giuditta and the three from Bellezza – Rodolfo, Luciano and Doctor Dethridge himself. It is our job to do what the guards cannot – protect the Duchessa of Bellezza and try to keep the peace for everyone else. And keep out of the Duke's way as much as possible, since he is against the Stravaganti.'

'And what am I supposed to do that you others can't?'

'That I do not know. Keep your eyes open and wait for the right opportunity,' said the friar. 'I'm sure it will come – otherwise you wouldn't be here – and I'm almost certain it will be at the weddings.'

*

Francesca di Chimici and the young Duchessa had rather surprisingly become good friends. The first time they had met had been when the young princess from Bellona had been forced to stand against Arianna in the election after the old Duchessa's 'assassination'. Forced too into marrying old Councillor Albani, from whom she had later been freed by the Pope's annulment.

But when they had next met, during the visit of Prince Gaetano to court the Duchessa in Bellezza, Arianna had softened towards the young woman she had been taught to think of as an enemy. It was clear that Francesca was both very unhappy and in love with Prince Gaetano herself, and Arianna had done everything she could to put the two cousins in each other's way.

And when Gaetano, acting under his father's orders in Remora, had finally brought himself to ask Arianna to marry him, she had been happy to refuse and glad to see the light in his eyes as she sent him off to ask

Francesca instead. Arianna liked Gaetano very much, something that made her more open to the idea that there were sympathetic di Chimici, but she didn't want to marry him.

Arianna and Francesca had travelled back to Bellezza at the same time and had become friends during the time that the di Chimici princess was packing up her belongings and extricating herself from Albani's house, before going back to Bellona.

And now she was in Bellezza again, as the Duchessa's guest. They never talked about politics and Francesca had no idea that Arianna's mother was still alive; even Gaetano didn't know that. Instead, they were in deep discussion about clothes.

'I didn't get a proper wedding last time,' said Francesca. 'And I hoped for something rather splendid in Giglia, but now we have to share the day with Gaetano's two brothers and cousin Alfonso, it's going to be a bit of a circus. Four couples – can you imagine? It would not have been my preference to share the day with three other brides!'

'But you will be the prettiest, I'm sure,' said Arianna, adjusting her green silk mask.

'Oh, as to that, I don't care,' said Francesca, tossing her black hair as well as she could for its pins and braids. 'But Gaetano and I will be the least important couple in the cathedral. And I did so want it to be special.'

'Nonsense!' said Arianna firmly. 'You will be the most important to each other – and to me. I don't know the Duke of Volana or his duchess-to-be and I've met Prince Fabrizio and Carlo only briefly and never seen their brides. I'm sure they are all very good-looking and important, but you and Gaetano are the only di Chimici who are my friends.'

Francesca flashed her a grateful smile.

'I've had an idea,' said Arianna. 'What were you planning to wear?'

*

Sulien and Sky drew into a small village, the horses sweating and panting. 'It will be a lot easier for them on the way back,' said the friar. 'It will be downhill all the way and my plants make one of the lightest loads for a beast of burden.'

After a few minutes' rest, he urged the two nags up a steep side path out of Colle Vernale to a friary at the very top of the hill. From the quiet grassy terrace outside, the view over the countryside was spectacular. Sky could see not only the city and its cathedral dome, snug in the valley, but the great river Argento which fed it, snaking down from the distant mountains. If he screwed up his eyes, Sky could trace the blue thread of it right back up to its source.

'The Argento is running high for this time of year,' said Sulien, following the line of his gaze.

'It's fantastic up here!' said Sky. 'Everything so far away but so clear. I feel as if I could touch the campanile of the cathedral if I just reached out a bit.'

Sulien smiled. 'Not yet,' he said. 'You are still a very new Stravagante.'

A brown-robed friar came bustling out to greet them.

'Welcome, welcome,' he said. 'Welcome to San Francesco.'

The friar must mean his Friary of Saint Francis, Sky thought. So Dominicans wore black and white and Franciscans wore brown. Just how many more religious orders were there to learn?

After introductions and instructions to a novice of his own to look after the horses, Brother Martino led them into his little church, which was cool after the sunshine and smelt of incense and candlewax. But they didn't linger there, crossing rapidly to a door into a cloister. When Brother Martino opened it, Sky was blinded by the light, overwhelmed by aromatic scents and almost deafened by the sound of birdsong.

The cloister was a herb garden. It was smaller than even the Lesser Cloister at Saint-Mary-among-the-Vines, and arranged around a fountain, whose spray sparkled in the sunlight. Low hedges clipped firmly into shape surrounded the herb beds. The wall nearest the church was one huge aviary, in which little birds like finches twittered and flew, singing at full throat.

Martino stopped to pull a pouch of seed from his belt of white rope and filled the feeders. The tuneful song immediately turned to squawking and squabbling.

The friars left the noisy cloister and entered the refectory, where Martino offered the Giglian visitors cold grape juice from a terracotta pitcher. Sky gulped it thirstily.

When they were refreshed, they went out to a yard behind the friary, where the horse cart was being loaded up by young friars. Hessian sacks gave off pungent and spicy scents.

'Fennel,' said Sulien, consulting a list. 'Lemon balm, valerian, pennywort, mallow, mint, burdock, borage, dandelion, bergamot.' He walked around the cart, crushing dried leaves between his brown fingers, and tying sacks tighter.

Sky was feeling dizzy. The smells reminded him of home and his mother's herb-based oils. What was he doing here, high up above a Renaissance city, wearing a friar's robe?

'The flowers are brought to me from all the meadows around Giglia,' said Brother Sulien. 'But the herbs I collect from Colle Vernale myself. I trust no one else to bring them to me with their properties undiminished.'

*

'Will you let me help you?' Arianna asked Francesca. 'My grandmother lives on one of the islands and makes exquisite lace. She makes it for all the most beautiful wedding dresses in the lagoon and can create any design. Shall we go there and ask her to make yours? I should love to give you your dress as my wedding present. And I haven't been to Burlesca for a long time.'

*

Camillo Nucci had an interest in herbs and plants himself, at least the poisonous variety. He had been brought up to hate the di Chimici family and he saw himself as the natural avenger of all his clan's insults and slights at their hands, not to mention the murders for which Duke Niccolò's family were responsible. It didn't bother Camillo that the di Chimici were growing in power and spreading over Talia; he wasn't interested in politics. All he wanted to do was even the score.

The upcoming weddings would provide perfect cover for an attempt on the di Chimici; the city was already filling up with merchants and pilgrims for Easter, and the public celebrations for the princes' marriage would only increase the numbers. Who could say whether a particular poison introduced into a di Chimici dish had come from within the city or from one of their many enemies from beyond Giglia?

Now he was closeted with an old monk from Volana, discussing with him the properties of the wild mushrooms that grew in the fields and forests around the city. But he had not noticed a scruffy street boy, who had trailed him to the family's old palazzo up near Saint-Mary-among-the-Vines and was now listening through a crack in the door.

'Now why does Camillo Nucci want to know about poisonous mushrooms?' Sandro asked himself. He made a mental note to pass this on to the Eel, then set off in search of Brother Tino.

*

The boatman rowed the Duchessa and her friend out across the lagoon to Burlesca. He was doing double duty as a guard, and the Duchessa also had a young Cavaliere with her, armed with a wicked-looking merlino-dagger. Luciano carried his weapon openly, but only he knew that Arianna had one of her own tucked into a garter. Her foster-brothers, true to an old promise, had given it to her when she turned sixteen, and Luciano had no doubt that she would use it if attacked.

'I came here with Gaetano last year,' said Francesca, happy at the memory.

Luciano looked at her curiously. Francesca never referred to the fact that her husband-to-be had been courting another woman the previous summer, a woman who was rapidly becoming her closest female friend. He himself had been all too aware of it, during the weeks when he had been in Remora, unsure whether Arianna would accept the di Chimici prince. His feelings about it hadn't been uncomplicated either, since he liked Gaetano, and had been having his own adventures with Georgia, the Stravagante. Not romantic ones, but their shared status as Stravaganti made their relationship special and had given him an insight into why the company of a Duke's son might be pleasant to a Duchess.

'Look, there's their house,' said Arianna. 'The white one among all the colours.'

The boat moored in the harbour and the young people moved through the village, receiving interested glances. Two good-looking women, richly dressed, both masked, were bound to attract attention.

'That's the young Duchessa,' was the whisper. 'Come to see her grandparents, no doubt.'

Paola Bellini sat outside her whitewashed cottage as usual, with her lace cushion. She had been mother and grandmother to a Duchessa, but had no desire to live anywhere grander than the little white house that had been her home for the last fifty years.

'Grandmother,' called one of the slender masked young women, hastening towards her. 'We need lace for a wedding dress!'

Paola's black eyes snapped towards Luciano but he met her glance with a slight frown.

'For my friend, Francesca,' Arianna continued smoothly. But she had seen the look and a flush crept up her neck.

*

Burlesca wasn't the only place where wedding dresses were being discussed. In Fortezza, the Princesses Lucia and Bianca were plaguing their father to death on the subject.

'Daughters, daughters!' Prince Jacopo exclaimed to his wife, Princess Carolina. 'Why did you give me nothing but daughters? I shall go mad if I hear another word about satin, silk, velvet or brocade!'

'What about taffeta?' asked Carolina, unperturbed. 'And I was of the impression that *you* gave the daughters to *me*.'

She was perfectly aware that Jacopo was devoted to his girls and, even if he was sad at the thought that his title would pass to the son of another di Chimici, he would not have exchanged them for all the boys in Talia.

'Tell them they can have what they like, as long as I don't have to hear about it,' said the prince, caressing the ears of his water-spaniel.

'But what about jewels?' asked the princess. 'They must have something special for their wedding day. Remember, Bianca will become a duchess and Lucia will be the Princess of Remora one day.'

'Haven't we enough in the palace treasury to kit

them out without ordering more?' asked Jacopo. 'You hardly ever wear the things.'

Carolina sighed. 'Fashions change, my dear,' she said. 'The gems I had at our wedding belonged to your mother and your grandmother before her. I didn't mind, but young women today are quite different. They may want something specially set in Giglia, where all the fashionable jewellers are.'

'Then let cousin Niccolò buy them,' growled Jacopo. 'He seems intent on masterminding these weddings.'

Princess Carolina let the subject drop. She knew how her husband felt about having their daughters married in the cathedral in Giglia. It had unfortunate associations for him. But she hadn't been his wife for thirty years without knowing how to manage Jacopo's moods. She would make discreet enquiries of Niccolò's daughter, Beatrice, and find out if he intended gifts of jewellery. If not, she would order something suitable for her daughters herself.

*

Rinaldo di Chimici was a changed man. At his powerful uncle's urging, he had entered the church. He was now Father Rinaldo, with good prospects of a cardinal's hat before long. Of course he was not a parish priest; he was far too grand for that. He had left the family's palace in Volana and become the Pope's own chaplain in Remora. It suited him very well to be so close to the Head of the Church in Talia, who was his uncle too, and he found the life of a clergyman in the Papal palace comfortable and easy.

And he had at last got rid of Enrico, who had gone to Giglia to spy for the Duke. Now Father Rinaldo was practising forgetting his life as an Ambassador when he had ordered the death of a woman, the last Duchessa of Bellezza, and was looking forward to assisting the Pope at the forthcoming di Chimici weddings.

Both his brother and sister were getting married – Caterina to Prince Fabrizio, who would one day be Duke of Giglia and head of the di Chimici family. Rinaldo was pleased with how his life was working out. He dreamed of a future in which he would be brother-in-law to Duke Fabrizio the Second and maybe Pope himself. It was a sweeter prospect than had faced him when he had failed to bring Bellezza into the family fold and had let that black-haired boy slip through his fingers. And if he were Pope it would put him in a position of power higher even than his older brother Alfonso.

*

In Volana, Duke Alfonso was closeted with his sister Caterina, also discussing the weddings. He was as relieved as Rinaldo that she was marrying so well within the family, so much so that he hadn't minded being assigned Bianca, Old Jacopo's younger daughter, even though she didn't bring a title with her. Besides, Bianca was very pretty and Alfonso had been a bit lonely in his castle since he had inherited the title four years before.

His mother, the dowager Duchess Isabella, had thrown off her widow's weeds and was entering into the spirit of the forthcoming celebrations.

'We must find out what your cousins are planning, my dear,' she said to Caterina. 'As bride to the Duke's heir, you must be the most splendid, mustn't she, Fonso darling?'

'My own bride must not be neglected, however, Mother,' the Duke said mildly. 'How would it look if the new Duchessa of Volana were cast into the shade by her sister-in-law?'

'These are delicate matters,' said the dowager, now in her element. 'But the weddings will be in Giglia, where the "figura" of their prince will weigh more than ours.'

'Still, we must do honour to our family too,' said Caterina, who secretly had no objection to outshining her new sister-in-law, though she had no reason to dislike Bianca herself. 'Perhaps we should take advice from Duke Niccolò?'

Her mother snorted in a most unducal manner. 'I think we've had quite enough advice from him.' Isabella would have preferred her son to marry the Duke's daughter, rather than the Fortezza girl, but she had seen the wisdom of going along with his plans for her family. And she quite understood that Niccolò was not ready to part with his Beatrice yet, after his recent bereavement.

Isabella sighed. She did not relish losing her own daughter to Giglia, even though it was such an advancement for Caterina. The dowager must learn to make do with her daughter-in-law.

*

'Brothers!' called Sandro when he saw them descending from the cart. 'Where have you been?'

'Collecting herbs,' said Sulien. 'And I must unpack and store them quickly, so perhaps you two would like to get yourselves something to eat in the kitchen.'

The two boys were drawn into the warmth of the kitchen, where Brother Tullio wielded the knife and ladle, assisted by two nervous novices. He was disposed to be cross till he heard Sulien had sent them.

'Ah, so the pharmacist is back,' he said. 'Brother Ambrogio, take him some refreshment to the storeroom. He won't stir from there till all his herbs are stowed. And as for you two, well, boys must be fed, I suppose.'

He gave them bread and sheep's milk cheese and tomatoes and hard little pears which were as sweet as they were tough.

'You know what he does with his plants?' said Sandro casually, as they took their booty out into the cloister and picnicked sitting on its low wall.

'Makes medicines, of course,' said Sky. He didn't want always to know less than Sandro.

'And?' persisted the little spy.

'Well, he makes perfume from the flowers, I know,' said Sky. 'And all sorts of lotions and potions.'

Sandro tapped the side of his nose. 'Close,' he said. 'But not just potions – poisons too.'

*

When they got back to the Palazzo Ducale in Bellezza, Arianna was tired but pleased with the day. She was sure that Francesca's dress would be magnificent.

Luciano left her at the door and returned to his home with Doctor Dethridge and Leonora, while Francesca went to change her dress for dinner.

Arianna and her maid Barbara were chatting about lace in her private room when Rodolfo came to see her. His expression immediately spelt trouble; she had rarely seen him look so disturbed.

'We have had another message from Duke Niccolò,' he said abruptly.

'He has no sons left unengaged to sue for my hand,' said Arianna, more lightly than she felt.

'It is not a marriage proposal this time,' said Rodolfo. 'It is a request to know your measurements. Niccolò di Chimici wants to send you a dress to wear at the weddings.'

Chapter 7

Deadly Nightshade

Sky found concentrating on his school work very hard the next day. Sulien had urged him to stravagate home early and he hadn't been reluctant. Sandro's information had knocked Sky for six. Could the friar possibly be a poisoner? Or at least a maker of poisons? It didn't make much difference really; if you made them, you knew what they were going to be used for.

Sky tried to remember what Brother Sulien had said to him in the Great Cloister on his first visit. 'The laboratory is where I prepare the medicines – and the perfumes, of course.' He hadn't said anything about poisons. Sulien was a good man – Sky was sure of it. But were good and bad the same in sixteenth-century Talia as now in London?

He was glad that school was breaking up soon for Easter. Georgia had warned him that he would get very tired during the day if he spent every night stravagating to Talia and today he understood what she meant.

Nicholas Duke was as good as his word and was waiting for Sky in the gym in the lunch break. Georgia had come along to watch. Nick handed Sky a mesh mask to protect his face and a foil with a sort of button on the end.

'You won't need padding for a trial session,' he said. 'I promise not to hurt you.'

Arrogant little prat, thought Sky, I'll show you.

But Nicholas was good, very good, and Sky couldn't get his foil anywhere near the younger boy's body. By the end of the session, he was sweating and panting and Nicholas seemed as cool as at the beginning. As Sky towelled his streaming face he was very glad that Alice hadn't joined Georgia to watch them.

'Good,' said Nicholas. 'You'll be a good fencer.'

Sky stopped, astonished. 'What do you mean? I was rubbish.'

'What do you think the point of fencing is?' asked Nicholas, looking at him intently.

'To slice your opponent,' said Sky.

'No,' said Nicholas. 'It is to prevent him from slicing you. Only assassins fight to kill the other person.'

Great, thought Sky. That's all I need – another younger kid to tell me what's what.

'It's true you didn't touch me,' continued Nicholas. 'But you didn't let me touch you many times either –

your defences are instinctive and that's good to work with.'

'Look,' said Sky, turning to Georgia for support. 'I'm not really going to learn to fence, am I? I just made that up to explain our being together.'

To his surprise, Georgia didn't back him up.

'Nick and I think it might not be a bad idea for you to learn,' she said. 'True, it will give us an excuse to spend time together – I often watch him in practice and matches – but we also think it might be useful for your protection in Talia.'

Sky felt the hairs on the back of his neck rise.

'What? You think someone may try to kill me?'

'Why not?' said Nicholas with a shrug. 'You're a Stravagante, aren't you? Let's go and get some lunch. I'm starving.'

Rodolfo, Luciano and Doctor Dethridge worked together late into the night in Rodolfo's laboratory in Bellezza. Luciano had been an apprentice to both older men and had learned a lot. Although he had been released from his apprenticeship and was supposed to be going to university the following year, he still felt he had much to learn. Now they were working together to see whether it would be possible for Stravaganti from the other world to travel to cities in Talia other than the ones their talismans came from.

'Wee coulde sende more thane one talismanne to eche Stravayger,' Doctor Dethridge had suggested, 'but it does not seme ryghte to mee to do such a thynge.'

'Nor to me,' agreed Rodolfo. 'But it does limit the usefulness of other-world Stravaganti to be able to travel to only one city. Luciano we now have with us always and everywhere and we are heartily glad of it, but he is one of our Talian Brotherhood now and no longer a traveller from the other world. Suppose we needed Georgia in Bellezza? Or this new one, Sky, might need to come here from Giglia.'

'Sky?' said Luciano, interested. There had been only one person with that name at his old school. He could just remember the young Sky Meadows from Year 10, but of course more than a year had passed since he had been 'translated' to Talia and then there had been that time lurch when Falco had died in Remora. Sky must be in the Lower Sixth now, he calculated, with Georgia.

'I saw him through Brother Sulien's mirror,' said Rodolfo. 'This time it is a young man and he is a Moor, like Sulien. I am very glad that Sulien has brought us another Stravagante. There is trouble brewing in the city.'

'Aye,' said Dethridge. 'Where the chymists have their home there will always bee daungere. In especial where the Duke ys to bee founde.'

'We had a message from him today,' said Rodolfo carefully, not looking at Luciano. 'He wants to send Arianna a dress to wear at the weddings.'

Luciano felt uneasy. 'Is that usual?' he asked.

'He has sent gifts before,' said Rodolfo. 'It is common between Heads of State. But he intends her to wear this garment and it is a much more personal gift than ever before.'

'Well, what does that mean?' asked Luciano.

'Yt meyneth somethinge ill, yow canne be certayne,' said Dethridge.

Luciano was used to the Elizabethan's antiquated way of talking by now and agreed with him that anything Duke Niccolò was planning would be bad news.

Alice was waiting for them in the cafeteria and seemed surprised that the chance meeting of the day before had already led to fencing lessons for Sky and a friendship among the three. But she didn't mind. It gave her the chance to get to know Sky better.

'Does Alice know about you two?' Sky asked Nicholas quietly as they walked back to lessons.

'What do you think?' said Nicholas. 'Would you ever have told anyone about Talia, if you hadn't known I came from there?'

'It must make it hard, though,' said Sky. 'Doesn't she wonder about your friendship?'

'Georgia told her she felt responsible for me,' said Nicholas, his face suddenly creased with pain. 'And Alice believes her, because Georgia was supposed to have found me in this world and taken me to Luciano's parents – Lucien, as you knew him.'

Sky saw how it was with the younger boy and felt sorry for him. Nicholas was obviously devoted to Georgia but feared she would never feel more than concerned friendship for him.

Quickly he changed the subject. There wasn't long before afternoon school and their lessons were in different buildings.

'Did you know Brother Sulien in your old life?' he asked. 'Do you think he could possibly be involved in making poisons?'

To his surprise, Nicholas continued to look agonised. He shook his head.

'No, I didn't know him then. There was a different friar in charge of the pharmacy when I last was there. But I know that Saint-Mary-among-the-Vines does supply poison. There is a second, secret laboratory somewhere in the friary. My family has got poison from there in the past.'

Duke Niccolò took Carlo into his confidence first. They had finished their weekly business meeting and were eating a private lunch together in the small dining chamber of the old palazzo, with only one servant.

'The weddings are less than two months away now,' said the Duke. 'On their eve, I shall make an important announcement.'

Carlo looked expectant, helping himself to polenta. He took a generous helping of wild boar stew but refused the dish of mushrooms proffered by the servant.

'The legislation is already in place,' said Niccolò, allowing the servant to add mushrooms to his much smaller helping. 'I intend to adopt the title of Grand Duke of all Tuschia.'

Whatever Carlo had expected, it was not that. 'Can you do that?' he asked, rather tactlessly.

His father raised his eyebrows. 'I don't see why

not,' he said. 'We have family members ruling in all the main city-states of the region of Tuschia – Moresco, Remora, Fortezza – and they would not dispute my claims to create such a title, as head of the family.'

'Of course not, Father,' said Carlo hastily. 'I'm sorry. I was just surprised, that's all.'

And the two men began to eat their meal in silence, each occupied with his own thoughts.

It took Sky a long time to stravagate that night. Normally he had no trouble sleeping; the busyness of his life at home ensured that. But that night he tossed and turned, thinking about poisons, fencing, unrequited love and all sorts of other things. Eventually, he got up and fetched some water from the fridge. He carried Remedy back to bed with him and settled down again with the cat in the crook of his arm and the glass bottle in his hand.

Then he had second thoughts and moved the tabby down to his feet; it would never do for Brother Tino to turn up in the friary with a miniature tiger in tow.

As soon as he arrived in Saint-Mary-among-the-Vines, Sky could see from the light that it was about midday. Sulien wasn't in his cell or the laboratory or the pharmacy. Sky wandered out into the cloisters; all was eerily quiet. He could hear the faint sound of chanting coming from the church.

And then a messenger burst into the Great Cloister from the yard. He took Sky for a novice and grabbed him by the arm.

'Where is Brother Sulien? He is urgently needed in the Via Larga – Duke Niccolò has been poisoned!'

*

Sandro was having his lunch bought for him in a tavern near the market. The Eel was in an expansive mood, as a result of soup and pasta and a large quantity of red wine.

'The Duke is up to something,' he was saying. 'You mark my words, Sparrow. There'll be an announcement soon.'

A flutter of movement in the corner of the market caught Sandro's eye. Black and white robes flapped as two figures ran through the square at an undignified pace.

'Look,' said Sandro. 'There go Sulien and Tino. What on earth can they be doing?'

'Only one way to find out,' slurred the Eel, throwing silver on the table. 'Come on!'

The two spies, master and boy, hurried after the friars. It was clear where they were heading. The great palazzo on the Via Larga almost backed on to the market and the square provided a short cut to it from the friary.

By the time Sulien and Sky had reached the palazzo gates, a small knot of people had gathered outside; news travelled fast in Talia and the rumours were already flying. The Duke was dead, the di Chimici had all been poisoned; the weddings were off.

Sky hadn't had any time to think. When the Duke's servant had arrived with his alarming news, Sky had found Sulien in the church and hurried with him to the pharmacy to collect bottles of medicine, before running all the way to the di Chimici palazzo. Now another servant led them, panting, up the great staircase to the Duke's bedroom, where he had been carried after his collapse.

The room had a foul stench of vomit and the figure on the bed was thrashing around on soiled sheets, in paroxysms of agony. His sons stood beside him wringing their hands, though the only one Sky recognised was Prince Gaetano. And he supposed the young woman trying to bathe the Duke's face was his daughter Princess Beatrice.

Brother Sulien took command as soon as he entered the room.

'Who was with the Duke when the poisoning took place?'

'I was,' said one of the young men. 'We were having lunch together.'

'Did you eat the same things?' asked Sulien, who had already crossed to the Duke and was trying to take his pulse.

'I didn't have the mushrooms,' said the prince, 'I don't like them. But Father had some.'

'And when did the signs of poisoning come on?'

'Almost immediately. He complained of stomach pains while we were eating some fruit. And then he started to vomit.'

'Can you hold him down, please?' said Brother Sulien. 'I'd like to examine his eyes.'

Sky was impressed by how the friar was taking

over; there were no 'your Highnesses' or ceremonious bows. He could see that speed was essential if the Duke's life were to be saved.

'I'll need clean linen and plenty of water heated up,' said the friar, after looking into the Duke's eyes, which kept rolling alarmingly back into his head. 'And warm coverings.'

He sniffed the bowl by the Duke's bed. 'Open the windows and air the room,' he ordered.

Princes and servants alike hurried to do the friar's bidding.

'Will he live?' asked the princess, pleading.

'It is not certain,' said Sulien. 'But if he can be saved I promise I shall do it. Now, Tino, hand me the phial with the purple liquid.'

Sky rummaged in the bag and found the right phial.

'I'll need a small glass of clean drinking water,' said Sulien, and Beatrice poured the water with an unsteady hand.

The friar took the stopper from the phial and added four or five drops of the dark purple tincture to the water, which turned a purplish black. It reminded Sky of the water he cleaned his paintbrushes in at school.

'He has to drink all this,' said Sulien. 'It's not going to be easy.'

The Duke was still racked with spasms and his teeth were bared in a ghastly rictus. It took all three princes and Sky to hold him still while the friar forced the purple liquid into his mouth. Niccolò struggled like a wild cat and Sky wondered if he thought he were being poisoned anew. After what he had heard from Sandro, the awful thought crossed Sky's mind that Sulien might actually be trying to finish the Duke off.

But he thrust it away again as he watched the Stravagante straddling the poisoned Duke on the bed, determined to get the antidote into the Duke's failing body.

Within minutes Niccolò di Chimici's struggles ceased and the whole room seemed to be holding its breath. The friar got off the bed and smoothed his robes down. The glass was empty.

'You can let him go now,' said Sulien. The princes rested their father back gently against the pillows. His white hair was plastered to his head and his eyes were staring, the pupils hugely dilated, but he lay still and the spasms seemed to have stopped.

'It is a miracle,' said Princess Beatrice, crossing herself.

'Just science,' said Sulien. 'I have given him extract of belladonna to calm the spasms. The poison was one of the muscarines found in some species of mushrooms. He will need rest, and no nourishment but water and some warm milk for twenty-four hours. You must see that he is washed and given clean linen and kept warm and that the room is well aired.'

'Of course,' said Beatrice. 'I shall wash him myself.'

Brother Sulien motioned to the princes to follow him into the next room, while the princess and servants fussed around the now apparently sleeping Duke. Sky followed his master, still dazed by what he had taken part in.

'We are eternally grateful to you, Brother,' said the handsomest of the princes, rather stiffly but with genuine emotion.

'Thank you, your Highness,' said Sulien, reverting

to the usual courtesies. 'May I present my assistant, Brother Celestino? Tino, this is Prince Fabrizio, the Duke's heir, and this is Prince Carlo, his brother. Prince Gaetano you have already met.'

Sky bowed to each in turn and they to him. 'We are grateful to you too, for your help,' said Prince Fabrizio.

Prince Carlo suddenly slumped into a chair. 'I thought he was going to die,' he said, dropping his head in his hands. 'It was terrible to see him.'

'Who made the dish with the mushrooms, your Highness?' asked Sulien gravely.

'I don't know,' said Carlo. 'I assumed it was made in the kitchens.'

'And who served it? Does the Duke not use tasters?'

'Usually,' said Gaetano. 'Did he today, Carlo?'

His brother shook his head. 'We lunched alone, with only one servant.'

'Which one?' asked Fabrizio.

Carlo shook his head as if trying to clear it. 'I don't know. I don't think I noticed.'

Sky wondered what it must be like to have so many servants that you didn't notice which one was on duty. Did these princes even know the names of any of the palace servants?

'We must find out,' said Gaetano. 'And about who cooked the dish. Could it have been an accident, Brother Sulien?'

'It is not impossible,' said the friar. 'Mushrooms are treacherous. You would need to know when and where they were gathered or whether they were bought from the market. But it is also possible that muscarine was introduced into the dish in the kitchens or by a servant, using ordinary mushrooms to disguise the taste.'

'The Nucci are behind this, without doubt,' said Prince Fabrizio, still white-faced with shock.

'Your Highness knows best,' said Sulien calmly. 'But I should think that it would be wise to conduct some investigations among the palace household before any public accusations are made.'

'Quite right,' nodded Fabrizio. 'It shall be done.'

'What else must we do for Father?' asked Gaetano.

'I shall leave this phial,' said Sulien. 'Three drops only, in water, to be given night and morning. No more. I shall return tomorrow to see how the Duke progresses.'

'Saint-Mary-among-the-Vines will be the richer for your work here today,' said Prince Fabrizio, shaking the friar's hand.

*

Sandro and the Eel got through the palazzo gate easily enough but a guard barred their way up to the Duke's chamber. So they had to cool their heels in the courtyard with the bronze nude statue. Enrico was consumed with curiosity about his master's state.

'Why did they let that friar up?' he fumed, pacing up and down. 'And that greenhorn of a novice, your friend, when they won't let me anywhere near him?'

It was about half an hour before Sulien and Sky came down the grand marble staircase.

'What happened?' Enrico asked eagerly. 'How is the Duke?'

'He will live,' said Sulien. 'At least, this time. He

was poisoned by a dish of mushrooms.'

Sandro remembered the discussion he had overheard between Camillo Nucci and the monk from Volana. He decided to tell Enrico as soon as he could.

'Can I see the Duke?' asked Enrico.

'I can't say,' said Sulien. 'That is up to his guards and the family. But he is sleeping now. I don't think he will see anyone for a while.'

Enrico set off, determined to try his luck with the guards again, but told Sandro to wait in the courtyard. Sulien went over to the fountain to splash cold water on his face.

Sky whispered to Sandro, 'You see he is no poisoner. He saved the Duke's life with something called belladonna. It stopped the spasms straightaway.'

Sandro was looking at him oddly.

'What?' asked Sky.

'Nothing,' said Sandro. 'Only belladonna is a poison, too. Deadly nightshade is its other name. I'm just wondering why Brother Sulien had a supply of it to hand.'

Chapter 8

Two Households, Both Alike in Dignity

Sky was silent over a late Saturday breakfast, wondering what on earth he should tell Nicholas about what had just happened in Giglia. How would *he* feel if someone brought him news of his mother from another world and he had to hear that she had been poisoned?

'How's the fencing going?' asked Rosalind.

'Fine,' said Sky, snapping out of his reverie. 'It was really good, actually. I mean, I wasn't very good, but Nicholas thinks I can be if I train hard.'

'Is he serious about teaching you?' she asked. 'If you're really keen, shouldn't we get you some paid lessons?'

'It's very expensive, Mum, and he's very good,' said

Sky. 'We're lucky that he's willing to do it for free.'

Sky got up and cleared the breakfast away, automatically loading the dishwasher and wiping the table. Then he checked Remedy's food and water bowl.

'What will you have for lunch?' he asked, opening the fridge. 'I'm going to meet Nicholas for another lesson – shall I make you a sandwich to eat later?'

'No, darling. I'm all right today. I can make something myself when I'm hungry.'

Sky looked at his mother. It was true; she did seem all right. He sat down at the table again, taking one of her hands in his.

'Are you really all right? You do seem a lot better.'

His mother nodded. 'I don't know why, but I feel as if I am coming to the end of a long tunnel. And it has been a long one, hasn't it? I don't know what I would have done without you.'

Sky escaped to meet Nicholas at the local gym, not wanting to stay and listen to her gratitude. If his life had stayed normal, he would have been feeling light-hearted now. His mother was getting better, the days were warming up and it would be the Easter holidays in a few weeks. But as a Stravagante, he found everything getting complicated. He had seen the most powerful man in Talia nearly die from poisoning and he was no longer sure who could be trusted.

※

It was a matter of honour to Camillo Nucci, the eldest of the young generation of his family, to loathe every di Chimici, and it was his dearest wish to avenge the murder of his uncle Donato, which had happened before he was born. His father, Matteo, was the richest Nucci so far and had commissioned the most splendid palace on the far side of the river, mainly to annoy Duke Niccolò. It was bigger than either the Palazzo di Chimici in the Via Larga or the grand Palazzo Ducale in the city's main square.

The Nucci were as old a family as the di Chimici and nearly as rich. But the two clans had been at war for as long as anyone could remember. It had most likely begun two hundred years previously when the first Alfonso di Chimici had been friends with the first Donato Nucci. The two young men had both courted the same young woman, the beautiful Semiramide. She was as haughty as she was lovely and the two suitors were less highly born than her.

It was the time when the two families were accumulating their first fortunes, the Nucci from wool and the di Chimici from distilling perfume. Each young man brought a gift for Semiramide. Donato's was a woollen shawl, warm and soft but not particularly elegant. Alfonso's was a crystal phial of lily cologne.

Semiramide was vain, it was summer, the shawl was set aside, the perfume applied to her wrists, and Alfonso's suit was favoured. For generations afterwards, when a Nucci met a di Chimici in the street, one would hold his nose and the other bleat like a sheep. The di Chimici's star rose rapidly; the money they made selling their perfumes and lotions brought them such riches that they were soon acting as bankers to half the royal houses of Europa and charging high interest on their loans.

Alfonso died in his sixties and his eldest son, Fabrizio, declared himself Duke of Giglia within eighteen months. The Nucci's fortune grew too and their acres of sheep farms ensured their continuing prosperity. But they could never catch up with the di Chimici, who gave themselves airs and wore fine clothes and acquired titles the way other men bought boots.

The Nucci could have rallied their supporters to form some kind of opposition to the di Chimici in Giglia. But they chose instead to brood over their wrongs and school their young people in hatred of the perfumiers and bankers.

Still, they were almost social equals, being richer than any other Giglian family, and it seemed as if the old enmities would be forgotten when young Donato was offered the hand of Eleanora di Chimici. But the original feud sprang up again a hundred times more fiercely after the insult to Eleanora and Donato's murder.

So it was with undisguised pleasure that Camillo received the news of the Duke's poisoning. His informant was a man who had removed his di Chimici servant's livery and run straight from the Via Larga to the Nucci's old palazzo.

'You stayed to see him taken ill?' pressed Camillo.

'Yes,' said the man. 'I served him with the mushrooms myself, the young prince having none, as you said would be the case. Then, when the main course was cleared and they were eating fruit, the Duke started to clutch his stomach. I waited until the vomiting began, then thought I should make myself scarce.'

'They will investigate the cook first, I don't doubt,' said Camillo. 'I should not like to be in his shoes.' He handed over a purse full of silver. 'Well done. And now I suggest you should take a little holiday – perhaps in the mountains – for a few weeks.'

*

Camillo would not have been so happy if he had seen Duke Niccolò a few hours later, sitting up in bed in a snowy nightshirt, his eyes glittering and his mind and body unimpaired.

His sons were around him and his daughter waited on his every need, but there was to be no deathbed scene – not this time.

'What did the cook say?' he asked Fabrizio.

'He swore that the mushrooms came from his usual supplier and were wholesome when he sent up the dish,' said the prince.

'And did you torture him to make sure his answer was honest?' asked the Duke, as he might have said, 'Are you sure it's not raining?'

'Yes, Father,' said Fabrizio. 'Not personally, of course, and not much. It was clear he was telling the truth. He has been in the family's service a long time.'

'No one is incorruptible,' said the Duke. 'No one. But I expect you are right. What about the footman?'

'No one has seen him since the meal was served,' said Prince Carlo. 'It is most likely that the poison was introduced by him. We have men out searching the city.'

'And what are they looking for?' said the Duke. 'A

man. That's all we could remember about him, isn't it?'

Carlo was silent.

'Let us waste no more time on the servant,' said the Duke. 'It is the master we want. I know I have many enemies, but this is not the work of the Stravaganti. Their methods are more subtle. It is to the house of Nucci that we must look for the origin of this attempt on my life.' He looked ready to leap out of bed and bring the culprit to book himself.

'Rest now, Father,' said Beatrice. 'You are still weak and must sleep in order to recover your strength.'

'Don't we need some proof before accusing the Nucci?' asked Prince Gaetano. 'It is only a guess that they were behind it.'

'Find proof, then,' snapped the Duke. 'But in the meantime, if I still have three sons loyal to their father, I shall expect this crime to be avenged.'

Sky waited till he and Nicholas were showering after their fencing lesson before telling him about the Duke. It was the only time he could be sure Georgia wouldn't be around. He didn't think she would approve of his passing on such disturbing news.

'Poisoned?' said Nicholas, standing still under the spray. 'Is he all right?'

'Yes,' said Sky. 'He's going to be fine. Brother Sulien gave him an antidote.'

'But who did it?'

Sky shrugged. 'No one knows.'

'It was the Nucci, I bet,' said Nicholas, as they

towelled themselves in the changing room. 'I can't bear it. I must go there.'

'To Giglia?' said Sky, surprised.

Nicholas sighed. 'But I can't, can I? My talisman comes from Remora and would take me to the City of Stars. I could ride to Giglia from there but it would take me at least half a day and I'd have to get back to Remora in the same day to stravagate back here.' He tugged his wet hair in frustration. 'And it's not that easy, going back. But I must. It drives me mad to think of my family in danger. What if someone tried to kill Gaetano?'

Carlo didn't consult his brothers. He took a dagger from the chest in his room and hid it down the side of his suede boot. Running down the steps of the palazzo, he bumped into the man he knew Duke Niccolò used as a spy.

'Come with me,' Carlo hissed at him. 'Take me to where the Nucci will be.'

Enrico knew vendetta when he saw it. He made no attempt to calm or dissuade the prince. If a di Chimici wanted to kill a Nucci that was family business. If Enrico could help they would be grateful, and whether the attempt failed or succeeded, he would have a hold over another di Chimici family member.

The two men left the palazzo, trailed by an inconspicuous street boy. The Eel recognised his young apprentice and smiled to himself; it wouldn't hurt at all to have another witness.

The Nucci would be at their palazzo near Saint-

Mary-among-the-Vines, Enrico thought, though that was a bad place to carry out revenge. He recommended waiting nearby till one came out. It was nearly dusk, and once the torches were lit, all of Giglia's fashionable families would dress in their best and join in the 'passeggiata' round the city's main squares.

Carlo was a complete amateur; he wanted to stab the first Nucci who appeared, in full sight of the people already gathering in the square with the two elongated pyramids, outside the friary church. But Enrico managed to restrain him until the little band of Nucci brothers – Camillo and the younger Filippo and Davide – had come out and were a good distance from the palazzo.

The three young men walked down an alley, taking a short cut to the Piazza Ducale. The two older Nucci walked on ahead while Davide, only eighteen years old and proud to be able to stroll out with his big brothers, stopped to caress a stray dog.

'Now!' hissed Enrico and Carlo felled the boy with a single thrust. Davide Nucci had no time to cry out. He felt the blade withdrawn from between his ribs and his life blood following it. Before his eyes closed, he saw the young prince's gloating smile and heard his feet padding away over the cobbles.

Camillo noticed that his younger brother had fallen back. 'Hurry up, Davide,' he called. 'The young ladies will be waiting!' He turned and saw a crumpled body at the far end of the alley.

Camillo and Filippo raced back to where their little brother lay dying. They did their best to staunch the blood but could see straightaway that the wound was fatal.

'Who?' demanded Camillo, cradling Davide in his arms. 'Who was it?'

'Di Chimici,' was the last thing Davide ever said. A small dog licked his blood from the cobbles while his brothers howled their grief to the darkening sky.

'What have you been saying to Nicholas?' whispered Georgia. 'He's in a very funny mood.'

As quickly as he could, Sky filled her in on the poisoning.

'You shouldn't have told him,' said Georgia.

'How could I just not tell him when he asked me what happened in Giglia last night?' asked Sky. 'It was upsetting for me too, you know, seeing a man nearly die of poison.'

'Yes, but it wasn't your father,' said Georgia, and immediately regretted it when she saw Sky's expression. She knew he had a single mum, knew vaguely that there was some mystery about his father and that he never talked about him; all the girls in their year knew that. She had put her foot in it. And it wasn't as if she didn't know what it was like to be fatherless. Even though her stepdad, Ralph, had become like a real father to her, she understood about families and the private sufferings they could conceal.

She put her hand tentatively on Sky's arm. 'Sorry,' she said.

And that was when Alice saw them. It hit her all at once that Sky was not interested in her at all; he just wanted to get to know her in order to get close to her best friend. She turned away, her cheeks scarlet.

'Damn!' said Georgia, catching sight of Alice. 'I'm getting everything wrong today. I'm just so worried about Nicholas. He says he wants to go back to Talia. I think he's regretting coming here.'

'You feel responsible for him?' asked Sky.

'Yes. If it hadn't been for me – and Luciano – he wouldn't be here. We tried to persuade him that he would miss his family too much but I can't tell you how determined he was. I've never met anyone with a will as strong as Nick's. And he was just a kid then.'

'Is that all it is?' Sky was surprised at his own boldness. A few days ago Georgia had seemed remote and intimidating; now he was asking her if she fancied a boy two years younger than her.

Georgia didn't flare up. 'No. It isn't all. I think Nick and I will always be together, because he's the only one who knows what it was like for me in Talia. You can't have an experience like that and just live the rest of your life normally as if nothing had happened. I know the real him and he knows the real me; it's as simple as that.'

'Not simple for him,' said Sky.

'It isn't simple for anyone, is it?' said Georgia. 'Why don't you ask Alice out?'

Sky was gobsmacked. It wasn't where he thought the conversation was going at all.

'You've wanted to for ages, haven't you?' asked Georgia. 'And she likes you, you know.'

Sky suddenly felt as if the sun had come out and all the birds were singing. His lungs felt too full of air to breathe properly. He grinned at Georgia and she smiled back at him.

'Go on, then,' she said. 'She's over there. Do it

before she gets the wrong idea about you and me. But I'll want to talk to you about Nick again.'

All was chaos in the Nucci palace. The brothers had carried Davide home, his blood staining their fine clothes, and laid him in the family chapel. Now their mother and sisters had begun to lament and their cries were heard through all the surrounding streets. The men left the body to the women and were huddled in Matteo's study. Servants brought wine and Camillo was drinking deep.

In a corner of his grief-maddened brain, he knew that he was in a way responsible for Davide's death. No di Chimici would have stabbed the boy if Camillo hadn't poisoned the Duke. But he simply couldn't afford to think like that. The only way to retain his sanity was to tell himself that the hated di Chimici had struck again. They had killed his little brother, just as they had killed his uncle, and only shedding more of their family's blood would make him feel any better.

The servant pouring wine for Matteo Nucci whispered something in his master's ear. The merchant started and fixed his eyes on his eldest son.

'I hear there was an attempt on Duke Niccolò's life today,' he said, slightly slurring his words.

'Hah!' snorted Camillo. 'Rather more than an attempt, I should say.'

'You had better say nothing!' snapped his father. 'The Duke lives. And my boy lies in the chapel.'

Camillo gaped. 'Impossible!'

The mild evening when Camillo had gone

swaggering out into the square, puffed up with his success in ridding the city of an arrogant tyrant, had turned to a black night of despair.

'You seem to know a lot about it,' said Matteo. 'But you don't know that the Duke has been healed by the Senior Friar at the church here. Don't you know better than to try and poison a family named for being chemists? They have remedies at their disposal that no one else has. And do they bother with poisons now? No, they avenge their wrongs with a knife.' And the old man wept.

'Forgive me, Father,' said Camillo, in anguish. 'But I shall avenge him. I shall avenge Davide's death. I shan't rest till the streets of Giglia run with di Chimici blood!'

'And what good will that do?' came a voice from the doorway. Graziella Nucci had already donned the black clothes she would wear for the rest of her life. 'Will that give me back Davide? No. All you will achieve is more deaths in both families, more lamenting women, more work for priests and gravediggers. I envy Benedetta di Chimici her place under the earth, where she no longer has to fear for the death of her children.'

Camillo loved and honoured his mother, but even as he respected and shared her suffering and promised her that he would not pursue the vendetta, he had every intention of breaking his word.

*

Sandro was rattled. He had never seen a man die before and this one was not much older than him. He picked up the little dog and carried him back to his lodgings. He didn't feel like eating much himself and was glad to give the animal half his dish of liver and onions. The dog wolfed it down and wagged his tail.

'You're as bad as me, I reckon,' said Sandro. 'Just a street stray, ready to do anything for a meal.'

He knew that it had been Prince Carlo who struck the blow, but he had seen the Eel lead him to the place and give him the nod when the boy got separated from his brothers, like a wolf singling out a vulnerable lamb.

So his master was a murderer as well as a spy. Well, he should have known. Giglia was a violent city, used to such things. Hadn't he himself always been fascinated by the stabbing in the little square? But now that he had actually seen blood spilt on the cobbles, Sandro's ghoulish imagination had drunk its fill.

The little dog was dozing on a rug.

'It's all the same to you, isn't it?' said Sandro. 'Blood and gravy. But that was a real boy, like Tino. Someone with a mother and father who loved him. Not like us. I don't reckon anyone would miss either of us.'

He was surprised to find tears running down his cheek. He rubbed them away fiercely with his sleeve. But he was glad not to be on his own that night. Even a scruffy stray dog was better than no company at all. He stretched out on the rug beside the sleeping dog.

'It looks as if we're stuck with each other,' he said, yawning. 'I'd call you after that young Nucci, but I don't know his name. Still, he was someone's brother. I'll call you Fratello.'

When Sky returned to Talia that night, he found Sulien pacing his small cell in deep thought.

'It has begun,' he said. 'The Nucci tried to kill the Duke and now someone has succeeded in killing the youngest Nucci. From now on, Giglia will be in a state of civil war.'

Chapter 9

Angels

Over the next few weeks tensions rose in Giglia. There were no more deaths but plenty of fights between the Nucci and di Chimici factions. It wasn't just family members; the majority of the city took sides with one clan or the other. Over the generations, hundreds of people had owed their livelihood to one of the two warring families. Now every night in the city bands of young men roved around, looking for trouble, and when rivals met, jeers and insults broke out. By day, many youths sported black eyes, bandaged heads and bloody noses.

The old Nucci palace was fortified with an ancient tower; many palazzos had such towers, left over from earlier days when life in Giglia had been even more violent and unpredictable. Now, ever since Davide had been buried, Matteo Nucci and his two remaining sons had been building up a supply of weapons to defend their family, in case those days returned.

Family members had gathered from all over Talia, rallying round the bereaved Nucci and filling the palazzo with strong young men. Di Chimici too would soon be assembling in the city for the weddings. Rumours were flying round that the Nucci would avenge the loss of Davide as soon as their period of mourning was ended.

Sandro's spying tasks increased but he wasn't happy about it; he kept out of the Eel's way as much as possible, just giving his reports and leaving. He no longer wanted to hang round Enrico and certainly no longer wished he had a father like him. Sandro passed most of his days up at Saint-Mary-among-the-Vines, which was convenient for spying on the Nucci and meant he could spend more time with Brother Tino.

Sky was relieved when the Easter holidays came and his mother was still getting better. It meant he could lie in late in the mornings like a normal teenager, which made up a bit for his nightly trips to Talia. His social life was becoming more normal too. He had taken Alice out twice before the end of term, once to the cinema and once just to a coffee bar, when they had talked for hours and really begun to relax with each other. Now he was looking forward to spending more time alone with her.

But a new problem had developed; Georgia, Alice and Nicholas often did things together and didn't mind Sky tagging along, but when he was with them he was torn between wanting to be with Alice and responding to frantic signals from the other two to tell them the latest news from Giglia. Seeing them on their own was difficult to organise too. Thank goodness for fencing! Alice was bored by it and had never come to watch Nicholas practise. Now that they couldn't use the school, Nicholas and Sky booked regular times at the local gym and it was natural for Georgia to come and watch. Meeting up in the cafe afterwards was their best time for exchanging news.

Nicholas was in a permanent state of agitation about his Talian family. Although Sky had assured him that the Duke had suffered no ill consequences from the poisoning, it had made the boy restless and the news about the stabbing of Davide Nucci had only made things worse. 'How is Gaetano?' – always his first question – had acquired a new urgency.

And worse was to come. Georgia dropped the bombshell at their first fencing session. 'You know I'm spending Easter in Devon with Alice? My parents are going to Paris.'

'What about Russell?' asked Nicholas.

Georgia snorted. 'As if I'd stay in the house with him!' Two terms at Sussex University had slightly improved her stepbrother but she still wouldn't want to spend any time with him. 'Anyway, he's back off to Greece. I think he's got a girlfriend there.'

Sky was stunned. No Alice and no Georgia. He tried out in his head the thought, 'My girlfriend's going away.' At least it sounded more normal than, 'My fellow Stravagante won't be around.' And he would still have Nicholas. But a day or two later even that ground was cut away. Nicholas had been down to Devon with Georgia before, where they all rode horses, and Alice had asked if he'd like to join them that Easter. The Mulhollands had no objections and Nicholas couldn't think of a convincing excuse, so he was going too. Sky was a bit hurt that Alice had asked Nicholas and not him.

Rosalind noticed that Sky was unusually quiet. 'What's up?' she asked, after he'd got off the phone with Nicholas.

'Everyone's going to Devon this holidays,' said Sky, trying to look positive about it. 'First Alice and Georgia and now Nick too.'

Rosalind was thoughtful. 'Perhaps it's time we visited Nana?' she said.

Giuditta Miele was virtually unaware of the mounting tension in Giglia. When she was beginning a statue, she thought of nothing else, day or night. She had made her first cautious cuts with the chisel on the Duchessa's block of marble. The young woman was in there somewhere, she knew, and her job was to uncover her. In spite of Duke Niccolò, the Duchessa would be portrayed as a symbol of her city's independence and autonomy.

Giuditta had decided to carve her almost like a ship's figurehead, standing at the prow of her state barge, as she did after her Marriage with the Sea. Arianna would be masked, with her cloak and hair streaming out behind her as she faced her city, returning to it after the ceremony that ensured its prosperity for the forthcoming year.

Now the sculptor worked all day, gradually excavating the statue she could already envisage. Her young apprentices watched and kept her supplied with food and drink. They were supposed to be working on a marble sarcophagus of a simple but effective design. It was like a large basket with rope handles – a style made fashionable by a tomb of a di Chimici ancestor in their family church of Sant'Ambrogio. It wasn't difficult and it kept them occupied, but there wasn't a would-be sculptor in the workshop who wasn't more interested in what Giuditta was doing.

'Come here, Franco,' she said to the best-looking of them now. 'Stand straight, looking towards the window. Pretend you are on the open sea at the front of a ship.'

Franco posed diffidently, trying to look like a sailor.

'No, no,' said Giuditta impatiently. 'You are a young woman. Don't plant your feet so sturdily. You are graceful, dignified, but also wild.'

It was a tough assignment but young Franco did his best. His skin was pale and his hair an unusual silvery blond; his mother came from northern Europa. He was much in demand by Giglia's many painters as a model for angels, but he was far from angelic and not effeminate at all. He adored Giuditta, who was the only artist he had met who was completely impervious to his charms.

'Mm,' said the sculptor. 'What would you do with your hands?'

'Grasp the ship's rail, Maestra?' hazarded Franco.

'Good,' said Giuditta, snatching up her pile of drawings and swiftly making some strokes with a piece of charcoal. 'You can go back to your basketry now.'

Then, to herself, 'I need the Duchessa here.'

*

The next time Sky arrived in Giglia, he found Sulien smiling.

'What's happened?' said Sky.

'Reinforcements,' said Sulien mysteriously. 'Can you manage to stay later tomorrow? It would mean sleeping through the morning in your world.'

Sky thought about it. It wouldn't be too difficult. Rosalind had a client the following morning, her first for ages, and she had arranged to have lunch afterwards with Laura, who still worked in the House of Commons. It would be perfectly easy to say that night that he wanted to sleep in.

'I think so,' he answered. 'Why?'

'Duke Niccolò wants us to come to dinner at his palazzo,' said Sulien. 'I think he wants to thank us for saving his life. And he will have some important visitors.'

But he would say no more, however hard Sky pressed him.

'Today I need your help in the laboratory,' said the friar. 'We are going to distil perfume from narcissus flowers.'

*

The Duchessa of Bellezza was entertaining some dear friends when the messenger arrived from Giglia.

Doctor Dethridge and his wife Leonora, the woman Arianna had been brought up to believe was her aunt, had arrived with Leonora's great friend, Silvia Bellini, Arianna's mother. The disguised former Duchessa had often sat in this same reception room, entertaining important foreign visitors. But plain Silvia Bellini did not miss the days of State occasions and gorgeous gowns. Now mask-less, she enjoyed a freedom that she had given up for twenty-five years in order to rule the city.

This little group and less than a dozen others were the only ones in Talia who knew that the old Duchessa still lived. Now they were drinking the blond sparkling wine for which the city was famous and catching up with the news. Silvia's constant companion, a tall red-haired servant, hovered behind her chair.

'Wants to give you a dress?' Silvia was saying, when the messenger was shown in. 'He never sent me one.'

Guido Parola coughed over her last words, so that the palace servant wouldn't hear them. Silvia was getting careless. The messenger being shown in was carrying a long box. He bowed as best he could and then presented the box to the young Duchessa.

'With the compliments of my master, the Duke of Giglia,' he said. 'His Grace, Duke Niccolò, asks that you wear this unworthy garment at the forthcoming nuptials of his sons.'

Arianna's startled eyebrows appeared above her rose-coloured mask. So soon? she thought. But she courteously thanked the messenger and sent him to get refreshment, while Barbara, her waiting-woman, took the box. The little group of people was expectant.

'Shall I open it, your Grace?' asked Barbara.

The tasselled silver cord was undone and the lid lifted, while Arianna resisted an urge to get down on her hands and knees and rummage in the tissue paper herself. Barbara lifted the dress out reverently; it was very heavy. 'Oh, milady!' she whispered.

It was an extraordinary garment. The cloth was a stiff silver brocade but it was almost invisible under the gems stitched into it. The wide skirt was criss-crossed with lines of pearls and amethysts, so that the whole dress sparkled and shone like the moon at dusk. The bodice was tight and the neckline cut low and square, the tops of the sleeves high in the Giglian style.

'It's beautiful,' said Leonora.

'The gemmes do matche thine eyes,' agreed Dethridge.

'You'll not be able to sit down in it,' said Silvia, casting a practised eye over the jewel-encrusted dress. 'But you'll look wonderful in it – fit to have your portrait painted.' She shifted her direct gaze to Arianna's eyes, so like her own.

'What do you really think?' the young Duchessa asked.

'I think you should contact Rodolfo and Luciano as soon as possible,' said Silvia.

*

Rodolfo and Luciano were already in Giglia. They entered the city as quietly as they could, but all visitors had to give their names in at the gates at a sensitive time like this, and news soon spread that the Regent of Bellezza and his assistant had arrived. They went first to their lodgings then set out to call on Giuditta.

The sculptor met them abstractedly and Luciano was immediately overawed by her. He had seen her just briefly when she came to sketch Arianna in Bellezza. She was the only female Stravagante he had met, apart from Georgia, and she was as different from the twenty-first-century girl as could be. Giuditta was tall and well-built, deep-bosomed and broad-shouldered. Her brown hair was streaked with grey – though whether from age or marble dust it was hard to tell – and was tied loosely back just to keep it out of her eyes. Her coarse working clothes made her look like a washerwoman rather than an artist and possessor of occult knowledge.

'Greetings, sister,' said Rodolfo, and Luciano saw a kind of transformation creep over the sculptor. Her spirit swam up to the surface of her eyes and it was as if she had suddenly woken from a deep dream.

'Rodolfo!' she exclaimed, smiling, and Luciano saw that she was attractive, with a lively intelligence and that total self-confidence that all Talian Stravaganti seemed to have. 'Does this mean the Duchessa is here too?'

'Not yet,' said Rodolfo. 'You remember my apprentice, Luciano, from your visit to Bellezza? He is a Cavaliere now and works with me as my assistant. We have come first, to ensure the city is safe for her.'

'I am told the city isn't safe for anyone,' said Giuditta, her eyes flicking back to the marble even as she spoke to them.

'Is that it?' asked Luciano. 'Arianna's statue?'

'It will be,' said Giuditta. 'I am still trying to find

her, but I know she's there. Go on, touch it. You know her. See if you sense the Duchessa inside.'

Luciano went and laid his hands on the white marble. It was cold and rough; only the polished marble of finished statues was smooth and shiny. He closed his eyes and thought of Arianna; it wasn't hard to do. But he saw only the warm, laughing girl of their first friendship, and this statue would have to be of the formal, public city-ruler who was still a stranger to him.

'No,' he said, opening his eyes. 'I'm sorry.'

'That's all right,' said Giuditta. She seemed quite amused. 'It doesn't mean she isn't there, only that you are not a sculptor.'

*

Sulien was still being mysterious when Sky arrived the next morning. It had been easy enough for him to feign tiredness when he had gone to bed in his own world; he had spent a lot of the day fencing and training and Nicholas was a hard master.

'I'm knackered, Mum,' he had said, scooping Remedy up to take him to bed. 'Is it all right if I don't set my alarm?'

'That's fine,' Rosalind had replied. 'I won't see you till late tomorrow afternoon. Remember I'm having lunch with Laura and she always has a lot of gossip to pass on.'

Now Sky was wondering what on earth dinner with the Duke would be like and what else was on the agenda besides.

'Come,' said Sulien. 'It is time you met another Stravagante.'

Luciano and Rodolfo were in their lodgings and the older Stravagante had unpacked his mirrors. He was adjusting them now, focusing the first, as always, where he believed his wife to be.

'Silvia does not seem to be in Padavia,' he said, frowning.

'You know how often she goes to Bellezza,' said Luciano. 'She takes awful risks.'

Rodolfo sighed. 'It is her nature and always has been.' He paused. 'Arianna is very like her, you know. Impetuous, certain her choices are right, and liable to walk into danger.'

'Do you think that's what she'll be doing here?' asked Luciano. He couldn't forget what it had been like when they had left the Duke in Remora after the death of Falco. Niccolò had been unconscious when they had removed hastily from the city, and this wedding invitation was his first overture to Bellezza since then.

'You know I would not let her do that,' said Rodolfo. 'But I shall not always be here to guide her. One day she must learn to make the right choices on her own. I can form my own opinion and advise her about any dangers, but she must be the one who decides if it's right to come to Giglia or not.'

Luciano saw the Ducal palace in Bellezza coming into sharp relief in one of the mirrors. Twisting the knobs and levers underneath, Rodolfo roved through the rooms of the palazzo until he found what he was looking for.

Bingo! thought Luciano, as the mirror showed

Arianna, her maid Barbara and Silvia in the Duchessa's private chamber. They were all looking at something which could not be seen in the mirror, and appeared worried. Rodolfo bent close to the glass surface and then focused another mirror on Leonora's house in the Piazza San Suliano. Immediately William Dethridge's large face swam into view.

'Maistre Rudolphe!' the Elizabethan's voice crackled. 'I was juste aboute to seke thee myselfe.'

'What is it?' asked Rodolfo. 'I have seen both Duchesse and they look worried. Has something happened?'

*

Sky couldn't believe his luck, getting into Giuditta's bottega. He had been interested in sculpture for a long time but didn't dare think about studying it, because it would mean a Foundation Year in art school, followed by at least another three years doing a degree, and he didn't think Rosalind could afford it. Whenever they talked about university, she assumed he'd do a three-year course in a subject like English.

But as soon as he walked into the bottega, Sky's heart leapt. He envied the apprentices who worked on their own projects while Giuditta's monumental work was created under their eyes. The workshop was full of maquettes and copies. In one corner stood a carved wooden angel holding a candle sconce, painted silver. Sky jumped when he looked from the angel to one of the apprentices; he had the same face.

The floorspace was dominated by a huge block of white stone on which Giuditta was working. She was chiselling furiously at the back of it and Sky wondered if she were making another angel; something very like wings seemed to be emerging. The sculptor's face appeared round the block of stone, whitened by the dust she was creating. Her hair too was like that of one of her statues, stiff and moulded to her head. When she saw the two friars, she climbed down from her ladder to meet them.

'You have come for your angel?' she asked Sulien, and Sky had the strangest feeling that if these two Stravaganti had been alone in the room together they would not have bothered to use words.

'And brought you the sky,' said Sulien. 'This is Celestino – Brother Tino, we call him. He comes from far away.'

Giuditta looked at him closely. If it had been anyone else, he would have been embarrassed.

'You have a good face,' she said, and he suddenly felt his chin grasped by her chalky fingers and his face turned towards the light.

'I like its planes and angles,' she said. 'But it is not a monk's face. And it would be a shame to trim all that hair to a tonsure.'

Sky felt thoroughly seen through, recognised as a Stravagante and fake friar and one with very unreligious thoughts about girls. But he didn't mind; Giuditta reminded him of Georgia, in a funny way. She had no small talk, just said what was on her mind. And he knew instinctively that she was honest and reliable.

'I wish I could be your apprentice instead,' he said truthfully, and was aware of suppressed laughter from the four young men who had downed tools and were watching him with curiosity.

'Art and religion?' said Giuditta. 'We don't separate them here. Come and look at this marble,' she said, and took him over to the block she had been working on.

'Is it another angel?' asked Sky.

'No,' said Giuditta. 'Those aren't wings. That's the Duchessa's hair and cloak.' She walked him round to the other side of the statue. 'Now, put your hands here, about halfway down. Can you sense her?'

Sky hesitantly put his hands on the marble. He had never seen Arianna but Georgia had told him about her. He guessed that he was touching the marble somewhere at the level of her middle. He expected to imagine sliding his hands round her slim waist, a strangely intimate gesture to make to someone unfamiliar and important, even though it was only a statue.

He frowned. Clear in his mind was a pair of white hands almost pushing him away. He opened his eyes, unaware that they had been closed till then. He found himself looking straight into the brown gaze of the sculptor.

'She resisted me,' he said. 'Her hands are here,' he indicated, 'pushing me away.'

Giuditta smiled. 'They are resting on a ship's rail,' she said. 'But only I know that, I and the apprentices. And now you too, Brother Tino. I think you must be an artist of our kind.'

Sulien and Sky carried the wooden angel with its candlestick back to the friary. It was wrapped in a bundle of sacking but still about the size and shape of a person, if you didn't count the wings. It made Sky feel as though they were carrying a corpse through the streets of Giglia.

*

'Yt is the dresse,' said Dethridge. 'Yt has arrived. And yt is worth a fortune. The Dutchesse asked me to telle thee. She is afeard. And so is her lady mothire. They thinke it bodes ille.'

Chapter 10

A Man's Job

Sky left Giuditta's bottega feeling ten feet tall. She really thought he could be a sculptor, like her! And that mattered so much that it took a while for him to realise that they had something else in common: they were both Stravaganti.

'You are quiet,' said Sulien, smiling, as they carried the angel home. 'I think our visit has taught you something?'

'Yes,' said Sky, 'but it just makes me want to find out more. I mean, what does it mean that you and I and Giuditta are all, you know, of the same Brotherhood? You're a friar, she's a sculptor, I'm a schoolkid. How does that make us the same and how are we like this mysterious Rodolfo and a boy who used to live in my world? Or Georgia and

Falco, who is now Nicholas?'

'Not all Stravaganti are practising scientists,' said Sulien quietly, checking that they were not overheard. 'Rodolfo, yes, and Doctor Dethridge, but many others of us follow other professions. In Remora, for example, there is a Horsemaster, and there is a musician in Volana. But we all know the ones in Bellezza and we communicate by means of a system of mirrors. As for the ones from your world, all we know is that the talismans seem to choose potential Stravaganti who are for some reason not happy there.'

He stopped and turned from his end of the angel to look in Sky's face. 'I feel that was true of you when the talisman found you. But I don't know if it still is.'

*

Rodolfo had asked William Dethridge to visit the Duchessa again and to get her to hold the dress up in front of the mirror in her chamber. He and Luciano were now staring at it.

'She can't wear that,' said Luciano decisively. 'She can't accept such an expensive present from the Duke. Or anyone, except perhaps you.'

'I couldn't afford it,' said Rodolfo grimly. 'Just look at those jewels! She's going to be more richly dressed than any of the di Chimici brides.'

'You don't mean she should wear it to the wedding?'

'I don't see how she can avoid it, without offending the Duke,' said Rodolfo. 'And with things the way they are, we must be very careful not to offend the Duke.'

'Is that why we're going tonight?' said Luciano. 'I really don't see why we have to go and meet him in his own palace – he might poison us both.'

'He might,' agreed Rodolfo. 'He is perfectly capable of it and would have the means, but I don't think he will. Remember, he is still fascinated by our Brotherhood and he wants to know all our secrets. He is much more likely to torture us than kill us.'

'Great,' said Luciano. 'Nothing to worry about there, then.'

*

Sandro was waiting back at Saint-Mary-among-the-Vines. He looked rather forlorn, lounging round the Lesser Cloister, watching friars weed the garden.

'No work today?' asked Sulien.

Sandro shrugged. 'Nothing new,' he said.

'Would you like to do something for me?' asked Sulien. 'Brother Tino and I are going to make liqueur.'

Sandro's eyes brightened. He would be in the laboratory, which had always fascinated him, and the Eel couldn't tell him off for that.

Enrico had asked him to find out what he could about the pharmacist-friar. But Sandro resolved not to tell his master about anything he found out.

Sulien's work on his list of formulas was progressing slowly. He was now making a new batch of the liqueur Vignales, for which the friary was famous, and whose recipe was a secret from all except the other friars. Sandro and Sky both felt honoured to be entrusted with even a part of the mystery.

'How do you know how to make it if you don't

have a recipe already?' asked Sky.

'It has been handed down through several pharmacist-friars to me,' said Sulien. 'I made it under the supervision of old Brother Antonino, my predecessor. More than once. But it's never been written down before.'

It took hours, filling a sort of cauldron with sugar, alcohol fermented from grapes and the various herbs and spices that Brother Sulien instructed the boys to supply from colourful ceramic jars. It soon became obvious to Sky that Sandro couldn't read and that Sulien was careful to instruct him in ways he could understand – 'please bring me the blue jar on the far left of the bottom shelf,' or 'the aniseed is in the tall green jar with the pink stopper,' and so on. To Sky he just said, 'I need cinnamon,' or 'fetch the ginger root.'

The pile of parchment, with recipes for perfumes, lotions, elixirs, tinctures and tisanes was growing slowly, but Vignales was an important addition. The three worked steadily and quietly for several hours until the cauldron steamed with a thick sticky blue liquid that smelt to Sky a bit like cough mixture. Still, Sulien assured them both that it was a highly prized and expensive drink, and they could certainly attest to the strength of its fumes. Sandro, who had eaten nothing all day, was beginning to stagger.

'Enough,' said Sulien. 'We can leave it to cool now and bottle it tomorrow. It must be getting late. Now, Brother Tino and I have to dine with the Duke but you, Sandro, look in need of a meal nearer home. Go to Brother Tullio and say you have been helping me all afternoon and I said to give you something to eat.'

Sulien took a bottle of the blue Vignales from a shelf. 'From my previous batch,' he explained. 'The Duke will be pleased to get it as a gift.'

'Here's one I made earlier,' murmured Sky.

'He's wonderful, isn't he?' Sandro said to Sky, and Sky was surprised that the scruffy urchin, so tough and hard-bitten when they were out exploring the streets of Giglia, was so impressed by the gentle and scholarly friar.

'I thought you said he was a poisoner?' he whispered.

'I don't really think he can be, do you?' Sandro whispered back. And Sky just had time to shake his head before they had to leave for the Via Larga.

*

'Why are we entertaining these Bellezzan charlatans?' asked Prince Fabrizio, brushing an invisible speck of dust from his white ruffled shirt. 'I thought they were our bitter enemies.'

'If you think diplomacy is about entertaining only people you like, then you have learnt nothing from me at all,' said his father, severely. 'It is true that Rodolfo is a Stravagante and that there is something sinister about his assistant, as he is calling him now. I haven't forgotten his involvement in Falco's death – how could I? But at the moment, we have problems nearer home than the Stravaganti. It was not they who tried to poison me.'

'The Nucci are planning something, I'm sure,' said Fabrizio. 'They'll not let Davide's death go unavenged for long.'

Both father and son knew who was responsible for that death but they would not say a word about it, even when alone with other family members. The expression 'walls have ears' might have been invented to describe the di Chimici palace in the Via Larga.

'Besides,' said the Duke, as if he had no thought of the Nucci, 'I must treat the Duchessa's Regent with due respect.'

'Huh!' said Carlo. 'It's not as if she showed us much courtesy, turning down Gaetano and rushing away from Remora the minute poor Falco died.'

Niccolò rounded on him and Carlo wondered if he had gone too far.

'I won't have a word said against the Duchessa,' the Duke said. 'And I shall expect you all to behave to her father with the same civility you would show to the lady.'

Gaetano remembered how hard he had needed to persuade his father that Arianna had intended no slight either in refusing the offer of a di Chimici marriage or in hastening back to her own city. For himself, he would have no trouble at all in being civil to Luciano, who was his friend, and he had a deep admiration for Rodolfo.

He couldn't help wondering what his father was up to.

*

Sky felt nervous walking to the di Chimici palazzo with Brother Sulien. It was one thing to explore it with Sandro, which he had done more than once, or to run there in an emergency as on the day Niccolò di

Chimici had been poisoned, but to enter it as the Duke's invited guest was quite another. The guard at the gate ushered them into the courtyard with the bronze Mercury, where another flunkey escorted them to the Duke's private reception rooms.

Sky had not seen them before and was overawed. The servant opened the double wooden doors and ushered them into a room more magnificent than anything the twenty-first-century boy had ever seen. But his awe soon turned to fascination. It was obvious that the Duke was a great patron of the arts.

Every wall was covered in paintings, of the kind Sky's art teacher had taught him were called trompe l'oeil, 'eye-deceivers'. Pillars, columns, staircases and balconies all appeared to grow from the walls but were two-dimensional painters' effects. Gods and goddesses leant from the balconies and nymphs danced round the columns, chased by satyrs. Sky stood open-mouthed until a cultivated voice cut through his reverie.

'I see your novice is a lover of the arts, Brother Sulien,' the Duke was saying.

'Indeed, your Grace,' Sulien replied. 'He is most impressed by all the great beauties of your family's city.'

Sky saw that Duke Niccolò was completely recovered. It was the third time he had seen him and he was an impressive figure, tall and well built, with the typical noble features of well-defined cheekbones and a thin bony nose. His white hair and silver beard were cut short and rather suited him. He was dressed in a crimson velvet robe over a lace-trimmed shirt and black breeches, 'like an aristocratic pirate,' thought Sky.

The young princes and the princess were now introduced to the friars, as if they had not met in that mad scramble to save the Duke's life. As indeed they might not have, so different were they now in their elegant clothes, with their composed manners. Sky soaked up every detail to tell Nicholas back home: Princess Beatrice, so dignified and graceful in her low-cut black satin (still in mourning for her brother), Fabrizio haughty and handsome but perfectly polite, Carlo rather nervous and Gaetano as ugly and charming as ever.

The Duke led the way into a second equally elaborately decorated room and Sky saw two figures waiting to meet them there.

'May I introduce Senator Rodolfo Rossi, the Regent of Bellezza?' said the Duke. 'Senator, I should like to present to you one of our most distinguished scientists, Brother Sulien of Saint-Mary-among-the-Vines – and his novice Celestino. You may have heard what signal service they did me recently when I was indisposed after a poisoner's attack.'

There were bows and polite murmurings, even though Rodolfo and Sulien were actually old friends.

'And this is my assistant, Cavaliere Luciano Crinamorte,' said Rodolfo, presenting him to the two friars. 'I think that he and Brother Tino are not far apart in age.'

'And close in age to my youngest son, Gaetano, too,' said the Duke.

Sky saw the little crease of pain that crossed Niccolò's face as he hesitated over the word 'youngest', but Gaetano quickly corralled him and Luciano and, under the excuse of taking them to admire a fine painting, got them away from the others, while servants brought wine.

So this was Sulien's surprise – for Sky to meet the mysterious Lucien! The two boys recognised each other straightaway, though one was dressed as a Dominican friar and the other as a Bellezzan nobleman.

'This is bizarre, isn't it?' said Luciano, as Gaetano pretended to explain the painting to them.

'Incredible,' said Sky.

It was the old Lucien Mulholland, all right, alive and well. He seemed at ease in his grand surroundings and to be on friendly terms with Gaetano, who now asked the usual question, 'How is my brother?'

'He's well,' said Sky. 'He's teaching me to fence.'

'Good idea,' said Luciano. 'You need to be careful here. Gaetano won't mind my saying that his father and brothers are dangerous people – even if they are on their best behaviour tonight.'

Gaetano shook his head sadly. 'But it's not just my family. The Nucci are gathering in their old tower and I dread what they might be planning for the weddings.'

'How's Georgia?' asked Luciano. 'You do know her as well as Falco, don't you?'

'She's fine,' said Sky. 'Off to Devon with her friend Alice. They're both going, her and Nicholas, I mean. You know that's Falco's new name?'

'Yes,' said Luciano. 'Georgia dreamed it up when we were planning his translation. I still find it hard to believe we actually pulled it off. It was mainly Falco, of course. It would all have fallen apart if he hadn't been so determined.'

'He's still that,' said Sky. 'In fact he's desperate to come here and see his family. But that would be madness, wouldn't it? Even if his talisman could bring him to Giglia, he'd be recognised. And he's supposed to be dead!'

'It would be wonderful to see him again,' sighed Gaetano.

'Rodolfo and I are working on the talisman problem,' said Luciano, 'with Doctor Dethridge. You know who that is?'

'The Granddaddy of them all,' said Sky, ruefully.

'We have so much to catch up on,' said Luciano. 'Can I come and see you at the friary tomorrow?'

Sky just had time to say yes, when dinner was announced and the Duke led the way into a dining room, even grander than his salon. Just the sight of the table made Sky feel nervous. Meals at home were eaten in the kitchen with Rosalind or on their laps in front of the television, and now here was a long, marble-topped table, with silver candelabra, wine goblets and a huge silver ornament in the middle.

Luckily he was shown to a seat between Luciano and Gaetano and opposite Beatrice so, although he couldn't talk about the things most on his mind, his position wasn't too terrifying. Rodolfo spent most of the meal in conversation with Sulien and the Duke, and Sky knew that the two older Stravaganti were under the same constraints as him and Luciano, which made him feel better.

Servants kept the red wine coming and Sky sipped his cautiously, noticing that the other young men knocked it back easily. He wasn't sure he liked it, but there was nothing else to drink and some of the dishes were quite salty. He noticed an extra servant, who stood permanently at the Duke's right elbow and who tried every dish and the wine too, before Niccolò allowed himself anything. His taster, presumably. What a frustrating job, thought Sky. Either you clutched your throat and fell down with agonising stomach pains, or the food and drink were perfectly OK and you couldn't have more than a sip or morsel of them.

The food was more recognisable than Sky had feared. There was a green soup which Gaetano said was made from nettles, but which was surprisingly tasty, and then a kind of white fish which was cold and soused in vinegar. That was not so nice but Sky was hungry. The next dish was a risotto with what turned out to be duck. But startlingly it was decorated with little pieces of silver foil – not the sort you'd wrap round a turkey in Sky's world but more like the thin slivers he had sometimes seen on Indian sweets. By the time that the servants brought a sort of sweet pizza, with raisins and sugar and cinnamon, and a dizzyingly sweet wine to go with it, Sky was quite stuffed.

He noticed that Luciano's attention was distracted. What had the Duke just said? He had asked after the Duchessa, Sky thought, but his brain felt a little fuddled, even after a small amount of wine.

'My daughter is very well, thank you,' Rodolfo was now saying.

'Charming young woman,' said Niccolò. 'It was a great disappointment to me that she refused to become part of my family.'

Luciano and Gaetano both tensed and Gaetano

started to blush.

'Not that I am not perfectly happy for Gaetano to marry his cousin,' the Duke continued smoothly.

'Indeed, Francesca di Chimici is also a very lovely young woman,' said Rodolfo.

'I have sent her a gift,' said Niccolò.

'Francesca?' asked Rodolfo, as if he didn't know all about it.

'The Duchessa,' said Niccolò. 'A paltry garment, which I hope she will do me the honour of wearing to the wedding.'

'The honour will be hers, I am sure,' said Rodolfo.

'Tell me,' said the Duke casually, 'do you think the young Duchessa would be equally averse to all members of my family?' Everyone round the table was surprised. Sky thought the Duke might be going to suggest yet another nephew or cousin of his, but all the others knew that the choice of di Chimici suitors would be very limited. The forthcoming weddings would tie up most eligible di Chimici males.

'I have been thinking,' continued the Duke, 'of re-marrying myself. 'And I think perhaps I erred in sending the Duchessa so young and inexperienced a suitor to court her, fond though I am of Gaetano. It perhaps proves the truth of the saying "Never send a boy to do a man's job." What do you think your daughter would say to the suggestion of becoming my Grand Duchess?'

There was silence around the table, but Sky had seen Rodolfo's eyes move straight to Luciano and the boy was fixed in his place only by the intensity of the message that gaze was sending. Both Rodolfo and Luciano had turned quite pale but it was Brother

Sulien who spoke first.

'Does this mean you are taking the title of Grand Duke, your Grace?' he said. 'May we offer our congratulations?'

It was clear that most of his children hadn't known what the Duke was intending; only Carlo looked less than amazed.

'I shall make a public announcement of my intention the night before the weddings, at the feast,' said the Duke. 'That is, as far as my new title is concerned. I think the time is right to become Grand Duke of Tuschia.'

'Then we must congratulate your Grace,' said Rodolfo diplomatically, raising his goblet as if in a toast. 'As for my daughter, I'm sure she will hear your suit with the honour due to it when she arrives in Giglia.'

Fabrizio was very torn. He had no objections to inheriting an even grander title when his father died, but Niccolò's plan to marry again appalled him. He didn't want a stepmother younger than himself, however beautiful, and he could see that Gaetano and Beatrice at least shared his view. None of them had any doubt that their father's courtship would succeed. Who could refuse such a man and such a title?

For Luciano, the rest of the evening was sheer torment. He couldn't wait to get out of the palace. In fact, the four Stravaganti left the palace together, after much tedious ceremony, and Gaetano had time only to whisper that he would meet the others at the friary the next day.

Sky knew that Luciano was still being restrained by the silent force of his master's will until they were well away from the Via Larga. But as soon as that control was relaxed, Luciano exploded.

'So that was what the dress was all about! And the grand dinner! We're supposed to be impressed. But I'll never let Arianna marry that monster. I'll kill him myself first!'

Chapter 11

Daggers Drawn

Sky woke up in the middle of the afternoon with a mini-hangover. He was surprised to find he could still taste the sweet dessert wine that he had gulped down in his nervousness at the Duke's announcement. He got up and showered and brushed his teeth extra thoroughly and drank two glasses of water before Rosalind got in.

He was just wondering what to eat and what meal to call it when he heard his mother's key in the lock. She was in a good mood but tired.

'Tea!' she moaned, falling into her chair in mock exhaustion.

'How was your lunch?' he asked, as he made Rosalind tea and himself toast and marmalade.

'Good,' said Rosalind. 'Laura's always a tonic. She's

a Councillor now, you know. I bet she'll end up an MP herself one day, instead of looking after them.'

'Perhaps she'll be Prime Minister?' suggested Sky. 'Imagine – there'd be laws making it illegal not to have parties every weekend.'

Rosalind giggled. 'I don't know where she gets her energy from. I used to think she'd stolen some of mine. Is that your breakfast, by the way? I know you said you wanted a lie-in, but I hope you didn't mean till four o'clock.'

Sky just grinned. 'Want some?' he asked. He couldn't decide if he felt tired because of spending a day and most of a night in Giglia or refreshed by having spent nearly sixteen hours in bed.

The phone rang. It was Nicholas. Sky took the phone into his bedroom. 'How did it go, dinner with my family?' was Nick's first question.

'OK, I suppose,' said Sky. 'I mean, no one got poisoned and I didn't spill my soup. But I still feel a bit drunk.'

'Who else was there?'

'Luciano and Rodolfo. Luciano recognised me straightaway.'

'He's nice, isn't he?'

'Yeah. I can see what Georgia saw in him.'

There was an awkward silence at the other end of the line.

'You know that, then?' said Nicholas quietly.

'Pretty obvious, I'd have thought.'

'Like you and Alice?'

'Touché,' said Sky. 'Don't worry – there's no future in it, with him stuck in the past, if you see what I mean.'

166

'I wouldn't be too sure,' said Nicholas. 'She's as keen as I am to go back, if something could be worked out about the talismans.'

'Luciano said something about that. I think Rodolfo and Doctor Dethridge are on the case.'

'I think the only thing that stops her is that Luciano is in love with Arianna,' said Nicholas.

'Um . . . about that,' said Sky. 'Your father made an announcement at dinner that didn't go down too well with Luciano.'

Sandro hadn't gone back to his lodgings. He had hung about the friary with his dog, feeling left out while Sulien and Tino were at the di Chimici Palazzo, and had eventually curled up in a corner of Sulien's laboratory, wrapped tightly in his thin cloak, with Fratello sleeping on his feet. The pharmacist found them after Sky had stravagated back home.

Brother Sulien covered the boy with his own thick black robe and didn't wake him then or when he got up early to walk the maze. Sandro was only beginning to stir when the friar came back from the church.

'Breakfast?' asked Sulien, and took the boy to the refectory for porridge and honey and milk still warm from the friary's goats. Fratello was banished to the yard but Sandro begged a bone for him from Brother Tullio.

It was only when they had both satisfied their appetite that they spoke.

'You seem to have moved in,' remarked Sulien conversationally.

'Only for one night,' said Sandro. 'I've got to be back outside the Nucci place tomorrow, so I thought why go home?'

'Where is home?' asked Sulien.

Sandro shrugged. 'Don't really have one. Not family, anyway. Just lodgings, up near where you were last night.'

'I know you were found by the orphanage near the Duomo,' said Sulien. 'Was there never any search for your mother?'

'Not that I know of,' said Sandro. 'She was probably glad to get rid of me. I expect she was an unmarried girl – or a whore, I suppose.'

'You are still bitter about it,' said Sulien. 'Come with me. I'd like to show you something, if you don't have to go on duty straightaway.'

They picked up Fratello and walked in the direction of the Duomo, but branched off left into a little piazza, called Limbo. It was quiet and deserted, with a tiny old church in one corner. In front of it was a little graveyard, full of small white stones.

'You know what this is?' asked Sulien.

'Yes, it's where they bury the babies.'

'The unbaptised ones, whose souls are in limbo,' nodded Sulien. 'They were born dead or died too soon after their birth to be given their names and welcomed into the church.'

'What are you trying to tell me?' said Sandro.

'There are lives which have a bad start, like yours, and there are those that don't start at all, like those of these innocent children,' said Sulien. 'But we are all in limbo unless we choose to let our lives begin and take us somewhere.'

'I must be getting back to the Nucci now,' said Sandro. But Sulien had given him something to think about.

'I don't believe it,' said Georgia flatly. 'If she wouldn't have Gaetano, who's a really nice guy, she won't take the Duke. Arianna hates the di Chimici – him most of all.'

But even as she said it, a little green devil lodged in her brain was thinking, But if she did marry the Duke, that would take her out of Luciano's reach for ever.

'I know that,' said Sky. 'But Rodolfo seems to think she can't just turn him down. And he's going to make himself Grand Duke now, whatever that means.'

'It means that my family will be even more important in Tuschia,' said Nicholas stiffly.

They were in Sky's room, discussing his latest visit to Talia.

'I'm sorry, Nick,' said Georgia. 'But you've got to stop thinking of them as your family. Vicky and David are your family now, not the di Chimici, and I can't pussyfoot around your feelings every time we talk about them. You know what your father is capable of.'

'It is not easy to stop thinking of those who are in Talia just because you can't see them any more,' said Nicholas, staring at Georgia till she changed colour.

'The point is,' said Sky patiently, 'I think it's going to mean more trouble. Luciano won't give her up without a fight – literally. Rodolfo was able to control him yesterday but that won't last for long. Arianna'll be in the city soon, for sittings with Giuditta the sculptor, and things will come to a head then.'

'What does Gaetano think?' asked Georgia.

'I don't know,' said Sky. 'He's coming to see me tomorrow. So is Luciano.'

'This is unbearable,' said Nicholas. 'I must find a new talisman and get back to Giglia. Can't you bring me something? You could have picked up a spoon or something at my father's table.'

Sky had a vision of what the Duke would have said if he had caught him smuggling silverware out of the palace.

'Don't be so stupid, Nick!' said Georgia, really angry. 'You know that Sky isn't trained to do that – only the Talian Stravaganti bring talismans from world to world.'

'You did it for me,' said Nicholas.

'It wasn't the same,' said Georgia, exasperated. 'That was the eyebrow ring I had with me all the time in Talia. But, while we're on the subject, I did it because you were so desperate to come here, remember?'

It was the closest Sky had ever seen them get to a row. Nicholas was flushed, his hands clenched, and Georgia looked as if she wanted to slap him.

'And now I'm desperate to go back!' Nicholas retorted. 'And so are you, admit it!'

Luciano hadn't slept all night. He tangled himself in the bed covers, thinking of what he would do if Arianna even pretended to listen to the Duke's offer.

He drove himself mad with visions of her as Niccolò's Grand Duchess, wearing dresses every day like the jewel-encrusted monstrosity she had been sent for the di Chimici weddings.

Ever since she had become Duchessa, the Arianna he had known and explored the canals of Bellezza with had seemed to be drifting away from him. She was still friendly and warm towards him, even flirtatious sometimes, but her many official duties and her necessarily grand lifestyle made her seem more and more remote in his eyes. And what was he? A Cavaliere of Bellezza, waiting to go to university. He didn't have a real aristocratic title, like a di Chimici, or even a job that would make him rich.

Now he longed to ride back to Bellezza and grab Arianna's hand and lead her, laughing, into a rowing boat and take her to empty her foster-brothers' lobster pots on Merlino or to eat cakes in her grandparents' house on Burlesca.

But it was no good. In a few days, the Duchessa would be here in Giglia, escorted by Dethridge – and Silvia, who could never keep away from where the action was, or from Rodolfo, for long. And here Arianna would have to be every inch the Duchessa, with her maids and her dressmakers and her hairdresser and her footmen and her bodyguards, and Luciano would be just another admirer she had to fit into her schedule.

He got up and dressed, and went downstairs, where he found Rodolfo already sitting having an early breakfast, served by their landlord.

'So, you couldn't sleep either?' said his master. 'I'm not surprised. These are deep waters we are in.'

The landlord, catching the last words, said, 'Indeed, masters, the Argento hasn't run so high in spring for a hundred years, or so people are saying in the city. It's the heavy winter rains we had. They reckon there's a real danger of flood by Easter.'

'Then I hope it drowns the Duke,' said Luciano gloomily.

The landlord looked shocked to hear such seditious words in his house.

'Take no notice of my young friend,' said Rodolfo. 'He drank too freely of the Duke's wine last night. And now he needs coffee and eggs.'

The man backed out hastily.

'Be careful what you say, Luciano,' warned Rodolfo. 'The city is full of spies.'

*

Francesca's wedding dress was finished. A frothy confection of white lace over a satin bodice and full underskirt, in which she would look every inch a princess. She was trying it on in Arianna's grandmother's parlour and the two young women and the old one were all admiring the effect.

'Gaetano is a lucky man,' said Arianna, smiling. 'No one will have eyes for any bride but you.'

'And what shall you wear, Arianna?' asked Paola Bellini, who had heard about the Duke's present.

'Oh, Nonna, I don't know,' said Arianna. 'If only I could just please myself and forget about diplomacy.'

'Then you would wear one of your old cotton frocks and go barefoot, I expect,' said Paola.

'Your uncle has sent me a dress, Francesca,'

explained Arianna. She hadn't mentioned it to her friend before. 'And it is much too grand and expensive for me to accept without granting him some favour in return. And the favour he has in mind is for me to sign his treaty with Bellezza – of that I am sure.'

'But you won't, will you?' said Francesca.

'No, I can't. It is what my mother spent her life resisting and I owe it to her and the city to continue the fight,' said Arianna. 'And yet, if I don't wear the dress, the Duke will be offended and that is undesirable too.'

'I see,' said Francesca. 'You have a dilemma.'

'It's too hard for me to decide,' said Arianna. 'I don't want to wear it but I can't do just what I want any more. I'm going to ask my father and Dottore Crinamorte what they think.' And my mother too, she thought to herself.

*

It was not long after Sky arrived back in Giglia that Luciano turned up at the friary. They were both short of sleep and went out to sit in the sunshine on the wall of the Great Cloister. Luciano looked at his own single shadow and sighed.

'I wish sometimes I had never been given the notebook,' he said bitterly.

'Notebook?' asked Sky.

'It was my talisman – the thing that brought me to Talia,' said Luciano.

'But, if it hadn't, wouldn't that mean . . .?' Sky hesitated.

'That I would be dead?' said Luciano. 'Yes. But I

think that may be going to happen anyway. I can't see how I can get out of this situation alive. If the Duke tries to marry Arianna, I will kill him – I would say "or die in the attempt" like some corny hero, except that in my case it will probably be "and" not "or", and I'm no hero.'

'You care about her that much?' asked Sky. 'So much you would die for her?'

Luciano didn't answer straightaway. 'Can you imagine what it was like to give up my family and my life in your world?' he asked finally. 'To leave everything I had ever known and be flung back over four centuries to live in the past in this world?'

'Not really,' said Sky. He had seen how comfortably the old Lucien seemed to fit into life in Talia and only now thought about what his feelings must have been when he had to leave his previous life.

'Oh, I know it gave me a second chance, that I *had* a life instead of what was going to happen to the old me,' said Luciano. 'And I'm not ungrateful, believe me. But I've had to become a different person, with a different future to look forward to, and it's only the people here who have made that possible. Arianna most of all. If I thought she was going to become the Duke's wife, I really think I would go mad.'

'But you don't think she'll accept him, do you?' asked Sky. He couldn't imagine a girl of seventeen preferring a white-haired man in his fifties to the good-looking Luciano, but he didn't know Arianna and he guessed a Duchessa couldn't always do what she preferred.

'I think it's unlikely,' said Luciano. 'But not impossible.' He couldn't forget how Gaetano's suit had not been turned down out of hand when it was first made. 'But if she does refuse him, then all our lives will be even more in danger, here in the di Chimici stronghold, with everyone armed and ready for a fight.'

A figure stepped out into the sunlit cloister to join them. It was Gaetano. 'What's this about fighting?' he asked.

*

The Eel was feeling pleased with himself. Word had flown around the palace that Duke Niccolò was going to marry the beautiful young Duchessa of Bellezza and Enrico lost no time in taking the credit for putting the idea into his master's head. He was pleased about the Duke's plans for a new title too; now he would be able to boast of being right-hand man to the Grand Duke. And once Bellezza had entered the fold, it would not take long for the remaining Talian city-states to follow suit. Enrico was quite sure that the Grand Duke would be king of a united Talia one day. If not this Grand Duke, then the next.

He made a mental note to cultivate Prince Fabrizio. The only fly in Enrico's ointment was that his spy network wasn't operating as efficiently as he would like. He wanted hard information about what the Nucci were planning. After all, they had made an attempt on a di Chimici life even before their Davide was killed, so they must be plotting something now. The only question was whether they would wait for the weddings when all the di Chimici would be in the city, or show their hand before.

This was the kind of work Enrico relished, collecting information, following suspects and perhaps having the chance to slide a knife between someone's ribs and be well rewarded for it. He had made himself indispensable to the Duke and looked forward to a rich future. True, he seemed to be losing his influence over his youngest spy, who had become sulky and elusive, but he had lots of others.

There was only one thing missing in the Eel's life and that was the comfort and companionship of a woman. Ever since his fiancée, Giuliana, had so mysteriously disappeared in Bellezza, Enrico had sworn off women. It had been inexplicable; they had been due to marry in a matter of days, Giuliana had ordered her dress and was apparently very excited about the wedding. Then, without a word or a note, she had vanished.

The only explanation he could think of was that she had met someone else and run off with him, someone who was such a good prospect that she had been prepared to leave not just Enrico, but all her family, without any farewell. So complete had been her deception that her father had come round and threatened Enrico for having taken his daughter away.

But that was some time ago and Enrico had been influenced by the Duke's decision to marry again. If a grieving widower could do it, so could a jilted spy, and Enrico was now open to the idea of another romance.

*

'You don't mean it,' said Gaetano. 'You're just upset. It may come to nothing.'

'I don't say what I don't mean,' said Luciano. 'I'm serious. I will kill him if he tries to marry her. I'm sorry he's your father, but I will do it.'

The three boys were still in the cloister. Sky was impressed by how close Luciano seemed to the di Chimici prince. He had heard something of their history together in Remora from Georgia and he knew that what had happened with Falco had forged a strong link between them.

'What do you think, Sky?' asked Luciano.

'What do I know?' he said. 'I've never known my father. I can't imagine what it's like for Gaetano to hear you threaten his.'

'I'm more afraid for you than the Duke,' said Gaetano. 'If you cross him, he can have you eliminated in an eye-blink. He wouldn't even let you get near him.'

'Perhaps Luciano should have fencing lessons too,' said Sky. He was joking, trying to lighten the atmosphere. But both the others turned to him eagerly.

'Could you teach me, Gaetano?' asked Luciano.

'Of course,' said the prince. 'Have you tried before?'

'A little, in Bellezza,' said Luciano. 'I've done a bit of rapier and dagger with Guido Parola.'

'Who's that?' asked Sky.

Luciano smiled for the first time since the Duke's dinner.

'He's a reformed assassin I happen to know,' he answered, remembering the first time he had met the red-haired Bellezzan, when he was trying to kill the previous Duchessa. 'He works for Rodolfo's friend, Silvia.'

'Well, he sounds like a good teacher,' said Gaetano. 'But we should start straightaway. I'll go and get a couple of rapiers and meet you back here.'

'Are you sure you don't mind?' asked Luciano. 'Remember that I shall want to use everything you teach me on the Duke.'

Gaetano smiled crookedly. 'Let's hope it doesn't come to that,' he said. 'But I want you to be able to defend yourself.'

Sky didn't stay late in Giglia; he was too tired. So he caught up on several hours' sleep and woke only when the telephone rang in the morning. He could hear Rosalind answering it and then she knocked on his door.

'That's all settled, then,' she said, coming into his room. 'Cinderella shall go to the ball!'

'What are you on about, Mum?' asked Sky, rubbing the sleep out of his eyes. But he was pleased to see her looking so happy.

'We're going to Devon tomorrow – for Easter,' said Rosalind. 'To visit Nana. And you can see your friends while we're there. Alice's house is less than twenty miles away. What do you think?'

Chapter 12

The Scent of Pines

The Nucci palace across the river was nearly finished. In the last few weeks, extra workmen had been hired to make sure that the second storey was complete, and others were busy laying out the extraordinary gardens, with their fountains, grottoes and radiating walkways. The city was about to see a display of di Chimici wealth at their family weddings and Matteo Nucci was determined not to be outshone.

Word had spread that the new palace was going to be bigger and better than anything owned by Duke Niccolò and people had taken to hanging about watching the workmen. The moving-in day for the Nucci had been announced for the day after the di Chimici weddings and already some of their furniture was being moved into the ground floor, while workmen finished tiling the roof.

Among the watchers was Enrico, who was not looking forward to telling the Duke what he had seen. Sandro had brought his master to see how rapidly the new palace was nearing completion.

'It's a deliberate snub to his Grace,' said Enrico. 'A way of saying that the Nucci are better than the di Chimici and at least as rich. The Duke won't like it.'

'It's a better way of saying it than killing people, though, isn't it?' muttered Sandro. 'Building a bigger and better house.' He bent down to stroke Fratello's ears.

'Now just you listen to me, young Sparrow,' said the Eel. 'Don't think that because they're building a house the Nucci have given up ideas of killing. They'll get their revenge for Davide, don't you worry.'

*

The Ducal carriage was drawn up on the mainland opposite Bellezza, waiting for the Duchessa. Some feet behind it was another less grand carriage with a red-haired footman standing by the door. Inside it sat an elegant middle-aged woman in a travelling cloak, with her personal maidservant.

'Another journey, Susanna,' she said. 'And this the most dangerous yet.'

'Yes, milady,' said Susanna. 'The Duke in his home city and not distracted by a dying son will be much more vigilant than he was in Remora.'

'Then I must be even more vigilant,' said Silvia. 'I want to know what he's up to, particularly as far as Bellezza is concerned.'

'Here comes the Duchessa,' said Susanna, who had been alerted by Guido Parola.

The red and silver barcone was beaching on the shore. The mandoliers who had rowed it now started carrying trunks over the shingle to the baggage carriages. And a white-haired man handed a slender figure on to a walkway of planks up to the road. Then came a small company of bodyguards. They were followed by the Duchessa's maid, Barbara, who was organising the luggage and scolding a burly young mandolier carrying a long silver box.

William Dethridge and Arianna stopped by the Padavian carriage and Guido Parola opened the door.

'Good morning, my dear,' said Silvia. 'And to you, Doctor. I trust you left Leonora well?'

'Excellently welle, good ladye,' said Dethridge. 'Bot a littil troubled by my voyage with the yonge Dutchesse here. Shee likes it not whenne I am from home.'

'You are fortunate in your marriage,' said Silvia a little pensively.

'Let's hope the di Chimici will be equally blessed,' said Arianna. 'I am sure that at least Gaetano and Francesca will be happy together.'

'If the Duke's ambition lets them,' said Silvia.

'I'm looking forward to seeing Giglia, anyway,' said Arianna. 'Gaetano spoke so highly of it.'

'Wel thenne,' said Dethridge. 'Lette us bee awaye. There is a longe road ahead.'

*

The Duke received Enrico's report in silence but he

181

sent for his architect straight afterwards.

'What progress on the palace?' he asked as soon as the man was shown in.

'Excellent, your Grace,' said Gabassi. 'The rooms are ready and I was going to say that we could start moving the new furniture in.'

'Good, good,' said Niccolò. 'Then let us begin. I shall move in with Prince Fabrizio and my daughter before the weddings and we shall host the celebrations in the piazza outside.'

When Gabassi had gone, the Duke went to a window that overlooked the main courtyard. 'Avenues and grottoes, indeed,' he muttered. 'Nucci is a farmer at heart and wants to bring the countryside into the city. I shall show him how a real nobleman uses his wealth.'

He rang the bell to call Enrico back. The Eel had not gone far.

'I want you to help Prince Fabrizio to move his apartments to the Palazzo Ducale,' said the Duke. 'And Princess Beatrice. I should like us to be in our new residence by the end of the week.'

'Certainly, your Grace,' said Enrico, rubbing his hands. This was his opportunity to make himself useful to the Duke's heir. And to the beautiful Principessa. She hadn't shown herself to be very warm to him in the past but perhaps that could be made to change.

*

Gaetano met Luciano at his lodgings, carrying two rapiers. They had tried a few passes the day before in

Sulien's cloister but now the real training began. They walked to a nearby piazza, where there was plenty of space to practise. The piazza took its name from the elegant Church of the Annunciation which made up one side of the square with its porticoed loggia. The square itself was amply big enough for swordfighting, if you stuck to the area between the two elaborate fountains, and a small knot of people had soon gathered to watch the two young men.

'Take no notice of them,' said Gaetano, driving Luciano hard back towards one of the fountains. 'You'll always have something to distract you if you are attacked. It won't be nicely organised, following rules of courtesy.'

'It's not them I'm bothered about,' gasped Luciano, who hadn't realised swordfighting was such a demanding activity. 'It's you. You're too good. Can we have a breather?'

Gaetano put up his weapon. 'Very well,' he said. 'Five minutes.'

They sat on the edge of the fountain, dipping their handkerchiefs in the water, and the small crowd dispersed.

'It's true I'm good,' said Gaetano, not boastfully. 'But my father's good too. And so are all the armed men you might encounter. Nobles in Talia are brought up to fight from a very young age – think of Falco – and assassins do it as if they've learned it as soon as they were weaned off their mother's milk.'

'Then there's not much hope for me, is there?' said Luciano, dripping the cool water on to his face. 'Whatever happens here is going to come about in the next few weeks. Even if we practise every day, I won't be able to catch up.'

'All we're trying to do,' Gaetano explained patiently, 'is teach you how to defend yourself. If you are attacked, your blood will run hot and your courage, together with the moves you have learned, may save your life.'

'Adrenaline,' murmured Luciano.

'But that doesn't mean you should lose your head,' added Gaetano warningly. 'If you lose control, you will certainly be killed.'

'But what about if I want to attack someone?'

'My father?' said Gaetano. 'I don't recommend it. Not with a sword, anyway.'

'Well, what else can I do? Poison? He has tasters, as I've seen, and besides, it seems cowardly compared with fighting face to face.'

'You can't really expect me to advise you how to kill my own father,' said Gaetano. 'Whatever he has done or is thinking of doing. Wouldn't it be better to talk to Arianna and find out what she thinks about the marriage?'

'The Duke hasn't even asked her yet,' said Luciano. 'But she'll be here in a day or two and I expect Rodolfo will tell her what your father is planning as soon as she gets here. Still, it's not easy. She didn't say anything to me all the time when you were courting her. I think a di Chimici proposal counts as politics with Arianna, not as an affair of the heart.'

'I think it probably counts as politics with my father too,' said Gaetano grimly. 'I doubt if he would be able to tell Arianna from one of his own nieces if she were not presented to him as the Duchessa of Bellezza.'

A scruffy boy with an even scruffier dog on a string was watching the two young nobles as they talked. He had noticed them fencing as he walked through the square on his way from his lodgings to the Piazza della Cattedrale. Then he had recognised one as the ugly di Chimici prince and his curiosity had been piqued.

Sandro was familiar with the Piazza of the Annunciation. He was fascinated not by the church but by the huge orphanage on one of the square's other sides. The Ospedale della Misericordia had the same porticoes as the church, but in one of them was the famous Ruota degli Innocenti, the Wheel of the Innocents, and that was what drew Sandro.

A wide, open window-space held a horizontal metal wheel, operated by a handle at the side. Desperate mothers with too many mouths to feed or no husband would come, usually at night, and place their babies on the wheel and crank the handle till their pathetic bundles vanished inside the Ospedale. The baby's cries would eventually rouse the nun on night duty and the infant would be accepted into the orphanage.

Occasionally one would be lucky and a rich woman with no children of her own would come and select a healthy smiling baby, usually a boy-child, and take it off to a life of leisure and luxury. That hadn't happened at Sandro's orphanage. Such women always went first to the sisters of the Misericordia. Time and again he had wondered why his mother had left him in the loggia of the Piazza della Cattedrale instead of on the Wheel of the Innocents in the city's only other orphanage. Was she saying she didn't want another mother to have him?

Such thoughts would make Sandro avoid the Piazza of the Annunciation for weeks, but he would always be drawn back to it like a tongue to a hurting tooth. Today he waited a little to see if the prince and his friend would start fencing again before he gave up and headed back to the Nucci's new palace.

Sky managed one snatched meeting with Nicholas and Georgia before they took the train with Alice to Devon. Nicholas had brought round a pair of foils.

'Bring them for us, since you're going by car,' said Nicholas. 'And we'll use them whenever we can meet up. Alice's place is huge.'

'She's not going to be too pleased if I turn up there and then spend all my time fencing with you though, is she?' said Sky. But he put the foils under his bed.

'Have you found out any more about the talismans?' asked Georgia. 'Are Luciano and Rodolfo any nearer to making them work for other cities?'

'I don't know,' said Sky. 'I haven't seen Rodolfo since the dinner at the Duke's, and Luciano seems to have other things on his mind.'

'Arianna,' said Georgia softly.

'More the Duke, actually,' said Sky. 'Gaetano's teaching him to fence, just like you and me, Nick.'

'My brother is teaching Luciano to fight my father?' asked Nicholas. His huge brown eyes were open wide. Sky smiled.

'Well, not specifically. I think he hopes it won't come to that. But Luciano is already quite handy with a weapon. He says that some bloke in Bellezza called Parola taught him.'

Georgia snorted. 'That would be Guido the assassin. He was trying to murder the Duchessa when Luciano met him.'

'Arianna?' asked Sky, surprised. He couldn't imagine Luciano making friends with anyone who had tried to hurt her.

'No. Her mother, the last Duchessa. He works for her now – as a sort of bodyguard-cum-footman.'

Georgia had told Nicholas ages before about how the mysterious Silvia she had met in Remora was really the Duchessa whom the di Chimici's second assassin was supposed to have blown up in her own audience chamber, but Sky hadn't known she was still alive.

'You can bet she'll turn up in Giglia too,' said Georgia. 'Just look out for a glamorous middle-aged woman somewhere near Rodolfo. That'll be her.'

'Who's a glamorous middle-aged woman?' asked Rosalind, putting her head round the door. 'Not me, I'm guessing.'

'No one you know,' said Sky quickly.

'We must be going,' said Georgia. 'Do you want to come and see Alice off at the station tomorrow?'

'No,' said Sky, suddenly embarrassed. 'I'll call her on her mobile.'

Sandro was waiting for Sky when he walked out of Sulien's cell the next morning in Giglia.

'Come and see how the new Nucci palace is getting

on,' he said straightaway. 'If Brother Sulien can spare you.'

Sandro's scruffy dog, Fratello, was waiting outside, tied to a metal ring in the wall. He jumped up and barked with pleasure when he saw his master and included Sky in his welcome too.

'What are those two wooden columns for, Sandro?' asked Sky. 'I've often wondered.'

'They're . . . ob-e-lisks,' said Sandro, trying hard to get the word right. 'We use them for markers when there are carriage races round the piazza.'

'Carriage races?' said Sky. 'I'd like to see that.'

The two boys and the dog walked through the centre of the city in the bright spring sunshine. Sky had got used to the smell of rubbish in the gutters and the juxtaposition of rickety wooden houses and grand palaces. They both looked up at the dome of the great cathedral with equal affection. It was so huge that you could see it from almost every street in Giglia, but the massive bulk of it was still always a shock up close.

They dipped down a side street off the square to pass through the Piazza Ducale, where there was quite a bustle round the Ducal palace. Workmen were carrying bundles of tapestries and pieces of furniture from carts in through the imposing front entrance.

'The Duke's moving house,' said Sandro. 'The next time he asks you to dinner, it will be here.'

'Why is he moving?' asked Sky. Sandro shrugged.

'Wants to live above the shop, with Prince Fabrizio, to keep a close eye on all the new laws being made. And he'll be able to keep an eye on the Nucci from here too – they'll be just across the river.'

They continued past the Guild offices and jewellery workshops, across the Ponte Nuovo. Sandro paused in the middle of it, letting Fratello sniff round the butchers' shops and fishmongers that lined both sides. The smell of blood was awful. Sky went to stand in one of the curved balconies in the middle of the bridge, looking out over the river. The water level was very high. Sandro came and stood beside him,

'The Argento will flood this spring,' he said knowingly.

'What? Into the city?'

'It happens often,' said Sandro. 'Though usually in the autumn. This bridge used to wash away in the old days, when it was made of wood. That's why they built this new stone one.'

'It doesn't look very new,' said Sky, looking at the grimy bricks and blood-stained cobbles and ramshackle food shops.

'It's been here two hundred years or more,' said Sandro. 'Stood up to floods all that time.'

They walked on to the street on the other side of the river, past one of the many small churches that punctuated the districts of Giglia. Within a few streets they were in sight of the surrounding countryside. Only the huge Nucci palace and its formal gardens separated the city from the fields around.

Sky was impressed. It was bigger and showier than either of the Duke's palaces. And, although it was built in a style he recognised as Renaissance architecture, it was so obviously modern and new that it suddenly made the grandeur of the di Chimici residences, with their frescoed chapels and trompe l'oeil reception rooms, seem outdated and stuffy.

Here too workmen were busy moving in furniture and hangings.

'Let's go into the gardens,' said Sandro.

'Is it allowed?' asked Sky.

'No one notices boys like me,' said Sandro. 'Or friars.'

They walked past the grand front face of the palace, at the top of a natural slope, and on towards what would one day be a gated side entrance to the gardens. Here all was innovation – radiating avenues of freshly planted trees encircling small lakes with fountains and statues. And every now and then the boys would come across an elaborate grotto, surrounded by vines and creepers carved from stone and bursting with statues of gods and nymphs.

They walked the whole circuit, following the upward slope of the ground, until they were at the back of the great house. In one direction the cupola of Saint-Mary-of-the-Lily dominated the blue sky; in the other lay fields of jonquils and asphodel. The air was fresh and laden with the scents of flowers and the mature pine trees that lined the avenue behind the palace.

'Wow!' said Sky.

'They've done it this time,' said Sandro. 'I don't think the Duke will let them hang on to it for long.'

*

The Duke was standing at the window of his new apartments at the top of the Ducal palace. It overlooked the river and from here he had a clear view of the newly risen Palazzo Nucci and its extensive gardens. Even from here he could see the bustle of activity that indicated the wool-merchant family were beginning to take possession of their new home. He was impressed and disgusted in equal measure but had no intention of showing the former emotion.

'There they are, the sheep-farmers,' he sneered. 'At least there'll be no shortage of mutton for their table. Their own grazing must start practically at the edge of their vulgar gardens.'

'Indeed, my Lord,' said Enrico, joining the Duke at the window. 'I hope it doesn't spoil your view.'

'I like to see the ants building their nest,' said Niccolò. 'But from here it feels as if I could tip a pan of boiling water over the whole colony. Just let them try anything else against my family and I will.'

'Fabrizio is here, Father,' said Beatrice, coming into the room. 'Shall I send for him to come up or do you want to take him to his rooms?'

'I shall come down and escort him myself,' said Duke Niccolò. 'This is a great day for the di Chimici family. We have moved to the centre of the city, where we belong. Let the Nucci play in their gardens, like the rustics and bumpkins they are. Politics are conducted in Council chambers, not in meadows.'

*

Sky lay in the as yet un-mown grass under the pines, breathing in the sharp and musky scent. Sandro and Fratello had flopped down beside him, glad of the shade in the warm mid-morning sun.

'I saw the young prince fencing yesterday,' said

Sandro conversationally.

'Which one?' asked Sky, though he thought he knew.

'The ugly one,' said Sandro.

'Gaetano?'

'Yeah,' said Sandro. 'He's the best of them, I reckon. Though the kid wasn't bad either, the one that died.'

'You knew Prince Falco?'

'Not to say knew,' said Sandro. 'Boys like me don't get on very close terms with princes. But he was all right. Fond of animals, especially his horses, till he had that accident. Complete wreck after that, of course.'

Sky wondered what Sandro would think if he could see Nicholas now.

'Anyway, his brother, Gaetano, the one that was closest to Falco, was teaching a young nobleman to fence. Don't know what sort of noble he was, mind you, that came from a family where he needed to be taught – probably a foreigner – but he's picking it up all right.'

'I expect that was Luciano, the Bellezzan,' said Sky cautiously. 'I met him when Sulien and I went to the Duke's.'

'Oh, Bellezza,' said Sandro, as if that accounted for it. 'I've heard they don't even have horses there. No wonder their nobles need helping by Giglians. They must be quite uncivilised.'

Sky rolled over on to his stomach, away from the boy with the dirty face and ragged clothes, to hide his smile.

'Shame, though,' said Sandro. 'He was much better-looking than our prince, though I can't imagine a

Bellezzan girl would have him if he needs so much polishing up, unless their girls are equally rough.'

'That's what the Duke thinks,' said Sky. 'He's planning to offer himself to the Bellezzan Duchessa, though I think she's far from rough. And I think she'd prefer Luciano.'

'Do you?' said Sandro, sitting up. 'That's very interesting.'

And Sky hoped he hadn't given too much away.

Chapter 13

Talismans

Lucia di Chimici was a redhead with fair skin, like her father Prince Jacopo, so she did not want to get married in pure white.

'Next to you I would look like a corpse,' she told her sister Bianca, who was dark like their mother. 'I shall wear gold.'

It was a bold choice for a Talian, because gold was a lesser valued metal than silver in their world and there was a danger of looking cheap. But there would be nothing cheap about Lucia's wedding dress. The gold taffeta would be oversewn with emeralds and she would wear her long dark red hair part loose and part plaited with gold and green ribbons.

She would look more dramatic than Bianca, whose choice was simple white satin rendered sumptuous by the addition of diamonds and pearls. Their father shuddered a little when he heard the cost, but he was proud of his girls' beauty and didn't take much persuading by his wife.

'They will be the two most beautiful brides,' said Carolina. 'And the honour of Fortezza is at stake.'

During the many fittings, the sisters had plenty of time to talk about their forthcoming marriages. At first they were too excited about the grandeur of the ceremony, with all its attendant celebrations and opportunities for fine gowns, to think of anything but the day itself. But as time went on, the seriousness of their lives' changes began to sink in. Neither girl had ever lived outside Fortezza and now they would both leave home together. Bianca would live in Volana with Alfonso, as his wife and his new Duchessa. And Lucia would be in Giglia with Carlo, living as she had been told with her cousins Gaetano and Francesca in the di Chimici palace on the Via Larga.

She had the advantage over Bianca, in that she and Carlo had always been fond of each other, from when the cousins were all small and played together in the summer palace at Santa Fina. At twenty-three, he was only one year older than her and they were well-matched. She wasn't exactly in love with him, but he was good-looking and clever and fitted the role of husband well enough to content her.

Bianca, at twenty, was seven years younger than her husband-to-be. The gap had seemed enormous during those long summers, when Alfonso and his skinny brother Rinaldo had been the two eldest, and she was still a bit in awe of him.

But he too was good-looking and had shown

himself perfectly willing to marry her, which was an excellent recommendation. And she was glad Duke Niccolò's choice had hit on him and not on Rinaldo when picking out a husband for her, as Bianca would have had to obey, whatever his decision.

All that spring the two princesses talked about their future in the di Chimici dynasty, imagining the children they would have and the city-states they would rule over.

'Duke Niccolò means Gaetano to have Fortezza when father dies,' said Lucia. 'I'm sure that's why we're getting such well-titled husbands. So that they won't contest Fortezza for themselves.'

'It is sad for Father to think on,' said Bianca. 'His line dying out in his own city. I hope we have boys, don't you?'

'I don't see why girls shouldn't inherit a title,' said Lucia. 'Look at Bellezza, where they always have Duchesse.'

'But they are elected,' said Bianca. 'The title isn't inherited like the ones in our family.'

'Still, this one's the daughter of the last one, isn't she?' said Lucia. 'It comes to the same thing.'

There was no way that Rosalind could drive all the way from Islington to Devon, even though she was much better. It was doubtful that their car would have made it, anyway. The dented Fiesta had belonged to Rosalind's father. When he had died four years earlier, her mother had given it to Rosalind, but life in London was harder for the car than in a Devon village and it was now the worse for wear.

Laura was going to drive them all in her new Rover; conveniently, she was visiting her family too.

'If I get frantic, tell me I can come and stay with you, darling,' she said to Rosalind as she drove very fast along the M4, window down and chain-smoking.

'Of course,' said Rosalind, smiling round at Sky. 'We wouldn't mind.'

He knew what she was thinking. Nana Meadows didn't approve of Laura and never had. 'Fast' and 'flighty' were her two favourite ways of describing her. Sky had once heard his mother stop his grandmother in her tracks by saying calmly, 'It's funny that you're so rude about my best friend. Particularly when you consider that I'm the unmarried mother and she's the one with a respectable job and decent income.' Of course, she hadn't known Sky was listening.

Laura had baulked a bit at their luggage, especially when she saw Sky's box of foils. But nothing ever fazed her for long and she had cheerfully re-packed the boot, piling the extras in the back with Sky.

'It's time you learned to drive,' she now shouted at him over her shoulder, sending clouds of smoke into the back of the car. 'I'll start teaching you in Devon, if you've got your provisional.'

It so happened that Sky had. And he had passed his theory and his hazard tests. But that was as far as it had gone. His mother couldn't afford driving lessons and she hadn't been fit enough until recently to think of teaching him herself.

At the next service station, Laura bought another packet of cigarettes and a pair of big red Ls for Sky; she never let the grass grow under her feet. Rosalind was feeling well enough to drive the next bit and Sky sat in the front with her, while Laura stretched out in the back. She was instantly asleep, looking much younger curled up on bits of luggage and without a cigarette in her mouth.

'What kind of a driving instructor do you think she'll make?' Sky asked his mother.

'Interesting,' said Rosalind, and they both laughed. 'Oh, I'm looking forward to this break,' she went on. 'I feel as if I haven't breathed any proper air for years. I bet I wouldn't have been so ill if we hadn't lived in London.'

'You don't want to move back to Devon, do you?' asked Sky, surprised.

Rosalind shook her head. 'No way,' she said. 'It may have better air, but a few days with your nana makes me long to be back in the smoke.'

'She's not so bad,' said Sky.

'Not to you. You're her blue-eyed boy – which is very strange, considering they're brown!'

It was true. Rosalind's parents had been appalled when she had told them she was expecting a baby, even though it wasn't unusual for unmarried girls any more. Then the golden boy with his chestnut curls had won Joyce Meadows over and it broke her heart when they moved to London. That had largely been Geoffrey Meadows's idea and his widow had often hinted she would like them to move back.

Up till now, Sky had thought that would be a disaster, but here he was speeding towards Devon and the girl he really liked and the two other people who now meant most to him in his life. And until as recently as a few weeks ago he had never spoken to any of them.

'It's enormous!' said Arianna, looking at the cathedral cupola. Fine as the Basilica of Santa Maddalena was in Bellezza, with its silver domes and mosaics, it couldn't rival Saint-Mary-of-the-Lily for size and grandeur.

She was staying at the Bellezzan Embassy in the Borgo Sant' Ambrogio. It was uncomfortably close to the Palazzo di Chimici in the Via Larga, and it was with relief that she learned that the Duke had moved further in towards the city's centre. Her Ambassador had refused as diplomatically as he could, on Arianna's behalf, all the offers for her and her retinue to stay at either palace, on the grounds that it was the first visit of a Duchessa of Bellezza to Giglia for nearly twenty years and that the Embassy must have the privilege of entertaining her.

She stood on the balcony of the Embassy's most splendid bedroom, looking down the Borgo towards the cathedral. In a few weeks she must attend the splendid weddings there and she still did not know what to do about the Duke's dress. Barbara was unpacking it even now, smoothing out invisible creases in the jewel-encrusted skirt, although it really was too stiff to crumple, even on a long journey.

There was a tap at the door. 'May I come inne?' said Doctor Dethridge, putting his grizzled head around it. 'Youre visitours have arryved.'

He was followed by Rodolfo and Luciano, and

Arianna's heart lifted to see them both. Her visit to Giglia might be a diplomatic quagmire but at least she was to be surrounded by people she loved, who were Stravaganti into the bargain. She would be much more comfortable with her father and Luciano living in the Embassy.

*

In another part of the city, two more Stravaganti were talking about the Duchessa's safety. Giuditta Miele was visiting Brother Sulien in his laboratory, drinking a tisane of mallow.

'Rodolfo has called a meeting of members of the Brotherhood for this afternoon,' Sulien was saying. 'With Doctor Dethridge now arrived in the city, there will be five of us. Six if you count young Celestino.'

'That will not be enough,' said Giuditta. 'You know my apprentice, Franco? The pretty one?'

Sulien nodded.

'He has been posing for Bruno Vecchietto, who has been painting angels all over the Nucci's new palace. And he told Franco there is definitely trouble brewing. Their armoury is stocked full of weapons, and they are not a military family.'

'But there is no reason to suppose their violence will be offered to the young Duchessa, is there?' asked Sulien. 'It is the di Chimici who are their enemies, and since Bellezza is opposed to the Duke's plans, I should have thought the Nucci would be on Arianna's side.'

'Violence is never tidy, Sulien,' said Giuditta. 'All it takes is for young men armed with swords and daggers to get their blood up and there could be a massacre. Can you be sure Arianna will be safe in such a mêlée?'

'What would you have us do?' asked the friar. 'Rodolfo will be open to suggestion.'

'If only there were another strong faction who could help keep order,' said Giuditta.

'The Nucci could have been useful,' said Sulien thoughtfully, 'but not since the death of Davide. If they see the opportunity to attack the di Chimici they will be caught up in that, not looking out for the Duchessa.'

'We need more Stravaganti here,' said Giuditta. 'I would have Rodolfo summon others of the Brotherhood from all over Talia. If it comes to a fight, it is not swordsmen we need, but those who can communicate without words and surround the Duchessa with their thoughts rather than their muscles.'

Sky moved into the little boxroom he always slept in at his grandmother's. It looked smaller than ever this time.

'Good heavens!' said his grandmother, looking in on him. 'You'll be bursting at the seams. I had no idea you had grown so tall!'

'Growth spurt, Nana,' said Sky. 'Don't worry – I'll be fine.'

'Next time, I'll put you in the back bedroom and let Rosalind sleep in here,' said Mrs Meadows. 'We can't have you cramping your young limbs. Are you sure you can fit in that bed? It's not even a full-size single.'

It was nice to be fussed over for a while but Sky was itching to get to see Alice. Next morning, after breakfast, he got Rosalind to drive him over to Ivy Court in Laura's car. Laura's parents lived within walking distance of Nana Meadows and Rosalind was quite happy to drive short distances on roads she knew well.

It was a fine spring day and the scent of flowers was in the air. It reminded Sky of Giglia. Particularly when they turned into the drive of Ivy Court and he caught the unmistakable scent of pine trees.

'Crikey,' said Rosalind. 'Your girlfriend must be loaded!'

Sky scarcely noticed that she had called Alice his girlfriend for the first time. His heart had sunk. Ivy Court was a red-brick Elizabethan farmhouse with imposing chimneys and a circular gravel drive. There seemed to be a lot of outbuildings as well. Nicholas had said that Alice had plenty of space but he had been very casual about it. Now Sky thought that it was all very well for Nicholas, who had been a prince in another life.

But it was Georgia who came round the corner; she was flushed and rather pretty – something Sky had never thought before.

'Oh, hi,' she said, smiling. 'Hello, Rosalind. We've just been for an early ride.'

'You obviously enjoyed it,' said Rosalind.

'Yes, it was great. There's something about the air down here. Come in and meet Alice's dad. I'll make us some coffee. Alice and Nick are still rubbing down the horses.'

Horses? thought Sky. She has more than one? He

moved into the house like a zombie.

Paul Greaves was sitting in the kitchen, reading the paper. He was relaxed and friendly and immediately started chatting to Rosalind while Georgia filled an enormous kettle and put it on the hotplate of a cream Aga. It was a comfortable, untidy room but Sky knew that it meant money. He thought of their kitchen at the flat, where they ate their meals. There was a wooden table and chairs in here too, but he was pretty sure that this house would have a proper dining room as well.

Georgia made six full mugs of real coffee and set out hot cross buns, and, by the time she was done, Alice and Nicholas had come in, smelling slightly of horse and with their hair ruffled and their faces glowing. Sky couldn't have felt less at home. But Alice gave him a beaming smile and he thought again how lovely she was and how lucky he was that she liked him.

'Did you bring the foils?' asked Nicholas, under his breath.

'They're still in the car,' said Sky, feeling glad that at least they had turned up in the new Rover and not his granddad's old Fiesta.

'Good,' said Nicholas. 'We'll start after coffee.'

'Start what?' asked Alice. 'Don't tell me you two are going to spend the holiday fencing?'

'Fencing?' said Paul. 'Are you another swordsman, Sky?'

'Not as good as Nick,' said Sky. 'But I'm learning.'

'He's obsessed,' said Rosalind. 'Every spare moment.'

'It's a good sport,' said Paul. 'I wish I could do it. It

203

always looks so glamorous and dashing.'

Alice laughed. 'You want to be dashing, Dad?'

Now it was Paul's turn to blush a little, and Sky saw where Alice got her looks from. He also noticed his mother looking appreciative, which alarmed him a bit.

'You know what an old romantic I am,' said Paul, putting his arm round Alice. 'It comes of being a country solicitor, who lives in the house he was born in,' he explained. 'I often think how unadventurous my life must seem from the outside, though I do like my job.'

'And it's a wonderful house,' said Rosalind.

'Alice tells me you were born round here too,' said Paul, and then the two adults were off on one of those 'Where-did-you-go-to-school and did-you-know-so-and-so?' conversations that meant the others could escape.

'You're not really going to start fencing, are you?' asked Alice. She was longing to be alone with Sky.

He felt torn in two. Insecure and lacking in self-confidence all over again, he would have liked to be on his own with Alice, too. But he also needed to talk to Nicholas and Georgia, who were obviously keen to quiz him about what was going on in Giglia.

'Come on, Nick,' said Georgia, coming to his rescue. 'Let's give them some space. I'm sure Alice would like to show Sky round.'

'We do need to get more Stravaganti here,' said Rodolfo, agreeing with Giuditta.

'Then send messages to Remora, Bellona and all the

other city-states,' she said. 'The brothers in Fortezza, Moresco and Volana could get here quickly too.'

'There is another way,' said Rodolfo. 'And one that wouldn't leave all the other cities vulnerable. It is bad enough that Bellezza is undefended.'

'Wee have been essaying to altir the nature of the talismannes,' said William Dethridge.

'How?' asked Sulien.

'You know how they bring Stravaganti from my old world always to one city?' said Luciano. 'It's a restriction we've been trying to overcome.'

'So that Celestino could travel to Bellezza, for instance?' asked the friar.

'Yes, though it's here he'll be needed,' said Rodolfo. 'But there are two others we could bring here.'

'Then you have succeeded?' said Giuditta.

'No,' said Rodolfo. 'Not yet.' He walked over to the window. He and Luciano had moved into the Embassy, to be closer to Arianna, and he was holding his conference of Stravaganti in one of its elegant reception rooms.

Luciano wondered if his old master had told Arianna about the Grand Duke's marriage plans. He hadn't been able to bring himself to ask; Rodolfo seemed so preoccupied with the safety of his daughter at the weddings.

'You sense the tensions in the city?' Rodolfo was asking Sulien and Giuditta. 'I don't think we can depend on the success of our experiments. I think you will have to take two new talismans yourselves.'

Rosalind stayed to lunch at Ivy Court. She couldn't remember how long it had been since she had liked someone as much as she did Paul. And it wasn't just because he was an attractive man. He was warm and friendly and willing to be interested in her and eager to show her round the house and grounds, not because he was showing off but because he loved them.

Lunch turned out to be a scrappy affair of things dug out of the freezer and larder. Sky was the best cook among them, which was not saying much, but they ended up eating a surprisingly satisfying concoction of rice and peas with what Sky said was chilli con carne. It was quite hot and Paul brought up cold beer from the cellar – it was the kind of house that would have a cellar. And his freezer was well-stocked with large tubs of ice cream – apparently a stipulation of Alice's when she was coming to stay.

'You'll need to get more with four teenagers in the house,' said Alice.

'I shall order a daily cartload,' said Paul grandly, and Sky felt pleased that he had been so easily accepted as just another friend of Alice's who was going to be around. But he was still reeling from his tour of the house and grounds. OK, it wasn't like a di Chimici residence, but it was still the grandest home he had been in outside Talia.

After lunch, Rosalind reluctantly said she must be getting back to her mother's. 'What time shall I collect him?' she asked Paul.

'Oh, don't worry,' said Paul. 'I'll drop him back whenever you want him.'

'Thanks. It'll be easier when Sky can drive,' said Rosalind. 'He's supposed to be having some lessons this holiday, so you mustn't let him spend all his time here.'

'I could give you some lessons, Sky,' said Paul. 'There's space for you to pick up the basics in the grounds, without going out on the road. It's an awkward stage, isn't it?' he said to Rosalind. 'Before they're quite old enough to drive but they're old enough to go out on their own and you end up ferrying them everywhere.'

Rosalind didn't feel quite comfortable agreeing; she knew that made it sound as if she was always doing things for her son, when it was usually the other way round.

'Now,' said Nicholas to Sky and Alice. 'If you love-birds are willing to be unstuck, Sky and I could do some fencing.'

Georgia nobly left them to it while she went off to talk to Alice and the two boys were able at last to talk about Giglia.

'I didn't go last night,' said Sky. 'And I'm hoping it will work OK stravagating from my nana's. I'll try tonight.'

'Georgia was able to get to Remora from here,' said Nicholas. 'What happened the last time you went?'

'Not a lot,' said Sky. 'I saw the new Nucci palace. It's huge.'

'The Nucci?' said Nicholas. 'They have a place up by Saint-Mary-among-the-Vines, don't they? The one with the tower?'

'They do. But they're moving to this swanky new one on the other side of the river. I don't think the Duke's too pleased about it.'

'I bet,' said Nicholas. 'He thinks swank is his prerogative.'

He was still holding a foil but not making any attempt to fence. He was too thoughtful.

'How am I going to get there?' he asked. 'I must be able to see what's going on for myself.'

'But wouldn't you be recognised?' asked Sky. 'Even if something could be done about the talismans?'

'I'll grow a beard!' said Nicholas.

They both laughed. 'You'd better start now, then,' said Sky. 'Do you even shave yet?'

'Just for that, I'm going to whip your ass,' said Nicholas. '*En garde!*'

The statue of the Duchessa was complete apart from the hands and face. She stood in Giuditta's studio, looking like a bird poised for flight, her marble cloak and hair streaming out behind her in the invisible wind.

'It's wonderful,' said Arianna. She was wearing a grey velvet cloak with a hood pulled up over her masked face and was accompanied by Barbara and two bodyguards. Franco the angelic apprentice was looking at Barbara in admiration, unperturbed by the two armed Bellezzans.

'I have never sculpted a face with a mask before,' said Giuditta.

'It's a pity,' said Arianna. 'But that's how I must appear, in a public statue.'

'Still, I should like to see your face,' said the sculptor. 'It would help if I knew what I was covering up.'

'Then everyone else must look away,' said Arianna.

'My guards know the penalty and would exact it.'

Giuditta gave the order and her apprentices turned away, watched over by Barbara and the guards. Arianna untied her mask and Giuditta looked long at her face, sketching swiftly with a stick of charcoal. She walked round the Duchessa for twenty minutes, drawing her face from several angles.

At last she said, 'It is enough for today. Thank you, your Grace.'

Arianna felt dismissed. She could tell that Giuditta was itching to get back to work on the marble. She re-tied the mask and put on her cloak. The tension in the studio lifted and she was sure she saw one of the apprentices wink at her maid.

When she had gone, Franco came over to look at the sketches.

'It can't be forbidden even to look at a drawing of her face,' he said, and the other apprentices clustered round.

'She's as beautiful as they say,' said one.

'She's OK,' said Franco. 'But I like the maid better.'

'How can you tell? She was masked too.'

But Giuditta took no notice of their chatter. She was concentrating on the macquette she was going to make of the Duchessa's head. It was taking her mind off the other thing she had agreed to do.

Chapter 14

Pictures in the Walls

Sky took the blue glass bottle in his hand with some trepidation. He had not stravagated the night before – the first time he had missed a night since his Talian adventures had started. He found it difficult to believe that he could arrive there just as easily from Devon as from London.

Everything felt different down here – the visit to Ivy Court had unsettled not just him. His mother had been unusually animated that evening, chattering about Paul and Alice, while he had retreated more into himself. He could see in his mind's eye the sort of boy Alice was supposed to get serious about – blond, rich and having ridden a horse practically as soon as he could walk – and Sky didn't fit any of the criteria.

It would be a relief to turn to his new friends in

Talia and his alternative identity as a novice friar and secret Stravagante with some serious involvement in politics and strategies. For weeks now he had been leading two parallel lives, and no one who knew him in his everyday world, apart from Georgia and Nicholas, would have believed that this lanky teenager with the long dreadlocks spent his nights striding round a mighty Renaissance city, dressed in black and white robes.

At the beginning, it had been like a game for Sky – a kind of dressing-up and play-acting that gave scope to his more flamboyant side that had been suppressed for years. And it had been a welcome break from being the only fully functioning person in his family. But as Rosalind continued to get better and some of the burdens had lifted at home, Sky had got more and more involved in what he was doing in Talia. It wasn't just adventures and role-playing; he had been sent there on a mission. Only he wasn't yet sure what it was.

The more time Sky spent with Brother Sulien, the more he came to respect and admire him. He could see that Luciano practically worshipped Rodolfo and wondered if that was always how it was with Stravaganti. Georgia hadn't said much about the one she met in Remora, but Sky knew that he was called Paolo and that Georgia still missed him and his family.

Still, it wasn't just the heady company of fellow Stravaganti that Sky enjoyed. He liked Prince Gaetano, who actually made him feel less uncomfortable than Alice's father, even though he lived in palaces and was rich beyond Paul Greaves's wildest dreams of a son-in-law. And then there was

Sandro, at the other end of the scale, with not much more status than the mongrel dog who trailed round after him. A novice friar was as much above Sandro as a prince was above Sky; the boy couldn't even read.

But he was Sky's friend nonetheless, because he liked him. Sky wondered, as he lay wide awake holding the bottle, whether Sandro ever wondered where he, Sky, had come from. He never asked. Just accepted that he was there. That was one of the things that was comfortable about Sandro.

Sandro had in fact been wondering about exactly that. He had been spending more and more time hanging round Saint-Mary-among-the-Vines and less and less with the Eel. Ever since the night of Davide's murder, his former admiration of his employer had started to wane. Certainly Enrico fed him and gave him lodgings, or at least gave him the silver that bought these things. But that was just payment for Sandro's services. Brother Sulien gave him food and shelter without wanting anything in return and Sandro loved him for it. And there was more; Sandro had a secret. Ever since the day he had helped Sulien and Brother Tino make Vignales in the laboratory, Sandro had been trying to learn to read.

Sulien was teaching him his letters from a big illuminated Bible. Sandro loved the pictures that went round the letters at the beginning of each chapter. 'A' for Adam, with its pictures of the first man and woman and the apple and the serpent, just like another picture in a chapel he had seen on the other side of the river. Sandro hadn't understood the wall paintings then, but now Sulien told him the stories that went with all the pictures.

The first man and woman had been very unhappy; Sandro understood that. When they had disobeyed their Lord they had been banished from their garden for ever. An angel barred the way back, and that began with an 'A' too. Sandro also knew what 'S' looked like because it began the name of King Solomon, as well as Sulien and Sandro. And, even more amazingly, his name began with an 'A' as well, because it was short for Alessandro. He was rapidly unwrapping the mysteries of language and the excitement of stories. And if he imagined the temple of Solomon as being rather like Saint-Mary-of-the-Lily, perhaps it did not matter very much.

No one had ever told Sandro stories before. The nuns in the orphanage had been too busy; they had taught him his catechism, so that he knew the words, but he had never known what any of it meant. Or that it related to something about which there were stories. His lessons with Sulien were nothing like those with the nuns anyway.

The pharmacist, having taught him a letter, would show him how to find it on his pots and jars. And, when Sandro's eyes were weary of letters, he would take him into the church and tell him stories about what was painted there. There were two paintings that Sandro knew now, about the poor man who had been nailed to a cross of wood. One was on a huge painted cross that hung down between the friars' stalls and the congregation's pews. It was so sad, with what looked like real drops of blood trickling from the hands and feet.

Sandro preferred the other one, which was a wall painting, showing the same melancholy scene, but with the man's father above him and a dove between the two of them. Sandro thought it must be a comfort for the red-headed man on the cross to have them there while he suffered.

'It's not just a comfort for him,' said Brother Sulien, 'but for all of us. You see, that Father is yours and mine, too.'

'Nah,' said Sandro. 'I haven't got a father – you know that.'

'You've got that one,' said Sulien. 'We all have. And he gave his own Son's life for us.'

'Not for me,' said Sandro.

'Yes, even for you,' said Sulien.

Then they would go and look at something more cheerful, like the frescoes in the Lady Chapel, showing the miracle wrought by the church's patron Saint. The first Alfonso di Chimici, when already a wealthy perfumier, had been taken ill one day during Mass and been carried through to where the infirmary now stood. The friars had not known how to help him, but a vision of the Virgin had appeared to the pharmacist-friar of the day and advised the administration of unripe young grapes from their vineyards. Within days, Alfonso was cured and gave a large sum of money to the church to build an infirmary.

Sandro liked this story, because it was about a friar curing a di Chimici. 'Just like you and the Duke,' he told Sulien. And it had a happy ending – unlike most stories about the di Chimici.

When Sky at last arrived in Sulien's cell, he sighed with relief. The friar wasn't there; the room was still and quiet and Sky lay on the cot for a few minutes letting his pulse slow. He stretched his limbs in his novice's robes and felt himself adapting to his Giglian role. Brother Tino. A young man without family, history or responsibilities. He suddenly felt ravenous and set off for the refectory.

There he found both Sulien and Sandro, tucking into bowls of frothy warm milk with cinnamon and freshly baked rolls.

'Ah, Brother Tino, come and join us,' called Sulien, moving along the bench. Most of the other friars had finished eating, so there was plenty of space.

'What news?' asked Sky, pouring himself some milk from an earthenware jug.

'Niccolò di Chimici has given us a farm,' said Sulien.

'Really?' said Sky. 'Why?'

'Because we saved his life,' said Sulien. 'Prince Fabrizio sent me the deeds. It's only a little homestead, on the other side of the Argento, but Brother Tullio is pleased, because he can grow more vegetables there.'

Wow, thought Sky. Fancy being so rich you could just hand over a farm as a thank-you present!

'And the Duchessa has arrived,' said Sandro, who had been bursting to tell what he knew. 'I've seen her.'

'What's she like?' asked Sky.

Sandro shrugged. 'Hard to say. She wears a mask. But she's got a pretty figure and lots of hair.'

'You shall see for yourself, Tino,' said Sulien. 'We

are invited to the Bellezzan Embassy for morning refreshment. Don't eat too many rolls now.'

'But "we"'s not me,' said Sandro, wiping his mouth with his sleeve. 'I haven't the manners for it. I'll see you later.'

*

Rodolfo was waiting when they arrived at the Embassy. He introduced Sky to William Dethridge and the Elizabethan held out both hands to the boy and studied him carefully, in much the way that Giuditta Miele had done.

'Aye,' he said at length. 'Ye'll do. Tell mee, how fares yonge George?'

It took Sky a moment or two, thrown by Dethridge's way of talking, to realise that he meant Georgia.

'She's fine,' he said. 'But anxious to get back to Talia. Almost as keen as, you know, Falco,' he added under his breath. 'Any luck with the talismans?'

It was Sulien who answered. 'We are to go to your world again, Giuditta and I, taking new talismans for Georgia and the young prince. Ones that will bring them here.'

'The only problem,' said Rodolfo, 'is that they will need to give up their old ones. How do you think they will respond to that idea?'

'I think that Georgia will not like it,' said a low voice, and Sky realised that the Duchessa had silently entered the room. He jumped to his feet, confused.

A beautiful young woman in a green silk dress was approaching. He had no doubt that she was beautiful, in spite of her mask. Behind it, violet eyes sparkled, and her glossy hair – lots of it indeed, Sandro, thought Sky – tumbled in carefully arranged long curls over her shoulders. She was followed by a woman Sky didn't recognise, an elegant middle-aged one, who stopped to talk to Rodolfo.

'Your Grace,' stammered Sky, attempting a bow.

'Call me Arianna, please,' she said, taking his hand and leading him to a new seat beside her. 'You are a friend of Georgia and Falco and a member of the same Brotherhood as my father. You are welcome in Talia.'

'Yow moste ask the yonglinges,' said Dethridge. 'Ask them if they wolde give up their olde talismannes to make the journeye to this grete citee where they are needed.'

'But they aren't in London at the moment,' said Sky. 'They are on Easter holiday with me, in Devon. I've come from there tonight – I mean today.'

'Easter?' said Sulien. 'I never thought to ask. Is it Easter in your world already?'

'It was Good Friday there today,' said Sky. 'When is it in Talia?'

'Not for another four weeks,' said Rodolfo.

'Is that because there's been another time shift in the gateway?' asked Sky.

'No,' said Sulien. 'It is because of the fact that Easter is a movable feast and your world is more than four hundred years ahead of ours. It would have been unlikely for the dates of Easter to match.'

'I can still ask the others about the talismans,' said Sky. 'But you mustn't stravagate to my world until we're back in London.'

'It is an unwelcome delay,' said Rodolfo. 'It means

we shall have less time to accustom them to this city before the wedding.'

'But it cannot be helped,' said Sulien. 'When do you all return home?'

Sky calculated. 'Four days,' he said. 'I'll come and tell you, the night we get back, and then you can come the next day. I can look out for you,' he added, feeling peculiar at the thought of the friar and the sculptor turning up on his doorstep. He must make sure Rosalind was out.

Just then, Luciano was shown into the room, his eyes sparkling and his cheeks glowing. Sky knew immediately that he had been swordfighting with Gaetano.

'Hi!' he said to Sky, and then made a more formal greeting to the others, first raising the Duchessa's hand lightly to his lips.

'You look well,' she said, smiling under her mask.

'I feel well,' he said simply.

Sky looked at them and felt sorry for Georgia. What a mess.

'What do you think, Luciano?' asked Arianna, as if reading his thoughts. 'Would Georgia give up her flying horse for a new talisman?'

'It would be hard for her,' he said. 'She loves horses and it's her only link with Remora and Merla.'

'We can but try,' said Rodolfo. 'We need her here. I am not so sure about Falco. It's a risky strategy. If he is recognised by any member of his family, except Gaetano, who knows his choice, there's no telling what might happen.'

'Yet he is the one more likely to accept a new talisman from here,' said Luciano. 'Giglia is his city, after all – not Remora.'

Luciano walked back to the friary with Sky and Sulien.

'Why does Doctor Dethridge talk like that?' Sky asked.

'Like what?' asked Sulien.

'It's because Tino and my foster-father come from the same world, centuries apart,' explained Luciano. 'I've got used to it, but to other English speakers from our world, Doctor Dethridge sounds as if he's speaking a very old-fashioned language.'

*

Arianna was going to change her dress but Rodolfo stopped her.

'There is something else I must tell you,' he said, but he waited so long to say what it was that Arianna thought he had forgotten she was there. Silvia had her eyes fixed on Rodolfo, waiting for his news.

At last he took Arianna's hand in his and, sighing, said, 'Duke Niccolò is going to ask you to marry him.'

Arianna felt numb. This was not like hearing that Gaetano was going to propose; this felt like being a small bird with a hawk circling in the air above her and she could see no way of escape.

'If you wear the dress he sent, at the weddings, he will assume you look kindly on his offer,' said Silvia.

'When?' said Arianna. She could scarcely find her voice. 'When is he going to ask?'

'I should think the night before the weddings – or perhaps the wedding feast itself, so that he can make the announcement in front of all his family,' said Rodolfo.

'Then I am trapped,' said Arianna bitterly. 'What will he do when I refuse him?'

'Not so hasty,' said Silvia. 'You don't have to refuse him outright.'

'Silvia!' said Rodolfo. 'You are not serious.'

'I am completely serious,' said Silvia. 'At least about getting my daughter and my husband out of this city alive. It may be necessary for Arianna to seem to go along with his plans. It will buy us time to work out what to do.'

Arianna shuddered. The Duke was repulsive to her. He was not unhandsome, even though so much older than her, and he was a cultured, civilised man, who valued art and literature and music. He was fabulously wealthy and could give her anything she might ever want. Except her freedom and the freedom of her city. But he was a murderer. And she did not, could not, love him. But her own mother was suggesting that she should not turn his proposal down out of hand.

Worst of all, Arianna guessed that Luciano knew of this development and had said nothing. What else was all this fencing about? It was pathetic; she didn't know whether to laugh or cry. Luciano against the Duke. She wished with all her heart that they had never come to Giglia.

Next morning, Paul himself came to collect Sky; the young people were out riding, he explained. He also explained that only one horse was Alice's, the one called Truffle. He was looking after Conker, the horse that Georgia rode, for a friend, and she and Nicholas had to take turns when they were both down together.

He clearly saw nothing odd in Georgia's friendship with the younger boy and nothing odd about his daughter's fondness for Sky either. He sat in Nana's parlour as much at his ease as in his own kitchen, chatting about horses and drinking her coffee, which was much less nice than at Ivy Court. Sky decided that he liked Alice's dad very much; he was the sort of person who was at home everywhere and accepted everyone on their own terms.

Paul hardly spoke to Rosalind, but he looked at her often and Sky wondered what he was thinking. He tried to see his mother as she might appear to Paul. A thin, pale-skinned, very fair woman in her late thirties, with a ready smile and expressive dark blue eyes. He wondered if she looked as fragile to Paul as she did to him. Sky suddenly felt fiercely protective of her. In all his seventeen years she had not dated anyone to his knowledge. Was it going to happen now? And with Alice's father, of all people! Sky couldn't imagine how that was going to affect his own relationship with Alice.

When they reached Ivy Court and found the others still out, Paul offered Sky the chance to drive his Shogun in the grounds. It felt enormous, sitting behind the wheel, but Sky managed to drive it without stalling and even changed gears with only one crunch. He was still in the driving seat when they finished a complete circuit and returned to the front of the house. Alice was waiting with her thumb stuck out.

'Any chance of a ride?' she smiled at him.

'Not till you've had a shower,' said Paul. 'I don't want my car reeking of horse. I have to drive it to my office, you know.'

But, horsey or not, Alice gave Sky a quick kiss when he got out of the car and, since it didn't seem to bother her father, Sky put his arms round her and kissed her back.

'You can go and get your sword-fighting out of the way while I shower,' she said. 'Nick says he's not going to bother till after – he'll only need another one after you've finished. He's waiting for you in the yard.'

Sky went round to the back and found Nicholas still talking to Conker. Sky himself was a little nervous of horses, never having had anything to do with them, and this one struck him as huge. But he was a handsome beast, with his arched neck and long mane. Seeing Nicholas with him reminded Sky of how little he knew about Georgia's stravagation and the time when the di Chimici's youngest prince had made his fateful decision.

'I miss having my own horse,' said Nicholas, looking up. 'I mean, I used to have them around all the time, before my accident.'

'But at least you can ride again now,' said Sky. 'And you would never have been able to do that if you had stayed in Talia. Or fence, come to that.'

'That's why I did it,' said Nicholas, but he sighed so deeply that Sky decided to tell him about the Stravaganti's plans straightaway.

'I'd be sorry to give back Merla's feather, of course,' said Nicholas, his eyes shining. 'But I'd do it if your friar could bring me something from Giglia.'

'That's what I thought,' said Sky.

'When are they coming?' asked Nicholas eagerly.

'As soon as we get back to London,' said Sky.

'So I could be back home in less than a week?'

'I guess.'

'Brilliant!' Nicholas punched the air, then stopped. 'What about Georgia?'

'Well, do you think she'd be willing to give up her talisman?' asked Sky. 'You know her better than I do.'

'I think it would be very hard for her,' said Nicholas. 'It was stolen twice, you know – by her awful stepbrother. The first time he broke it and the second time he kept it for nearly a year. We couldn't go back and it was agony. She was so happy when the horse came back. It means a lot to her.'

'More than seeing Luciano again?' asked Sky softly, but Nicholas couldn't answer that.

Giuditta had finished the macquette of the Duchessa's head. The hair was only suggested, because she had already sculpted it; it was the face she had made it for.

'Remarkable,' said Rodolfo, who had accompanied Arianna to her latest sitting. 'You have caught her to the life.'

'Will you hold on to the back of this chair, your Grace?' asked the sculptor. 'I should like to sketch your hands as if holding a ship's rail.'

Arianna was quite happy with this arrangement, which left her free to talk. Giuditta was taciturn as always, but her workshop was, unusually, empty, so

Arianna and Rodolfo were free to speak to her about private matters.

'Is it true that you are going to Luciano's old world?' Arianna asked the sculptor.

'Yes. Please don't tighten your fingers. Thank you.'

'Giuditta has of course been before, more than once,' said Rodolfo. 'But not to take a talisman for another Stravagante.'

'What will it be?' asked Arianna and saw Giuditta's dark eyes glance up, startled.

'I don't know yet,' Rodolfo answered for her. 'It must be from Giglia and Giuditta must choose it herself.'

'Do you think that Georgia will come?' Arianna asked Rodolfo.

'I think she will want to,' he said, looking thoughtful. 'And she is brave and loyal. But it would mean giving up her connection with Remora, and that will not be easy for her.'

Giuditta was listening, though she appeared to be totally concentrated on her work. So this girl she had to fetch was going to be difficult to persuade. Giuditta had hoped that, since Georgia was already a Stravagante, her work would be almost done. Now she could see this was far from true.

'Give up the flying horse?' said Georgia. 'Why on earth would I want to do that? They must have gone mad!'

'It's the only way to get you to Giglia at the moment,' Sky explained. 'And they all seem to think you'll be needed there. As well as Nicholas.'

Georgia was flattered, but the enormity of what she would need to do overwhelmed her.

'Can't I just take the other talisman and leave the horse here?' she asked.

'It doesn't work like that,' said Sky. 'Don't ask me why. They all know more about that sort of thing than I do. If Doctor Dethridge says that's the way it is, I'm not going to argue.'

'And they'll be here in a few days, as soon as we get back to London?'

It cast a shadow over the three of them for the rest of the weekend, making them edgy and anxious. Alice picked it up but had no explanation for it. Her time with Sky had started so well but now, inexplicably, he seemed to want to be with Nicholas and Georgia more than with her. And Georgia herself was remote and scratchy; the only times when things felt right were when they were out riding.

As for Nicholas, he was moodier than Alice had ever known him. Normally they got on well; it had been hard at first to accept him, but he and Georgia were so close that, over time, Alice had come to like him in his own right. But now he had become just a monosyllabic teenage boy and whenever they were all together, no one had anything to say except Alice. Paul was hardly ever there; he seemed to be spending a lot of time with Sky's mother.

In the end, Alice could think of only one reason for their behaviour, and she decided to confront them. It was the afternoon before they were due to go back and the weather had turned very warm. The boys had finished their fencing practice and were flopped on the lawn at the back of the house. Georgia had been watching them as usual. And Alice had been watching them all, from her bedroom window.

The three of them were talking quite animatedly. What did they find to talk about when they would say nothing to her? As soon as she reached the garden, the others fell silent.

'There's no need to stop,' said Alice. 'I've worked out what it must be. If you two want to be together,' she said to Sky and Georgia, 'then that's all right.'

Then she turned and walked back to the house, so that they wouldn't see she was crying.

Chapter 15

Visitors

Luciano's swordsmanship was improving. Twice he had managed to disarm Gaetano and hold a rapier to his throat. He was naturally quick and light on his feet and getting better at predicting his opponent's moves. When he wasn't practising in the piazzas and parks of Giglia, he often fought imaginary assailants with invisible weapons, whirling and twisting in the largely empty rooms of the Bellezzan Embassy. Many were the innocent statues and mirrors menaced by his increasing skill.

'You are quite alarming, even without a sword,' said Arianna, coming upon him alone on one such occasion.

He stopped, confused. They had hardly been alone together since Arianna had come to Giglia and he felt self-conscious. Here, in the Embassy, she was still very much the ruler of her city, and he felt more distant from her than ever. He still didn't know whether Rodolfo had told her about Niccolò's marriage plans and couldn't bring himself to ask.

'Why are you doing all this?' she asked now. 'I know Gaetano has been teaching you to fight. Do you know of some danger you are keeping from me?'

Luciano said nothing. If Rodolfo hadn't told her, then he had his reasons. Or if he had told her perhaps she didn't see it as a danger. In the old days, he would just have asked her, but now that she was Duchessa, he had to think before he spoke.

'Of course if you think it is safer for me not to know . . .' she said, turning her head away so that he should not see the sadness in her face. It pained her that Luciano no longer confided in her; the old Luciano of their early friendship in Bellezza would not have been capable of keeping anything a secret from her. She was longing to share her fear of the Duke's proposal with him but she couldn't raise it herself, couldn't talk to Luciano, of all people, about being asked to marry another di Chimici.

'It is nothing,' said Luciano stiffly. 'Just that, you know, Rodolfo and Doctor Dethridge and Sulien all seem sure that something bad will happen at the weddings. Even Gaetano seems to think the same. I just want to be ready if there's trouble.'

'And that's why they want more Stravaganti here? Even though bringing Falco back would be such a risk?'

'Yes,' said Luciano. 'I think Sulien and Giuditta are going to take the new talismans tomorrow.'

'Together? That's unusual, isn't it?'

'I don't think it's ever been done, but Giuditta hasn't taken a talisman before and she's a bit nervous, so Sulien offered to go at the same time.'

'Giuditta – nervous?' Arianna laughed, and Luciano smiled too.

'I know,' he said. 'It's hard to think of her being scared of anything.'

'I find her quite terrifying,' said Arianna. 'I'm glad she's on our side.'

'Me too,' said Luciano. 'She makes me feel about five years old. But I don't think she means to – it's just that she's so involved with her work that she doesn't see anything else as being important.'

'Well, she must think stravagation is important, or she wouldn't have done it.'

'How's the statue going?'

'Pretty well, I think,' said Arianna. 'We have only a few sittings left before the weddings.'

'Will you go back to Bellezza straight afterwards?' asked Luciano.

'Yes. I have invited Gaetano and Francesca to come back there for their honeymoon. It was where their courtship began – even though Gaetano was supposed to be wooing me at the time.'

'Did you ever consider accepting him?' asked Luciano. He had never dared to ask before but now he really needed to know.

'I had to *consider* it, Luciano,' said Arianna seriously. 'As Duchessa I have to think for my city, not for me,' she added, thinking of the coming proposal more than the last.

It wasn't an answer that Luciano found reassuring.

Carlo had been jumpy ever since the murder of Davide. He was unnerved by the apparent lack of reaction of the Nucci clan and he kept a bodyguard with him at all times. His bride was due to arrive in the city in a few weeks, with her sister and parents, and his uncle Jacopo would demand to know how his daughters were to be kept safe. Carlo didn't know the answer.

Several Nucci would be present at his wedding to Lucia, when the four couples would process into the great cathedral. Each couple would have their own entourage and it would be possible to introduce some armed guards into the procession; the bridegrooms themselves would all wear swords as part of their ceremonial dress. But it was unimaginable that they should be drawn in the cathedral. The very thought of it brought Carlo out in a cold sweat.

'I wish these accursed weddings were over and we were all married!' he said to Fabrizio.

'That's no way to talk about your approaching nuptials,' laughed his brother. 'Lucia wouldn't find it romantic at all.'

'You know what I mean!' said Carlo. 'I've no objection to marrying Lucia, but the more I hear about Father's plans for the occasion, the more certain I am that the Nucci will strike then.'

'Still, what would you have him do?' asked Fabrizio. 'Three di Chimici princes and a duke all marrying on the same day cannot be a jug of wine and a plate of olives affair!'

'I know, but Father has decided to make it the

biggest exhibition of di Chimici wealth and power in the history of Talia! And if he can also announce the Grand Duchy and his betrothal to the Duchessa of Bellezza at the same time . . .'

'I know,' said Fabrizio. 'I have the same fears as you. It's just going to provoke the Nucci and their allies. But Father's chief spy is working to find out what he can and he will be in charge of our safety at the weddings.'

'The Eel?' said Carlo, uneasily. 'I hope he knows what he's doing.'

Sky was utterly miserable. He had tried to explain to Alice that he had no interest in Georgia and they had sort of made up. But he couldn't give her any reason for why he needed to spend so much time with Georgia and with Nicholas. It wasn't just his secret, so he made a poor fist of being convincing. Their sunny holiday had fizzled out in suspicion and jealousy.

And to make it worse, Rosalind hadn't noticed anything wrong and had chattered happily about Paul Greaves all the way home. Laura seemed almost as peeved as Sky about this. She knew Paul's ex-wife Jane, Alice's mother; they were councillors together in Islington and had sat on several of the same committees. Since Jane was Laura's friend, she couldn't believe that Paul could possibly be a good person.

'You know why they got divorced?' she demanded, driving too fast as usual, with the window open, so that she had to shout over all the noise.

'Because he was a serial killer? He held orgies at Ivy Court? He beat her up?' suggested Rosalind, stung by Laura's know-all attitude.

'Because he was controlling and didn't want Jane to lead her own life,' said Laura. 'He was always sure he was right about everything.'

'Alice says it was because they were too different,' said Sky. Wretched as he felt about his own relationship, he didn't want Laura to squash his mother's happiness. He couldn't remember when he had last seen her as carefree and relaxed as she had been over this long weekend.

Rosalind had been exhausted by the time they got back to London though and had gone straight to bed. After a not very satisfactory phone call with Alice, Sky had followed suit and hurled himself towards Talia for a quick dip into his Giglian life – just long enough to tell Sulien that they were back.

The next morning he was up early, making breakfast, determined to be first to the door when the Talian Stravaganti arrived. He didn't know how he was going to get his mother out of the flat. Remedy wound round his legs, torn between pleasure at having him back and indignation at having been fed by a neighbour for so long. Sky picked him up and held his long, purring body over his shoulder. The doorbell rang.

It was Nicholas and Georgia. Rosalind came into the kitchen, looking young and tousled, in her dressing gown.

'Oh, hello, you two,' she said, smiling. 'Can't keep away, can you? Alice not with you?'

Everyone mumbled something uncomfortably and

Sky smoothed the moment over with offers of coffee and toast, while his mother went off to shower.

'I don't know how I'm going to get rid of her,' he said. 'She's so tired after yesterday's journey. I can't just shove her out of the house.'

'Perhaps we should wait outside for them,' suggested Georgia.

'It'll look a bit odd, won't it?' said Nicholas. 'Us just hanging around on the doorstep all day.'

'It wouldn't be all day,' said Sky. 'They're going to get here some time this morning.'

There was a muffled knocking from the front door in the hall.

'Too late,' said Georgia. 'I bet that's them.'

Sky came out of the flat and listened. He could hear voices outside the front door of the house and then it opened. His neighbour, Gill, from upstairs, the one who had been feeding Remedy, was letting herself in. She had a newspaper under her arm and a paper bag from the local patisserie in her hand; he could smell the warm, fresh croissants.

'Sky,' said Gill. 'There's a sort of priest here, asking for you. Shall I let him in?'

Beatrice was adapting to her new home in the Palazzo Ducale. She had a much larger chamber than her old one in the Palazzo di Chimici and a pretty little sitting room with green silk on the walls, next to her father's suite of rooms and sharing its view of the river. Her life was busier than ever, turning the lofty, elegant rooms into something that felt like a home, and she would soon have guests to welcome at the old palazzo in the Via Larga. Members of the di Chimici family would be converging on Giglia from all over Talia, to celebrate the weddings.

The last time so many family members had been together in the city had been for Falco's funeral, and Beatrice was determined to chase that memory away with the warmth of their welcome for the happier occasion. She wondered if her father had the same idea as she heard more about his elaborate plans for the celebrations. Three days of feasting, tournaments, pageants and processions were being prepared for, and the princess, as the only female di Chimici of the Giglian branch, had to oversee everything as hostess.

She had very few moments to herself and, though she was glad of the help she was offered by Enrico, her father's confidential agent, she wearied of the way he seemed always to be there, one step behind her.

On this day, a week after having moved into her new home, Beatrice stood at the window of her sitting room, enjoying a few minutes of solitude. The year was warming up; it would be April soon and the weddings were just over three weeks away. The river was running very high, she noticed, remembering how wet the winter had been. At least the rains seemed to be over now; it would be an awful shame for the brides to have their finery drenched, she thought. She looked across to where the new Nucci palace stood and its grand gardens beyond.

Beatrice sighed. She didn't understand why things had got so bad between the two families; she could remember a time when they visited with one another reasonably civilly. Although rivals with a bloody history, they were the two wealthiest families in the city and that meant at least some social intercourse. A smile played round her mouth as a day came back to her from childhood when the three Nucci boys and their two sisters had visited the di Chimici in the Via Larga. The grown-ups had been interminably talking and drinking wine and the children had all been turned out like puppies into the courtyard. Camillo Nucci and her own brother Fabrizio had devised a plan to clothe the bronze Mercury in the middle of the flower beds.

It had been Beatrice who had fetched the scarves and necklaces and a petticoat from her mother's room, but Camillo, Fabrizio and Carlo had done the draping, while the little princess had looked on with Filippo Nucci and the little boys and girls. It had been before Falco was born and Davide had been no more than a toddler in his big sister's arms, thought Beatrice, looking back fondly on how ridiculous the Mercury had looked in his finery and how the Duke and Matteo Nucci had scolded them.

And now Davide and Falco were both dead and the families were bitter enemies. On the few occasions when Beatrice had passed any of them in the street, they had looked sternly ahead, even though Graziella had sat and mourned with them after Falco's death and Beatrice had sent words of sympathy on their own bereavement.

A knock at the door roused her from her reverie.

'The confectioner is here, your Highness,' said Enrico. 'Wanting to speak to you about marzipan.'

'I shall come directly,' said Beatrice.

It would take a quantity of sugar to sweeten the

inevitable coming together of the two families.

Sulien and Giuditta stood on the doorstep. Brother Sulien looked just like a monk or friar from any modern monastery or friary; his robes were a kind of uniform that hadn't changed over more than four centuries. But Giuditta did not look as if she belonged in the twenty-first century at all. She wore a long green velvet cloak with its hood flung back over her ordinary working clothes, and Sky was sure he could see marble dust in her hair. But she was as calm and impassive as she was in Giglia, with the stillness of one of her own statues.

'Can we come in?' asked Sulien, and Sky couldn't think of any way of saying no.

They walked along the short passage to the kitchen and suddenly he found himself introducing four Stravaganti to one another. Giuditta recognised the young di Chimici prince, changed though he was, but Nicholas had not met Giuditta before. The Giglians were looking round the kitchen with interest when the freshly showered Rosalind came in and saw them.

'Good heavens,' she said, startled. 'We are having a lot of early visitors this morning. Who are your friends, Sky?'

Sky had no cover story ready; he had been banking on getting his mother out of the way before the Stravaganti arrived. But it was, surprisingly, Giuditta who handled the situation.

'I am Giuditta Miele, the sculptor,' she said, holding out her hand. 'And this is Fratello Suliano Fabriano.

He brought your son to my studio and I saw that he was interested in sculpture.'

It was one of the longest speeches Sky had ever heard her make and he could see it was full of holes. But his mother was nothing if not polite and she latched on to the bit she could understand.

'Yes, he's very good at art; it's always been one of his favourite subjects. Can I offer you some coffee, Ms Miele? And Frat . . .'

'Please call me Sulien,' said the friar, with a winning smile. 'Sky always does. I'd love some coffee.'

Sky was already busy washing up the cáfetière.

'Should I know your work, Ms . . .?' Rosalind began to ask Giuditta.

'Giuditta,' said the sculptor. 'I doubt it. It is in another place.'

'Italy, is it?' asked Rosalind. 'Your English is very good, both of you.' She was struggling to incorporate these two strangers into her frame of reference. How could this handsome friar have taken her son to the sculptor's studio if it was in Italy? And how did Sky come to know him? They seemed old friends.

Nicholas came to the rescue. 'She has a wonderful reputation,' he said. 'Giuditta Miele is one of the most famous artists in Europe.'

'Really?' said Rosalind. 'Please forgive my ignorance.'

Georgia had been sitting dumbstruck, appalled by the awkwardness of the situation. She wondered what she would have done if Paolo the Horsemaster, 'her' Stravagante in Remora, had ever turned up at her house and sat drinking coffee in the kitchen. Remembering how her mother Maura had got the wrong end of the stick about her relationship with the old antique dealer who had sold her the talisman of the flying horse, she began to feel hysterical laughter rising in her throat.

Nicholas kicked her under the table and she turned it into a cough. The phone rang and Rosalind went to take the call in the living room.

'Thank goodness,' said Georgia. 'I thought I was going to burst. You can't get away with this, Sky. She's bound to smell a rat. You don't just have friends who are sculptors and friars who live in Italy without ever mentioning them to your mother.'

'I can make her forget all about meeting us if you like,' said Sulien. 'If you think it would be less worrying for her?'

'You don't mean with one of your potions, do you?' asked Sky apprehensively.

'I would never administer anything that could harm her,' said Sulien gravely. 'But no, I meant something simpler.'

Rosalind came back into the room looking pink and pretty. 'I'm awfully sorry, but I'm going to have to go. A friend is unexpectedly in town and wants to see me. I'm sure Sky will look after you.'

To Sky she whispered, 'It's Paul. He came up on the night train last night. He wants me to meet him at his club. Will you be all right here?'

'Of course,' said Sky. Then said, 'His club?' with a quizzical look.

Rosalind suppressed a giggle. She went to get her bag and jacket, then took her leave of the group in the kitchen. As she shook hands with Sulien he gazed into her eyes and said some words that no one in the room, except perhaps Giuditta, could understand. Rosalind shook her head slightly, her blue eyes suddenly cloudy. Then she said goodbye to the three teenagers, as if there were no one else in the room, and left.

'Phew,' said Sky. 'That was horrible. Thank goodness for Paul.'

'We are wasting time,' said Giuditta. For all her apparent confidence, she did not yet feel at ease out of her own world.

'Prince Falco,' said Sulien. 'I have come because I hear you are willing to try stravagating to Talia again.'

'More than willing,' said Nicholas eagerly. 'I'm dying to go back.'

'But the talisman you have takes you only to Remora,' said the friar. 'Do you have it with you?'

Nicholas pulled a glossy black feather, about the size of a swan's, out of his jacket and laid it on the table. It was beautiful. Sulien took from his pocket what at first looked like an identical feather and put it beside the first one. Then Sky saw it was in fact a very fine quill pen. Nicholas took it up and admired it; it had a bluish sheen.

'You understand that if you take it, you have to give up the other talisman?' said Sulien. Nicholas nodded; he seemed mesmerised by the quill. Sulien took the black feather and stowed it in his robes.

'Simple, isn't it?' said Georgia, and Sky saw that she was glaring at Giuditta. 'I suppose you now offer me something and I'm supposed to hand over my flying horse?'

She took a bubble-wrapped package from her pocket and began to open it. Giuditta said nothing. She had said nothing to Georgia at all so far. At last the winged horse stood on the table between them. Sky had never seen Merla, the miraculous horse with wings that both Georgia and Nicholas had ridden in Remora, but he could see how much the little figure meant to Georgia; she was fighting tears as she said, 'What can you offer me to set beside that?'

'Nothing,' said Giuditta. 'The exchange can be made only if the Stravagante is willing. I did bring a new talisman for you, but if you do not want to give up your right to travel to Remora, I cannot make you.'

This was not what Georgia had been expecting. She struggled with her curiosity to see what the sculptor had brought and her desire to keep the little horse. But it seemed churlish to ask to see the new talisman when she had no intention of accepting it.

Giuditta took something from a pocket in her work-dress and put it, wordlessly, on the table. It was an exquisite figure of a ram.

'I made it myself,' she said impassively.

'For me?' asked Georgia. Giuditta nodded. 'Can I hold it?'

Georgia took up the small animal. It was quite different from her original talisman – Renaissance in feeling beside the Etruscan figure, more sophisticated in its detail, with the tiny curved horns and woollen curls meticulously sculpted. And it touched her that this gifted, if severe, artist had made it specifically for her.

'It's beautiful,' she said simply, handing it back.

'But you are not going to take it?'

Georgia shook her head, miserable.

'Georgia,' said Nicholas, taking her hand. 'If you

took it, we could be in Giglia together tonight! I could show you my city. And we could see Gaetano again. You'd like that, wouldn't you?'

Georgia was crying, silently.

Giuditta stood up. 'Do not attempt to compel her,' she said sternly. 'An unwilling Stravagante would be no good to us in time of danger. Sulien, I think we should leave.'

She put the ram away but Sky did not think she was offended; if anything, she seemed to be on Georgia's side. Giuditta asked if she could lie on his bed to stravagate back to Talia and he led her to his room; Sulien would follow as soon as the sculptor had disappeared. When Sky got back to the kitchen, he found Sulien spooning honey on to a piece of toast and making Georgia eat it.

'You are trembling, my dear,' he said. 'You have been through an ordeal and must have something sweet to restore you.'

'Please don't be so nice,' said Georgia, her mouth full of crumbs and stickiness. 'I know I'm spoiling all your plans. And the ram was really lovely. But I just can't give up the horse.'

'Then we must just make some new plans,' said Sulien.

While Beatrice spoke of sweetmeats and silvered almonds, the Duke was giving a very special commission to a jeweller from the nearby workshops. The Grand-Ducal crown of Tuschia was to be kept a secret, on pain of death. It was to be a circle of silver with the Giglian lily in front, bearing a great oval ruby that was already in Niccolò's possession. All the way round rose points of silver, every other one terminating in a miniature lily, and the whole was to be set with gems, square-cut and round.

And the jeweller had a second even more secret commission: a smaller crown, for a Grand Duchess, a copy of that to be worn by her lord and master. And if he wondered who was to wear it, since the Duke was a widower, he valued his own life far too much to voice the thought. And he was going to be busy; the Duke had also ordered a choker of pearls and diamonds, a sleeve pendant in the shape of a Bellezzan mandola and two silver collars, 'large enough for a big dog.'

'Any particular dog, your Grace?' hazarded the jeweller. 'Such as I might measure?'

'They are not for dogs at all,' said Niccolò haughtily. 'I have ordered two spotted cats from Africa; the collars are for them.'

'It doesn't matter, really,' said Nicholas for the umpteenth time, but Georgia was inconsolable.

Sulien and Giuditta had both gone. Sky had been feeding Georgia sweet tea for shock but she was still in a terrible state.

'I do want to go to Giglia with you, more than almost anything,' she was saying. 'It's just that I can't give up the chance of going back to Remora and seeing Paolo and Cesare again and their family – and the horses. It was what stopped me going mad all that time when Russell was bullying me.'

The doorbell rang again and Sky went to answer it.

'I understand, honestly,' said Nicholas. 'I didn't mean to make it harder for you. You know I wouldn't do anything to upset you.'

Someone was following Sky into the room; it was the last person he had expected to find on his doorstep.

'Hello, Georgia,' said Luciano.

Chapter 16

Mapping the City

The Pope was feeling testy. He was accustomed to being treated as less important than his older brother, the Duke; it had been going on all his life. But he was Pope, after all, and Prince of Remora into the bargain, and he did think he might have been consulted about the arrangements for these weddings, especially since he was going to officiate at them. Now his chaplain, his nephew Rinaldo, was telling him that he would have to travel to Giglia soon after celebrating Mass in the cathedral of Remora on Easter Sunday, in order to be there in time for a great tournament the next day.

In truth, much of his bad humour came from the fact that it was nearly four weeks into Lent and Ferdinando di Chimici hadn't had what he considered a decent meal since Shrove Tuesday. Easter Sunday's dinner was something he had been looking forward to. The Pope was a great trencherman and Lent was a sore trial to him.

'I shall have terrible indigestion if I travel by coach after dinner on Easter Sunday,' he complained.

'But, your Holiness,' said Rinaldo, who was well aware of his uncle's weakness, 'you would not wish to miss any of the feasts planned by your brother the Duke. He has told me himself of the splendour and magnificence of the banquets. Perhaps if you took a light lunch after Mass on the Sunday, you could travel in comfort? I am sure the Duke will entertain you sumptuously when you reach Giglia.'

The Pope was mollified. 'Tell me about the banquets,' he said.

Georgia was quite hysterical.

'I know why you've come!' she hissed at Luciano. 'They thought you could persuade me to swap talismans. I bet you've got that ram with you, and I know it's beautiful, but I'm not going to take it. It's not fair to ask me!' And all the time she was thinking, It's Luciano, after all this time, and I'm all red-faced and teary – I must look a sight.

'I'm not going to ask you,' said Luciano calmly. 'I came to tell you I've thought of another way. I haven't got any ram.'

His voice was husky, as if his throat hurt, and Georgia was suddenly seized with remorse, as she remembered how hard it was for him to stravagate in this direction. She wondered if he'd had to go first to his old home and whether his parents had seen him.

'Give him some of your sweet tea,' she said to Sky. 'He looks as if he needs it.'

Luciano accepted the tea and looked admiringly at Nicholas, while Georgia escaped to the bathroom to repair the damage done by all the crying.

'You look amazing, Falco. I should hardly have recognised you.'

'Thanks,' said Nicholas. 'Do you think I'll be recognised in Giglia? I mean, I'm a whole year older than I should be, as well as being alive when I'm supposed to be dead.'

'I think you'd be fine,' said Luciano, 'except with members of your family. They'd know you but they'd have to see you up close.'

'I told Sky I'd grow a beard,' said Nicholas. 'But I can't wait for that. I want to go to Giglia tonight.'

'Without Georgia?' asked Sky.

Nicholas paced the small kitchen. 'Of course I don't want to go without her! But you'll be there, won't you? And it doesn't look as if she ever will.'

'That's why I've come,' said Luciano.

Georgia came back; she was calm now and ready to listen to his idea.

'It's simple really,' said Luciano. 'Although we thought there wouldn't be time for you to get from Remora to Giglia and back within one night's stravagation, there's something we've all been forgetting.'

They all looked blank.

'We've been thinking of doing it by carriage or horse, using the road between the two cities,' he continued. 'It would take several hours each way on the sixteenth-century highway – it's not like a motorway. But the distance between Remora and Giglia is not so very great – at least, not as the horse flies.'

Georgia saw it in an instant, although the other two were a few steps behind her. She flung her arms round Luciano, no longer embarrassed, and he smiled into her radiant face.

'Brilliant!' she said. 'That's it! I could go to Paolo's and see Cesare and the family and then fly to Giglia on Merla. And then do the same in the opposite direction before darkness falls in Talia. I could keep my talisman and still come to Giglia!'

Now she hurled herself at Nicholas and made him dance round the kitchen with her. Everyone was grinning. Suddenly it seemed as if they were all about to embark on an exciting and glamorous holiday.

'When can we go?' asked Nicholas.

'Hang on,' said Sky. 'We've got to plan this properly. If I understand it, you've both got to have proper clothes waiting at the other end and Nick's at least will have to be some sort of disguise. And how is Georgia going to land a flying horse in the middle of a city? They don't exactly have airfields in Giglia, and she hasn't been there before – how will she know where to meet us?'

That slowed everyone down a bit.

'We can contact Paolo and tell him about Georgia going to Remora,' said Luciano. 'Rodolfo can do it through his mirrors. And I'm sure we can make some arrangements in Giglia, but Sky's right; you can't go tonight, Falco. Your disguise and cover story are going to take a bit of planning.'

'How about him being another novice, like me?' said Sky. 'My black robe has a hood, which he could pull up over his face if there was anyone around who might recognise him. And Sulien could organise that.'

'Where will I arrive?' asked Nicholas. 'The only time I've done it before, I turned up in Paolo's stables, because my talisman was Merla's feather, but I don't know where the quill comes from.'

'I think Sulien brought it from his cell,' said Luciano. 'But I'll check on that and on the novice friar idea. I can tell Sky when he stravagates tonight.'

'Oh, this is too frustrating!' said Nicholas. 'I have the talisman and I still can't go! How long is it going to take?'

'Not more than a day or two,' said Luciano. 'I must tell Gaetano, and we Stravaganti need to talk about where you should go and where you should be during the weddings. And Paolo will need to organise some clothes for Georgia. Nicholas isn't the only one who has changed since he left Talia.'

Georgia felt a blush beginning. Luciano hadn't been in Remora when she and Nicholas had made their dramatic stravagation there six months ago and found that their worlds had been separated by an extra year. She knew she was no longer the awkward, flat-chested girl who had harboured a secret crush on Lucien Mulholland. The constant admiration of Nicholas and the increase in her confidence that her adventures in Remora had given her had turned her into quite a different person. In all respects but one. Just seeing Luciano sitting in Sky's kitchen, wearing the simplest white shirt he could find and undisguisably black velvet trousers, she was overtaken by a wave of the old despair. The only boy she had ever really loved was separated from her by hundreds of years and a dimensional barrier she couldn't begin to understand. And yet he had come back to tell her his idea himself, when he could have just explained it to Sky in Talia.

'I wore one of Teresa's dresses when I went back last time,' she said quickly, to hide her feelings. 'I expect I could do that again.'

Luciano nodded. 'We could organise that.' He passed a hand across his face, suddenly weary. 'I'd better get back. Can I lie on your bed, Sky, to stravagate home?'

'Help yourself,' said Sky, showing him the way. 'It's been like an airport terminal in there today.'

When Sulien stepped off his maze the next morning he found two colourful figures waiting silently in the pews. A young man and woman, tall, with long dark hair, wearing the vivid, be-ribboned clothing of the Manoush. Sulien gestured to them to follow him into the cloister. He hadn't met these two before but he knew others of their tribe; now he realised that the man was blind. The woman said, 'Brother Sulien? Rodolfo sent us.'

Sulien nodded.

'I am Raffaella,' said the woman. 'And this is Aurelio. Rodolfo thinks you may need us.'

Before he could ask why, a rather dishevelled and tired-looking Luciano joined them; clearly he knew the Manoush. Aurelio raised his fine head towards him as soon as he heard Luciano's voice. But before they had finished exchanging greetings, Sky too had appeared. The five of them moved to Sulien's laboratory.

Luciano laid out the problems about getting Georgia from Remora to Giglia.

'She will come on the zhou volou?' asked Aurelio. 'We can look after the horse for her while she does whatever you need her for in the city.'

'Where could she land?' asked Sky. 'She doesn't know Giglia.'

'There are fields all round the city,' said Raffaella. 'We just need to agree a suitable place. It must be somewhere where we can keep the flying horse safely hidden until Georgia comes back for her.'

'It also has to be somewhere she can find by easy landmarks,' said Luciano. 'You could draw her a map, Sky, showing her what to look for.'

'The river and the cathedral are the two main landmarks she will be able to see clearly from the sky,' said Sulien. 'They will guide her course when she flies in from Remora.'

'And what about the new Nucci palace?' suggested Sky. 'I bet that's visible from quite high up.'

'Is it safe to land near there?' asked Aurelio. 'Is it not from the Nucci that you fear danger?'

'From what I've heard,' said Sky, 'they aren't moving into that palace until the day after the di Chimici weddings. Until then they'll be living in their home near here. Besides, we have a little farm there. It used to belong to the di Chimici family but Niccolò gave it to the friary recently. Georgia's Merla could be kept safe there.'

He fetched paper and pen and unrolled a parchment

with a map of Giglia on it. They all contributed ideas, until there was a rough sketch that Sky could memorise and reproduce for Georgia.

'What about, you know, Nicholas?' he asked Sulien warily, looking at the Manoush. He didn't know quite what to make of these new people, but the friar seemed to trust them and Luciano obviously knew them.

'Do you know what happened to Prince Falco?' Luciano asked them.

'We know it was not what was given out,' said Raffaella. 'Our friend Grazia, in Remora, told us that she saw him win his own memorial Stellata, on the zhou volou.'

'Many there said it was a ghost who rode in that race,' said Aurelio. 'But the Manoush can tell spirits from living people. I would guess he now lives in the other world – the one known to you Stravaganti.'

'You are right,' said Sulien. 'But he, like Georgia, will come back here to strengthen our numbers in the troubled times ahead. I myself took him a new talisman to bring him here – one of my own quill pens. He will arrive here, Sky. You can stravagate together.'

*

Rodolfo and Paolo faced each other in the mirror. Arianna and Silvia watched in silence.

'So we shall see her again, our little champion?' said Paolo.

'Not for long,' said Rodolfo. 'She will take Merla, if you are willing, and leave you swiftly for Giglia. There will be no time for her to linger in Remora.'

'It will still be a pleasure, if a fleeting one,' said Paolo. 'And it will not be a single stravagation, if I understand you.'

'She will need to learn the city, if she is to be of use to us when danger strikes,' said Rodolfo.

'And she will need clothes?' asked Paolo.

'A young woman's costume, as before,' said Rodolfo. 'Luciano tells me she has grown up.'

'So,' said Arianna, when Rodolfo turned away at last from the mirrors. 'Georgia is coming back.'

'Do you mind?' he asked.

'Not if you need her,' said Arianna.

'I need them all,' said Rodolfo. 'And even with them, with eight Stravaganti in the city, I still don't know if it will be enough.'

'I wish it were all over,' said Arianna. 'And that we were back in Bellezza and out of the Duke's clutches.'

'As to that,' said Rodolfo, 'have you decided what to do about the dress?'

Rosalind had looked very pleased with herself when she returned from her meeting with Paul. If she remembered that her kitchen had been full of Stravaganti when she left, she said nothing about it.

'How was the *club*?' Sky teased.

'It was OK,' she said. 'But we didn't stay there. Paul was supposed to be meeting a work colleague in London, but after we'd had coffee, we went out and ended up having lunch together in Soho.'

'You really like him, don't you?' said Sky.

'I do,' said Rosalind. 'Does that make it difficult for you and Alice? I've noticed you seem to be, well, having problems.'

'It's not because of you,' said Sky. 'Though it is a bit weird when your girlfriend's dad fancies your mum. We had a misunderstanding in Devon. Alice thought I preferred Georgia.'

'I'm not surprised,' said Rosalind. 'You do spend an awful lot of time with her. But aren't she and Nicholas together? I've often wondered.'

'It's not that simple,' said Sky. 'Sorry. There are things I can't tell you because they're not my secrets.'

Rosalind didn't press him. But Sky wasn't happy. The new developments in Talia meant that he was going to be spending even more time with Georgia and Nicholas and their shared secrets were going to grow. How could he explain it to Alice? She was already suspicious and, try as he might, he couldn't see how he was supposed to have a normal relationship with a girl while he spent every night stravagating to another world.

The first problem arose the next day. He was round at the Mulhollands, reporting to Nicholas on the progress of plans for getting him to Giglia. Georgia was there too, and the two boys were trying to draw her a map of the city. But Sky was trying to remember Sulien's sketch and Nicholas kept telling him he was getting things wrong.

'Geography homework in the holidays?' asked Vicky Mulholland, seeing them all bent over the dining table. 'You are keen.'

'Vicky,' said Nicholas. 'Have you got any maps of Italy?'

'Somewhere,' said Vicky. 'Let me think. Yes, up in David's office. Do you want me to get them?'

'I'll find them,' said Nicholas. 'Thanks.'

'I'll come with you,' said Georgia.

'Would you like some coffee, Sky?' offered Vicky and he went with her into the kitchen.

Now that Sky had met Luciano, he was fascinated by Vicky Mulholland. She had the same black curly hair as her son but she was small and energetic. Nicholas towered over her and so did Sky. As he watched her deft movements about the kitchen, grinding beans, assembling mugs, tipping biscuits on to a plate, he wondered how on earth she had coped with losing one son and gaining another so mysteriously.

What would Rosalind have done if he had died and, a year later, a Sky lookalike had turned up, in need of a home?

'How's the fencing going?' Vicky was asking.

'What? Oh, yes, very well, thanks,' said Sky. 'I'm nowhere near as good as Nick, of course, but he's a good teacher.'

'I'm glad to hear it,' said Vicky, pouring the coffee into mugs. 'He's been a bit, well, restless lately. I'm glad he's got something to occupy him.' She hesitated. 'You know how he came to live with us?'

Sky felt wrong-footed. He had just been thinking about it and what he knew was very different from the Mulhollands' view of events. 'He was abandoned, wasn't he? By asylum-seekers or something?'

'I don't think exactly abandoned,' said Vicky slowly, 'but it was something like that. He had been badly injured and I think mentally scarred too. He had lost his memory. Only – well, it's silly really – I don't like to ask him about it in case it upsets him, but lately I've been wondering if he has remembered something – if he's been thinking about his old life.'

She looked at Sky with her big dark eyes, so like both Luciano's and Nicholas's, and he felt very uncomfortable indeed; she was closer to the truth than she realised.

'Has he said anything to you?' she asked.

He was saved from answering by the return of the others, triumphantly waving a handful of maps. They had struck gold and found one of Italy and an old battered one of Florence. They took their coffee into the dining room and spread the maps among their bits of paper. Vicky disappeared with her mug, looking a bit wistful. It was another complication, but Sky had to push it to one side as they pored over the outline of the city that both was and was not Giglia.

'Florence is almost due north of Siena,' said Georgia. 'So, if Giglia and Remora are in the same positions as them, I'd need to set my course and fly virtually straight till I reach the city walls.'

'And you'll see the river running almost across the middle,' said Nicholas, 'with Saint-Mary-of-the-Lily on the far shore.'

'The Manoush think you should land before you reach the river, though,' said Sky. 'There's a breach in the southern wall between the fields and where the gardens of the Nucci palace begin. They'll meet you there if we agree on a day and time.'

'And they'll look after Merla?' she asked.

'Yes, they offered. They seemed to know all about her,' said Sky.

'They were there when I won the Stellata,' said Georgia, remembering. 'And Cesare flew over the Campo on Merla. I'm sure Aurelio saw her, even though he's blind. I'd rather trust her to them than anyone else outside Remora.'

'Now, you need to know how to get from there to a place you can meet us,' said Nicholas. He was flushed and excited, trying to trace the lines of his old home under the sprawl of the modern city. 'Oh, this is so frustrating! It isn't Giglia at all!'

'Of course not,' said Sky. 'It's Florence. It's a different city in a different world over four hundred years later. What did you expect?'

But Nicholas ploughed on. 'Just walk past where Sky says this new palace is, towards the river, and you'll come to a stone bridge – the Ponte Nuovo.'

'Just follow your nose,' said Sky. 'It stinks. It's full of butchers and fishmongers.'

'Then cross the river and turn right and you'll come to a square on your left,' said Nicholas, ignoring him and closing his eyes, visualising a walk he had done many times when he was little. 'That's where the silversmiths have their workshops, under the Guild offices. Turn left and walk through that square to the next one – it's huge. That's the Piazza Ducale with all the statues.'

'That must be where the Piazza della Signoria is today in Florence,' said Sky, pointing it out to her on the map.

Gradually they pieced out a route from Georgia's landing place to the piazza with the great cathedral in it.

'I think we should meet in Giuditta's bottega,' said

Sky, 'if she'll let us.'

Georgia squirmed. 'Must we? She probably despises me for making it all so difficult when I could just have stravagated straight there with her model of the ram.'

'It's central,' said Sky firmly. 'And right by the one thing in Giglia you can't miss. It's on the north side of the big bit of the cathedral – where the little domes are. And it's Stravaganti territory – near neither the Nucci nor the di Chimici, so we should be safe.'

Georgia committed it all to memory. She was getting excited now too. She didn't expect to love this city the way she had Remora, but it had been Nicholas's home when he was Falco and it was where Luciano was now.

Someone came in and they didn't look up, assuming it was Vicky. But it was Alice. They had been talking so animatedly that they hadn't heard the doorbell.

'I think it's time you told me what's going on,' she said quietly, and they all looked up, as guiltily as if they'd been caught planning a bank robbery. 'There's something that you're all in on,' said Alice. 'And I'm not leaving till you tell me what it is.'

Chapter 17

My Enemy's Enemy is My Friend

'So you and Georgia are time travellers and Nicholas is from another dimension?' said Alice coolly. 'Like something out of *Buffy*?'

'More *Roswell High*, really,' said Sky. 'The site of our school was where the first Stravagante had his laboratory in the sixteenth century. That's why the talismans always end up near it.'

'Well, thanks for clearing that up,' said Alice. She seemed so calm that it took a while for the others to realise that she was in a white-hot rage. 'Now would you like to tell me what's *really* going on?'

When she had arrived at the Mulhollands' and demanded an explanation, it had taken only a few exchanged looks before they decided there was no way out but to tell her the truth. And now she didn't believe them.

'I don't blame you for not believing us,' said Georgia. 'I wouldn't if I were you. But it's true. I found my talisman in Mortimer Goldsmith's antique shop nearly two years ago. I started travelling to Talia then and I met Nicholas there – Falco, he was then.'

'I decided to come here because I couldn't walk in that world,' said Nicholas. 'You remember what I was like before I had my operations? I'd had a terrible accident with a horse and I couldn't be cured in Talia.'

'And I pretended to find him outside this house,' continued Georgia.

'And you're seriously trying to tell me that you kept all this Talia stuff from me all the time we were becoming friends?' said Alice.

'I didn't want to,' said Georgia. 'But you wouldn't have believed me – you don't believe me now. Or any of us!'

'Let me show you the talisman,' said Nicholas suddenly, taking the quill pen out of his shirt.

A few moments passed and Georgia took the winged horse out of her pocket. Sky followed suit with the perfume bottle. The three talismans sat on the table among the sketch maps and the coffee mugs. Alice was visibly shaken.

'I don't understand,' she said. 'All these come from the other world, according to you. But Nicholas doesn't go there, does he? If what you told me is true, he came from there to here. His talisman should be a – I don't know – a GameBoy or something!'

They all smiled at that, even Alice herself. She suddenly sat down.

'I don't know why I'm even trying to bring logic

into this,' she said. 'It's too crazy even to discuss.'

They explained about how Nicholas had used Georgia's old silver eyebrow ring to stravagate from his old world and had been back to it only once, using a feather from the flying horse. And how the quill was a new talisman, to take him to Giglia.

'You're saying they came here – two travellers from this other world?' asked Alice.

'That's how the talismans always get here,' said Sky. 'Stravaganti bring them from Talia so that we can go there. I know it sounds fantastic, but it's true. That's why I've spent so much time with Nick and Georgia. I found out about them while I was there.'

'OK, then,' said Alice. 'Prove it. Take me with you the next time you go.'

'You can't just come with us,' said Nicholas. 'We've explained that a talisman has to be brought by a Stravagante from Talia before someone from here can travel there.'

'Then how can I believe anything you've said?' said Alice. 'If I can't see it for myself?'

'Well, I could ask Sulien, I suppose,' said Sky. 'When I go there tonight. We hope that Nicholas and Georgia will be able to go back tomorrow.'

'You mean you're going there tonight?' said Alice.

'Yes,' said Sky. 'I go there nearly every night, for as long as I can.'

'He won't let you bring another talisman,' said Nicholas.

'How can you be so sure?' said Alice. 'How come you and Sky and Georgia are so special but I'm not worthy to have one of your little trinkets? Why shouldn't I be a Stravagante? Oh, God, I can't believe

I'm even asking this. It can't be anything more than a crazy story you've made up.'

'Why would we make up a story to keep you out?' said Georgia. 'Look, the talismans seem to find people who are unhappy, or ill, even. The first person to go from our school was Lucien – the Mulhollands' son – you know, the boy I told you about. And he was so ill he died.'

'But you're telling me he's still alive in this Talia of yours?' said Alice.

Georgia looked round nervously. 'Keep it down,' she said. 'You don't want Vicky to hear. She doesn't know anything about it.'

'Well,' said Alice bitterly. 'If you have to be unhappy, then I qualify. How do you think it feels to have a boyfriend who's always busy seeing your best friend or playing sword games with her . . . whatever Nicholas is? And when you ask for an explanation, all you get is fantasy fiction.'

Sulien showed Sky the second set of novice's robes he had ready for Nicholas.

'When he stravagates, you should both arrive here,' the friar said. 'I'd like him to walk the maze before you take him out into the city. I think from what I saw of him in your world he will be too excited to be careful and I want him to leave here in a calm frame of mind.'

Sky nodded. He had walked the maze himself a few times now and it always steadied him; it would do Nick good. He wished he could do it himself now, after the row with Alice. But there was too much to organise and he wasn't quite ready to tell Sulien about her.

'It's going to get crowded in your cell of a morning,' he said. 'Especially if Sandro is hanging around too.'

Sulien smiled. 'He certainly spends a lot of time here.'

'What shall we call Nicholas while he's being a novice?' asked Sky. 'He can't be Brother Falco!'

'No, nor Brother Niccolò, really. What do you think?'

'I'll ask him,' said Sky. 'Is everything ready in Remora? And with the Manoush?'

'There is no reason why you should not all make your first trial stravagation tomorrow,' said Sulien. 'You can meet at Giuditta's workshop as planned.'

'It will be so odd to have them both here,' said Sky. 'I sort of think of it as my place now.'

'The young prince will help you know it even better,' said Sulien. 'But Georgia will need you both to help her find her way around.'

'She needs a Sandro,' said Sky.

'I've been meaning to talk to you about Sandro,' said Sulien. 'Do you think he knows about you?'

'I don't think so,' said Sky. 'He's never said anything about anyone being a Stravagante.'

'But he knows Prince Falco by sight,' said Sulien. 'And it will be difficult to keep the two of them apart. Yet I would rather that Sandro were on our side than working for the di Chimici. He's very observant.'

Sky had been putting it off too long. 'There's been a bit of a complication in my world,' he said.

It was the Warrior's fiftieth birthday. April the first – April Fool's Day – and he felt the irony. Loretta was giving him a party to which, bizarrely, she was inviting all his ex-wives, girlfriends (at least the ones she knew about) and his many children and grandchildren.

'That woman is a saint,' said Gus, getting rather sentimental over the champagne. 'To put up with you and all your brood.'

The singer just grunted. He knew how lucky he had been with Loretta but he wasn't going to agree with Gus about anything that didn't involve a contract.

'Only it's not quite all, is it?' said Gus, nudging the Warrior in the ribs. 'There's one Colin sprog she doesn't know about.'

The Warrior shot him an evil look. 'Don't call me that!' he said automatically. But Gus had got him thinking. He had been a rotten father to most of his children, but to Sky Meadows most of all; he had never even met him. It had been Sky's seventeenth birthday recently and he had a new photo of his secret son. The boy was old enough to be a father himself, he thought; the Warrior had certainly made his own first kid at that age, even though he wouldn't recommend it.

He was suddenly overwhelmed by the feeling that he was getting old.

'Loretta,' he said to his wife that night, when all the visitors had gone home and the guests who were staying over in his Hollywood mansion had gone to bed, 'I want to go back to England. There's someone I want to see.'

‡

'That is a complication, indeed,' said Sulien when he had heard Sky out. 'I don't think anyone has ever volunteered to be a Stravagante from your world to ours before. I'll have to ask Doctor Dethridge about it.' He didn't seem fazed by the idea of Alice turning up in Giglia.

'Wouldn't it be too dangerous, though?' asked Sky. 'I mean, she can't fight and you all seem to think there's going to be trouble coming.'

'It's dangerous for all of you,' said Sulien. 'She won't be as experienced at stravagating as you or Georgia and she won't know the city as well as Falco does but, if the others agree, she'll have more than two weeks to get used to it before the weddings.'

'She might not want to keep coming,' said Sky doubtfully. 'It's just supposed to convince her that we're telling her the truth.'

'I don't think Doctor Dethridge will agree to taking a new talisman for just one journey,' said Sulien. 'But stop looking so worried. Nothing can be decided until I've spoken to the others.'

It was so unusual for Sky and Sulien to be on their own together these days that Sky decided to ask him about something else. They were in Brother Sulien's cell and the friar had been working on his collection of recipes and formulas when Sky arrived. It looked nearly finished. Sky looked at what he had been writing down; it was a cure for tiredness.

'I shall need some of that soon,' he said, trying to smile. 'All this stuff with Alice and coming here every night is wearing me out.'

Sulien scrutinised his face. 'If it gets too much for you, you must tell me,' he said seriously. 'We can't have you getting ill.'

'I'm all right really,' said Sky, embarrassed. 'And my mum is so much better. I wanted to ask you – is that because of my visits here? Could that be helping to cure her of her ME?'

Sulien was thoughtful. 'I don't think so,' he said at last. 'After all, she doesn't come here herself. We don't have the illness you speak of in Talia, unless it is like the sleeping sickness. But from what you have told me about it, I gather that it can get better quite suddenly, after a period of years?'

'That's what the doctors kept saying,' agreed Sky. 'Just give it time, they said.'

'And that is what has happened,' said Sulien. 'Just be thankful. Now, why don't you go and find Sandro?'

Sky was glad to get out into the city. He found Sandro and Fratello in their usual position loitering outside the Nucci palace. The boy's face brightened when he saw Sky.

'Ciao, Tino!' he said.

'What's happening?' asked Sky.

'Nothing,' said Sandro, lowering his voice. 'None of the Nucci have come out yet today.'

'Do you have to stay and wait for them?' asked Sky.

Sandro shrugged. 'There aren't any rules about it. As long as I keep bringing little bits of information back to my master.'

But at that moment, Camillo came out of the palace and looked in their direction.

'Quick,' said Sandro. 'Pretend I'm talking to you.'

'You are talking to me,' said Sky, smiling.

'No, I mean about something serious!' said Sandro. 'So he doesn't think I'm watching him.'

Camillo Nucci glanced around him, focused for just a moment on the little dog, frowning, and then set off towards the cathedral.

'Come on!' said Sandro. 'We'll follow at a distance.'

The two boys strolled along the busy streets and Sky felt his worries over Alice lift. The sky was the same blue it always seemed to be in Talia and the sun beat warm on his robes; it was almost too hot. At every window and doorstep, window boxes and flowerpots spilled pink and red petals and trailing greenery. And the scent of flowers hung in the air, covering up the worse smells coming from the gutters and the streets.

Sandro picked a bloom from one of the plants and stuck it in his cap. When they reached the cathedral square, they were just in time to see Camillo disappear into the door of Saint-Mary-of-the-Lily.

'We can't take Fratello in there, surely?' said Sky.

'Come with me,' said Sandro mysteriously.

They walked further round the cathedral, towards Giuditta's workshop, and stopped by a side door. Sandro tied Fratello to a rail and the little dog immediately sank down with his nose on his paws. Sandro slipped through the door, beckoning to Sky to follow. But instead of going into the body of the great echoing building, he led Sky up a stone staircase. They climbed until they were both out of breath, pausing only once, at a sort of landing, before resuming the upward curve of the steps. Just when Sky thought his lungs would burst, they were out on a narrow balcony that ran round the base of the dome. There was only a wooden banister between them and a sheer drop to the floor of the cathedral.

Sandro leaned casually on the banister. 'All right?' he asked.

Sky's heart was pounding. From up here he could see the floor of the cathedral, inlaid with designs so that it looked as if it were covered with marble carpets. They reminded him of Sulien's maze. There was no service at present but there were always visitors in the cathedral. The people seemed tiny from here and he noticed how few of them looked up. It was the perfect place for a spy. Sandro nudged him.

'See Camillo,' he whispered, pointing to the Nucci's distinctive red hat.

Camillo seemed to be measuring the length of the aisle from the cathedral door to the high altar, pacing it out. It wouldn't have looked odd from ground level but from up here it seemed clear that he was planning something.

'This would be a good place to position archers,' said Sandro.

'During a wedding?' said Sky.

'That's when the di Chimici expect the attack to come,' said Sandro. 'They'll have archers up here, all the way round, mark my words.'

Camillo seemed to have finished his measuring.

'Do you want to go right up to the top?' asked Sandro.

'Can you get further?' asked Sky.

Sandro led him round half the circumference of the dome's base and through another door. The steps began again and Sky realised that they were climbing up inside the dome itself, up hundreds of stairs – so many that he lost count – until they emerged inside the white stone lantern at the very top.

The two boys sat hanging on to the wooden rails, with their legs dangling over the side. Sky wished he had brought some water. His robes were sticking to him after the hot climb. But there was a welcome breeze up here and the view made it worth it.

The whole city was spread out beneath him. He could see the Piazza Ducale and the river and the new Nucci palace on the other side and the stretch of green that was their gardens. He could even see the avenue of pine trees where he had been with Sandro just over a week ago. And beyond that, the city wall and the meadows of flowers that surrounded the city, alternating with green fields dotted with white blobs that were sheep.

Tomorrow, if their plans worked, Georgia would land somewhere over there on Merla. Sky wondered if he would ever get the chance to see the flying horse.

Rainbow Warrior had two homes in England: a mansion in Gloucestershire, where he spent hardly any time but which he felt was an important part of his image to keep up, and a flat in Highgate. Whenever he went on tour in the UK, he spent a bit of time in north London and it was here he decided to stay for a few days shortly after his birthday. On the spur of the moment, he asked Loretta to accompany him; he was nervous of telling her about Sky but even more so about the prospect of meeting his son on his own.

It would be unusual for him to be back in the country of his birth without having any gigs to play. He could visit his mother, of course. She had taken a lot of persuading to leave the estate where he was born and had spent only a few years in the house he bought her in Esher before needing to go into a residential home. She was wandering in her mind a bit now and scandalised some of her fellow residents with the language she sometimes came out with.

But there were his brothers and his sister as well and he didn't look forward to their knowing he was in town. The Warrior had given them a lot of money over the years and none of them had made anything of their lives. One brother had a half-hearted career as a record producer; the other was unemployed and always asking for handouts. His sister was a bitter woman, jealous of his success, which had made her discontented with her job as a nurse, her husband and the house her brother had bought her in Clapham.

She sneered at him for the articles in *Hello!*, his many marriages and his regular albums. But she bought the magazines, accepted flights out to the weddings and boasted to her friends when the albums sold well.

Sometimes the Warrior thought that the only person he had ever met who had never asked him for money was Rosalind, who had been prepared to bring up a child on her own. He had sent money, though, a lot of it the first time. But neither she nor her son had ever expected anything from him and that intrigued him.

He told his PA to book the flights straightaway.

'Can I ask you something?' said Sky when he was alone with Brother Sulien.

'Of course.'

'You said when I first came that Duke Niccolò di Chimici was dangerous and hated all Stravaganti.'

'That is still true.'

'But he seems to be more of an enemy of the Nucci at the moment. Does that mean that we and the Nucci are on same side?'

'If the Nucci knew anything about us, it's true that they might want us to help them in their vendetta against the di Chimici,' said Sulien. 'But the Stravaganti are not to be used in such feuds. We are only on the opposite side from Niccolò because we believe that he wants to take over all Talia. The Nucci long ago ceased to care about the government of Giglia, let alone Tuschia or Talia as a whole. They just want all the di Chimici dead, because of Davide.'

'I can see that it would be a bad thing for Niccolò to rule all Talia, because he's a bad man,' said Sky, frowning. 'But would it be a bad idea for Talia to get together under someone? I mean, in my world Italy is one country, not lots of little dukedoms and so on.'

'I know it must seem to you as if we are interfering in politics,' said Sulien. 'But it is not like that. We are protecting the gateway to your world from the uses the di Chimici would make of it.'

'What uses, exactly?' asked Sky.

'If Niccolò had the secret of travel in time and

space, he would not respect the rules we have developed,' said Sulien. 'He would take cheap gold from here and use it to buy weapons and drugs that have not been invented here.'

Sky could just see it – di Chimici with swords and daggers were bad enough, but the thought of them with an arsenal of chemical weapons was terrifying.

'There's nothing I can do till the Stravaganti have made their decision,' Sky told Alice on the phone next day.

'But you're all still going tonight – you and Nick and Georgia?'

'Yes, it's all arranged,' said Sky.

'Then I'm at least going to be at Georgia's while she stravagates,' said Alice.

'You do believe us, then,' said Sky.

'I don't know,' said Alice. 'I want to. I don't want to think you would lie to me. But it just seems too incredible.'

As soon as she got off the phone to Sky, Alice called Georgia and went round to her house.

Maura O'Grady was used to finding Alice in her house when she got home from work, and if she thought things were a little tense between the two girls, she put it down to teenage hormones and worries about the coming term's exams. She certainly had no objection to Alice staying the night. In fact she was relieved that Georgia was spending more time with her best female friend; it bothered her how often her daughter was with Nicholas.

After a supper of takeaway Chinese – much to Georgia's relief because Maura was a dreadful cook – the girls had an early night. They said they were going to watch videos in Georgia's room.

'So how exactly does it work, then?' asked Alice. 'Do you just hold the talisman and say "abracadabra"?'

'No,' said Georgia, a bit reluctant to go into details. 'You have to fall asleep with it in your hand, thinking of where you're going in Talia.'

'And what will it look like when you've gone?'

'Just the same, I think. My body will still be here. I have another body in Talia, one without a shadow.'

Alice shook her head. 'So you won't be able to prove that you've been anywhere?'

'I'll tell you everything about it when I get back,' said Georgia. 'And you can ring Sky first thing and check it all with him. Then you'll know we're not making it up.'

But she secretly wished that Alice were not there. It was going to be hard getting to sleep with her best friend watching her.

Early next morning Cesare was in the stables as usual but he kept glancing up at the hayloft. He hummed under his breath as he filled the horses' water troughs from a bucket and mucked out the dirty straw. Arcangelo, the big chestnut, was restless and bent his great neck to huff in Cesare's ear.

'I know, boy,' he said, grinning. 'She's coming back.'

His father, Paolo, came in with a bundle of clothes.

'Any sign yet?' he asked.

Cesare shook his head. A small grey cat wound its way round the stable door and leapt on to the ladder to the loft. There was a rustling sound and the cat paused, its ears pricked. The trapdoor was raised and a tawny head appeared.

'Giorgio!' said Cesare, then stopped, confused. 'I mean, Georgia. It's good to see you!'

Chapter 18

Flight

While Alice slept and Georgia crossed worlds, Sky was spending the night at the Mulhollands'. Nicholas was so excited about stravagating back to Giglia that he kept them both awake talking about it. And then he fell silent and Sky, anxious that Nicholas was going to arrive in Giglia before him, tossed and turned a lot longer, unable to give up the hold on consciousness that was preventing him from slipping into his other life.

Gaetano had arranged with Sulien to come to the friary early so that he could be there when his brother arrived. It had been over six months since Falco had died in Talia. Gaetano had seen him a month later, riding the flying horse, and he had been told that, for Falco, a whole extra year had passed. Yet he did not know what to expect. There was so much that he didn't understand about the gateway between the two worlds, and he found it hard to believe that his little brother had caught up on him by a year and was now fit and well, able to walk unaided and to ride. But Gaetano clung on to one thing: Falco was coming back.

Sulien was awake and waiting in his cell. It was a bare room – just a cot of a bed, a chest, a table and a chair – whitewashed and dominated by a large wooden cross. The bed was empty and Sulien was sitting in the chair. He rose when the prince entered but Gaetano gestured him back.

'I shall sit on the floor,' he said, and settled himself with his back to the wall. 'How long do you think it will be before they come?'

'It depends on how hard they find it to fall asleep in their own world,' said Sulien. 'It perhaps will not be easy for your brother. It may be that Sky will arrive ahead of him.'

The two of them sat in silence, waiting. Gaetano rested his arms on his knees and cast his cloak over his head. He must have dozed a little but was woken by a sigh. On Sulien's bed lay a figure stretching and yawning, a young man with curly black hair, worn loose and rather long. He swung his long legs over the edge of the bed and stood up tall and straight.

Gaetano got to his feet, stiff from the wait. Sulien left the cell as the brothers embraced.

*

Georgia had greeted every horse in the stable. Most of them knew her – Arcangelo, Dondola, Starlight and the miraculous Merla. The black winged horse was now fully grown, glossy and well-muscled. Georgia had no doubt she would be able to carry her to Giglia.

'I have ridden her that far and further,' said Cesare. 'And I weigh more than you do.' He couldn't stop smiling; he was so pleased to see Georgia again.

'I wish I could stay and catch up with all your news,' she said, longingly. 'But I must leave straightaway if I'm to meet the others in Giglia. I'll see you tonight, though.'

Paolo and Cesare led Merla to the meadow where she could take off. The horse was glad to be out so early in the warm spring morning and was already flexing her wings. Georgia was going to ride bareback, so she was glad of a leg-up.

Once astride Merla's back, she looked down on her friends' faces, sad to be seeing them so briefly but exhilarated at being back in Talia and the prospect of another flight on the winged horse.

'Go safely,' said Paolo.

And Cesare slapped Merla on the rump.

The young mare broke into a trot, then a canter and was at full gallop before she unfurled her mighty wings. With a few lazy flaps she was aloft and Georgia saw the rose-coloured City of Stars dwindling beneath them. She clutched Merla's mane, ready for their next adventure.

*

When Sulien re-entered his cell the two brothers were sitting on the bed with their arms round each other. He smiled at them.

'Welcome, Prince Falco,' he said.

'Alas, I am that no longer,' said the new Stravagante, slipping back into his former way of speech.

'What shall we call you?' asked Gaetano. 'You'll have to have a new name while you are here.'

'How about Benvenuto?' said the boy. 'If I am really welcome.'

'Brother Benvenuto indeed,' said Gaetano.

'And now we must give you your disguise,' said Sulien, opening the chest and taking out a set of robes.

'I hope they fit him,' said Gaetano. 'He is taller than me now.'

When he was dressed in the robes, Nicholas looked the part of a Dominican novice. He tried pulling the hood up over his face and Gaetano said, 'No one would recognise you now – even the family. You are so much taller, and of course they would not be expecting to see you.'

'You made it all right, then?' said Sky and they turned and saw him, already robed, on Sulien's cot.

The two novices faced each other. Nicholas couldn't wait to get out into the streets of Giglia, but he also wanted to spend time with his brother, and the others had to remind him how dangerous it would be to be seen with the prince.

'You may look very different from when you left,' said Sulien, 'but you don't want anyone to make the link because of seeing you two together.'

Gaetano stayed with them for breakfast and they met Sandro in the refectory. The boy showed no signs of recognising Prince Falco.

'Another novice?' he said suspiciously, when Sulien introduced him to the new 'Brother Benvenuto'. 'How many are you going to have?'

'As many as are called,' said Sulien. 'There is always room in God's house.'

Sandro was disposed to be jealous of the new novice. He regarded Brother Sulien as his personal property and wasn't at all pleased that he had to share him with another young friar. And this Benvenuto seemed much too friendly with Brother Tino, who was also Sandro's own discovery.

When the prince left and the two novices went out into the city, Sandro trailed alongside them, as his dog trotted after him.

'Where are you going?' he asked.

'We have a commission to Giuditta Miele, from Brother Sulien,' said Sky. 'Why don't I meet you later, back up here?'

Sandro recognised that he was being got rid of and remained, sulking, in the piazza outside Saint-Mary-among-the-Vines.

*

It was a glorious day and the sun warmed Georgia's right side as she flew north on Merla. She was wearing a russet-brown dress of Teresa's and it felt awkward riding with a full skirt. But she had bunched it up around her and left her legs bare to the sun. They flew over fields and meadows, the people of Tuschia tiny beneath them, tilling the earth and pulling vegetables like the little figures in a book of hours. The countryside was gently undulating, with small green hills crowned by cypresses and brick farmhouses with terracotta roofs. She could see miniature cattle and sheep and the blue threads of streams winding between green banks.

After about three quarters of an hour of Merla's steady flight, Georgia began to see in the distance the signs of a great city, much bigger than Remora. It was surrounded by meadows of flowers of every colour; Georgia could detect their scent even from this height. Strong defensive walls encircled the city and Georgia looked out for a gap in them, which would show her where to land.

She whispered in Merla's ear and the flying horse began her descent. She landed on the edge of a meadow of bluebells, where two figures waited, as colourful as the flowers. Georgia climbed off the horse, shook out her skirt and clasped hands with the Manoush. Merla whickered a greeting and went with them happily.

'We shall take good care of her,' said Aurelio, stroking the horse's nose. 'We are taking her to a small homestead that belongs to the friary.'

He pointed out to Georgia a cluster of buildings in a field, then Raffaella took her as far as the road.

'It's that way to the river,' said Raffaella. 'You know how to go from there?'

'Yes,' said Georgia. 'Thank you. I'll be back well before nightfall.'

She walked towards the city. On her right stood the great edifice of the Nucci palace, gleaming in its newness, with its vast fringe of gardens. It was her first glimpse of Giglia and she was impressed. Past the little church, she set foot on the stone bridge and smiled as its smells assailed her. She stopped and looked out over the river. It looked like a picture postcard of other people's Italian holidays. But there was no time to look longer; she had to get to her meeting place.

Giglia was very different from Remora, full of grand buildings and squares. Georgia followed the map in her mind and crossed the great piazza with its statues. Soon she reached the cathedral, whose cupola dominated the city and had beckoned her here to its centre from a great distance. She skirted it warily, following it round to the east end. How was she to tell which was Giuditta's bottega among this jumble of little buildings?

*

The statue of the Duchessa was finished. Sky and Nicholas gazed at it in admiration. Nicholas had never seen its subject; he had already been unconscious when Arianna came to Remora. And Sky had met her only once so far. And yet both of them knew the statue was a masterpiece.

Two of Giuditta's apprentices were polishing the marble of the white figure. Arianna stood oblivious of their caresses, grasping the rail of her ceremonial barge. She looked proud and independent, most unlikely to yield to persuasion or intimidation. Her creator stood opposite her, almost a mirror image of determination.

'She's made the Duchessa look like her,' whispered Nicholas.

'Only more beautiful,' said Sky.

'Perhaps,' said Nicholas. 'But Giuditta is beautiful too – in her own way.'

'Don't let her hear you say that,' said Sky. 'I shouldn't think she likes to be flattered.'

'That reminds me,' said Nicholas. 'I wonder if Georgia's all right?'

'I'll go and look for her,' said Sky.

It had been Nicholas's first test as Benvenuto, walking to Giuditta's workshop, and no one in the streets had given him a second glance. He thought that one of Giuditta's apprentices – a blond boy with angelic curls – had stared at him a little too long, but put that down to natural curiosity. Now Nicholas gazed at Giuditta, fascinated. He knew that she had sculpted his memorial statue and it made him feel very peculiar to think about it.

Sky stood outside the workshop in the lee of the cathedral, making sure to stay in the doorway so that his absence of shadow would not be seen. He was soon rewarded by the sight in the distance of a familiar figure with a head of red, white and black hair. He could not greet her out loud, as it would hardly be seemly for a novice to hail an attractive young woman in the street, but he closed his eyes and concentrated his thoughts on her, using the fact that they were both Stravaganti to guide her to him.

He opened his eyes to see Georgia coming towards him, a relieved look on her face. He beckoned her inside the workshop. Franco looked up appreciatively at this new arrival and Sky suddenly saw Georgia through the apprentice's eyes. A tall and quite graceful figure in a simple russet dress, with her dramatic hair colouring, she could be an aristocrat in disguise or a woman of the streets. Either way, she didn't look like a suitable friend for two young novice friars. Giuditta must have thought the same, because she shooed all the apprentices out of the workshop and told them to take a long break.

The Stravaganti were alone together. But not for long. A well-dressed middle-aged woman entered from the street before they could even greet one another properly. She had the air of a wealthy woman who had wandered in to commission a portrait bust of her late husband, perhaps, and was accompanied by a tall red-headed servant. Sky had a vague half memory of having seen her somewhere before. His heart sank at the interruption but Giuditta made no attempt to get rid of the woman.

And the woman went straight up to Georgia and said, 'I don't think we could pass you off as a boy now, Georgia,' and embraced her.

Sky and Nicholas stared at each other. Then light dawned on them simultaneously: this could only be the previous Duchessa of Bellezza, Arianna's mother, who was supposed to have been assassinated by a di Chimici agent in her own audience chamber. And Sky remembered where he had seen her: in the Bellezzan Embassy, with Arianna and Rodolfo. Georgia made the introductions. Silvia took Nicholas's hand in hers and scrutinised his face.

'We have something in common, Prince Falco,' she said in her low, musical voice. 'We are both supposed to be dead. I hope your disguise will be as effective as mine.'

Then she turned to Sky. 'And you are the new

Stravagante,' she said. 'You have joined us at a time of great danger.'

'I know,' said Sky. 'The Nucci and the weddings.'

'And the new threat to the Duchessa from the Duke,' said Silvia, nodding at the statue. 'You have caught her perfectly, Giuditta. Helmswoman of the ship of state.'

'Or figurehead,' said a voice from the door. Guido Parola's hand moved to the hilt of his sword, as a white-haired figure entered. Nicholas shrank into the shadows, pulling his hood up over his face.

'Good morning, Maestra,' said the Duke to the sculptor. 'Good morning, Brother Celestino. I trust your master is well? Good. Won't you introduce me to your charming patroness, Giuditta? Clearly she knows something of the beautiful ruler of Bellezza.'

'This is Signora Silvia Bellini,' said Giuditta, almost truthfully. 'From Padavia. I believe the Signora has seen the Duchessa on a visit to the city.'

'That is so, your Grace,' said Silvia, suddenly playing the part of a flustered and foolish woman thrown into confusion by the presence of the great man. She curtseyed and gestured to her servant to bow to the Duke. 'My late husband had connections in Bellezza and I have seen the young Duchessa there on State occasions.' She placed her hand to her heart as if it were fluttering at the honour of being in the Duke's presence.

'Delighted,' said the Duke, putting Silvia's other hand to his lips. 'Pray don't let me disturb your discussion with the maestra – I came merely to look on the work she has created, whose reputation is already spreading in Giglia.'

Thank goodness Luciano isn't here, thought Sky. He would probably try to run the Duke through. As it was, Guido Parola still had his hand on his sword. Duke Niccolò walked over to the statue and caressed its white marble cheek. The tension in the workshop was unbearable.

'So,' he said. 'She is clearly *not* holding a treaty.'

'I made her as I saw her, your Grace,' said Giuditta.

'I have finished my business here, my Lord,' said Silvia, gesturing silently to Sky to leave.

'And so have I,' Sky said, taking his cue. 'We shall return to the friary.'

'And what about the other charming lady?' asked the Duke, not taking his eyes off the statue. So he had noticed Georgia.

'She is one of my models,' said Giuditta. 'You can take a break now and come back when the apprentices do,' she told her.

Slowly they all left the workshop, backing out of the Duke's presence, leaving him alone with the sculptor. As soon as they got outside, Silvia beckoned the others to follow and took them into a nearby tavern. As they collapsed on to wooden benches, she ordered red wine, even though it was only the middle of the morning, and they all drank deeply when it came.

'That was awkward,' she said pleasantly, but Sky saw that the hand holding her goblet was shaking. Parola took his wine and stood by the door. Now that Nicholas had thrown back his hood, his face appeared white and frightened.

'I would not have recognised him,' he said. 'I would have said it was here that extra years had passed – he looked so old.'

'It was young Prince Falco's death that did it, they say,' said Silvia quietly.

'Thank goodness he didn't notice Nicholas,' said Georgia.

'He didn't mention him,' said Silvia. 'But that is not the same thing at all.'

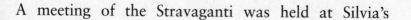

In the middle of the night Alice woke suddenly. She was sleeping in Georgia's bed and Georgia was in a sleeping bag on the floor. She looked across at the body of her friend, her chest rising and falling gently with her breath. Georgia had told her that there would be nothing to see when she stravagated, but Alice peered carefully at her all the same.

Then she found it hard to get back to sleep. She lay for what felt like hours, imagining the three others in their secret world; it was too fantastic to believe that their bodies lay sleeping in this world while three alternative ones had adventures in another. She wouldn't – couldn't – believe it unless she experienced it herself. And yet, if it were true, it made her feel afraid. Talia seemed to be such a dangerous place. Sky hadn't told her everything, but there had been enough about stabbing and poisons to make it sound thoroughly alarming.

Alice wondered what would happen if she tried to shake Georgia awake; she felt terribly lonely.

A meeting of the Stravaganti was held at Silvia's

lodgings that afternoon. Sky felt guilty that he was neglecting Sandro but he couldn't miss out on the meeting. And he was beginning to see that he couldn't really turn up at the friary with Georgia in tow; for the first time, his novice's disguise was a hindrance.

Silvia felt it too; she offered Georgia a red scarf to hide her hair. But not before she had been caught in a bear hug by William Dethridge and greeted by Rodolfo and Sulien. Best of all for her, though, was the embrace from Luciano, a long heartfelt hug even though only one between friends.

'Eight of the Brotherhood in one room,' said Rodolfo. 'It is an honour to have you all here. We can hope to save the city in its time of danger.'

'Um,' said Sky. 'Would it be even better to have nine?'

Sulien had already heard about Alice, and of course Georgia and Nicholas knew about her, but that still left four to convince that they should bring yet another talisman to their world. Luciano at least knew who Alice was, but the others were surprised at the idea of someone volunteering to come to Talia.

'It's the only way I can convince her that we're not lying,' said Sky. He felt terribly embarrassed at having to talk about his girlfriend with these distinguished grown-ups. Georgia came to his rescue, emboldened by being with Luciano again.

'Alice is my best friend,' she said simply. 'And she was very unhappy because she thought that Sky had something going on with me. He's been spending a lot of time with me and Nicholas, what with the fencing and all the talk about Talia.'

'So it is our secrets and our problems that have brought about your own difficulty?' asked Rodolfo. 'You are prepared to risk your life in Talia to save others and yet we have done nothing for you. I think we should grant your request. What does everyone else think?'

'The more the merrier, as far as I'm concerned,' said Luciano, rather wildly. He felt that the whole business of Stravaganti from his world was getting out of hand; was the whole of Barnsbury Comp going to turn up here? They could charter an inter-dimensional bus at this rate.

'Hold harde,' said Dethridge. 'If the mayde is to stravayge, who is to take hir talismanne? Shee can not arrive in a house of brothires of Saint Francis.'

'It must be me then, I suppose,' said Giuditta. 'I have done it before.'

Georgia felt most uncomfortable. Everyone in the room knew that she had rejected Giuditta's talisman and she couldn't bear the idea of Alice having the ram that had been made for her.

'I shall take her something from my workshop,' continued the sculptor. 'And she will arrive there. But my counsel is that she should come for only one stravagation, to confirm the truth of her friends' story.'

*

Sandro was bored with spying. He no longer believed that there was any danger from the Nucci, in spite of their defensive tower and their many weapons. Their attempted poisoning of the Duke and the loss of their youngest family member were in the past now and he thought they might be a spent force. Now he was tired of hanging about outside their old palace; he would have far rather been out exploring the city with Brother Tino.

Then he remembered that Tino had gone off with the new novice without even a backward glance, and felt annoyed. Fratello was his only real friend after all, thought Sandro, and he bent to ruffle the dog's ears. And found himself looking at a pair of feet in black shoes with silver buckles. An unpleasant scent in the air and the growl in Fratello's throat alerted him to the presence of his master.

'How is it going, little Sparrow?' said Enrico genially. 'Anything happening with our friends over there?'

'Nothing,' said Sandro. 'Nothing to report at all. Can't I go somewhere else?'

'That's the minute something will happen, if I know anything about it,' said Enrico. 'What about at the friary? Anything interesting going on there?'

The most interesting thing in the friary as far as Sandro was concerned was that he was learning to read there, and he didn't want the Eel to know that.

'There's a new novice,' he said instead. 'Brother Benvenuto.'

'Another one?' said Enrico. 'They'll have more novices than full friars soon. Perhaps you'd better keep an eye on this one – let me know if there's anything fishy going on. I'm never quite sure whether that Sulien is loyal to the di Chimici or not.'

Sandro said nothing. He knew now what being loyal to the ruthless di Chimici might involve and he also knew that it wasn't a good idea to be found wanting.

*

'Now,' said Rodolfo. 'Alice or no Alice, we must plan our strategy for the days of the wedding.'

'*Days?*' said Georgia. 'You mean they take more than one day to get married?'

'The ceremony itself takes not much longer than an ordinary Mass,' said Sulien. 'But there will be a grand tournament the day before, with a banquet in the evening, various pageants and processions on the day itself, and a final party the day after.'

'And we moste kepe vigillant atte all these tymes,' said Dethridge.

'How, exactly?' asked Nicholas.

'A circle of strength,' said Giuditta. 'If all eight – or even nine – Stravaganti are together, we can surround the likely targets with our linked minds, see where the danger is coming from and protect them from harm.'

'And who are the likely targets?' asked Sky.

'I'm afraid that is what we don't know,' said Rodolfo. 'My daughter is my main concern, but any member of the di Chimici and Nucci families is at risk.'

'And if vyolence comes,' said Dethridge, 'thenne every one and eny one canne be harmed. Inne a church or a square – wheresomever there are crowdes – a small acte with a blade canne lead on to mayhem overal.'

'Wait a minute,' said Georgia. 'I can see about the circle of minds, I think, though I'd like to practise it. But what if we do see a threat coming from a particular person. What can we do about it? Can the Stravaganti disarm an armed man with their thoughts?'

'No,' said Rodolfo. 'That is why Luciano has been learning to fight. We and our allies have to be ready to defend ourselves and others.'

'Gaetano will be ready,' said Luciano.

'But he will be getting married,' protested Georgia. 'How much use can he be? You surely don't expect him to break off the ceremony to fight a bit and then carry on with it.'

'We shall all go armed to the wedding,' said Giuditta.

'And Guido here won't be getting married,' said Silvia. 'He is a handy fellow with a blade.'

Sky realised that this was the assassin Luciano had told him about.

'I don't think you will be invited to the wedding, Silvia,' said Rodolfo, smiling. 'The Duke doesn't know you, and you should be grateful for it.'

'As to that,' said Silvia, 'I met the Duke only this morning and I think he was disposed to be charmed by me. But what do I care for invitations? I shall be at these weddings, invited or not.'

*

Sandro and the Eel walked into the centre of town, though Fratello was careful to keep on Sandro's side, as far away from Enrico as possible. As they neared the cathedral, the spy suddenly clutched at the boy's sleeve.

'Is that him?' he hissed.

Two young Dominican friars were coming out of a palazzo.

Sandro nodded. 'That's the new one, with Brother Tino.'

The novices were followed out of the building by a striking-looking young woman with stripy hair. And then Luciano and Rodolfo, the two Bellezzans, with an older white-haired man whom Sandro didn't recognise. Finally Giuditta Miele came out of the door, in conversation with Brother Sulien.

'Now that is something worth reporting,' said Enrico. 'What are they up to? And who exactly is that new brother?'

He had pulled Sandro back into a doorway. They hid as the party from the palazzo passed on the opposite side of the road.

Enrico gasped. 'Look!' he said. 'Look at that new novice! He has no shadow. And, come to that, nor does your Brother Tino! I think the Duke might be very interested in that.'

Chapter 19

Flowers of the City

Georgia woke feeling stiff and disorientated. She had flown back to Remora soon after the meeting of Stravaganti, spent a few sweet moments with Cesare and his younger sisters and brothers, and fallen easily asleep in her old hayloft. It took her a few minutes to adjust to being back in her room.

'At last,' said Alice when she saw that Georgia's eyes were open. She herself was already showered and dressed. 'Do you know what time it is? Your parents have already gone to work.'

Georgia sat up blearily. 'Give me a minute,' she said.

'Sweet dreams?' asked Alice.

Georgia wasn't sure she liked this new aggressive version of her friend. But as far as Alice was concerned, she still needed to be convinced that what the others had told her was true and that she could still trust Sky. Georgia decided to let it pass.

'I went to Remora, flew to Giglia and met the others there,' she said. 'I saw the old Duchessa in the sculptor's workshop and then Duke Niccolò came in. We had a meeting of Stravaganti at Silvia's place and then I did the journey back.' She stretched. 'Can I go and have my shower now?'

'Did you see, you know, Lucien?' asked Alice.

Georgia nodded. 'He's one of the Stravaganti who was there. But I don't want to talk about it.'

'Fair enough,' said Alice. 'I'll get us some breakfast, shall I? And then we can go round to Nick's.'

Sandro was feeling uneasy. He hadn't taken kindly to the idea of sharing Brother Tino and Sulien with anyone else, but he didn't want the new novice to fall foul of the Eel; he knew what his master was capable of. But he was puzzled by the business of the shadows. That wasn't natural, surely? Everything had a shadow – even Fratello. Sandro separated from Enrico as soon as he could and went straight to Saint-Mary-among-the-Vines.

The friars were all at prayer; it was the hour of Vespers. Sandro was not allowed to take his dog into the church, so he waited outside the main door until he heard the chanting stop. Then he put his head round the door and called softly. Sulien heard him and came towards him.

'You are troubled?' he said straightaway, seeing the

boy's distress.

'What does it mean, Brother, when a man has no shadow? Is it the work of the Devil?'

Sulien didn't answer directly. 'Tie your dog up and come inside,' he said.

Not all the friars had left the church. Sandro watched as Sulien walked over to a side aisle and pulled back a threadbare carpet to reveal a strange circular pattern of black and white. Meanwhile, a line of friars was forming, waiting to step on to the circle. Sandro had never seen this before.

Sulien came over to where Sandro sat in the pews and said, 'Watch what they do. I want you to walk the maze just before me.'

'Why?' asked Sandro. 'What does it do?'

'You can tell me that yourself afterwards,' said Sulien.

The girls walked round to the Mulhollands' house in silence. Vicky let them in.

'I'm afraid they aren't up yet,' she said. 'Shall I call them?'

'Well, if you're sure,' said Georgia.

'It's late,' said Vicky. 'It's time they were up. Why don't you put the kettle on?'

Twenty tense minutes later, Nicholas and Sky joined them in the kitchen. To the relief of all, Vicky had gone shopping. The boys were tired but, after a few cups of tea and a lot of toast, were willing to talk. By then Alice was ready to explode.

'Well?' she asked Sky. 'I've heard Georgia's version

of last night. What's yours?'

He could scarcely recognise her; she seemed so cold.

'Nick got to Giglia first,' he said. 'And when I got to Sulien's cell, he was already there with his brother. We walked to Giuditta's workshop and then Georgia came. And Silvia, Arianna's mother, turned up.'

'With her bodyguard,' added Nicholas.

'And then the Duke arrived,' said Sky.

'My father,' said Nicholas. Alice saw that he had dark circles under his eyes. 'He had come to look at Arianna's statue.'

'And then we all went to a tavern and drank wine,' said Sky. 'It'd been a bit of a shock, meeting the Duke like that.'

'We had a meeting of Stravaganti in the afternoon,' said Nicholas.

'And we asked them about you, Alice.'

'Oh yes, what did they say?'

'They were pretty much OK about it,' said Sky. 'Giuditta said it would have to be her who brought you the talisman.'

'Well, congratulations,' said Alice. 'Your stories match perfectly.'

'They're not stories,' said Georgia. 'They're accounts of what we actually did. And I for one am getting fed up with you not believing us.'

Alice looked surprised.

'How often do I have to tell you that I'm not the slightest bit interested in Sky as a boyfriend?' said Georgia, warming to her theme. 'Why would I invent all this about Talia? Why would any of us?'

'Stop it, both of you!' said Nicholas suddenly. 'I can't take any more of you two arguing about whether my country exists or not! My father was poisoned there and the other members of my family may be attacked at any time. I can't waste any more time on this stuff with Alice. Believe us or not, as you like. I want to talk about going back.'

'Well, we can go back tonight,' said Sky.

'No,' said Nicholas. 'I don't mean tonight. I mean permanently.'

Sandro put one foot tentatively on to the maze. He didn't understand why Sulien wanted him on it, but gradually, as his feet traced the pattern of the marble, he felt himself calming down. He looked down, shuffling slowly forwards behind the black and white robed friar in front of him, till the colours of the maze and the colours of the robes blurred. When he found himself in the middle, he sank to his knees, suddenly tired. He would have liked to stay there for ever.

He became aware that Sulien had joined him. The last of the other friars had finished walking out from the centre. Sandro realised that he was kneeling on the figure of a woman. Her robes and hair were outlined in black against the white marble and she had a sweet, loving face that made him want to cry. There were twelve stars around her head. Sandro got to his feet and silently, slowly, traced the path back to the outer world. By then the light was waning in Talia and the sky outside the church windows was darkening.

'I must get Fratello,' he said to Sulien. 'He'll be lonely.'

'Bring him in through the cloister,' said the friar.

'You can both sleep in the laboratory tonight.'

'Then will you explain about the shadows?' asked Sandro.

'I will,' said Sulien.

*

'I just wondered, my Lord,' said Enrico, 'whether there's any chance that the Nucci could be in alliance with other enemies of yours.'

'More than likely, I would have thought,' said the Duke. 'Which enemies did you have in mind?'

Enrico wasn't quite sure how to proceed. When he and his master had returned from Remora after the young prince's memorial race, the Duke had been obsessed with a group of people led by the Regent of Bellezza. Enrico knew they were called 'Stravaganti' but he didn't know what that meant. He believed they were a powerful Brotherhood of magicians and he feared what Senator Rodolfo might be able to do to him.

He knew that the Senator's young assistant, Luciano, had learned more than science from his master, and he feared the young man too. There had once been something unnatural about him but that was so no longer. Enrico had captured Luciano with his own hands and knew that at one time he had been without a shadow.

The Eel's old master, Rinaldo di Chimici, had been most interested in that fact, even though it had crumbled to dust when brought to the attention of a People's Senate in Bellezza. Enrico had never known what it meant; it was one of those things he pushed to the back of his mind, like the disappearance of his fiancée. Luciano certainly had a shadow now and so did Rodolfo. It must be something to do with their magic powers. But now Enrico had seen two more people without shadows in Giglia and they were both connected with the Moorish friar who had saved the Duke from poisoning.

So had it been a double bluff? Was Sulien softening the Duke up for a later occasion when he would finish him off? This was the sort of thing the Eel was supposed to know and normally would have been happy to investigate. But any suggestion of magic unnerved him; he was afraid of the evil eye.

'Well?' said the Duke. 'Have you information or not?'

'There is a new novice at Saint-Mary-among-the-Vines, my Lord,' said Enrico hesitantly.

'That is hardly momentous,' said the Duke. 'I think I may have glimpsed him with young Brother Celestino in the sculptor's workshop. What of him?'

'How sure is your Grace of the loyalty of the friars up there?' asked Enrico.

'Tolerably certain,' said the Duke. 'Brother Sulien did save my life recently.'

'It's just that . . . well, neither this new novice – Benvenuto, he's called, according to my information – nor that Brother Tino seems to have a shadow.'

The Duke was silent. His memory of the events in Remora was clouded – by grief and, he suspected, by sorcery. But he knew that there was something deeply significant in this information. Something connected with his son's death. He had never believed that Falco had killed himself. That Luciano and his stable-boy friend who seemed to have disappeared had something to do with it. But the Duke had a private plan of his own for how to deal with Luciano.

'Look into it,' he said abruptly. 'Find out all you can about this Benvenuto and bring the information direct to me. Speak to no one else about it.'

Nicholas's announcement had stunned them all.

'I'm tired of being Nicholas,' he said simply. 'I don't even want to be Brother Benvenuto. I want to be Falco again, living in my own city, with my own family.'

'But you can't just turn back the clock,' said Georgia. 'You're dead and buried in Giglia – with a statue by the great Giuditta Miele on top.'

'How do you know I can't?' asked Nicholas. 'When I was translated here, this world leapt forward a year. Perhaps if I went back, it would move in the opposite direction.'

'But wouldn't you end up just the way you were before?' asked Sky, 'with your leg all hurt?'

'It's worse than that,' said Georgia, who had seen it all in a flash. 'He'd have to die in this world. Are you really prepared to do that to Vicky and David, Nicholas?'

'There may be a way to make it work out all right for them,' he muttered.

'Stop it!' said Alice. 'You three are freaking me out! OK, I believe you about this other world of yours. There's no need to go on about dying.'

'Look,' said Sky. 'You're tired and it must have blown your mind to be back in your world. We can go back tonight – every night if you like. But you can't just go back to live in Talia as if nothing had happened.'

'Have you ever wondered about where Brother Tino came from?' asked Sulien.

'Anglia, you said it was,' said Sandro.

'And that is true,' said the friar. 'In a way. But both he and Benvenuto come from an Anglia that is in another world – and from a time hundreds of years ahead of us.'

Sandro made the Hand of Fortune, to ward off the evil eye. Such talk was the last thing he expected to hear from a man of the church. Sulien smiled.

'There is nothing to be afraid of,' he said. 'They are good people. And they belong to the same Brotherhood as I do.'

'The Hounds of God?' asked Sandro.

'The Stravaganti,' said Sulien.

'What's that?'

'Travellers,' said Sulien. 'Travellers in time and space. There are several gathered in the city at the moment. They – we – have plans to save it from bloodshed at the approaching wedding festivities.'

'So Brother Tino isn't really your novice after all?' asked Sandro. 'Is he even a friar?'

'No,' said Sulien. 'I'm afraid that was a story to give him a reason for being here.'

Sandro felt strangely pleased. 'Tell me about the shadows,' he said. 'You said you are one of these travellers, but you have a shadow. I've seen it.'

'We have a shadow in the world we live in because that is where our real bodies are. It is only in the world we travel to that we are without our shadows.'

'So where do you go?'

'To Tino's world,' said Sulien. 'And there I have no shadow. I am just a visitor.'

'Could I go?' asked Sandro.

'Who knows?' said Sulien. 'Maybe one day. But you couldn't take Fratello with you – dogs can't be Stravaganti. Anyway, what I have told you is a secret. It would be very dangerous for us if anyone else knew it – particularly the di Chimici.'

'Even Prince Gaetano?' asked Sandro.

'No,' said Sulien. 'Gaetano knows about us. But you mustn't tell anyone else. I have told you our great secret, because I believe you can be trusted. You have changed in the last few months and I don't think you are as much of a di Chimici man as you used to be. You wouldn't do anything to put Brother Tino and myself in danger, would you? But you must be careful in front of that man up at the palace, the one who works for the Duke.'

'He already knows about the shadows,' said Sandro, anxious to show himself worthy of Sulien's trust. 'We saw you all coming out of a palazzo in the city today. Tino and that Benvenuto came out first and Enrico spotted that they didn't have them.'

'Then we are already in danger,' said Sulien. 'I must tell the others.'

Nicholas was so restless that the four of them left the

house and walked back to Sky's flat. Georgia was really worried about Nicholas. There had always been a danger in letting him go back to Talia but she had never thought it would hit him as badly as this. All the anxiety about him and the problems with Alice were spoiling her enjoyment at having been back to Talia herself. She longed for the old days when no one else knew about stravagation but her.

Sky let them in and heard his mother talking to someone. But the last person he expected to see at their kitchen table was Giuditta Miele. His heart sank; what on earth had the two of them found to talk about?

'Oh, hello, darling,' said Rosalind. 'You have a visitor. We've been waiting for you. Hello, you lot. Make yourselves at home – I'll get another chair.' She went off to the bedroom to fetch one.

'Alice,' said Sky. 'This is Giuditta Miele. I've told you about her.'

'It's Alice I've come to see,' said Giuditta. 'I've brought something for her.'

She took out a piece of paper, smaller than A4, with a red crayon sketch on it.

'Oh, that's Georgia, isn't it?' said Rosalind, coming back in with a chair. 'It's very good.'

'Thank you,' said Giuditta.

Alice took up the sketch, which showed Georgia hiding from the world's gaze behind a long sweep of tiger-striped hair.

'You made her look sort of Renaissance,' said Rosalind, 'in spite of the hair. How did you do that?'

'I drew what I saw,' said Giuditta simply.

'Well, I must leave you all to it,' said Rosalind. 'I

have a client to visit. Sky will look after you.'

'Is that my talisman?' asked Alice when she had gone. 'The drawing of Georgia?'

'Yes,' said Giuditta. 'It will bring you to my workshop in Giglia.'

'And I'm to go tonight?' said Alice, stunned. She no longer had any doubts that her friends had been telling the truth and she wasn't sure that she wanted to go to Talia any more. It seemed to bring nothing but trouble. But the others were all looking at her eagerly, as if something wonderful had happened, so she just said, 'Thank you.'

Wherever Beatrice went, her father's agent was at her elbow; she was beginning to think that the Duke had ordered this man to be especially helpful to her and she wished fervently that he had not. Enrico had a rank body odour – as if he rubbed himself with onions – and he stood too close. She took to applying more of the cologne that came from the pharmacy in Saint-Mary-among-the-Vines, so that she moved in a cloud of her own scent. But although it kept something of the man's smell at bay, it did not get rid of the man himself.

Today she was trying to arrange what would be necessary by way of flowers for the weddings, and it was no small task. Beatrice set off for the Garden of the di Chimici, a large tract of ground near their old palace, where Dukes as far back as Fabrizio the First, a hundred years ago, had grown flowers in the heart of the city. She had a key to the iron gates in the bunch hanging from her girdle, so she let herself into the garden, reluctantly allowing Enrico in after her.

'Paradise on earth!' he exclaimed. 'Just look at those colours!'

'I like it for its sweet scents,' said Beatrice.

'Never had much of a sense of smell myself,' said Enrico cheerfully. 'But I like flowers. You get plenty of them in this city but I've never seen anything like this garden.'

The garden was full of bees and butterflies. Gardeners worked in beds of all shapes – crescents, circles, octagons, diamonds, trefoils – divided by gravel paths. But Beatrice walked straight to the glass hothouses, where she knew the head gardener would be. Here were plants which would normally flower later in the year, like roses and carnations and lily-of-the-valley, brought on to bloom early and grace the Duke's dinner table. Here too were the exotic flowers collected by her father, not her favourites, because of their fleshy petals and their absence of scent. But they needed specialist care so the senior gardeners looked after them.

'Principessa!' said the head gardener, coming towards her wiping his hands on a sacking apron. 'We are honoured. What can I do for you?'

'I have come to talk about the wedding flowers,' said Beatrice.

'I think I'll wait outside, if you don't mind, your Highness,' said Enrico, mopping his brow with a lace handkerchief. 'It's too hot for me in here.'

Beatrice watched him go with relief. It was indeed stifling in the hothouse but it was worth it just to be rid of the man's presence.

'We need flowers for each bride, of course,' said the princess. 'And for their attendants. The cathedral itself must be a mass of blossoms and we shall need more flowers for the palazzo and the procession to the Church of the Annunciation that comes after the wedding ceremony.'

'We cannot supply so many from our own beds,' said the gardener. 'But the brides' flowers and those for the banqueting table, those we can provide from among our finest blooms here. The rest will come from the meadows outside the city, picked fresh on the day.'

Beatrice bent to smell a white orchid with purple splotches: no scent, as usual. She had a sudden vision of her father's own wedding, perhaps only a few months away, to the beautiful young Duchessa. He would want her to wear these waxy, lifeless flowers, as like real ones as statues to living, breathing people. And what then? Would the Duchessa look after Niccolò the way his own daughter had?

Beatrice feared there would be no place for her in the Grand Ducal palace once it had its Grand Duchessa; it pained her to think of her little riverside sitting room turned into a dressing room for a stepmother some years younger than herself. Best to leave for a new home of her own, with a husband. But who? The only unmarried di Chimici cousin left after the coming weddings would be Filippo of Bellona, Francesca's brother, unless you counted cousin Rinaldo. Beatrice's mouth curled up at the very thought. But Filippo was all right, thought Beatrice, a kind man and not unhandsome. She would try to find out if her father's plans tended that way.

All this flashed through her mind in the time it took to sniff an orchid.

They were all going to stravagate separately that night. Alice had reasoned that, since she wouldn't arrive in the same place as Georgia, there wasn't much point in their leaving together. And she felt shy about being watched. Giuditta had promised to have clothes waiting for her in the workshop, but she hadn't much confidence in what they might be like.

Her relations with Sky were still strained and Georgia was obviously worried about Nicholas, who was still muttering darkly about translating back to Giglia full time. Alice was happy to spend some time on her own. But she found an unexpected complication.

It was one of the rare evenings when Jane Greaves didn't have a committee meeting and she was disposed to stay up late and chat. Normally this would have made Alice happy, but she wanted to get an early night in case the stravagating took a long time to get the hang of. Giuditta had said she must arrive in the workshop before the apprentices were up and she didn't want to be late.

'What's the hurry?' asked her mother. 'You've got another week off school. You can lie in after I've gone to work – lucky you. Besides, we haven't talked properly for ages.'

It soon emerged that what she wanted to talk about was Rosalind Meadows.

'I gather your boyfriend's mother made a big hit

with your dad,' she said, a little bit slurrily, since she was drinking her way through a bottle of red wine.

'Well, she's nice,' said Alice defensively.

'I'm sure she's lovely,' said Jane, waving her glass. 'She's Laura's best friend, you know, the one who's on the same scrutiny committee as me? Known each other since they were at school. She told me about Sky's father.'

Alice was burning to ask about him but thought she shouldn't; Sky would tell her when he was ready, she supposed.

'Doesn't it make it a bit awkward for you, though, his mother and your father being together?' asked Jane.

'Don't exaggerate, Mum,' said Alice. 'They're not "together" like that – they just got on well in Devon. That's all.'

'Not what I heard,' said Jane. 'I spoke to Laura this evening and she told me they spent last night at Rosalind's flat. Sky was out or something.'

Yes, thought Alice; he was at Nick's, stravagating to Talia. It made her feel very peculiar to think of her father and Rosalind as a couple, and she wondered what Sky would say. Her brain was buzzing with thoughts. What was her father doing in London without contacting her? Was he going to be here all weekend? And where had he been when they called round at Sky's flat this morning? Had he left before Giuditta arrived?

'I'm sorry, Mum,' she said. 'I'm dropping. I really must go to bed.'

Giuditta was always up before her apprentices. She was still working on the Duchessa's statue, polishing, chipping minute fragments off it, polishing it again. It was always hard for her to decide when a piece was finished. Sometimes she felt that something was complete only when it left her workshop, collected by the patron who had ordered it. At other times the finishing point was the moment when she started something else. Certainly, she didn't yet feel that her connection with Arianna was over.

She stoked the fire that heated the stove in her little kitchen at the back of the workshop and put on a pan of milk to simmer. Giuditta had a bedroom of her own above the workshop, but the apprentices slept on the floor among the statues and blocks of stone. She had stepped over them on her way to the kitchen and none had stirred. She made a mental note that Franco was not among them – catting about with one of his many conquests in the city, she supposed.

Giuditta was about to sit down in the kitchen's one chair, when an ethereal figure materialised in it. A fair, slender girl in a long blue shift with the mysterious word 'fcuk' written on the front of it, solidified in the chair. She looked terrified.

Giuditta silently gave her some warm milk and stirred honey into it. Alice drank it gratefully, thankful too that she recognised this large, calm woman as the sculptor who had brought the drawing of Georgia, which Alice was still clutching, rolled up in her hand.

'I am in Talia?' she whispered.

Giuditta nodded. 'Stay quiet here,' she said. 'I'll fetch you some suitable clothes. And don't go in the workshop – there are boys sleeping in there.'

She was back soon, holding a simple blue cotton dress. 'My niece's,' she said, helping Alice into it and giving her a pair of dark blue ankle boots. 'You and she are much of a size, as I guessed.'

The dress had a complicated bodice with laces and Alice suspected she might look a bit like the soppy love interest in a pantomime, but there was no mirror in Giuditta's kitchen and at least now she could go out into the street.

'I must give the boys their breakfast,' said Giuditta. She seemed almost motherly, warming bread in the oven and pouring spiced milk. Alice helped her carry bowls and platters into the workshop. One apprentice was opening the shutters and letting in the bright morning light. The other two were stretching and yawning. A fourth boy, older than the others, slipped in through the door and was cuffed round the head by Giuditta before being given his breakfast.

They were all amazed by the sight of Alice.

'My new model, Alice,' said Giuditta, only she gave the name three syllables – Ah-lee-chay. She gestured to Alice to keep out of the sun; the girl jumped back quickly when she saw she had no shadow.

She was suddenly ravenous and ate bread and butter and a delicious preserve made from berries. They all breakfasted in silence, but when the apprentices were rolling up their bedding, Sky and Nicholas arrived. Alice had never been so glad to see anyone before.

Giuditta gave them a sheaf of drawings and said,

'Please take these to Brother Sulien. Alice, you can go with them and bring me back any comments he has.'

The three Stravaganti waited outside the workshop for Georgia to arrive. Alice flung her arms around Sky.

'I'm so glad you're here,' she said. 'It's all so strange.' She was gazing up at the vast cathedral, unable to accept that she was here and not in her bedroom at home.

'It'll be stranger still if anyone catches you embracing a friar,' said Nicholas. 'I think we'd better work out a different cover story.'

Chapter 20

The River Rises

After that once, Alice never stravagated again. Sky and Nicholas and Georgia all looked at home in Talia, as if they understood their role there. But she felt out of her depth the whole time. They took her to meet the other Stravaganti and they were perfectly welcoming. But Alice felt nervous of them; she was acutely aware of being an intruder into someone else's world.

She didn't like the way the city and its people smelt, the fact that all the men carried swords or daggers unnerved her and, worst of all, she had the feeling all the time of arriving in a play where she hadn't seen the earlier acts. Everyone seemed tense and worried about these weddings and she still couldn't sort out everyone's names and which person was getting married to which.

'Even my talisman isn't really for me,' she told Georgia the next day. 'It has your face on it.' And she took Giuditta's sketch and had it framed and hung it on her bedroom wall.

At least the tension had gone out of her relationship with Sky and the others. She was in on their secret, which would prove useful in providing future alibis, and she now understood why they all spent so much time together. She was included in their conversations and even joined Georgia when she watched the boys fencing. It no longer seemed boring now that she knew why they needed those skills.

Gradually, as they went back to school and started revising for exams, Alice felt her world swivel so that from being an outsider she became someone who was included, who could be told secrets that no one else in the world, literally, would understand. She didn't want to go back to Talia herself but she wanted to hear all about what was going on there. And with a part of herself she knew that the life the others were leading in the City of Flowers would come to a climax in less than two weeks' time and, for good or ill, Sky's role there would be over. And she would still be here, waiting for him.

In Talia, preparations for the big di Chimici event were in full swing. An additional kitchen was being built on to the back of the Palazzo Ducale in order to cope with all the planned feasting. The tournament on the day before the weddings was going to be held in the great Piazza Ducale, followed by an open-air banquet, and one of the main worries of the Duke's steward was the weather.

For the first two weeks in April, it rained steadily in the city, causing the already swollen river to rise even higher. The Duke's men were erecting a wooden platform on one side of the square, which was to hold tables seating hundreds of guests. It was to have a canopy bearing the di Chimici arms, but the weather was too wet to put it up yet.

When Arianna walked through the square, the sight of all the preparations made her heart sink. So far she had met only two or three times with the Duke and he had said nothing of his intentions towards her, but by the time the banquet was held he would surely have made his proposal formally and she would have to give him an answer. And she still didn't know what to do about the extravagant dress.

She picked her way through the puddles, attended by Barbara and her bodyguards, glad of a break in the rain to get out of the Embassy and visit her mother. The sky was still dark with rain clouds.

'If I believed in augury,' said Silvia after their greetings, 'I would think the gods were against at least one of these marriages.'

'Well, it wouldn't be that of Gaetano and Francesca,' said Arianna. 'I never met such a lovesick swain. Gaetano hasn't stopped talking about her since I arrived. I'll be glad when Francesca gets here herself, so that she can look after him.'

'And give you more time to look after your own swains?' asked Silvia.

'What do you mean?' asked Arianna. 'You are surely not referring to the Duke? He's a little old for a swain, I think.'

'Well, he is one of them, though he has made no declaration yet,' said Silvia. 'And I wish you would pay some thought to what you will say to him when he does.'

'I think about it all the time,' said Arianna. 'But to no avail.'

'Perhaps because your affections are already engaged?' suggested Silvia. 'That need not determine how you handle the Duke.'

'But he has no feelings for me,' said Arianna, exasperated. 'It is my city he wants, not me. It's all politics.'

'So it must be dealt with politically,' said her mother. 'Not romantically at all. It must not matter that he doesn't care for you – or that you don't care for him.'

'How could I care for him? He was behind the plot to kill you and as far as he knows he was successful. I think he was also involved in killing that young boy in the Nucci family and goodness knows how many others.'

'All the more reason to be careful how you refuse him,' said Silvia. 'You know what a dangerous man he is. And if he suspects that it is because you prefer another, that person's life would not be worth a scudo.'

*

Enrico hadn't been able to find out anything about the new novice, and it bothered him. Sandro had been quite useless in bringing him information on Brother

Benvenuto, or anything else at the friary recently, come to that. Though he was still keeping an eye on the Nucci.

Saint-Mary-among-the-Vines niggled at the back of Enrico's mind whenever it wasn't occupied by the arrangements for the wedding, helping the Principessa or spying on the Nucci. He knew that the pharmacy used to be the seat of the di Chimici's experiments, which were only partly into distilling perfumes. It was common knowledge that the family continued to be supplied with poisons from there for generations. But what about now? Enrico couldn't quite see Brother Sulien handing out deadly potions to the Duke if he asked for them. And yet he had no reason to suppose that the friar wasn't loyal. He had been prompt enough to save the Duke in his hour of need.

No, and besides, Sulien definitely had a shadow; Enrico had checked. He could not be one of those occult masters that the Duke feared and hated. So why did he entertain two novices who were under suspicion of belonging to that secret Brotherhood? It was one of those things that irked Enrico – like what had happened to his fiancée.

The Warrior had been in London for nearly two weeks and had not yet plucked up the courage to go and see Sky. Loretta knew he was worried about something and wisely said nothing. She had known what she was taking on when she married him and knew that if they were to have any future she mustn't be jealous of his past.

They had been married for six years now and there had been no babies, which was a sadness for her; she had long passed the youthful stage of thinking that children would ruin her figure and would have liked one of her own now. But she could see that Rainbow, as he liked to be called, was not exactly broody. He had so many children of his own already.

It was a mild spring in London, with the parks full of daffodils and no likelihood, as so often, that they would end up battered under a layer of late snow. Loretta filled the flat with flowering plants until it was full of the scent of hyacinths and the exotic blooms of orchids and hibiscus. And she waited.

One warm April morning while they were drinking cappuccinos outside the Café Mozart and the Warrior had signed just the right number of autographs to keep him happy – he was still a celebrity but didn't want his privacy disturbed – he said, 'Loretta, there's something I've got to tell you.'

At last, she thought, and took another bite of sachertorte.

The State coach of Fortezza, with its crest of the lily crossed by a sword, rumbled into the Via Larga late in the evening of Maundy Thursday. Princess Beatrice, who had spent all day supervising the making up of beds and airing of rooms, was first to greet Prince Jacopo and his family. Even though the di Chimici palazzo was large, she was glad that she and the Duke and Fabrizio had already moved into the Palazzo Ducale; there were more visitors expected. Francesca would be brought from Bellona by her brother Filippo, who would be giving her away. And cousin Alfonso would arrive next, from Volana, with his sister and mother. Thank goodness, thought Beatrice, that Uncle Ferdinando had a Papal residence in Giglia too, where he and cousin Rinaldo would stay; the di Chimici palace would be stretched to its limits, particularly since the bridal couples must be kept strictly apart.

'Welcome, welcome!' she said now to Jacopo and Carolina, receiving hearty kisses on both cheeks, and hugging Lucia and Bianca with genuine affection. Beatrice had always been fond of that branch of the family and intimate with these two cousins, who were distant in blood but near to her in age. These weddings were going to bring everyone closer.

'Little Beatrice!' growled Jacopo, gripping her like a bear. 'Why no husband for you in the cathedral next week? You are as pretty as your mother and shouldn't keep the young men waiting.'

'Father is not ready to part with me yet,' said Beatrice, blushing. 'He will be here soon, to greet you. Fabrizio too. Let me show you to your rooms.'

Liveried servants, of both the Fortezzan and Giglian branches of the family, carried the considerable baggage of the brides-to-be and their parents up the staircases, while maids scurried to bring heated water and lighted candles.

'Come and talk to us while we change, Bice dearest,' said Lucia.

'We want to show you our wedding dresses,' said Bianca.

'And I want to see them,' said Beatrice.

'Will Carlo be at dinner?' asked Lucia.

'Yes, yes,' said Beatrice. 'He is anxious to see you. And Alfonso will be here on Saturday,' she told Bianca, 'and Francesca. By the day after tomorrow all four couples will be able to sit down to dinner at the same table, even though you know you must not be alone together.'

'That's all right,' said Lucia. 'After next Tuesday, we will have a lifetime of being alone together.'

*

Sandro was watching the di Chimici palace from the street with Enrico. The Eel thought it was part of his young spy's education to show him the family members as they arrived. Sandro shuddered when he saw Prince Carlo came back with his father and older brother; Fratello growled softly.

'Now, you are straight about which prince is going to marry which princess?' asked Enrico. 'The little redhead who came from Fortezza tonight gets Carlo.'

'Poor her,' said Sandro under his breath.

'What was that?' asked Enrico.

'Which one is the dark sister going to marry?' asked Sandro, to distract him.

'Duke Alfonso of Volana,' said Enrico promptly. 'He's coming on Saturday. His sister is Caterina.'

'The one that Fabrizio is going to marry?' asked Sandro.

'Well done,' said Enrico. 'And their brother is?'

Sandro shook his head. 'No idea.'

'My old master, Rinaldo,' said Enrico. 'I worked for him when he was Ambassador to Bellezza. A real pansy. He works for the Pope now. They won't be here till Monday because the Pope has to say the Easter Mass in his own city of Remora.'

'The Pope's the Duke's brother, isn't he?'

'His younger one, yes. Now, who is Prince Gaetano's bride?'

'Francesca of Bellona,' said Sandro, screwing up his face with the effort of remembering. 'He's always talking about her.'

'Right then, you know all our lot. Now how about the Nucci? How many are there at the tower now?'

'Well, you know about Matteo,' said Sandro, 'and Camillo and Filippo. There are at least eight others – cousins I think or uncles – whose names I don't know.'

'But you know them by sight? You'd recognise them?'

Sandro nodded.

'Good lad,' said Enrico. 'You'll be useful on the day of the weddings.'

*

Sky had a second disguise in Giglia now. Gaetano had given him a set of clothes to keep up at the friary; they were the plainest he had and yet they still made Sky feel the part of a young nobleman. Now he was Brother Tino within the walls of Saint-Mary-among-the-Vines and ordinary Messer Celestino when he went out into the city. In this way he could consort with Georgia without comment and, if they usually had another young friar with them, that lent more respectability to their association. Nicholas continued to need his disguise and the abandonment of Sky's identity as a novice wasn't without its dangers. He had to be careful not to be seen by Nicholas's brothers or the Duke. But the nobles were all involved in the wedding preparations and it was good to stride about the city in clothes that accommodated a sword and dagger at his belt.

On the day after the Fortezzas arrived, Good Friday in Giglia, Sky and Nicholas set out to meet Georgia at Giuditta's workshop a bit later than usual. As novices, they had been required to attend a special service before leaving the friary. In their own world they had been back at school a week and hadn't missed a night's stravagation to Talia. They were tired, their senses a little dulled in both worlds, or they might have been quicker to realise what was happening in the narrow street off the Piazza della Cattedrale.

Most of the streets around the piazza were deserted, since the majority of the people who would normally have been out were still attending a long service in the cathedral. Gaetano and Luciano had used the emptiness of the Annunciation piazza for an early-morning practice with the foils.

They too were on their way to meet Georgia at the sculptor's workshop when they suddenly found their way barred by a small group of the Nucci faction. It was Camillo and two of his cousins and all three were armed to the hilt. Luciano didn't know any of them and was taken by surprise when these obviously hostile youths started to hold their noses and jeer the name di Chimici. He didn't know that the traditional response was to bleat like a sheep and crow 'Nucci!'

Gaetano was not responding; he and Luciano were

outnumbered and he had no desire to provoke a fight so he said nothing.

'See what lily-livers these lily boys are!' cried Camillo. 'They don't like a fair fight, these flower-arrangers! They prefer secret stabbings in an alley!'

'I have no quarrel with you,' said Gaetano finally, as evenly as he could manage. 'I am sorry for the death of your brother, but it was not my doing.'

'Maybe so,' sneered Camillo. 'But you can't deny your family had a hand in it.'

'I am not my family,' said Gaetano. But it was no use. His attitude was incomprehensible to red-blooded Giglians. In the City of Flowers family was everything. The three Nucci came closer until Camillo's face was only centimetres away from Gaetano's. Meanwhile one of the others gave Luciano a shove. The prince glanced sideways for an instant at his friend and that was time enough for Camillo to draw his dagger and aim it at Gaetano's ribs.

But Gaetano had excellent reflexes and blocked the blade with his left arm and hit him smartly in the face with his right fist. Luciano backed off and drew his rapier and soon his new fighting skills were being used in deadly earnest.

That was when Sky and Nicholas turned the corner and saw what was happening. They both rushed into the fray, Sky drawing his sword awkwardly and Nicholas launching himself at Camillo's back and pinning his arms. Suddenly the odds were against the Nucci. Camillo was disarmed, with Gaetano's blade at his throat, and his cousins found themselves faced by two other armed and ferocious young men, even though one of them was a friar.

'Call off your men,' said Gaetano, and Camillo nodded gingerly. His cousins sheathed their swords and at a further sign from Camillo retreated into the distance. Gaetano lowered his weapon.

'Go back to your family,' he said. 'I say again I have no quarrel with you and nor do my friends.' He signalled to Nicholas to release his hold and Camillo Nucci loped off after the others, cursing all di Chimici as he went.

'You're bleeding,' said Nicholas to Gaetano, as the others put up their weapons.

They were fortunately near Giuditta's workshop by then and took the wounded prince in.

'It's not a bad wound,' said Gaetano. 'The dagger just glanced off my arm.'

'Just a scratch, I suppose?' said Georgia hysterically. She realised that they had all been in mortal danger.

Giuditta sent her to boil water on the stove, while she eased off Gaetano's doublet and shirtsleeve. The apprentices crowded round; this was better entertainment than they had expected on the long penitential day of Good Friday.

It was indeed only a flesh wound, though it bled impressively. Giuditta tore up a cotton sheet to bandage it.

'Will it heal by Tuesday?' asked Gaetano, not so much worried about it impeding his wedding as about whether he would be able to fight then if called upon.

Giuditta nodded. 'It will knit together well enough in a few days if you do not use it. I don't recommend your taking part in the tournament on Monday.' She pulled his shirt and doublet back on gently and made a sling from more of the sheet.

'So I shan't be able to conceal today's encounter,' he said wryly.

'Be thankful it was not worse,' said the sculptor. 'And that you had friends at hand.'

'But it irks me that Gaetano has taken hurt while the Nucci walked away unscathed,' said Nicholas, surprising the apprentices. They would not have expected a novice friar to be so bloodthirsty.

*

Beatrice was with her other family members in the church of Sant'Ambrogio, and had no idea what had happened. But her thoughts were not altogether concentrated on the service. Because of the religious obligations of this day and of Easter Sunday, there was effectively only Saturday left in which to finish getting everything ready for Monday's tournament and banquet, which would lead rapidly on to the weddings themselves. And Francesca and Alfonso and their wedding parties would arrive on Saturday and need housing and entertaining.

Thank goodness I'm *not* getting married on Tuesday too, she thought, or nothing would be ready in time.

By the time they left the church, it was again raining heavily in the city and the di Chimici party had to make an undignified run to the palazzo.

When Sky returned home after school the next day, there was a red sports car outside his flat. He didn't think for a moment that it had anything to do with him and let himself in as usual. But in his kitchen sat a very glamorous couple. A middle-aged black man with greying dreadlocks and a silk suit, and a stunning long-legged bronzed young woman, sitting perched awkwardly on a kitchen chair with Remedy on the minimal lap of her very short skirt. Rosalind was looking dazed.

But she didn't need to make any introductions; Sky remembered the *Hello!* article when he was eleven. He felt his hackles rising.

'Hi there, Sky,' said the Warrior awkwardly.

Sky couldn't say anything. What could he say after seventeen years? He moved instinctively close to Rosalind, remembering how the singer had ignored his appeal of three years ago.

Loretta held out a perfectly manicured hand with scarlet nails and Sky took it, fascinated.

'I've only just heard of your existence,' she said to him. 'Yesterday, in fact. I'm sorry. If Rainbow had told me, I would have invited you to visit us in the States.'

'I wouldn't have come,' he said instantly, appreciating her forthrightness. 'I wouldn't have left Rosalind.'

'I understand,' said the Warrior. 'You don't want anything to do with me and I don't blame you. But I didn't want to die never having met one of my sons.'

'Are you dying, then?' asked Sky rudely. 'Why should I care? You didn't seem that bothered when Rosalind was ill.'

They all looked at him equally blankly.

'You know, when I wrote you that letter?' he added. 'Asking you to find her a good doctor.'

The Warrior shook his head. 'I never got no letter,'

he said. 'You never told me you'd been ill,' he said to Rosalind.

'I'm getting better now,' she said. 'It was tough on Sky for a while – it was ME.'

It was clear from the Warrior's face that he didn't know what she was talking about. Sky felt something beginning to unknot in his stomach. But he was puzzled by the singer's attitude. It sounded as if he and Rosalind had kept in touch, which was not what Sky had been told.

'I'm sorry,' said the singer. 'Sorry I didn't get the letter, sorry that your mum's been ill – sorry for being such a rotten father. But she did say that she wanted to bring you up on her own. And I'm not dying – I just wanted to see you in the flesh. All these photos are great but it's not the same.'

He took an envelope from his inside pocket and tipped out a cascade of photographs on the table. Sky saw his whole life spread out in random order, from chubby brown baby to six-foot teenager. The pictures were all tatty round the edges, particularly the older ones, as if they had been handled and looked at often.

For the first time, he saw that he looked like his father.

It rained the whole of the rest of that weekend in Giglia. Then, miraculously, on Easter Sunday in the afternoon, the sun came out and the city began to steam in the spring heat.

'God be praised!' said the Pope, in his carriage on the way from Remora.

'Goddess be thanked!' said the many workmen and tradesmen busying themselves about the weddings. They worked late into the night, Easter Sunday or not, carrying tables out into the Piazza Ducale, plucking and arranging flowers, spreading ornate cloths and di Chimici banners, creating fantasies of sugar and marzipan in the kitchen.

Monday dawned fair and clear, to the relief of grooms and armourers and all the young men taking part in the tournament. Sky and Nicholas got to the piazza early, meeting Luciano and Georgia in the loggia with all the fine statues. They wanted to get a good view of the tournament, even though their own favourite, Gaetano, would not be taking part.

He had greeted his bride two days before, with his arm still in its sling. Francesca had cried out when she saw him but he had reassured her that it would be better by Tuesday and that he would marry her with two strong arms. The Duke had been furious to hear of the Nucci attack, but Gaetano and Beatrice had prevailed on him not to take any revenge before the weddings.

'You got visitors, Gloria,' said the care assistant.

'Mrs Peck to you,' said the old lady. This was one of her better days.

Sky wasn't at all sure about this. His other grandmother, Rosalind's mum, had been a part of his life as long as he could remember. But this tiny black woman seemed to have even less to do with him than the ageing rock singer did. He would have appreciated

Loretta's company on the drive down, but there was room only for two in the sports car and she had stayed to talk to Rosalind.

So Sky had been enclosed in a small space with the man he could not think of as his father. He supposed it hadn't really been any more awkward for him than for the Warrior. But he had no intention of making it any easier.

'I really never got that letter, you know,' said his father, as soon as they were heading south.

'I believe you,' said Sky. 'It's OK.'

'Your mum always writes care of my agent, Gus,' he went on. 'And I've always got her letters – the ones with the photos. Regular as clockwork, once a year.'

'I didn't know she was doing that,' said Sky.

'I expect you hate me, don't you?' said the Warrior, after a long silence.

'No,' said Sky, thinking about the way the Nucci felt towards the di Chimici. 'I don't hate you. I just don't know you. I don't feel as if you have anything to do with me.'

The Warrior winced. 'Fair enough,' he said. 'But there is a connection. I mean, blood's thicker than water, isn't it?'

'Is it?' said Sky. 'I don't think we've got anything in common except our DNA. I may look more like you but Rosalind's the one I'm really like.'

'Only because you've been with her all this time,' said his father.

Sky shook his head. 'I don't think so,' he said.

'Well, then, I suppose I'll just have to settle for the DN whatsit,' said the Warrior.

'It'd be useful if you ever needed a kidney or a bone

marrow transplant,' said Sky, but even as he said it, meaning to be sarcastic, he thought of all those episodes of *ER* he had watched with Rosalind and couldn't help smiling.

'You taking the piss?' asked his father, glancing sideways at him. 'Nothing wrong with my kidneys.' Then he relaxed just a bit. 'Might need some liver one day though – used to drink like a fish before Loretta took me over.'

'She's nice,' said Sky and meant it.

'Yeah, she's a real diamond,' said the Warrior.

'Nice car, too,' ventured Sky.

'You want a go?' he asked. 'Have you got your licence yet?'

'Only the provisional,' said Sky. 'I'm only just seventeen.'

'Course not,' said the Warrior. 'It's different in America. Kids can drive as soon as they're fifteen in some states. But I tell you what. Have a spin round the grounds of the home after we've seen your granny – OK?'

Sky wasn't quite sure how he'd been talked into this visit. The Warrior had asked if he'd go with him to see his old mum in a home in Surrey and Sky had the strangest feeling that the singer wanted someone with him to act as a buffer. He had explained that the old lady sometimes got a bit confused.

She seemed bright as a button when Sky first caught sight of her, her eyes darting back and forth between them.

'Hello, Mum,' said the Warrior, bending over to kiss her. They had stopped on the way to buy flowers and he now presented her with a huge bouquet of hothouse roses.

'There now, Mrs Peck – isn't that lovely?' said the care assistant before taking them away.

'Say hello to your granny, Sky,' said the Warrior.

Sky didn't feel he could kiss a perfect stranger. He held out his hand to her. A puzzled look crossed the old woman's face.

'Is it Kevin's boy?' she asked her son.

'No, Mum,' said the Warrior. 'This is my son, Sky. You haven't met him before. Nor had I till today. He lives with his mum.'

'Another one?' said Sky's grandmother. She didn't seem very pleased to meet him. 'He looks like you, Colin. And your dad – poor bugger.'

Sky didn't know if she meant him or his grandfather. But he was amused to discover that the millionaire Rainbow Warrior was really Colin Peck, with an old mum who stood no nonsense from him. He felt a bit sorry for him, really. What with his feisty mother and Loretta taking him in hand, it seemed as if the glamorous rock star was a bit henpecked.

'What you laughing at?' said Mrs Peck. 'Let's have a proper look at you. Mum's white, I see.'

Sky nodded. He wasn't going to discuss Rosalind with this woman.

'Well, you've got the looks. I suppose you want to be a singer too?'

'No,' said Sky. 'I want to be an artist. I don't even like his kind of music.'

Then he realised he was being unnecessarily rude. They were both staring at him. He suddenly had a very strong feeling that he was young and had all his choices ahead of him. This old woman, who was biologically his grandmother, looked as if she didn't have much of her life left. And the Rainbow Warrior wasn't a bad man; he'd just led a very different life from Sky.

'There – don't they look lovely?' said the care assistant brightly, bringing back the roses arranged in a glass vase. 'Would you like me to make you all a nice cup of tea?'

Chapter 21

The di Chimici Weddings

The young Stravaganti sat on the steps of the loggia, watching the preparations for the tournament. The loggia itself was filling up with food stalls for all those not fortunate enough to have been invited to the banquet. Luciano bought them all thick slices of frittata between pieces of coarse bread and a jug of cold ale to share. Nicholas sat slightly apart, his back against one of the statue plinths and his hood pulled up to shade his face.

The di Chimici party came out of the Palazzo Ducale. A special stage had been built for them to sit on and watch the games. All four di Chimici bridegrooms escorted their brides, and there was also the Duke, Princess Beatrice, the Duchessa of Bellezza and her father the Regent, and the Pope himself, who stood and gave his blessing on the crowd before the games began. Prince Fabrizio announced his bride to the spectators as Queen of the Tournament. As future wife of the di Chimici heir, Princess Caterina of Volana merited that honour. And the crowd were delighted to see the pretty young woman blushing as the prince placed the wreath of olive leaves on her golden hair.

The tournament began with a great procession of bullock wagons carrying models of all the cities that were under di Chimici rule – Remora, Moresco, Fortezza, Volana, Bellona – finishing with a perfect model of Giglia itself, complete in every detail (apart from the marked absence of the new Nucci palace) and dominated by the miniature of the great cathedral. By then the edges of the square were full of spectators.

'No Bellezza, you see,' Luciano whispered to Georgia. And he knew that Arianna, sitting in splendour across the piazza, was thinking the same. 'You'll never see a model of the City of Masks carried on a cart to glorify the Duke in Giglia.'

Not unless Arianna accepts his proposal, thought Georgia, but she carefully kept that thought to herself.

When the last wagon had rumbled past the Palazzo Ducale, two men came and set up a quintain at the south-east end of the L-shaped piazza. It was a stuffed dummy of a man with a shield in one hand and a weighted whip in the other. Riders ran at it with a lowered lance and once they had struck the shield had to jink out of the way to avoid the whip as it swung round. The first two or three were easily knocked off their horses.

Nicholas was on his feet booing with the rest of the crowd. 'I was very good at this,' he told Sky. 'Oh, if only I had a horse and a lance!'

Fabrizio, Carlo and Alfonso had left the wooden stage now and entered the lists. They were wearing only light armour and no helmets. Gaetano scanned the tops of the surrounding buildings carefully for archers but the only bows he could see were di Chimici men, archers from the Duke's private army. He was almost as frustrated as Nicholas that he couldn't tilt at the quintain but Francesca held him tightly by the hand.

The flower of Giglian youth was at the tournament – not just di Chimici and Nucci but every family that had any claim to ancient lineage in the city. The Aldieri, the Bartolomei, the Donzelli, the Gabrieli, the Leoni, the Pasquali, the Ronsivalli and the Salvini were all represented, and each family was in allegiance with either the perfumier-bankers whose weddings were being celebrated or the wool merchants and sheep farmers who were their enemies.

The young men were lining up to try at the quintain while in other parts of the square jugglers and acrobats and musicians entertained the crowd while they waited for the main joust. And not just nobles; every boy and youth, no matter what their estate, was in the square, greedily absorbing the sights and sounds. Sandro and Fratello were on the edge of the crowd, watching.

Prince Fabrizio won the quintain and was rewarded by Caterina who bestowed his prize of a silver chain round his neck. He whispered in her ear as she put it over his head and the crowd roared their approval.

For the main joust, the combatants all put on metal helmets. Sky couldn't believe that he was going to see real riders and horses charge at one another with metal-tipped lances. But for the others, who had seen the excesses of the Reman Stellata, it was not so surprising. The clash of lance on shield and sword on sword rang round the square and no quarter was given, even though this was supposed to be a wedding celebration.

The jousting lasted for hours until only Camillo Nucci and Carlo di Chimici were left in the lists. By then many young men were nursing broken limbs or bleeding from sword slashes. Fabrizio and Alfonso had both retired with minor wounds because their brides-to-be insisted on their remaining in one piece for the next day.

'Surely someone will get killed?' said Sky.

'Not usually,' said Nicholas.

Camillo and Carlo thundered towards each other along the short run the piazza permitted. Their lances both made contact and both riders were unhorsed. The loose horses charged on, stopped only by the fearless grooms who caught their harness. The two young men leapt to their feet, swords drawn. Camillo had dropped his shield but was thrown another by his brother Filippo.

The combatants circled each other like gladiators while the crowd bayed for blood. This was the pinnacle of the day's entertainment for most of them. Georgia found herself cheering 'Carlo! Prince Carlo!' and then stopped, wondering why. The only di Chimici she liked were Gaetano who wasn't fighting and the translated Falco who was standing beside her dressed as a friar and yelling for his brother to win, in a most unecclesiastical way.

'What do you reckon?' Sky whispered to Luciano.

'They're pretty evenly matched as to size and skill, I'd say,' Luciano replied. 'But it's not like fencing. Look at the weight of those swords!'

The two armoured men stood and exchanged blows. There was not much space between the metal plates to inflict a wound, but that wasn't what the endgame of a tournament was all about. It was enough for one to disarm the other or force him to the ground. They were both nimble and good at swordcraft but the weapons were heavy and it was not a subtle contest.

'That's for my brother,' hissed Carlo, lunging at Camillo's neck.

'And this for mine,' retorted Camillo, deflecting the blow with his shield and aiming one of his own.

After twenty minutes, Camillo had wearied his opponent into submission and Carlo sank to his knees. The joust-master stopped it there, seeing that Camillo would have pulled off Carlo's helmet and inflicted a final blow. So the prize was awarded to a Nucci, which left half the crowd howling for revenge and the others crowing with delight.

To her distaste, Princess Caterina had to bestow a handsome silver and bronze war helmet on her family's enemy. The di Chimici applauded politely, their smiles painted on. As he came down the steps Camillo very lightly pinched his nose, provoking more cheers and catcalls. The exhausted Carlo was sitting on the steps of the loggia, his helmet off and drinking a cup of ale. As Camillo passed him he saw a ragged boy and his dog that he had often spotted hanging round outside their family's palace.

The boy and dog were hurrying across the piazza to where the next event was going to take place. Their route took them past Carlo, but the dog suddenly swerved and barked at the prince. It was over in an instant, with the prince cursing at the dog and the boy dragging him away on his piece of string, but at that moment, Camillo Nucci remembered where he had seen the mongrel before. And he knew which of the di Chimici had killed his brother.

But then it was time for the fencing and half a dozen pairs of young men were suddenly ferociously thrusting and parrying all over the square.

'Come on!' said Luciano to Sky. 'Let's have a go!'

A groom gave them a couple of bated weapons and they fought together for the first time. For Sky it was the most exhilarating moment of his journeys to Giglia so far. The sun was shining on their weapons, they were young, alive and well-matched and he was just another well-dressed Giglian noble taking part in the city's great day of rejoicing. But the sixteenth-century rapier was so much heavier than the fencing foils that Sky was used to that Luciano was soon able to beat his weapon out of his hand. As Sky went back to sit with the others, Georgia grabbed him by the arm.

'What on earth did you think you were doing?' she railed at him. 'Imagine if you'd won the whole thing and had to collect a prize from the princess. I suppose you think Giglia's so full of black brothers with dreads that the Duke wouldn't have realised you're the one who's supposed to be a friar!'

But she wasn't listening for an answer. Luciano was now fighting with Filippo Nucci and she was in agony that he might get hurt. Several of the fencers had lost the buttons off the end of their rapiers and there were cries as sharp blades met flesh. But Filippo pressed Luciano hard and soon disarmed him, catching Luciano's weapon on the elaborate cross-guards of his own rapier.

Luciano came back to join them, out of breath. They watched as a revived Prince Carlo saved the honour of his family by defeating Filippo Nucci in the final encounter. His soon-to-be sister-in-law smiled much more happily as she gave him his prize of a silver drinking cup. Nicholas applauded loudly. Georgia shuddered; all these encounters with sharp weapons brought home to her the fears everyone had expressed for the next day's wedding ceremonies.

'I'm glad Alice isn't here,' she whispered to Sky.

'Me too,' he said. He realised that he wouldn't be able to concentrate on what the Stravaganti had to do the following day if he had to keep one eye on his girlfriend. He had distractions enough at home without having them in Talia too. Deliberately he thrust the thought of his father to the back of his mind and concentrated on what was going on across the square.

The di Chimici were leaving the wooden stage and going back into the palazzo. Swarms of servants were finishing laying the tables for the banquet on the platform in the north-west corner of the piazza. Others brought out bowls of warm water scented with rose petals or lemon peel so that the arriving guests could wash their hands. The platform had been constructed to encompass the fountain with its central statue of Neptune and its basin spiked with cologne so that there was a continuing fragrance and the sound of purling water throughout the meal.

The canopy was now in place, made of turquoise cloth threaded with silver and hung with swags of greenery and hothouse roses and lilies. Escutcheons with the di Chimici crest hung on every supporting pole. Guests were divided into male and female, young and old, so that the brides were all at one table with Beatrice and Arianna while the grooms sat at another with the two Nucci sons and various other nobles. Theirs was the most tense gathering at the feast.

Isabella, the dowager Duchessa of Volana, presided over the table of older women, which included Francesca's mother Princess Clarice of Bellona, Princess Carolina of Fortezza, and Graziella Nucci. At a very lavishly decorated table near the fountain sat the Pope in his grandest robes, with his brothers, the Duke of Volana and Prince of Bellona, and his cousin, Prince Jacopo of Fortezza. Rodolfo sat there too and Matteo Nucci and it was of course presided over by the Duke himself.

'Aha, what have we here?' said the Pope as the first course was brought in.

'Capon in white sauce, your Holiness,' said the servant, who had been instructed to serve him first. 'And those are silvered pomegranate seeds.'

Bronze cauldrons filled with water kept cool the greenish wine from Santa Fina while the bottles of Bellezzan and Giglian red had warmed gently in the afternoon sun.

The young Stravaganti, none of whom were invited

to the banquet, quelled their hunger with sugared pastries and watched the comings and goings across the square, like spectators at a theatre.

'That will go on for hours,' said Sandro knowledgeably, coming to join them on the steps of the loggia. Nicholas ruffled Fratello's ears. Ever since Sulien had told him about the Stravaganti, Sandro had spent more and more time with them. They were aware that he knew their secret and that Brother Sulien trusted him.

'I must leave long before the end,' said Georgia regretfully. The next day was a school one and she couldn't risk oversleeping. And, unlike the boys, she had a long flight before she could stravagate back.

'I'll tell you all about it tomorrow,' said Luciano, giving her one of his heart-stopping smiles.

'Me too,' said Sandro. 'I'll name you all the dishes. Enrico will know them all, even though he's not grand enough to sit down with dukes and princes.'

'Or clean enough,' said Luciano. 'They'd have had to fill the fountain with every perfume in Sulien's pharmacy if he'd been invited.'

It bothered Luciano that Sandro was still working for the Eel, even though it was Sulien who had advised the boy not to break off his connections with the di Chimici. Luciano knew what Enrico was capable of, including murder, and he didn't like the idea of the boy risking exposure as a sort of double agent.

Georgia left the square as the candles were being lit in the di Chimici silver candlesticks and the lanterns hanging from the canopy. Sky and Nicholas stayed just long enough to watch a great confection being carried in of spun sugar in the shape of a giant perfume bottle surrounded by lilies. Then Sky had to drag Nicholas back to Saint-Mary-among-the-Vines.

Luciano sat on in the darkening square with Sandro, while the sated guests nibbled silvered almonds and figs and listened to the band of musicians who played on the balcony of the palazzo. When the music stopped, the speeches began, and Luciano realised he must have dozed off, because Sandro was shaking him awake.

'The Duke's making some big announcement,' he said.

The two of them got up and strolled closer to the banqueting platform, which was now an island of light and flowers in the dark. Duke Niccolò, resplendent in a fur-trimmed scarlet velvet doublet, was standing holding a silver goblet full of red wine. His speech was slightly slurred and he swayed a little but he was still very much the master of the feast.

'My brother, his Holiness the Pope, Lenient the Sixth, here to celebrate the union of eight of our closest family members in the cathedral tomorrow, has conferred upon me the honour of a new title.'

The Pope also rose, even more unsteadily than his brother, and took the new crown from a page who had borne it to the platform on a purple velvet cushion.

'By the powers invested in me as Bishop of Remora and Pope of the Church of Talia,' he said, 'I here declare Duke Niccolò di Chimici, Duke of Giglia, to be the first Grand Duke of all Tuschia.'

He placed the Grand-Ducal crown, which looked rather like one of the kitchen's finer confections, on his brother's white head.

The new Grand Duke adjusted it as the applause rose from all the tables.

'This crown I hope to pass on, with the title, to my heir Fabrizio and his descendants,' said Niccolò. His eyes sought out one person among his guests. 'And now, before we adjourn to the palazzo for dancing, I ask you to join me in one final toast, to our most welcome guest, the beautiful Duchessa of Bellezza!'

There was some whispering among the diners at that; such a signal honour coming straight after the announcement of the Duke's new title must mean something of significance. Luciano gripped Sandro's shoulder tightly. But there was no further announcement; the Grand Duke had no secret understanding with Arianna. The most important guests were moving into the central courtyard of the Palazzo Ducale for dancing, and Arianna passed out of Luciano's view.

'Would you like me to stay here and wait for her to come out?' asked Sandro.

Luciano was touched. 'I think I'll stay myself, thanks,' he said.

'Then I'll keep watch with you,' said Sandro.

The servants were clearing the platform, so they went and sat on the edge of the scented fountain and soon found themselves partaking of leftovers from the feast – even Fratello got some fragments of goat liver that had fallen from the tables.

In the piazza outside Saint-Mary-among-the-Vines, carriage races were being held round the wooden obelisks but Sky was not there to see them.

In all the other piazzas of the city bonfires were lit in celebration of the new Grand Duke and of the weddings on the morrow. Silver coins were thrown into the crowds by Niccolò's men and the people cried, 'Long live Grand Duke Niccolò! Long live the di Chimici!'

*

In the courtyard of the Ducal palace, couples were forming for a dance. Arianna sought out her father for a quick conference but was forestalled by the Duke himself.

'Ah, your Grace,' he said, bowing rather carefully and unsteadily. 'Please do me the honour of being my partner.'

Arianna was quite startled till she realised he was just referring to the dancing. All round the first floor of the inner courtyard ran a loggia, to which the musicians had now removed. Torches flickered in iron brackets fixed just under this gallery and the players themselves had their music illuminated by many-branched candelabra. The air was heavy with the scent of lilies and high above the dancers the stars came out. It was the perfect night for romance.

The four couples who were to marry the next day clearly thought so and so, alarmingly, did the Grand Duke.

'I have a present for you,' he said to Arianna, as they executed the formal movements of the dance.

'Your Grace has already been more than generous,' she said.

The Duke took from his doublet a black velvet bag.

Goddess save us, thought Arianna, not during the dance with everyone looking. But it was not a ring. It was a silver sleeve-pendant in the shape of a mandola, encrusted with precious stones.

'It's lovely,' said Arianna. 'But –'

The Duke held up his hand. 'That is a word I do not care for,' he said. 'There are no conditions to accepting it – let us call it a gift from Giglia to Bellezza.'

'Then Bellezza thanks Giglia,' said Arianna.

'Here, let me pin it to your sleeve,' said the Grand Duke, and they stepped aside from the other dancers so that he could fix it to the left sleeve of her blue satin gown. When that was done, he signalled to a servant and led her into a small side chamber. She looked frantically around for Rodolfo but he was nowhere to be seen.

'There is something more,' said Niccolò.

A servant led into the room two beautiful spotted cats, the size of boarhounds. Each wore a silver collar of entwined fleur-de-lys with a long chain attached. Arianna couldn't help showing her pleasure; she loved animals.

'You may touch them, my Lady,' said the servant. 'They are quite tame.'

Arianna stroked their magnificent fur and admired their large brown eyes, which were underlined with black, like those of the most fashionable Giglian ladies. Her own eyes were shining and the Duke looked pleased.

'Are they really for me?' asked Arianna, like the girl she still was.

'Another token of Giglia's esteem,' said the Grand Duke. 'And a sign of the closer friendship I hope will develop between our two cities.'

Completely captivated by the glamorous cats, Arianna was quite heedless of the way this encounter was moving. Niccolò was beginning to feel jealous of the caresses lavished on the animals and ordered his man to take them away.

'You heard my announcement after dinner,' he said, showing no signs of wanting to rejoin the dance.

'Indeed,' said Arianna.

'And saw my crown?'

Arianna noticed that the crown was displayed on its velvet cushion on a small table in the chamber. Niccolò clicked his fingers and another servant brought in a second crown. It was smaller and more delicate but equally sparkling with gems.

'Can you guess who this is for?' he asked.

Arianna said nothing.

'I had it made for my Granduchessa,' said Niccolò, taking the slender silver crown from the servant. 'I should like to see if it would fit your Grace.'

Arianna protested. 'I couldn't wear it,' she said, adding, 'and I know not how to address you, my Lord, under your new title.'

'Niccolò is my name,' he said, lifting the small tiara of diamonds from her hair and putting the crown in its place. 'There! A perfect fit, I would say. It looks well on you, my dear – Arianna, as I would call you. Won't you honour me by wearing it always and being my Granduchessa?'

It has happened, thought Arianna, and it feels like one of those dreams when you try to run and your legs won't move and everything slows down. At that moment a battery of rockets went up and stars of purple and green and gold exploded above the courtyard, so she was excused from speech. Not as good as Father's, she thought, but they came just at the right moment.

The new Grand Duke looked annoyed. Arianna took off the crown and restored her tiara. 'Do let us return to the courtyard to see the fireworks,' she said, as calmly as she could manage.

'There is no need to answer straightaway,' said Niccolò, raising his voice over the sound of Reman candles. 'You can tell me tomorrow, after the weddings. I'd like to make an announcement in the evening. In fact, you do not have to tell me. Just wear the dress I sent you and I will know your answer is favourable.'

At that moment, all Arianna could think of was getting away from him. 'Yes,' she said. 'That would be acceptable.'

Then she hurried out of the room, leaving Niccolò to look at the pair of crowns. Among the crowd whose upturned faces were illuminated by the fireworks was Rodolfo, and Arianna almost ran to his side, she was so relieved to see him. He put his arm round her.

'He has asked me,' she said simply and pressed herself close to her father's side, suddenly shivering in the warm night air.

'I hoped I had let off the rockets in time to prevent it,' he said.

'They saved me from having to give him an answer now,' said Arianna. 'But the fireworks aren't yours, are they?'

'I was taking a professional interest,' said Rodolfo, with the ghost of a smile. 'Unfortunately for the firework master, I set off the display a little ahead of time.'

Arianna was exhausted and, as they made their excuses and farewells and slipped out into the night, her bodyguards closed up around her, carrying torches to light her back to the Embassy. The fireworks continued to explode over the Palazzo Ducale and Luciano, waiting in the square, saw that Arianna's face was bereft of all colour except what their light shed on her.

*

Next morning the Palazzo di Chimici on the Via Larga rang with the cries of ladies' personal maids calling for warm water, curling irons, hairpins and combs, as four brides were arrayed for their weddings. In the Piazza della Cattedrale a baldachino of blue velvet studded with silver stars was erected to provide a covered walkway to the cathedral's east door, and a red carpet decorated with silver fleur-de-lys was unrolled underneath it to reach right to the end of the piazza, where the princesses would descend from the Ducal carriage.

The cathedral itself was filled with lilies – and soldiers. Members of the Duke's private army lined the walls, and up in the gallery above the High Altar, a body of archers encircled the base of the dome. In the vestry the Pope was being helped into his silver brocade cope. All morning guests kept arriving and filled up the pews of the body of the building.

Rodolfo and Sulien were invited but not Dethridge, Giuditta, Luciano or Sky. And certainly not Nicholas or Georgia, who weren't even known to be in the city. So two Stravaganti would be inside the cathedral and the remaining six outside among the celebratory crowds. Silvia and Guido would also be among the observers. Many Giglians had been up since dawn establishing their viewpoints and bringing their own food and drink. Every window and balcony that overlooked the Piazza della Cattedrale was filled with spectators.

In the Embassy, Arianna was in a panic of indecision. The cursed di Chimici dress was laid over her bed alongside the equally elegant – and much more comfortable – green and blue brocade she had brought from Bellezza. She paced up and down in her lace shift, her chestnut hair loose and tangled about her shoulders, to the despair of Barbara the maid, who was trying to dress it.

Arianna had not slept the night before and was glad of a mask to wear to conceal the dark circles under her eyes – but was it to be the diamond-studded silver one sent by the Grand Duke to match the dress or the green and blue shot-silk one that went with her Bellezzan gown? Rodolfo had advised against wearing Niccolò's present, once he had heard about the proposal and this way of giving an answer. But Silvia thought not wearing it would provoke a dangerous diplomatic incident at the weddings.

'How can you be so unsure, my Lady?' asked Barbara, who was about Arianna's age and on very confidential terms with her mistress. 'I would love to have the chance to wear that diamond one.'

Arianna stopped her pacing. 'That's it!' she said. 'You shall, Barbara! Why not? My mother used a double often enough and you and I are much of a size. If I wear the dress, the Duke will take that as my consent to his proposal. But if I can later say it wasn't myself in it, I will have bought myself a little more time. Say you'll do it!'

*

The Grand Duke was visiting the young brides in the Via Larga. There was a flutter of screens and towels and dressing gowns when he put his head around their doors. But the Duke just laughed; he was in an excellent mood and all these pretty young relatives of his just served to remind him that he might have a young bride of his own soon. He had brought them their wedding chests, each cassone painted with the scene that was soon to take place at Saint-Mary-of-the-Lily, of the four couples entering the cathedral under the di Chimici baldachino.

And inside each were the thick ropes of pearls and rubies he had ordered as their wedding gifts. The princesses were thrilled with the jewels and held them up against their wedding dresses, kissing the Duke with their hair still loose about their shoulders. He left their rooms in high good humour.

*

The guests in the cathedral craned their necks to see the lovely Duchessa of Bellezza enter on the arm of her father and take a seat of honour near the High Altar. She was resplendent in a dress of silver so oversewn with pearls and amethysts that the brocade could scarcely be seen between them. A silver veil covered her hair and she was masked as usual, but that did not stop the Giglian crowd from declaring her the most lovely young woman they had ever seen.

The Grand Duke, sitting in his place of honour, saw her come in wearing the silver dress and smiled. He sat back and prepared to enjoy the weddings; it would not be long before there would be another, even more important one, in his family.

The Duchessa was attended by a maid in a plain but rich dark green gown, who was herself remarkably pretty, though she wore her hair twined in a double plait around her head and no jewels in it. The Pope and his attendants entered, taking their places at the altar with the Bishop of Giglia who was to assist at the ceremony.

Outside the cathedral the Ducal carriage had arrived at the edge of the square and a great flurry of dresses and veils was gradually emerging from it. Four nervous bridegrooms waited on the red carpet to receive their brides. First to extricate herself from the carriage was Caterina, in a dress of silver and white brocade. Then came the two Fortezzan princesses, the redhead in her green and gold and the brunette sister in her pure white satin scattered with white jewels.

Finally came Francesca in her Bellezzan white lace with her black hair full of pearls. Each groom thought his bride the loveliest, which was quite as it should be. They took hands under the baldachino and processed slowly into the cathedral, the three Giglian princes preceding their cousin Alfonso.

At various points around the cathedral the Stravaganti linked minds with the two of their

Brotherhood who sat inside it. Power flowed back and forth among them, creating a force-field which held the great building suspended in their protection. The wedding procession music came to an end and the Pope intoned the opening words of the Nuptial Mass.

Camillo Nucci, sitting with his parents and his brother and sisters looked up at the gallery and saw the archers, their bows already strung and arrows nocked. 'Not here, then,' he murmured to Filippo.

It took an hour and a half to marry the di Chimici nobles to their brides. By the end of the ceremony, the young Stravaganti were exhausted by their concentration on their task. As the bridal couples stepped out on to the red carpet and the crowd cheered and the silver trumpets blared and the bells rang from the slender campanile, they allowed their minds to relax.

And at that moment a dark rain cloud blotted out the sun.

Chapter 22

Blood on Silver

The Church of the Annunciation was a traditional place of pilgrimage for newly-weds. It sat at right angles to the orphanage, in the square where Luciano had fought so often with Gaetano. Three hundred years earlier a monk had painted on one of its walls a fresco of the Angel appearing to Mary with news of her expected child. At least, he had started to. The Virgin was depicted at a prayer desk and there was the body of a winged angel on the left, carrying a sheaf of lilies. But the unnamed monk didn't know how to paint the Angel's face.

The legend was that he had prayed for help and in the night the Angel himself had come and finished the picture. Over the generations a custom had developed for just-married couples to take bouquets of flowers to lay in front of the miraculous picture, so that the Angel would bless their union with children. If he did, they were fruitful and, if not, well, there was always the orphanage nearby, where there would be a supply of babies to fill the gap.

The di Chimici were no less superstitious than any other Giglian and the Duke was anxious to have grandchildren, so it had always been a part of the wedding plans that the four couples would go in procession to the Church of the Annunciation and lay their wedding flowers before the Angel. It was only a short walk from the cathedral.

The narrow street linking the two squares was lined with cheering citizens, and more hung out of the windows, greedily soaking up the sight of the fine dresses and jewels. Since the church was much smaller than the cathedral, only some selected guests followed the young people, the rest going on to the Palazzo Ducale, where another banquet was in preparation. The first fat drops of rain started to fall as the bridal procession left Saint-Mary-of-the-Lily.

Rodolfo and Arianna were among the procession, the Duchessa still accompanied by her maid. But it was a nightmare for her bodyguards in that narrow street. A thought-message from Rodolfo sent Sulien and the other Stravaganti running up the parallel side roads, so that they could reach the Piazza of the Annunciation before the wedding party. They were joined there by Guido Parola, sent on by Silvia, who was alarmed at seeing her daughter disappear up the narrow Via degli Innocenti. The square was full of spectators – all the people who couldn't get into the Piazza della Cattedrale had crowded in and were perching on the fountains and lining the arched loggias of the church and orphanage.

Among them was Enrico the spy. He hadn't been invited to the wedding, the blessing or any of the banquets and he was feeling a bit peeved about it. Hadn't he been involved in all the safety precautions and kept the Duke informed every step of the way? He could see now that the procession was virtually unguarded and he shrugged. Amateurs, he thought.

The red carpet that had been laid all the way from the cathedral to the church was darkening with the rain and the brides were jostled by the crowd as servants tried in vain to cover their heads against the worsening weather. The archers and soldiers from the Duke's private army streamed into the piazza, pushing spectators out of the way, aware that they had been held up by the crush on the way there.

Sulien and Dethridge tried to marshal the Stravaganti into a new circle of strength, but the rowdiness of the crowd, who had been drinking from their wineskins since early in the morning, and the confusion developing round the procession, made it hard for them to concentrate. Sulien could feel the younger ones slipping out of the link.

*

To the east of the city was a tributary of the river Argento. It had been filling all winter and the rains of earlier in the month had taken it to the top of its banks. As the di Chimici couples had left the cathedral in the city below, a thunderstorm had broken out and the tributary had overflowed. The Argento, already full to the brim, could not sustain any more water and broke its banks. Waves of turbulent river water spilled out over the city, hurrying through the centre.

*

The di Chimici newly-weds were glad to get into the safety and cover of the church. They filed along the aisle to the fresco in a chapel to the side of the High Altar, where they were greeted by the priest in charge. The Grand Duke, the Pope, the Duchessa and many other notables, including the Nucci, crowded into the church behind them. But there was not enough room for all the di Chimici armed men and many of them were stuck in the atrium outside the church's front door.

And that was when the Nucci struck. Camillo had been seething ever since he had seen the little dog snarl at Carlo in the Piazza Ducale. He had sat all through the long wedding service, watching the man he was now sure was his little brother's cold-blooded killer, while he smiled at his pretty bride, surrounded by all the pomp and splendour the di Chimici coffers could provide. And now he was being blessed by another priest with the promise of children. Where was the bride for Davide and the hope of his descendants? Locked in the grave.

As the couples walked slowly back up the aisle, accepting the greetings and congratulations of their friends, Camillo leapt in front of Prince Carlo and stabbed him in the chest.

The church erupted. Lucia snatched a candlestick from a side chapel and brought it down hard on

Camillo's head. Fabrizio, who had been just in front of them, swiftly slit the Nucci's throat. Filippo Nucci, howling with rage, hurled himself into the fray. And then all was a confusion of knives and swords.

More soldiers pushed into the little church. But Sky, Nicholas and Luciano, alerted by the cries from within, were before them. The Grand Duke and Fabrizio were both fighting with Filippo but he wasn't without supporters. There had been more Nucci and Nucci-sympathisers in the church than anyone had realised. The priest and the Pope and his chaplain were trying to herd the women up to the altar and away from the fighting, but Luciano arrived in time to see a young man strike at a slender figure in a pearl and silver dress.

Luciano ran through the crowd, his rapier drawn, but a red-haired figure had already tackled the assailant and was engaging him in fight. Before Luciano had reached them the Duchessa's maid had whipped out a merlino-dagger and stabbed her mistress's attacker.

Out of the corner of his eye the Grand Duke saw the famous silver dress, stained with bright blood, and saw its wearer collapse in the arms of two young men. He had time only to notice that one of them was the black-haired Bellezzan who had been Falco's friend, before he had to fight off the opponent who pressed him.

Fabrizio and Alfonso were also in single combat with Nucci. Nicholas snatched up a fallen blade and went to fight beside them. Guido Parola left the wounded woman with Luciano and ran to the side of Lucia, who was lying over the body of her dead husband, and dragged her with him back to the altar. She was hysterical. The clergymen were having the greatest difficulty keeping Caterina and Francesca out of the fray.

When the frantic Georgia at last managed to get into the church, ducking between blades, she saw a scene of chaos. She ran to Luciano, who was uninjured, but stricken, holding the body of Arianna in her fantastic dress.

'She isn't dead,' said the Duchessa's maid in a familiar voice and Georgia found herself looking into violet eyes. 'She mustn't be dead,' repeated the maid, who was not Barbara at all. Luciano continued to hold the inert body of the real Barbara, who was still breathing. Arianna in the maid's dress was holding a wicked-looking blade, still dripping with blood.

'We must get you both out of this madness,' said Georgia.

She could see Sky fighting beside Gaetano, the two of them assailed by three Nucci, and Gaetano went down even as she watched. And then Rodolfo was there, wielding a sword that she had assumed was merely ceremonial, defending Sky and wounding two of the attackers.

But gradually the Nucci riot was put down, as more and more di Chimici men got into the church. The remaining Nucci, including old Matteo, were held; they had suffered many casualties. Camillo was not the only one dead and Filippo was seriously injured. But the di Chimici had lost Prince Carlo and both Fabrizio and Gaetano were badly wounded. It looked as if three of the new brides could be widows before the day was out.

The Grand Duke strode round the church from body to body, blood welling from a gash on his forehead. Flowers lay trampled and stained underfoot. Sulien came and stood by his side, laying a hand on his shoulder.

'All my sons,' said the Duke wildly. 'They want to take all my sons!'

'Prince Carlo I cannot save,' said Sulien. 'But trust me with the others. Let me take them back to Saint-Mary-among-the-Vines and I will do all I can.'

But by the time litters had been made for the wounded and they had been carried out into the square, they found it inches deep in flood water – and rising rapidly. All the spectators had left, running back to save what they could of their own property. But such had been the noise and chaos within the church that no one had heard the shouts of warning outside.

'Quick,' said Giuditta, who had been out in the square with Dethridge and had organised everything. 'We must get the survivors to the upper floors of the orphanage.'

The door of the Ospedale was already open and the nuns waiting to help nurse the injured. One by one they were carried up – Fabrizio, Gaetano, the Duchessa and even, at the insistence of Beatrice, Filippo Nucci. Four soldiers carried the dead prince and laid him in a room on his own. The body of Camillo Nucci was tossed unceremoniously into a corner. The walking wounded followed, including Sky and the Grand Duke, but not before the latter had ordered any surviving Nucci to his dungeons, even the women.

The Pope brought the four brides up too, since there

was nowhere else safe to take them in time, above the level of the swirling waters. So, gradually, all the remaining guests at the most splendid weddings the city had ever seen found their way to the upper floors of the orphanage. Babies were crying, temporarily abandoned by their nurses, who were all needed to tend the wounded.

Giuditta corralled the shocked Georgia into tearing up bandages, cutting away clothes and fetching basins of warm water. Silvia materialised as if from nowhere, ashen when she heard that Arianna had been wounded.

'Where is she?' she asked, tight-lipped.

'Luciano is with her and her maid,' whispered Georgia. 'I think they swapped clothes.'

Silvia closed her eyes and Georgia thought for a moment she was going to laugh. But she just hugged her and said, 'Goddess be thanked!'

Sulien was going back and forth among the wounded. Fabrizio, Gaetano and Filippo were the most seriously injured and were unconscious. Sky had a slash on his arm that hurt like hell but he knew he had been lucky.

'Have you seen Nick?' he asked the friar.

'No,' said Sulien. 'Is he not among the uninjured?'

Duke Alfonso of Volana, though he had fought bravely, had suffered no hurt and had been put in charge of the women and of the other unwounded who had been taken up to the top floor.

'I'll go and look,' volunteered Sky. 'How's Gaetano?'

Sulien looked worried. 'They are all badly hurt. I don't know how I'm to help them if I can't get back to my pharmacy.'

'How bad do you think the flood will get?' asked Sky. 'When will we be able to leave here?'

'Not today,' said Sulien. 'We have had many such floods in the city before. Some are worse than others – usually the spring ones are less severe than the autumn ones. But even they can rise to six feet or more.'

Sky knew that would mean he and Nicholas couldn't stravagate back from the friary but he decided not to worry about it yet. He had more pressing worries, such as where Nicholas was.

*

In the Piazza Ducale the water had risen above the level of the loggia steps and invaded the banqueting platform. Servants had carried all they could into the palazzo as soon as the flood hit the square, and wedding guests who had not been invited to the Annunciation blessing had taken shelter inside the building, swarming up the great staircases to the upper floors. They now looked down over the wreckage of the feast and the shining surface of the waters, where only the day before young nobles had jousted in the sun.

Some startled guests came face to face with two large spotted cats who had been brought up to the roof by their handler. But the beasts were well-behaved and chained to a pillar by their silver collars. They shared a side of meat that the cooks had provided.

The soldiers who had been entrusted with the Nucci had not been able to march them back to the palazzo, whose dungeons were anyway flooded. The squad had broken up into a second riot as soldiers and prisoners scrambled for their lives out of the way of the incoming waters. Matteo and Graziella ran with their daughters and remaining supporters to a nearby tower of the Salvini family, who were sympathetic to their faction. They hammered on the doors for entrance, the water now up to their waists. Ladders were let down from an upper floor and they climbed up, the women hindered by their sodden wedding finery. But at last they were all safe, at least until the waters went down, and could give way to their grief for Camillo and their fears for the only remaining Nucci son.

*

Arianna tended Barbara herself, undoing the fastenings on the dress that had betrayed her into danger. Luciano refused to leave them, even though the maid was now in her shift and her white breast exposed, with an ugly bleeding gash in it.

'It was my fault she got hurt, Luciano,' sobbed Arianna. 'I didn't mean anyone but the Duke to think she was me. He said if I wore the dress, he'd know my answer to his proposal.'

'So he did ask you, then?' said Luciano, thinking how odd it was to be talking about this while people lay dying and the waters swirled through the city.

'You knew he was going to?'

Luciano nodded.

'It was last night, during the dance. He put the vile crown on my head.' She shuddered. 'And now Barbara may die because I was too much of a coward to say no straightaway.'

'Not if I can help it,' said Sulien, coming to the girl's bed. He examined the wound carefully and asked one of the nuns to bring him the remedies he needed. 'It's not too deep,' he said. 'A little lower and the blade would have pierced her heart. The attacker cannot have had a clear aim.'

'Parola foiled him,' said Luciano. 'But Arianna finished him off.'

Arianna was shaking. Her mother ran to her and caught her in her arms. 'You are all right?' she asked.

Arianna nodded. 'As you see,' she said, 'Barbara took the blow meant for me.'

'Quickly,' said Silvia. 'Get into that wretched dress and lay the maid's one across the bed.'

'Why?' asked Arianna.

'Because we don't know who attacked you and why,' said Silvia.

'It was one of the Nucci,' said Luciano. 'I saw him.'

'And you know a Nucci sympathiser from a di Chimici agent?' asked Silvia. 'The Grand Duke must have taken your wearing the dress as assent, Arianna. Let him go on thinking that for a while.'

Silvia helped Arianna out of the plain green gown and into the Grand Duke's gift. Her daughter hated it even more now that it was slashed by a dagger and stained with blood.

'Don't just stand there,' Silvia said to Luciano, who was trying to keep up with the turn of events. 'Get Arianna's hair out of those plaits, while I try and turn Barbara back into a maid.'

Arianna's hair tumbled down as Luciano uncoiled and released the braids. He passed her the silver mask and veil while Silvia undid the elaborate coiffure Arianna and Barbara had constructed together a few hours earlier. While she gently teased out the curls of it, Barbara revived. She looked at Silvia out of cloudy eyes.

'Brave girl,' said Silvia. 'You have saved the Duchessa's life.'

'And Parola saved hers,' said Luciano. 'He deflected the blade.'

'Did he now?' asked Silvia, interested. 'What a remarkable young man he is. Sulien, what can you do for the girl?'

Brother Sulien was bathing the wound with an infusion of herbs brought by the nun.

'This will help,' he said. 'But I'll need to sew the wound together. It will hurt, so I must give her a soporific. But I am greatly hampered by not being able to fetch things from my pharmacy.'

'I'll go,' said Luciano. 'Make me a list.'

'It's too dangerous,' said Arianna. 'The flood waters are still rising. How will you get there?'

'Don't worry – I'll find a way,' said Luciano.

*

Georgia ran into Sky on the stairs up to the higher floor of the Ospedale.

'Thank God,' she said. 'You're all right?'

'I've got a slash in my arm,' he said. 'But not too bad. Did you see what happened to the others?'

Georgia nodded. She didn't want to think about the bodies which she had seen carried out of the church.

'How's Nick?' she asked instead.

'I'm looking for him,' said Sky. 'I'm hoping he's upstairs with the uninjured people.'

They clung together for a moment on the stairs.

'It was so horrible,' said Georgia. 'I don't think I'll ever be able to forget it – the blood and the smell.'

'Me neither,' said Sky, patting her back awkwardly. He thought again how glad he was that Alice had decided not to return to Giglia. It hadn't been exciting and glamorous when the wedding attack came. It had been the most horrible quarter of an hour of his life. And in the end the Stravaganti had been powerless to stop it.

'Do you know if Gaetano is going to be OK?' asked Georgia.

'No,' said Sky. 'I reckon if anyone can save him, Sulien will. But he's cut off from his medicines.'

They walked up to the top floor, where Duke Alfonso had organised some fortified wine for the women and the other people who had not been hurt. His bride, Bianca, clung to his arm, terrified. He was the only uninjured groom and she could not believe that he had survived unscathed. His mother fussed over all the girls, especially her own daughter, Caterina, whose new husband lay badly hurt on the floor below.

Lucia, who had fought so bravely to save Carlo, though in vain, sat shocked and cold on the far side of the room. There was no sign of her parents, Jacopo and Carolina. Guido Parola had put his cloak over Lucia's shoulders and was trying to get her to sip the wine. The Pope, revived by the strong drink, turned to Alfonso.

'We must get them warm. They are all soaked and

shocked. Where are all the nuns?'

'Tending to the wounded, I expect,' said Alfonso. 'Perhaps Cousin Beatrice could help?'

'I'll find her,' said Sky. 'I know what she looks like.'

'Well, I have no idea who you are,' said the Pope. 'But if you can find my niece, I'll be grateful.'

'Have you seen a young Dominican friar anywhere?' asked Georgia. 'He was fighting in the church and we don't know if he's all right.'

But no one had seen Nicholas.

They found Beatrice with the Duke, who was sitting, dazed, while she bound his head. Sky ducked out of Niccolò's view and Georgia delivered the message.

'I'll come,' said Beatrice. 'Will you be all right if I leave you, Father?'

'I shall go to my sons,' he said, his voice slurred, as if from strong drink.

'That's probably where Nick is,' said Georgia to Sky. 'With Gaetano.'

They followed the Duke at a distance to a separate cell. Gaetano and Fabrizio lay very still on beds next to each other. Sulien stood over them with a grave face. But there was no sign of Nicholas. They looked into the room next door and Georgia could not suppress a cry. There was just one bed in this cell and on it lay the body of Prince Carlo, his wedding finery soaked in blood. Curled up between the bed and the wall, looking like a bundle of black and white rags, lay Nicholas.

*

Enrico's first instinct when the flood waters had entered the square was to climb up to the top of the orphanage. From the roof he had seen bodies and wounded people carried out of the church and he knew that everything had gone horribly wrong, even though he couldn't tell who had been hurt. His first thought was that he might be held to blame – his intelligence hadn't helped to prevent a slaughter. But he didn't even know if the Grand Duke had survived; he waited alone on the roof for some time before deciding he would have to find out.

Cautiously he descended the stairs, looking into a room which he at first thought was full of nuns. But they had curled hair and their pale faces still bore rouge and they wore jewels at their throats. It was the princesses, who now looked like the widows they might be, for all Enrico knew, clad in black robes brought for them by the nuns. Their sumptuous wedding dresses lay crumpled and sodden on the floor, including one that had once been of gleaming white lace. It reminded Enrico of the one his Giuliana had ordered for their wedding.

His eye was drawn to the little red-headed princess; she was being comforted by a similar-looking tall young man, who must be some relative. The only prince in sight was Alfonso, who seemed to be all right. Enrico sighed with relief; there was one di Chimici bridegroom left standing at least. There was no sign of the Grand Duke.

He went down another flight, to the first floor. There, the large dormitory, usually full of babies and children, had been cleared and the wounded laid on their beds. Enrico couldn't see any of the di Chimici princes. Sulien was busy among the wounded. A flash of silver suddenly caught the Eel's eye. He moved slowly into the room.

A screen was partially obscuring the bed beside which the Duchessa sat and she was surrounded by bodyguards, but Enrico could see that, although the silver and gems of the dress she was wearing were encrusted with blood, the Duchessa herself did not seem hurt. She was holding the hand of her maid, who clearly *was* wounded. The squeamish spy stuffed his fist in his mouth when he saw the mutilated breast. There was another, older woman, sitting by the bed, whom he scarcely registered. But his mind was racing. Why would the maid be hurt and the Duchessa be unharmed? And why was the Duke's gift-dress so stained if no one had attacked the Duchessa?

*

Luciano didn't leave Arianna until Silvia had rounded up the remnants of her bodyguard and posted them round the bed where her daughter sat, holding her servant's hand. Then he went to look out of the window and was shocked by what he saw. The piazza where he had so often fenced with Gaetano was a sheet of water. The tops of the two fountains stuck up out of it and gave him some idea how deep the flood was. About five feet, he calculated, and probably still getting deeper.

The tops of the buildings were all full of people waving and shouting in a kind of parody of the way they had behaved when the wedding procession entered the square. Luciano couldn't believe how much had changed in such a short time. But, in spite of his promise to Sulien, he didn't see how he was to get to the friary, collect medicine and bring it back here.

He went out on to the landing and met Georgia and Sky, with Nicholas slung between them like a sack of potatoes.

'What is it?' he asked. 'Is he badly hurt?'

'I don't think so,' said Sky, lowering the boy to the floor and wincing as his arm took the weight. 'He was with Carlo.'

'We think it's shock,' said Georgia. She was shaking herself. Suppose the Duke had gone next door to see his dead son and found two of them!

'I'll fetch Sulien,' said Luciano.

The friar was busy. He had left the two princes for the moment, having their wounds bathed by nuns, and was attending to Filippo Nucci, but he came straightaway when Luciano told him about Nicholas. He lifted the boy and took him over to the stairs, where he examined him for signs of injury.

'He has a wound much like yours, Sky,' he said. 'But I think his mind has closed down. He has seen one brother killed and two others wounded. He needs rest and medicine.'

'I'm going to the pharmacy,' said Luciano. 'Have you got that list?'

As Sulien gave him a scrap of parchment, Georgia asked, 'How are you going to get there?'

'Swim, I suppose,' said Luciano, trying to smile.

'Don't be daft,' said Sky. 'We need to find some kind of a boat.'

'We?' asked Luciano. 'Are you coming too?'

'Of course he is,' said Georgia. 'It was probably what he was sent here to do.'

'Oh my God,' said Sky. 'I'm hallucinating.'

He pointed outside the window and they all saw the black wings of the flying horse, with a brightly dressed Manoush on her back.

Chapter 23

Drowned City

Sandro hadn't been at the wedding or the blessing either. He had drifted back to the Piazza Ducale, pleased that there hadn't been any attack and hoping to find some more scraps for him and his dog when the next feast started. He was hanging around the platform when the rain began and minutes later the flood water came swirling into the square.

He ran, then, up the steps of the loggia and sat at the top, hugging the scared Fratello and sheltering from the rain. He didn't think that it would last for long. Sandro had heard a lot about floods in Giglia but hadn't seen one in his short life. The little dog was trembling but Sandro himself was not frightened.

At least not then. The water was only inches deep. But then he saw wedding guests hurrying into the palazzo and the water still rose. And later, citizens came splashing through the piazza shouting about an attack. They hadn't stayed to hear what had happened in the Church of the Annunciation but rumour spread through the city: all the di Chimici had been assassinated; the Grand Duke was dead, stabbed by the Duchessa of Bellezza with his own sword.

Sandro thought he would let the news settle down like the flood water and leave a silt of truth he could sift through later. But the water had now reached the top of the steps and Sandro couldn't swim. He tucked Fratello under his arm and began to climb on to the back of a lion sculpted by one of Giuditta Miele's ancestors.

*

Georgia ran up to the roof with Sky and Luciano. Never had she been so glad to see anyone as Raffaella and the flying horse. It had been nagging at the back of her mind that she didn't know how she would get back to Remora by nightfall if she couldn't get to Merla on the other side of the river. But she had felt bad even for thinking about it when she didn't know if Gaetano would survive his injuries.

Sky stood gazing at the winged horse in wonder. In spite of everything he had been told about Merla, the reality of her was so much more overpowering than any description.

Rafaella dismounted.

'Aurelio sent me,' she said. 'He seemed to know where you would be.'

'Can you help us?' asked Georgia. 'We need to get

medicine from Saint-Mary-among-the-Vines. Is the whole city flooded?'

'Certainly between there and here,' said Rafaella. 'But I can take Merla up again and look for a boat.'

'Do you think she'd carry both of us?' asked Georgia. 'Perhaps I could bring one back?'

No one liked the idea but Georgia persuaded them on the grounds that she was the lightest and the best rider.

'It's not the riding I'm worried about,' said Sky. 'It's the dropping into a boat.'

He and Luciano watched the two young women take off on the flying horse.

'She's got guts, all right,' said Luciano.

From the air the city looked like a dreamscape: only the biggest buildings seemed the same. But the piazzas were lakes and the streets canals; fountains and statues and pillars poked up above the water like drowning people waving desperately for help. The river, no longer defined by its banks, had spread like a stain into every corner of the city.

But in the end Georgia did not have to be dropped into a boat. Raffaella landed Merla on the Ponte Nuovo. The horse didn't like it: it was narrow and dangerous for her wings and the water rose over her hoofs. But it was only inches deep here and Georgia was able to splash through it down to where boats bobbed on the surface of the flood, tugging at their painters tied far below the water. Raffaella cut the rope of one with a dagger from her belt, as far under the surface as she could reach.

'I'll take Merla back to the orphanage roof,' she said. 'You'll still need her to get back to Remora tonight.'

Georgia nodded. She was struggling with the boat. She had never rowed one before, except once on the Serpentine in Hyde Park, and everything was wet. Her dress and hair were soaked, the bottom of the boat slopped with rainwater and the oars were slippery and very heavy. A cold wind lashed the flooded river into waves and she couldn't at first see where she was going for her wet hair whipping into her face. And she hadn't quite got the hang of travelling backwards and was scared of bumping into hazards she couldn't see.

But gradually she managed to steer the boat up between the pillars of the square where the Guild offices were. The city was eerily quiet and she shivered as she rowed awkwardly into the Piazza Ducale. It was so weird to think her boat was sliding forwards nearly her own height above yesterday's tournament lists. The last thing she expected was to hear her name shouted.

It was Sandro, sitting on a stone lion with his little dog clutched in his arms. Cursing under her breath at this new complication, Georgia tied the boat to the lion's leg and coaxed him down into it. It was doubtful whether Sandro or the dog was more alarmed by the rocking motion of the boat as they got into it. But Sandro's teeth were chattering and he had been very frightened, alone with no prospect of the water withdrawing.

'I'll take you to the orphanage,' said Georgia. 'That's where all the others are.'

'What happened?' asked Sandro, trying to warm the dog inside his jerkin.

'Where do I begin?' asked Georgia, casting off again. 'Do you know how to row?'

'I can try,' said Sandro.

Georgia looked at his skinny arms and undernourished frame.

'No, it's OK. I can manage till I get there. But then I'm leaving it to Luciano and Sky.'

'Brother Tino?' asked Sandro. 'What are they going to do?'

'They're going to the friary to fetch medicine for Brother Sulien,' said Georgia. 'You know the Nucci attacked at the church?'

'I heard people shouting something,' said Sandro. 'But I was stuck on the loggia and couldn't find out anything.'

'Lots of people have been killed or hurt,' said Georgia. 'Gaetano and his oldest brother are seriously injured and Prince Carlo is dead.'

Sandro jumped so violently it rocked the boat. 'I'm not sorry,' he said. 'He was a murderer.'

'But Gaetano isn't,' said Georgia. 'And we must do what we can to save him.'

They had reached the drowned Piazza of the Annunciation. Sandro helped Georgia navigate past the fountains and up to the orphanage. The front door was still open and the ground floor flooded in spite of the steps leading up to it. They had to pull the oars in while the boat slipped through the door, but once inside they were able to tie it up to the stone banister of the staircase. Fratello leapt out of the boat, shaking himself, and ran gratefully up the steps, looking back to check that Sandro was following.

Sky was amazed to see the little spy, particularly when he told him how he had got there. Georgia soon appeared, looking very bedraggled. Sulien was relieved to see her but still anxious to get what he needed for his patients.

'I'd go myself,' he said. 'But I am needed here. You're sure that you and Luciano will manage, Sky?'

Sky's arm had stiffened up and was really hurting. He didn't think he'd be much use at rowing but he knew where to find most things in the pharmacy. And Luciano was the least afraid of water of any of them; he was a first-class swimmer and lived in a city where the streets were canals.

'Take this key,' said Sulien. 'The most important thing I need, and the one I can't replace quickly, is in a locked cupboard in my cell. The jar says "argentum potabile" and it's the only thing that will save the young princes.'

'Right,' said Sky, more confidently than he felt. He put the key in his pocket.

'Let me come too,' said Sandro. 'I'm not heavy and I know where everything is.'

Sulien agreed. 'Take him,' he said. 'He might be very useful.'

'Only look after my dog,' said Sandro. 'He won't want to get back in that boat.'

'I'll look after him,' said Georgia, taking the sodden length of string round Fratello's neck. She suddenly felt exhausted, but there was plenty of work left to do in the orphanage and Giuditta needed her.

The boys ran down the staircase to the drowned hall. Luciano took the oars and Sky sat at the other end, with Sandro crouched damply in the bottom of the boat.

They glided out into the piazza as Luciano struck out west from the orphanage, trying to find a navigable street that would take them south to the Dominican church. Saint-Mary-among-the-Vines lay even closer to the river and had been one of the first areas to be flooded. When they reached the piazza in front of it, they could see just the tops of the wooden obelisks sticking up through the water.

'The cloisters will be flooded,' said Sky, 'and the pharmacy will be under at least five feet of water. What are we going to do?'

'We've got to try,' said Luciano. He manoeuvred the little boat through an archway beside the black and white church and steered right into the Lesser Cloister.

The arched cloister was underwater and Sky realised that all the plants and vegetables would be ruined. They had to take the boat across to the far corner of the cloister and steer it along a corridor, with their heads almost grazing the ceiling. But then they were through and out into the Great Cloister where the pharmacy and Sulien's cell were. Sandro cried out when he saw the devastation caused by the water.

The door from the cloister to the laboratory had been open when the flood came. Alembics and crucibles floated about, and bottles and jars had been smashed by the force of the water pouring in.

'This is hopeless,' said Luciano after a few minutes' fruitless search. 'There's nothing in one piece from his list.'

'How about the stuff in his cell?' asked Sky. 'The medicine in the locked cupboard might be OK.'

But here was a problem: the door between the laboratory and Sulien's cell was closed, with a weight of water holding it shut. They manoeuvred the boat back out into the cloister.

'Look,' said Sandro. 'There's a skylight I could climb through.'

It was true. There was a small, glazed fanlight that led into Sulien's cell, and neither of the other two would have been able to wriggle through it. Luciano smashed the glass with an oar and Sandro took the key from Sky. They watched as he climbed in, then heard a splash and a cry as he landed on the other side.

'Oh God, don't tell me he can't swim!' said Luciano.

*

Enrico flitted from room to room in the orphanage. He had seen the body of Prince Carlo and the near-corpses of the other two princes. But something else was niggling at the back of his mind and preventing him from concentrating on the present scene. Something to do with the Duchessa and her maid.

He was jolted out of his trance by the Princess Beatrice.

'There you are!' she said, for once pleased to see him. 'I need you to help me.'

Beatrice, Giuditta and Georgia had formed a sort of nursing team with the nuns, carrying out instructions from Sulien and Dethridge. There were all the orphans to look after as well as the injured and the roomful of traumatised princesses. The nuns were also in a great flutter at having the Pope himself under their roof, not to mention the Grand Duke of Tuschia. They kept

Enrico busy running up and down stairs on errands. It was not long before he found himself taking wine to his master, and he didn't know how he would be received.

But Niccolò did not hold Enrico responsible for the attack; he knew very well whom to blame. Had he not seen with his own eyes Camillo Nucci stab his second son? Enrico recognised the feverish look in his master's eyes; the Duke had been the same when young Falco was dying. Now the only thing consoling him for Carlo's death was the thought of the revenge he would take on the Nucci. It didn't seem the right moment for the Eel to tell his master that the young Duchessa hadn't been wearing the expensive dress he had given her; he would try to let him know later that it was the maid who had been hurt. But perhaps he wouldn't mention that she had been impersonating the Duchessa at the time. Enrico had a feeling that information would make the Grand Duke very angry, even though he was too distracted at the moment to think of courtship.

*

Sandro surfaced, spluttering. He was terribly afraid. The water was cold and his feet couldn't touch the bottom. He flung out an arm and found himself clutching the top of the wooden crucifix on the wall. He held on to it as to a lifebelt; he knew what it was – the suffering man, like the one who hung in the church. The princes were suffering too and perhaps he, Sandro, could save them. He waited, floating on the top of the water, anchored only by his hand on the cross, getting his bearings in the little room.

A face looked anxiously through the skylight. Sandro waved with his free hand and then saw the cupboard. It was a triangular wooden one high up in one corner. It had a keyhole and a wooden knob in the door. Sandro launched himself across the room, sank again, resurfaced and grabbed at the knob. It surprised him how little purchase you needed on a fixed point in order to stay afloat. He had the key clutched in his hand. The water came up nearly to the keyhole but he was able to unlock it and wrench the door open.

The shelves inside were full of packets and bottles, Sulien's most precious remedies. 'Ar-gen-tum pot-a-bil-e,' Sandro spelt out from the label on one bottle; he had no idea what it meant.

'He's got it,' said Sky outside the fanlight.

Sandro thrust the hand with the bottle in it as far towards the little window as he could. He pushed himself as far away from the cupboard as he could manage without letting go of the door. There was still a gap of about six inches. Sky reached his arm through, cutting it on the broken glass.

Suddenly Sandro thought, It doesn't matter if I drown. What matters is getting Sulien's medicine to the people who need it.

He thrust away from the cupboard. Sky grabbed the bottle as the boy sank.

*

The rain had stopped. The water in the city was no longer rising, though it would be a while before it began to sink. The friars at Saint-Mary-among-the-Vines had taken shelter on the upper floors. Brother Tullio looked out over the drowned cloister, shaking his head. How was he to feed the brothers with all his produce underwater? He just hoped something had been saved at the new farm across the river, which was on slightly higher land.

Tullio blinked. There was a boat in the cloister, rocking dangerously just under a broken window. His first thought was looters, then he saw that although the two young men in it appeared to be nobles of the city, one of them was young Brother Tino.

He watched while they poked an oar through the window and a bedraggled, wretched figure appeared clutching the end of it. It was clearly a rescue mission, not a burglary.

*

Sandro had panicked when he went down and found himself on the floor of Sulien's cell. But the water was not far above his head. He opened his eyes and saw he was just by the wooden chest in which Sulien kept robes. He managed to get one foot up on it and push his head above the water, shaking his hair out of his eyes. And there was the oar. Sky pulled him towards the fanlight, nearly capsizing the rowboat in the attempt. But once Sandro had reached the window frame, he wriggled through and collapsed in a wet and shivering heap on the floor of the boat.

'Tino! Brother Tino!' shouted a voice from above them. Brother Tullio stood waving from a window on the upper floor. Luciano rowed over until they were underneath it.

'Where have you come from?' said Tullio.

'From Brother Sulien,' explained Sky. 'There has been a terrible fight at the blessing ceremony and there are people badly injured. He sent us for medicines but everything is ruined in the pharmacy and the laboratory. We've only got what Sandro managed to find in his cell.'

Brother Tullio peered down. 'Is that drowned rat young Sandro?' he asked. 'What does Sulien want?' he continued. 'The brothers brought everything up to the top floors that we could salvage.'

It wasn't long before a basket full of medicines was lowered to the boat and the boys were able to make the voyage back. Sky put the precious bottle in the basket with the other remedies and just then realised how lucky they were to have it.

'You read the label,' he said to Sandro and the street-boy grinned, trying not to let his teeth chatter.

*

It was beginning to get dark, and Georgia was wondering how much longer she dare stay in Giglia. But she didn't think she should leave with Nicholas still unconscious. How was he going to get back to his own world? Sky and Luciano had brought back the medicines, and a delirious Fratello had hurled himself at the filthy wet bundle which was Sandro. Sulien was even now administering his precious 'Drinking Silver' to the most seriously injured patients. There was very little of it because it was so costly and time-consuming to make; it was a secret process, taking months. He gave five drops each to Fabrizio and Gaetano and then made his way to where Filippo Nucci lay moaning and feverish.

'I forbid you to give it to that wretch,' said the Grand Duke.

But Sulien took no notice and measured out a dose for Giuditta to administer to the young man. Princess Beatrice herself restrained her father's hand or he might have attacked the friar in his grief.

'Very well,' he said, struggling to collect himself. 'Let him live. There will be one more Nucci for me to hang.'

Sulien went next to the Mother Superior's room, where he had hidden Nicholas, and gave him a drop of the valuable liquid. The boy's eyelids fluttered and Sulien breathed a sigh of relief. But he could not rest. Now that his medicines had arrived, he moved among the patients, stitching wounds and giving soporifics to ease pain.

By the time Georgia climbed wearily up to the roof, everyone who needed treatment had received some. But there were a lot of cold, wet and exhausted people for whom there was no food; all the stores had been on the ground floor and only a few bottles of wine were still usable. Merla was waiting for her, her wings drooping. She didn't like the water. Raffaella sat patiently with her, soothing the horse with one of her strange-sounding songs.

The two of them lifted off on Merla as she made her run off the roof, relieved to be heading back out of Giglia and towards dry ground.

*

It took all Sky's powers of persuasion to get Nicholas to leave with him. As soon as he was awake, the boy was determined to stay and see his brothers recover.

'Look,' said Sky. 'It's already getting dark outside and we're going to have to leave from here rather than the friary. Who knows if we'll even arrive back in the right place? And what do you think it'll do to Vicky if she finds you unconscious in the morning? Don't you care about your new family at all?'

'I won't be able to go to sleep anyway,' said Nicholas. 'Not with Gaetano and Fabrizio like that.'

'You can't be with them,' said Sky. 'You'd be recognised by your father or sister. And you can come back tomorrow.'

'I'll give you both something to help you sleep,' said Sulien. 'You do have your talismans with you? All you have to do is think of your home in the other world. And I promise you I shall do everything in my power to keep your brothers alive until you return.'

'What on earth have you done to your arm?' said Rosalind when she went to wake Sky up. She thought he had just overslept but of course he had stravagated back late. Sky was so relieved to find himself in his own bed that it took him a few minutes to register what she meant about his arm. There was a very un-modern looking bandage round it and he could see the flesh round it was swollen.

'I cut it fencing,' he said, which was the best he could manage.

'Well, why didn't you say something last night?'

demanded his mother. 'Let me see if it needs stitches. We must get you to the hospital if it does.'

'It's been stitched, Mum. Don't fuss,' said Sky. He felt awful – deathly tired and his arm was throbbing – but he had to find out what was going on at Nicholas's and somehow get through a day at school.

'What do you mean?' asked Rosalind. 'When did you go to the hospital?'

He was saved any more questions by the phone ringing. He sat up groggily, nursing his arm. Remedy came and head-butted him. Sky felt like bursting into tears – delayed shock, he supposed. He was just beginning to realise that he could have been killed in Talia, stabbed like Carlo. He couldn't get the image of the dead prince out of his mind.

'Well, that's that!' said Rosalind from the doorway. 'No more fencing for you! That was Vicky Mulholland on the phone. She says that Nick's been injured too and won't tell her how it happened. You're both going to have the day off and we're taking you to the doctor. I want those stitches looked at – Nick told Vicky he'd had some as well.'

She let him have breakfast first though, and he was ravenous. Sky managed to ring Alice on her mobile.

'How was the wedding?' she asked.

'Awful,' he whispered. 'We're all right, but Nick and I were both wounded and his brother Carlo was killed.'

'Wounded?' gasped Alice. 'Are you OK? What happened?'

'I'm OK but Mum's suspicious. Other people were hurt too – I can't say any more now. Mum and Vicky are taking Nick and me to the doctor. Get Georgia to tell you everything and I'll see you after school.'

Silvia looked out of the orphanage window over the dark city. She was no longer worried about Arianna; even Barbara was sleeping peacefully, her wound having been stitched. But it was going to be a long night, with no lights in the city and no warmth in the orphanage and very little food. And then she blinked, unable to believe what her eyes were seeing.

Prince Jacopo was standing in the prow of a large boat, lit with torches and laden with supplies. At the other end stood a tall dark figure holding aloft a glowing red stone.

'Rodolfo!' said Silvia and ran down to meet him.

The barge was too big to get in through the main door, so the little rowboat found by Georgia was used to ferry people and provisions into the orphanage in stages. Jacopo left his men to unload and demanded to be taken to his daughters. Lucia flung herself into his arms and wept properly for the first time. It shocked Jacopo to see her and Bianca dressed as nuns, reminding him of his sisters. He knew that Lucia's bridegroom was dead but he was relieved to see Alfonso alive and looking after Bianca.

'Where are the other princesses?' he asked Beatrice.

'With their husbands,' she answered. 'Oh, Uncle, we don't know if Fabrizio and Gaetano will last the night.'

'We have brought food and drink and dry clothes and blankets,' he said. 'The Regent of Bellezza has been helping. You must all take heart. Things will look better in the morning.'

'Not for me,' said Lucia. 'Nothing will ever be better again.'

Rodolfo went from room to room, placing his firestone in hearths and warming whole wards of patients. He found Arianna sleeping fitfully on the floor beside Barbara's bed and covered her with a warm blanket. Her bodyguards were still on duty around the screen. All those who were awake were given food and wine. Sulien was still working, his face looking grey with fatigue in the candlelight. The Grand Duke and his daughters-in-law kept vigil over the unconscious princes.

Rodolfo and Silvia made Sulien sit down and have something to eat. Dethridge, Giuditta and Luciano joined them.

'You have done all you can tonight,' said Rodolfo.

'And yet we failed,' said Sulien. 'Eight Stravaganti and we could not stop the slaughter.'

'Perhaps it would have been worse without us,' said Giuditta.

'And you and Doctor Dethridge were marvellous about getting this place turned into a hospital,' said Silvia.

'Thatte was just physicke,' said Dethridge. 'Brothire Sulian is righte. Wee sholde have bene able to forestalle the murthers.' He cast his cloak over his head.

'Do not despair, old friend,' said Rodolfo. 'There is work yet to do and other deaths we may prevent. The Duke will need restraining even if both his remaining sons survive.'

Doctor Kennedy was completely perplexed by the two sword wounds.

'They have both been expertly stitched but with very out-of-date materials. Where was this done?'

Neither Sky nor Nicholas would answer.

'I doubt if the wounds were even sterile,' she said, frowning. 'Were you given anti-tetanus?'

The boys shook their heads and were both given shots by the nurse. Doctor Kennedy wrote out prescriptions for antibiotics and strong painkillers.

'Just to be on the safe side,' she said. 'But it would cause more trauma than it's worth to restitch the wounds. Whoever was responsible for this bit of fancy embroidery knew what he was doing.'

The boys would say nothing more than that they had both been hurt fencing, however much the women nagged them. Sky couldn't explain the scratches on his other arm, from the broken glass, and Nick had the beginnings of a black eye.

Vicky said she was going to phone the school and complain to Mr Lovegrove but Nicholas stopped her.

'We weren't in school,' he said. 'It was an accident.'

Even that cost him a lot, letting Vicky and Rosalind think that they had done this to each other when all their injuries were the fault of the Nucci. The two women didn't know what to make of it, but it seemed clear to them that there was no hard feeling between Sky and Nicholas and that it was safe to let them be together. The two boys spent the rest of the day at the

Mulhollands' house. Their foils were taken from them and locked in a cupboard, though Vicky was surprised to find them unstained and still bated.

Chapter 24

God's Puppy

Dawn broke in Giglia over a dismal scene. The flood waters had retreated and the fine city was filled with evil-smelling sludge and mud. For the new Grand Duke, however, it was a welcome sight. He didn't want to sit by his ailing sons' beds any more; he had lived through that experience once before. He had a city to organise. And Enrico was at hand to help him.

Beatrice was left in charge of the sick and injured at the orphanage while her father strode about giving orders, marshalling his army to collect sodden debris into heaps that could be dried out in the sun and then fired. Then every bucket and broom in Giglia was commandeered to bring well water and wash the squares and streets. The bodies that had been left in the Church of the Annunciation were brought out –

those of the Nucci faction to be hung by the heels on display in the Piazza Ducale, those loyal to the di Chimici washed and clothed in silk and laid in the chapel of the palazzo in the Via Larga. And first among them Prince Carlo.

The Pope was dispatched to purify the church itself from the bloodshed within, but not before he had gone to his Residence for a change of clothes and a large breakfast.

Damage to houses was less than it would have been in an English city; very few people had carpets or soft furnishings on the ground floor. And the Talian sun, which had so often been absent of late, was now back in full strength, shining into doors and windows, dispelling all mustiness from the wet floors and walls. The whole city seemed to steam in the morning heat.

Guido Parola had been sent by Silvia to the Bellezzan Embassy, for the State carriage, and he came back to the orphanage to collect Arianna and the wounded Barbara. Silvia went with them and Luciano rode on top with Parola. Gradually the nuns were losing their unexpected guests and were able to concentrate on cleaning up and looking after their usual charges.

A fleet of Ducal carriages took the exhausted princesses back to the Via Larga, to be tended and cosseted by their maids and their families. Soon the only ones who were left at the Ospedale were the two di Chimici princes and Filippo Nucci, being nursed by Beatrice, Giuditta and Sulien. Rodolfo and Dethridge had volunteered to go to the friary to see whether it could be made suitable to receive the patients. Sulien was anxious to have them near his supplies of medicine, depleted though they were.

He administered a second dose of Drinking Silver to the three injured young men but there was little of the precious liquid left. Both princes had intermittently regained consciousness, but not Filippo, who had lost even more blood than they had.

It did not take long for the Grand Duke to realise that his prisoners had escaped. He sent one team of men to comb the city for Nucci; they went from palazzo to palazzo and tower to tower of those families known to be sympathisers. It would be only a matter of time before they were brought to justice.

The new palace, into which the Nucci should have moved on that very day, had escaped damage altogether. It had been built on raised ground on the far side of the river and the flood water had not reached even up to its front gate.

Matteo Nucci doubted that he would escape with his life, let alone be allowed to take possession of his new home. He knew that they would not remain safe for long in the Salvini tower. He didn't fear so much for himself – what had he to live for now if all his sons were dead? – but he couldn't be sure that Graziella and his daughters would be spared Niccolò's wrath.

'Go now, my dear,' he told his wife. 'Take the girls and leave the city with what you stand up in. See if you can get to Classe and my brother's family. Amadeo Salvini will lend you some money, I'm sure.'

But Graziella wouldn't hear of it. 'With Camillo's body and perhaps Filippo's too still lying unburied in Giglia?' she demanded. 'Am I a mother or a monster? I am going nowhere, unless the . . . Grand Duke of Tuschia,' she spat, 'chooses to dispatch me.'

Alice and Georgia went round to Nicholas's after school, where he and Sky were still recovering from the Giglian battle. Alice couldn't rest until she'd seen their wounds.

'It's all right,' said Sky. 'Sulien did a good job of stitching us up and we've got all sorts of pills from the doctor.'

'That's more than my brothers have,' said Nicholas. He was very pale.

'But that stuff Sky brought back from the friary must be pretty good,' said Georgia. 'I'd back Sulien against Doctor Kennedy any day.'

'Really?' said Nicholas. 'I seem to remember I had to give up my entire life in Talia because no one there could cure me and your doctors could.'

Georgia was really worried about Nicholas. Ever since his first stravagation to Giglia and his wild idea about translating back, he had been a different person. She and Sky had both talked endlessly to him about the craziness of this idea, about the hurt he would inflict on the Mulhollands, the danger that his disability would return, the impossibility of taking up his old life in Giglia. And he had seemed to listen to them and accept what they said.

But now that he had seen his family attacked, it was different. There was a hardness and determination about him that reminded Georgia of his stubbornness when he had first decided to leave his world and come where he could be cured. Only this time she was not in his confidence; he said nothing to her about what he was planning and that made her very uneasy. And she didn't like to admit how hurt she was that he could think of abandoning her so easily to return to his family. Georgia had got used to being all-important to Nicholas.

'Are you going back tonight?' asked Alice.

'Of course,' said Nicholas, though it was Sky she had been asking.

Niccolò agreed to let his sons be moved to Saint-Mary-among-the-Vines, once he had inspected the infirmary. He had sent some of his own men to help with clearing up the mess left in the friary and its church. But he did not want Filippo Nucci to be nursed with them. In this, however, he was completely overruled by Beatrice.

'He is a young man as precious to his people as Fabrizio and Gaetano are to us,' she said firmly. 'Don't you remember how our two families played together when we were children? Why, Mother herself used to take him on to her lap and tell him stories. Where is his own mother now – dead or missing? For pity's sake, we should care for him, as we would want others to care for my brothers if we were not by.'

Niccolò was not used to this fierce side of his daughter and he let her have her way. But Sulien did not trust him and ordered three of his friars to keep a round-the-clock watch by Filippo's bed.

Giuditta had at last made her way back to her workshop, where she found that her apprentices had made a start on the clearing up. Their bedding was hung out to dry from the balcony outside her bedroom and the kitchen stove had been re-stocked with dry logs. The mud had been swept and washed from the tiled floor of the studio. But they had not touched the statues, which were all stained with a muddy high-tide mark, even the beautiful white Duchessa of Bellezza. Fortunately, she was on a raised plinth and looked as if she had been gazing out over the flood waters from her state barge.

'Maestra,' said Franco. 'We are glad to see you safe. We didn't know what had happened to you – there were rumours of bloodshed in the Piazza of the Annunciation.'

'Not rumour,' said Giuditta. 'Cruel fact. I have been tending the wounded.'

Stories about the slaughter had spread through the city. The bodies of the Nucci hanging in the Piazza Ducale and the black ribbons on the doorknocker at the Palazzo di Chimici had told some of the tale, and it was soon embroidered. But nobody expected the sight that was to be seen in the late morning. Matteo and Graziella Nucci, still in their bloodstained and muddy wedding finery, walked proudly from the Salvini tower to the Palazzo Ducale to demand the body of Camillo Nucci. It was not among the corpses displayed in the piazza, much as it grieved them to see nephews and brothers hanging there.

The Grand Duke himself came to the door when he heard who his petitioners were.

'It is not often that the fox comes willingly back to the trap,' he said, when he saw Matteo Nucci.

The old man knelt then in the muddy square.

'Do with me what you will,' he said. 'I care not. But

let us first bury our son and tell us whether there be another body, that of his brother, to bury with him. Then you will have robbed us of all our sons and we shall be ready to join them.'

'*I* rob *you*?' said Niccolò, incensed. 'I have a son of my own lying dead in my chapel and a daughter-in-law made a widow on her wedding day. And two more whose husbands' lives are in the balance, all because of your murdering boy. But you shall have his body, if someone cares to remove it from where my soldiers threw it in the orphanage. And as for the other, he lives and may yet survive to feel my vengeance.'

Matteo Nucci stood. 'I offer myself as hostage,' he said, 'if you will let my wife visit Filippo.'

'You are in no position to bandy terms with me,' snarled Niccolò. 'I could have you and your beldam hanged beside your relatives here, to make food for crows – yes, and your daughters too!'

'But you will not,' said the Pope, appearing beside his brother on the steps of the palazzo. 'There has been enough killing. Camillo Nucci must have his funeral rites, and these other poor wretches too. And I shall myself take Signora Graziella to see her son at the friary. As for Signor Matteo, there is no dungeon here dry enough to put him in. I suggest that he and his daughters and any of those remaining who took part in the attack surrender themselves to my authority. I shall house them at the Papal Residence under guard until they can be brought to trial.'

The Grand Duke could not show how displeased he was. His brother was Pope, after all, and ruled as Prince over the most important city in Talia, even if

Niccolò was head of the di Chimici family. Never had Ferdinando defied him before – and in public too.

Rosalind was at her wits' end. Just as she was feeling physically better than she had for years and was embarking on her first proper relationship with a man since Sky had been born, his father had suddenly appeared out of nowhere. And now Sky seemed to be going off the rails. It perhaps wasn't surprising that he hadn't wanted anything to do with the Warrior. But this business of injuring Nicholas, and getting hurt himself, in what had obviously been a no-holds barred fight, and then clamming up about who had treated their wounds – well, that was completely unexpected.

He had been a model son for the last three years, devoted and coping cheerfully with all the extra demands that her illness had placed upon him.

'Perhaps that's why,' she said to Vicky Mulholland, the day they took the boys to the doctor. 'It hasn't been a natural life for a teenager, never going out and having all that extra responsibility. Perhaps, now I'm getting better, he'll break out with all the stuff he's been suppressing for years.'

'But that doesn't account for Nick,' said Vicky. 'He's younger, of course, but David and I have never had any trouble with him until the last few weeks. He's been so – I don't know – depressed, somehow, and he never was through all that dreadful treatment and the operations.'

'It's a good thing they've got each other,' said Rosalind. 'And I would have said it was a good thing they had their fencing – until this morning. What do you think happened there?'

Vicky shook her head. 'I honestly don't know.' She hesitated. 'You'll think I'm crazy, I know, but there's always been something a bit, well, inexplicable about Nicholas.'

The Bellezzan Ambassador to Giglia was more than a little startled when his footman told him there was a man at the door with two leopards.

'He says they belong to the Duchessa,' explained the servant.

'Oh, my cats,' said Arianna. 'The Grand Duke gave them to me. They are not exactly leopards, but they are quite tame. Perhaps I could house them in your stables until I return to Bellezza?'

Enrico entered the audience chamber, without waiting for permission, with the two spotted cats on their leashes.

'Pardon the intrusion, your Grace,' he said. 'My master, the Grand Duke, asked me to deliver these to you, and a message to say that he would call on you this afternoon to see how your Ladyship is and to talk about his other gift.'

Arianna, blushing fiercely under her mask, hid her confusion by stroking the magnificent beasts. They already recognised her and rasped her hands with their rough tongues. She couldn't believe that the Grand Duke would pursue his suit while he had one son lying in state and two others on the brink of death. But then she remembered how he had ordered

Prince Gaetano to propose to her when poor Falco lay dying. He was as unstoppable as the flood.

'Take them to the stables,' ordered the Ambassador. 'And tell my people how they are to be fed and exercised.'

*

Nicholas and Sky were relieved to find that they were not under several feet of water when they stravagated back to Giglia that night. Sulien's cell was greatly damaged but more or less dry. They found Sulien himself with the wounded in the infirmary.

'It's over then, the flood?' asked Sky, while Nicholas went to his brothers. They were sleeping more naturally now.

'The waters have retreated,' said Sulien. 'But it will be some time before everything is back to normal. I'm glad you are both here. How are the wounds?'

He made them roll up their sleeves to show him. Nicholas was in his novice's robe, but it was damp and muddy. Sky was still in Gaetano's old clothes and they were stained with both blood and flood water.

Sulien nodded approvingly. 'You are healing well, with no fever. But you can't wear those wet clothes. All the robes in my chest were ruined, but go to Brother Tullio and he will kit you both out in dry ones. He rescued so much from the ground floor. Then come back to me – I have an errand for you.'

Brother Tullio had laid all the logs for his ovens out to dry in the sun in the Lesser Cloister; there had been no porridge for the friars that morning. But there had been beer saved from the barrels that floated on the flood and a great deal of Easter bread consumed. Sandro was eating some of it on the cloister wall, sunning himself beside his dog.

When Sky and Nicholas were newly clad as novices in clean dry robes, he joined them. Sandro had no desire to find his official master or to go back to the orphanage, where he had seen dead bodies. All his instincts kept him tied to the friary and the life-giving Sulien.

Sulien told them that Brother Tullio had rescued his parchment with the precious recipes and kept it safe on the top floor. Now he wanted Sky to go up to the Franciscan friary in Colle Vernale above the city and collect fresh herbs to restock the pharmacy.

'Do you think you could drive the cart?' he asked.

Sky hesitated just a little; he was honoured to be entrusted with such a mission but he really was not comfortable with horses.

'I can,' said Nicholas.

'And I know the way,' said Sandro eagerly. 'I'll go with them.'

So the three boys and the small dog left the city and rose above the smells and the factions and up the hillside to the friary. Sky couldn't believe how much had happened since he had first gone there with Sulien less than two months before. Giglia lay spread out beneath them, calm and beautiful in the sunshine. From here there was no sign of the violent events of the day before; it was hard to think that so few hours had elapsed since the outbreak of carnage and the flood that had overtaken it.

They rested the horses in the village and Sandro

dropped off the cart to race Fratello to the top of the hill.

'I love it up here, don't you?' asked Sky.

'Yeah,' said Nicholas. 'You can forget what a stinking mess the city is and just enjoy the beauty.'

'Are you all right, really?' asked Sky. 'I'm sure your brothers will get better. Sulien knows his stuff.'

'No,' said Nicholas. 'I'm not all right. Look, could you drop me off before we get back to the friary? The horses will know the way and I want to see Luciano. I guess he'll be at the Embassy with Arianna.'

*

Arianna was longing to get back to Bellezza but she couldn't leave while Gaetano's life was in danger. Both Francesca and Barbara needed her; her friend was in an agony of fear for her new husband's life and her maid was still in a lot of pain.

'Whatever I put my hand to seems to bring disaster,' Arianna said to Rodolfo. 'I should never have become Duchessa. It is too hard.'

'We are in a tight corner now, I agree,' said her father. 'But we have been in tight corners before and come out of them. You have to be brave a little longer – just long enough to refuse the Grand Duke without offending him.'

'And do you think he'll just accept my answer and let me go back home without taking any revenge?'

Rodolfo was silent. He had believed that he and all the other Stravaganti would have been able to prevent the kind of attack that had followed the di Chimici weddings. True, Arianna was safe, but many others had died or been injured. Could they still keep her safe if Niccolò di Chimici turned against her?

He pressed her hand. 'You'll have me and Luciano and Doctor Dethridge. Once you've refused the Grand Duke we won't leave your side till you're back in Bellezza.'

'His Holiness Pope Lenient the Sixth and the Grand Duke of Tuschia,' announced the footman.

*

Luciano was in the courtyard at the Embassy, making a few desultory passes with a rapier at a statue in the middle of a fountain. It was mud-stained up to its middle. He was relieved when the figure of a tall Dominican novice was shown into the court.

'Your technique isn't quite right,' Nicholas told him and took the weapon from him, showing him how to improve his grip. 'That's why Filippo Nucci was able to disarm you.'

'How is Filippo?' asked Luciano. 'And your brothers?'

'Sulien thinks they will all recover,' said Nicholas.

'That's wonderful. You must be so relieved.'

'Yes, of course,' said Nicholas. 'But that's not what I wanted to talk to you about. Luciano, do you ever feel homesick?'

Luciano was taken aback. 'Sometimes, yes,' he said. 'Is this about you? About wanting to come back?' Georgia had filled him in a bit.

'Not just me,' said Nicholas. 'It's about your parents too – Vicky and David, I mean.'

Luciano had never asked Nicholas about his living

arrangements in the other world; it was too painful.

'What about them?' he said, his face closed.

'They haven't got over it, you know,' said Nicholas. 'Losing you, I mean. I'm a good substitute but that's all I'll ever be. It's not like being their real son.'

'Why are you saying this?' asked Luciano. 'You know there's nothing I can do.'

'That's just it – there is,' said Nicholas. 'I've got a plan.'

*

Upstairs in the Embassy, the Bellezzan Ambassador was serving the famous red wine of his city to his most illustrious guests. The Pope was interested in the almond cakes that the Duchessa had brought with her from Bellezza; he was a great authority on sweetmeats.

'I have never been in the Embassy before, Ambassador,' he said good-humouredly. 'Perhaps you would care to show me around? I could bless any parts damaged by the flood. My chaplain here has a phial of Holy Water.'

'Certainly, your Holiness,' said the Ambassador. 'I would be honoured.'

'Won't you join us, Regent?' the Pope said to Rodolfo. 'I believe you were acquainted with my nephew when he was Ambassador to Bellezza, before he found his present vocation?'

Rodolfo and Rinaldo exchanged the thinnest of smiles; there had been no love lost between them at that time.

Rodolfo did not want to leave Arianna with the

Grand Duke but she motioned him to go. She wanted to get the forthcoming audience over with and she didn't believe she would be in immediate danger. After all, she had killed a man since Niccolò made his proposal. Arianna shuddered, remembering the feeling as she had plunged her dagger into the chest of the man attacking Barbara. There was no doubt that she had killed him, and she had no idea who he had been. For a moment she had understood what it must be like to be Grand Duke Niccolò di Chimici and to regard another human being as completely expendable.

But even while she was thinking these thoughts, the Duchessa of Bellezza had already asked after the princes and seen that Niccolò was genuinely concerned about them.

'I shall be happy to entertain your Grace's daughter-in-law Francesca here as long as I am in the city,' she said.

'That is most kind,' said the Grand Duke. 'And only what I would expect from such a gracious lady. I believe one of your own retinue was also injured. I am greatly relieved to see that you yourself are unhurt.'

'My maid took the force of the blow intended for me,' said Arianna. 'She will make a complete recovery.'

'I was honoured to see you wear my gift at the wedding,' said Niccolò. 'May I take it that you look kindly on my proposal? Of course we must delay the announcement until after Carlo's funeral and until Fabrizio and Gaetano are quite recovered, but it would give me great joy to be able to look forward to it.'

'What would you expect to happen to my city if I were to be your Grand Duchess?' stalled Arianna. Her mouth was dry and her heart pounding.

The Grand Duke was delighted; this was going better than he had hoped. 'Well, my dear,' he said confidentially, 'you would of course live here with me in Giglia. Perhaps the Regent could look after Bellezza for a while, but he will not live for ever. And your city is used to a female ruler. I thought perhaps my daughter the Princess Beatrice could become its Duchessa in due course.'

'So it would be a di Chimici city,' said Arianna softly. 'And I a di Chimici bride. Forgive me, but that does not seem a very safe occupation this morning.'

'Nowhere is safe in Talia,' said the Grand Duke. 'Least of all Bellezza if it stays out of alliance with my family. Come, my dear, it is time to put aside all enmity – what is your answer?'

'I prize the independence of my city too much to put it in your hands,' said Arianna.

'But you wore the dress,' said the Grand Duke impatiently. 'The dress was to have been your answer.'

'I did not wear it,' said Arianna. 'That was my maid. And she suffered for it. The blow was meant for me.'

'Ah, I understand now,' said Niccolò. 'You fear for your life if you marry me? Be assured that I shall look after you. No harm will come to my Granduchessa.'

'You could not protect Carlo,' said Arianna, more bluntly than she had meant to. The Grand Duke flinched. 'But that is not my only reason,' said Arianna, bracing herself. 'I cannot marry where I do not love.'

'That is a girl's answer, not a ruler's,' said Niccolò impatiently. 'I am not offering love, but good political sense.'

'I am a good ruler of my city,' said Arianna. 'But I am a girl too. And I am in love with someone else. If I can't marry him, I shall stay single.'

Niccolò was furious but remained icily polite. 'Might I ask who is my rival for your Grace's hand? Who can equal the offer of a Grand Duke of Tuschia?'

'That is a matter for my own heart,' said Arianna. 'There is no other offer and no engagement. I am very sensible of the honour you do me but I must decline. I cannot marry without love.'

And then it was over. The Grand Duke swept out of the room, white-lipped with rage. Arianna was shaking. She had always known that she could not accept his offer but she hadn't known how to do it. And in the end she had been on her own, without Rodolfo or Luciano to support her. She had gone head to head with the most powerful person in Talia and had no doubt that he would exact a terrible revenge.

*

Sandro and Sky got the cart safely back to Saint-Mary-among-the-Vines and unloaded Sulien's supplies. While the sacks of dried herbs were being used to restock the unbroken jars in the pharmacy, the Eel wandered in.

'Good day, Brothers,' he said, doffing his rather bedraggled blue velvet hat. 'I came to enquire after the princes. But I see my little Sparrow is here helping you. Good, good.'

'The princes are recovering well,' said Sulien. 'And I am grateful for the loan of the boy – Sandro has been most useful. Indeed, if it had not been for his efforts yesterday, I doubt the princes would have lived to see this day.'

Enrico was surprised. He couldn't imagine what Sandro could have done that would be medically useful, but he made a mental note that the boy was well regarded by the pharmacist-friar.

Sandro looked from Sulien to Enrico and made a decision. He was not officially apprenticed to the Eel; no papers had been signed. What he knew of his master was that he had taken Carlo to find a Nucci to murder. And he didn't doubt there were other murders in the Eel's past. But all his experience of Sulien was of healing and care for others, even to the point of teaching a street boy his letters and telling him stories. Sandro didn't want a life of running errands and telling tales for the Eel.

'I'd like to stay here,' he said to Enrico.

'Good idea,' said Enrico. 'You can bring me messages as to how the princes are getting on. And I want that Nucci kept an eye on too,' he added, lowering his voice.

'I don't mean that,' said Sandro. 'I mean I want to be a friar here at Saint-Mary-among-the-Vines.'

Sky and Sulien were as surprised as the Eel.

'But you can't even read or write,' said Enrico. 'How could you be a friar?'

'I think you'll find that he can read,' said Sulien. 'And we can teach him to write. That is, if you are serious about this, Sandro?'

'I am,' said Sandro. 'I want to be a Brother, like

Tino and you.'

Enrico didn't like it. He felt in some way that he had been robbed. But he made no objection; somewhere under the layers of his years of crime he had a glimmer of conscience that told him Sandro had made a good choice.

*

'You are seriously insane!' said Luciano, throwing aside his rapier and pacing up and down the courtyard. 'There is so much wrong with that idea, I don't know where to begin.'

'Why?' asked Nicholas. 'We've both done it before. And it would make everything right for our families.'

'Let's see, shall we?' said Luciano, ticking off reasons on his fingers. 'We'd both have to die again – I can't believe I'm even saying this – my parents would have to lose their foster-son and all my friends here would have to lose me. Then, if it did work, my parents and I would have to move away somewhere so that they didn't have to explain how come their son who had been dead for two and a half years had suddenly turned up again. And, oh yes, Prince Falco would also have suddenly risen from the dead, much to the delight and surprise of his family in Giglia. Good God, Nick, this is la-la land!'

'Not really,' said Nicholas. 'Talia is much more open to the supernatural than England is. I could probably get away with it here. I agree you couldn't pull it off in Islington, but I bet Vicky and David would be willing to move away if it meant they got you back.'

Luciano couldn't deny that.

'And perhaps it would get my father off the Stravaganti's back?' said Nicholas. 'He's never really believed our cover story about my suicide.'

'But what about my mum and dad?' said Luciano, tugging at his hair. 'I wouldn't even think of putting them through that again.'

Nicholas looked at him calculatingly. 'I could tell them,' he said.

'Tell them?'

'Yes. They know you're alive in another world. You told me yourself that they've seen you stravagate back a few times. I could tell them the whole plan. Just think about it, Luciano. You must want to see them again properly.'

And the awful thing was, although he still thought the whole idea was madness, Luciano knew that Nicholas was right. He did want to see his parents again – very much.

Chapter 25

Exile

The Pope's men brought the body of Camillo Nucci to the church of Saint-Mary-among-the-Vines and laid it out in a chapel, alongside five other Nucci corpses recovered from the Piazza Ducale. Graziella Nucci and her daughters found it there after they had visited Filippo in the infirmary. A friar had been sitting by the Nucci's bed when the women entered. Gradually Filippo was surfacing from his death-like sleep. Brother Sulien had given him the last few drops of the *argentum potabile*. And the Princess Beatrice was helping to nurse him as well as her brothers.

Graziella had shed tears of joy to see her last remaining son returning to life. But it was another matter when they were taken into the church.

'We shall have them all washed and anointed,' said

Sulien. 'The Pope has authorised it. They shall receive decent burial wherever you wish.'

Graziella bent over Camillo. 'Let him be buried with Davide in the same grave,' she said. 'And the others in the same chapel. Who knows how many of us shall join them?'

But she and her daughters stayed to help with preparing the bodies; it was the last thing they could do for their kinsmen.

*

The new Grand Duke was in a slowly simmering rage. He barked at his servants and wouldn't wait for his tasters but tossed back many goblets of wine and sent for Enrico. He had lost another son, been overruled by his brother and his daughter and now had been turned down by a chit of girl in favour of a youth a third his age. Niccolò had no doubt who was meant when the Duchessa had referred to 'someone else'. Who could it be but that black-haired Bellezzan youth, the Regent's assistant, who seemed to dog his every step?

And the Duchessa preferred this callow boy to a mature man with all the wealth and prestige of his house to offer her! It made him livid to think of the silver dress, the African cats and the costly brooch. Not that he wanted his gifts back; he would disdain to have them. He was not mean. But he was proud, and the slight to his honour and his person was more than he could bear.

Still, as he drank more, his angry mood settled into an equally dangerous calm. It was not that he had failed to anticipate this. He had always known that

Arianna might refuse him for this reason and he had a plan for how to turn it to his advantage.

'You sent for me, my Lord?' said Enrico.

'Yes,' said the Grand Duke. 'I want you to take my glove to that Bellezzan boy at the Embassy and challenge him to a duel.'

*

Arianna slipped out of the Embassy, accompanied by Guido Parola and her bodyguards, to visit Giuditta. The sculptor's apprentices were still cleaning her statue.

'It looks as I feel,' said Arianna. 'Stained.'

'The stain can be removed from marble,' said Giuditta. 'What has tainted the original?'

'I am ashamed of what happened to Barbara,' said Arianna. 'She is weak and in pain from a wound that should have been mine. But there is something else – the Grand Duke made his proposal a few days ago and I refused him finally today. He made it very clear that his offer was not motivated by love, and yet I fear he is deeply offended and therefore dangerous.'

'Did you give him a reason?' asked the sculptor.

'I gave him one I thought he would understand – that I was in love with someone else. But that is not all. He wants to take my city from me – the city my family has fought so hard to keep free and independent of the di Chimici.'

'Did you tell him who the other person is?' asked Giuditta.

'No, but I fear he will guess. Now I am worried that I have put Luciano in danger. It will be like Barbara all over again – maybe worse. It always seems to be others who suffer the consequences of my actions.'

'Why are you telling me this?' asked Giuditta. 'Why not talk to your mother or Rodolfo?'

'My mother thinks only of politics and they are both too concerned with my safety. I thought perhaps, as a Stravagante but not a politician, you might advise me.'

'I think it might be advisable to leave the city – at least for Luciano, if not yourself.'

'But don't you think he will be watched?' asked Arianna.

Their conversation had been conducted quietly, only Parola standing near enough to hear them, but now Giuditta raised her voice.

'I think we had better make arrangements for carrying your Grace's statue back to Bellezza,' she said.

Georgia had not stravagated to Talia the day after the weddings. She wanted to give Merla a rest, since the horse had made some of her journeys with two riders. And Georgia herself felt weary to her bones. She just couldn't face another night without sleep and full of exhausting adventures in Talia. So the two boys had gone with the pledge that they would tell her all about it the next day, which was Saturday in their world.

Georgia's parents were going to be out for the day so they were all going to meet at her house – Alice too. On the Friday, Georgia had an early night, leaving the model of the flying horse on her chest of drawers, where she could see it but not be tempted to hold it.

But in spite of these precautions, she dreamed about Giglia, reliving the moments in the Church of the Annunciation – the screams and the blood and the sight of people she knew and trusted turned into sword-wielding nightmares. And people she had always feared like Niccolò di Chimici appeared even larger than life in her dreams. He was standing with a bloody sword over the body of Luciano.

She woke in the middle of the night, sweating, and wondered whether to stravagate after all, just to check that Luciano was still alive. But she lay in the dark instead, thinking about him and about how little progress she had really made in getting over him since he had walked away from her in the circular Campo in Remora over a year ago.

The Pope had prevailed over his brother about the Nucci's lives but they were not to get away with their crimes unpunished. The Grand Duke issued a proclamation that anyone bearing the name of Nucci and any known to have fought by their side at the Church of the Annunciation were banished from Giglia in perpetuity and their property sequestrated.

'I see their new building was unaffected by the flood,' said Niccolò. 'Send Gabassi to me,' he ordered a servant. 'I shall take their palace in payment for Carlo,' he told the Pope. 'I no longer wish to live in the Palazzo Ducale. It has unpleasant memories. I shall live in the Nucci's extravagant folly and let

Fabrizio have this place. And I shall get Gabassi to build me a covered walkway above the city, elevated over any future flood waters, that will take me from the seat of government here to my new home there. It can cross the Guild offices and the bridge.'

'That is reasonable,' said his brother. 'I agree that Matteo Nucci should forfeit his property and be driven into exile. But let the wife and daughters remain until Filippo is fit enough to be moved from the city.'

'Very well,' said Niccolò. 'But they must stay in their old palazzo; I won't have them take possession of the new one. And I want another proclamation issued that Camillo Nucci was a murderer and would have been executed publicly if he had not already had the penalty exacted by Prince Fabrizio. I want that family disgraced and their name wiped from the memory of this city, except as the felons they are.'

*

Luciano was waiting for Arianna when she got back to the Embassy.

'I must talk to you,' she said.

'Me too,' he said.

She dismissed her guards. The two of them sat in silence for a while in the blue salon of the Embassy. Arianna was wearing one of her simplest dresses and a white silk mask, which she now took off. The Duchessa of Bellezza went unmasked only with her personal maid and her nearest family members; it wasn't often that Luciano saw her face now that she was ruler of a great city. It made him feel sad to see how tired she looked and so full of cares, compared with the light-hearted girl he had met in Bellezza.

But her beauty moved him as it always had, and the vulnerability she showed in unmasking before him made him feel even more protective of her than usual.

'You go first,' she said.

He took her hand.

'Nicholas has come to me with a strange proposal,' he said. 'He wants us to change places. For him to become Falco again and for me to go back to my parents.'

It was the last thing she had expected. But it made her shiver.

'Would that work?' she asked, playing for time. 'I mean, with the extra year's difference and everything? And wouldn't he be crippled again? And you, would your disease of the Crab return?'

'Is that what you would care most about?' asked Luciano, holding her hand tightly and looking her straight in the eye. 'That I would be ill again in my old world?'

It wasn't. But it was too much of a shock for Arianna to say what she really thought. Why was he telling her this unless he was seriously thinking of doing it? And how could he even think of leaving her if he felt as she had always hoped he would?

'What do you think?' persisted Luciano.

'I think you should talk to Rodolfo,' said Arianna shakily, 'and Doctor Dethridge and any other Stravagante. I'm sure there must be rules against translating back, or the Doctor would have suggested it after – you know – what happened to you in Bellezza.'

It was not what Luciano wanted to hear. He wanted her to beg him not to go, to say she couldn't live without him.

'What did you want to tell me?' he asked.

'The Grand Duke came for his answer,' she said.

'And what did you tell him?' he asked.

'I told him that I could not accept him, that I could not let Bellezza become a di Chimici city – he wanted Princess Beatrice to rule it.'

She did not repeat the other reason she had given Niccolò; she could not bring herself to say it now that she knew Luciano was considering leaving her for ever.

And so they parted at cross purposes and Luciano was completely unprepared for Enrico's visit.

He had glimpsed the Eel on more than one occasion in Giglia and always kept well out of his way. He aroused memories of the worst days of Luciano's life, when he had been kidnapped in Bellezza and held beyond the time he should have stravagated back to his own world. Well as the old Lucien had adapted to his new life, the Bellezzan Luciano could not look back on that time without pain.

And now his kidnapper had turned up at the Embassy, cool as a lettuce, and walked straight up to him and struck him in the face with a long leather glove! Luciano raised one hand to his smarting cheek and his other flew to the hilt of his weapon.

But Enrico raised his own hand to stop him.

'Hold there,' he said pleasantly. 'The blow was not from me and should be repaid to him who sent it. The Grand Duke Niccolò di Chimici challenges you to defend the insult given to his honour. He will meet you at dawn on Friday in the grounds of the new Nucci palace. You may bring two seconds.'

Luciano felt as if he were having a bad dream.

'What insult? There must be a mistake. I have not spoken to the Grand Duke since I dined with him a month ago. And I have never knowingly insulted him.'

'Too bad,' said Enrico. 'The Grand Duke has issued his challenge and if you refuse it you will be branded as a coward and subject to his persecution.'

'That's completely senseless,' said Luciano.

'So you refuse the challenge?' asked Enrico.

Luciano suddenly felt reckless. He had said he would kill Niccolò if he asked Arianna to marry him and now he had the opportunity to do it legitimately. It didn't matter that she had refused the Grand Duke; she had done it for the wrong reason. He would kill him anyway.

'Tell your master I'll be there,' he said.

Sky stravagated back to his world early that night, without waiting for Nicholas. He was as exhausted as Georgia and wanted to catch up on some sleep. He was confused about his role in Talia now. The Stravaganti hadn't prevented the deaths at the weddings, he had done what he could to help the injured and he no longer knew why he was supposed to be visiting the other world.

Perhaps it had all been to save Sandro from the Eel? The boy certainly wouldn't have offered himself as a novice friar, Sky was sure, if he hadn't befriended 'Brother Tino' and become closer to Sulien. Georgia had warned him that the reason he had been brought to Talia might be different from what he thought. She had believed she was needed in Remora to help Falco translate into Nicholas, but in the end she had replaced Cesare in the mad horse race and struck a further blow for the independence of Bellezza. But Sky didn't see what that had to do with him and his visits to Saint-Mary-among-the-Vines. In fact it made his brain hurt even to think about Talia. It had all got so complicated.

It had been much more straightforward when it had just been him and Sulien in the friary, and now it was all tangled up with Nicholas and Georgia, and even Alice. It had been much easier at the beginning to separate his daily life from his nightly journeys to the other world. Now they seemed to be sort of leaking into one another.

He woke early and set out for Georgia's house as soon as he reasonably could. Paul was going to be in town again and Rosalind was singing while she washed her hair. It seemed to Sky that being an adult was much less complicated than being a teenager – particularly a teenager who was a Stravagante.

When Sky got to Georgia's house it was Alice who opened the door. He put his arms round her, burying his face in her hair; it smelt good. He wondered if she had sung in the shower at the thought of spending the day with him.

'Are you OK?' she asked.

'Pretty much,' said Sky. 'My arm's a lot better and I came back early last night – I was so knackered.'

Georgia let them in and the three of them waited for Nicholas to arrive. Her parents had already left and the house felt calm and quiet. They made mugs of instant coffee and took them out into the garden with slabs of a chocolate cake Maura had bought. It was sunny and still warm, as it had been in Devon, and tulips were beginning to come up in the flower beds among the daffodils. They sat at the wooden pub table where barbecues were eaten in the summer and Georgia shared her worries about Nicholas.

'He's shutting me out,' she said. 'I've always known what he was thinking and planning before, but all I know now is that the signs aren't good.'

'Do you think he still wants to go back to Giglia?' asked Alice. 'Even though he's been stabbed there?'

'I think he wants it more than ever,' said Georgia. 'He's seen what his family has been through the last few days and it's bound to make him want to be with them.'

'I'd have thought he was well out of it,' said Alice, shivering in the warm sunshine. She couldn't wait for her friends to finish their Talian adventure. She just didn't understand the fascination it held for them.

'Georgia's right,' said Sky. 'I think he has got some sort of plan. He went to see Luciano today, after he'd checked his brothers were doing OK.'

The doorbell rang and the three of them jumped guiltily.

A body of the Grand Duke's soldiers accompanied Matteo Nucci and a dozen of his followers to the north-east gate of the city. He was glad that his route to Classe did not take him past the new palace where he and his family would never live. He had been allowed only the clothes he wore and the horse that would take him away from Talia. But Matteo Nucci had money in cities other than Giglia.

Graziella had accompanied him as far as the gate, promising to bring Filippo and the girls on to Classe as soon as possible.

'Believe me, I shall not stay a minute longer than I have to in this city,' she said bitterly. 'I can think of nothing better for us now than to live in a city where the di Chimici do not rule.'

They embraced then and parted.

*

In another part of the city, a young boy was being robed as a Dominican novice. He had to make his preliminary vows in the church; then he would be entitled to eat all his meals and spend all his nights quite legitimately at Saint-Mary-among-the-Vines.

'But you must give up swearing, gaming and keeping loose company,' said Brother Tullio solemnly.

'And you won't be able to keep the dog,' said Brother Ambrogio. 'Friars aren't allowed to have pets.'

Sandro looked absolutely stricken.

'Don't tease him,' said Sulien. 'Fratello sounds like a friar already. He shall be Brother Dog and live in the kitchen with Tullio. We need something to keep down the rats. Now, are you ready to take your vows?'

Sandro looked round; he wished that Brother Tino and Brother Benvenuto could be there to see him through the ceremony, but he understood that they could not be in Giglia at night-time; it was all to do with their shadows and their lives in the other world. But the encouraging smiles he was getting from Sulien and the others were enough to make him feel he belonged. He was going to get a family at last – not the kind of brothers he had once imagined and neither the Father nor Mother were where he could see them. But it was enough.

'I'm ready,' he said.

It was much worse than any of them had thought. Nicholas hadn't wanted to discuss it at first, but of course Georgia had wanted to know everything about his seeing Luciano, since she had missed a day in Giglia.

'Well, he told me he has to fight a duel with my father,' said Nicholas. It was true, but he had found this out only later. If possible he was going to keep from the others the plot he hoped Luciano would agree to. But this news was startling enough.

'A duel?' said Georgia. 'But surely he can't beat Duke Niccolò?'

'*Grand* Duke Niccolò,' Nicholas corrected her. 'It's true that Gaetano won't be able to help him. It will be weeks before he's strong enough to hold a sword. But Sky can be one of his seconds. He's allowed two.'

'How can you be so calm about it?' demanded Georgia. 'Even if Luciano could beat Niccolò in a fair fight – which I doubt – how can we be sure the Grand Duke will fight fair?'

'Why has he challenged Luciano now?' asked Sky.

'You'd have thought he'd be grateful for what he did when we got the medicine.'

'Luciano said his challenge was about an insult to his honour,' said Nicholas. 'But he didn't know what.'

'Maybe Arianna turned Niccolò down,' suggested Alice.

They all turned to her in horror; what she said made a kind of sense. If Niccolò was jealous, challenging Luciano to a duel was just the sort of thing he would do.

Georgia felt a pang – would Luciano fight the Grand Duke if Niccolò had proposed to her? Then the absurdity of the very idea overtook her and she laughed, a bit hysterically.

'He'll be killed, for sure,' she said. 'And there'll be no other life for him this time.'

Nicholas couldn't bear to see her so upset; he thought he would be able to console her.

'I wouldn't be so sure,' he said.

*

Niccolò di Chimici took possession of the palace over the river the next day. But Giglians kept the name for it; though generations of di Chimici grand dukes and princes would live there and no member of Matteo's clan ever set foot in it again, it was never known as anything other than the Nucci palace.

Niccolò had a good reason for moving in; his sons were recovering and he wanted them back under his own eye. The Palazzo Ducale felt tainted to him; he would always connect it with the remnants of wedding-feast finery washed up against the steps, his public humiliation by his brother and his proposal to the Duchessa on the night before the weddings, which had been all in vain.

The Nucci palace, undamaged by the flood, represented a new start, and the Grand Duke was good at new starts. He walked through the fine reception rooms, admiring the taste and wealth behind their decoration and furnishings. He ordered all the Nucci portraits to be taken down and representations of his own family put in their place; the Nucci coat of arms was also hacked off the stonework and hastily painted wooden escutcheons with the arms of the Giglian di Chimici fixed in their place.

Enrico walked through the palazzo too, a few steps behind his master and the architect Gabassi. The Eel was also in need of a new project and he was as taken with the grandeur of the palace as Niccolò was. He had a vision of becoming the Grand Duke's steward in his new home; what vistas of opportunities for skimming off silver into his own pocket were opening before him!

They moved up the grand staircase to the upper floors. The rooms were all furnished, the cupboards and chests full of linen and the library full of codices and manuscripts. All this was now di Chimici property because of the blow struck by Camillo Nucci in the Church of the Annunciation. The Grand Duke allocated bedchambers for himself and Beatrice and temporary ones for Fabrizio and Gaetano and their brides. They would keep Fabrizio here until he was well enough to go back to the Ducal palace and Gaetano until he could return to the Via Larga, where he would live as planned with Francesca.

Poor Carlo would have no more need of a palace and Niccolò made a mental note to talk again to Lucia. She would presumably want to go back to Fortezza with her parents, but she would go as a widowed di Chimici princess, one robbed of her future role as wife of the ruler of Remora.

He had already thought about Remora – Gaetano must have that title now and there would have to be another plan for Fortezza. The weddings had been such a promising scheme for increasing the number of di Chimici heirs, but the family had been robbed of two of its young men and both Fortezza and Moresco were without males to inherit their titles.

'A husband for Beatrice,' mused Niccolò to himself. 'Perhaps she could marry the ruler of one of the city-states we have not yet won. If Bellezza can't be brought into the fold just yet, then I shall concentrate on treaties with Classe and Padavia.'

*

Silvia had sent for Guido Parola. He was not far; since the day she had taken him into her service as his punishment for trying to assassinate her, he had never been very many paces from her side. When he entered her presence, she gave her maid Susanna permission to leave.

'Ah, Guido,' she said, scrutinising him carefully. 'You are looking pale. Are you quite recovered from your hurts?'

'Yes, my Lady,' said Parola. 'I was very fortunate and took only slight flesh wounds.'

'Sit down, Guido,' ordered Silvia, indicating the

place beside her on a chaise longue.

'My Lady?' asked Parola hesitantly.

'Stop being my servant for a moment,' said Silvia. 'I want to talk to you properly and you are much too tall for me to do it if you don't take a seat. You're making my neck ache.'

He sat nervously on the edge of the chaise.

'Don't look so worried, Guido,' said Silvia. 'I am very pleased with you. You saved the life of that girl Barbara and, as far as I am concerned, the life of my daughter, since she was the one intended for that blow.'

'Do you think it was the Nucci?' asked Parola. 'I went back to the church the next day, but I couldn't say which of the bodies was the man the Duchessa dispatched.'

'I think it was,' said Silvia. 'Not even Niccolò di Chimici would engineer an attack on his family to provide cover for assassinating Arianna. Besides, he hadn't then been told that she wouldn't marry him, and his plan was to take Bellezza by matrimony, not violence.'

'And the Nucci thought the Duchessa might accept him?'

'I doubt if they even knew about the proposal,' said Silvia. 'But she was an honoured guest of the di Chimici and wearing his handsome gift, as they thought. You can be sure that he himself had spread the rumours that Bellezza was about to form an alliance with Giglia. And he isn't the sort of man to keep quiet about the lavishness of his presents. So as far as the Nucci were concerned, she was a fair target.'

They were silent a few moments, reliving the horror

of what had happened in the Church of the Annunciation.

'Guido,' said Silvia. 'I am going to release you from my service.'

He looked stricken, and started to protest, but Silvia held up her hand.

'Let me finish. You are a nobleman. I know your family's fortune was gambled away by your older brother, but you should be at university completing your education as a gentleman, not acting as a footman to me. You have paid many times over for your original crime – which was one of intention rather than commission – but you are now fully pardoned and should be making your own way in the world.'

'But I don't want to leave your service, my Lady,' said Parola. 'Don't dismiss me. I want to go on protecting you.'

'I am not dismissing you, Guido,' she said gently, taking his hand. 'I am, very regretfully, letting you go. You will have an ample financial reward for all that you have done for me. I forgive you for trying to kill me and I want you to regard me now as a sort of godmother. You can escort me back to Padavia. But after that, what would you say to going to university in Fortezza?'

Chapter 26

Corridor of Power

Rinaldo was nervous about remaining in Giglia. He had not carried a sword at the di Chimici weddings – he was a priest now, after all – but it had been frustrating, brought up as he had been, to be unarmed in the midst of such slaughter. He had helped his uncle get the women, including his sister Caterina, first to the sanctuary of the High Altar and then into the orphanage. But not before he had seen people killed and wounded.

Now he was anxious to get back to the comfortable life he lived in the Papal palace in Remora. His uncle and master, the Pope, was not loath to leave Giglia either, but he would not go until the young princes were out of danger. The Grand Duke too was in a strange mood. He had been thwarted of the bloody revenge he wanted to take on the Nucci, and this idiotic plan to move out of the Ducal palace after only a few weeks was part of his frenzy. The Pope wanted to keep an eye on him and sent Rinaldo across the river to see how his cousins were faring.

He was walking near the great cathedral when he glimpsed a tall figure he thought he recognised coming out of one of the palazzi. He had noticed him before in the Church of the Annunciation, fighting and later taking care of the Princess Lucia, but in the chaos of the slaughter and its aftermath during the flood he had forgotten all about him. It niggled at the back of Rinaldo's mind, the sight of this red-headed youth; he knew he had seen him somewhere before but couldn't think where.

*

Luciano was waiting for Sky and Nicholas at the friary when they stravagated to Giglia. He had bumped into Sandro, almost unrecognisable in robes just a little bit big for him.

'So you are Brother Sandro now?' asked Luciano, smiling.

'Yes,' said Sandro. 'And Fratello is Brother Dog. He works in the kitchens. You are waiting for Tino and Benvenuto?'

Luciano nodded. He had to remind himself that Benvenuto was Nicholas, who once had been Falco. Was he going to be Falco again? Luciano thrust the thought down. He needed to talk to them both and to Brother Sulien.

The boys arrived within minutes of one another and

came out to find Luciano and Sandro in the cloister. They went together to the infirmary and found Gaetano sitting on the edge of his bed. There were no other friars about so Nicholas threw his arms around his brother.

Sandro suddenly realised who he was. He had seen the memorial statue of Prince Falco many times but never made the connection until he saw 'Benvenuto' in Gaetano's embrace. He turned to Luciano, eyes wide, but the Bellezzan just put his finger to his lips. Sandro understood. He was a friar now, not a spy, and was going to have to learn how to keep secrets, not pass them on.

'Gaetano!' said Nicholas. 'You really are all right? Where is Fabrizio?'

'Gone with Sulien and Beatrice to Father's latest palace. I shall join them soon. You know that we have taken over the Nucci place?'

'I wanted to talk to you about that,' said Luciano. 'Your father has challenged me to a duel tomorrow and he wants us to meet in the gardens of the Nucci.'

Gaetano looked horrified. His arm was in a sling and his head was bandaged but he made as if to grab his sword, then realised he didn't have one.

'A duel?' he said. 'But why?'

Luciano shrugged. 'What does it matter? He's made up his mind to fight me. I don't think anyone refuses a challenge from the Grand Duke.'

'This is terrible,' said Gaetano. 'I won't be able to lift a rapier for several weeks.'

'But you've given me lots of lessons,' said Luciano. 'I'm not going to learn any more in a day. I'm either ready to meet him or I'm not.'

Georgia was not going to miss another day in Talia. And she had the idea that she might be better able to persuade Nicholas out of his crazy idea if she could get him on his own in Giglia and show him how impossible it would be to return there as if nothing had happened. But the awful thing was, although she knew it was a fatally flawed plan for Nicholas, she couldn't get it out of her mind that it could work to save Luciano's life – which would certainly be at risk if he fought this duel with the Grand Duke.

If Vicky and David were somehow made to understand, they could be ready to take their restored son away somewhere far from Islington. And one day Georgia could go and find him, wherever he was. It would put him for ever out of the reach of Arianna, just as she would have gone out of Luciano's if she had accepted the Grand Duke. And who else in the world would the new Lucien turn to if not Georgia?

There was so much wrong with this picture that Georgia knew it was really a fantasy, and yet she couldn't shake it out of her head. There was only one thing to do: she must talk to the Stravaganti about it, the way they hadn't when she and Luciano had helped Falco translate across worlds.

She started with Giuditta, who was beginning to pack up Arianna's statue when Georgia arrived at her workshop that morning. The head, with its streaming hair, was still poking out of the layers of straw and sacking, the Duchessa's masked face staring out defiantly. Georgia felt a bit guilty about her thoughts;

she had come to admire Arianna, even if she could never stop feeling jealous of her.

'Good morning,' said Giuditta. 'I think we can stop for a while, boys. You can have half an hour's break.'

When they had gone, Franco lingering to give Georgia a lascivious backwards look, the sculptor boiled a pan of water on her kitchen stove and made a tisane of lemon verbena for them both.

'You look as if you need it,' she said to Georgia. 'Drink it while you wait for the others to get here.'

Georgia was grateful. 'There's something I want to ask you about,' she said. And then she told Giuditta Nicholas's plan.

*

'We should go and meet Georgia,' said Sky to Nicholas, when Gaetano had been removed to the Nucci palace.

'I'll come with you,' said Luciano.

The three of them walked in silence to Giuditta's bottega. The cleaning-up operation was continuing in the city, helped by the cloudless sky in which the sun burned as if rain were an unknown phenomenon. Sky had to admit that the Grand Duke was a good administrator. Everywhere they went they saw bands of citizens and soldiers working together to burn debris, clean monuments and repair damage. Their route took them through the Piazza Ducale and they saw that the banqueting platform had been taken down as quickly as it had been erected; there was no sign of all the canopies, flowers and lanterns that had adorned the square the night before the weddings.

Notices had been pasted to various columns proclaiming the exile of the Nucci and the sequestration of all their lands, houses and goods, even down to the least lamb in their flocks, by the house of di Chimici in compensation for the treasonous uprising against their authority and the loss of Prince Carlo. An idealised woodcut of Carlo appeared on the handbills but Nicholas scarcely noticed. He walked, head down, with his hood pulled over his eyes.

When they reached the Piazza della Cattedrale, unusually Giuditta was waiting for them outside her bottega, with Georgia.

'I want Luciano and Brother Benvenuto to come with me,' she said seriously. 'Georgia and Tino can meet us later. We are going to the Bellezzan Embassy.'

So Sky and Georgia were left on their own, making an odd couple – the friar and the artist's model. In order to escape curious looks, they went into the baptistery and sat one behind the other. It was a much smaller building than the cathedral, and the clearing up from the flood had finished there, so that they could talk relatively undisturbed.

'She's going to see if the other Stravaganti can make them see sense,' said Georgia.

'Them?' asked Sky. 'I thought it was only Nick who wanted to do it. Luciano's surely too sensible?'

'Yes, well, you'd have thought so, but with this duel hanging over him, I think Nicholas is going to try to persuade him to take the easy way out,' said Georgia. 'Drink poison in Giglia and stravagate to Islington before it works. Nicholas does the same, maybe with sleeping pills, in the Mulhollands' house. Then, Bob's your uncle: they both end up with real bodies, complete with shadows in the worlds they started from.'

'I never heard anything so ridiculous,' said Sky. 'Surely Luciano would never buy it? I mean he's got a lot going for him here, if you know what I mean.'

'Yes,' said Georgia calmly. 'You mean Arianna.'

'Among other things,' said Sky. 'And what would people say here?'

'That he killed himself rather than face the Grand Duke in a duel,' said Georgia. 'That part would be just about believable, at least by outsiders.'

'But what about Nick? What would Vicky and David tell everyone, even if they were in on the swap?'

'That he had been depressed and difficult lately,' shrugged Georgia. 'He wouldn't be the first fifteen-year-old to kill himself.'

'I don't buy it,' said Sky. 'I mean, they're pretty attached to him, aren't they?'

'But just imagine if he were giving them the chance to have their own son back. I bet they'd consider it.'

'There isn't time for all this anyway,' said Sky. 'Nick would have to explain it all to them and get them to agree tomorrow, if Luciano was going to – you know – take poison before the duel.'

'I think,' said Georgia slowly, 'that if they both agreed to do it, it could just about work as far as the time is concerned. But the Stravaganti would have to give their blessing within the next few hours.'

'And you said Giuditta was against it, so they're not likely to give their blessing, are they?'

'I would have said not, but Sky, if Luciano doesn't do this, he might be killed by Niccolò tomorrow. With no second chances. Finito!'

'He's asked me to be one of his seconds,' said Sky. 'I think he means to go through with it.'

'And who else?' asked Georgia. 'It can't be Nicholas – it's too dangerous.'

'Or Gaetano. You couldn't expect him to support someone against his own father. I think he might be going to ask Doctor Dethridge.'

*

'Here are the rapiers you asked for, my Lord,' said Enrico. 'They are well balanced and matched to perfection.'

'Ah, yes,' said Niccolò. 'We must be seen to be scrupulously fair.' He showed his teeth in a humourless smile. 'What about the poison?'

'The poison, my Lord?'

'Yes, man, poison,' he said. 'Am I to go and ask Brother Sulien for it myself? To say, "Thank you so much for saving my sons' lives with the medicine Cavaliere Luciano helped bring through the flood and now can I have some poison to make sure that I kill him?" No – Sulien must not know.'

'I see, my Lord,' said Enrico, scrambling to keep up and trying to be indispensable. 'Of course you have none here?'

The Grand Duke gave him a quelling look.

'No, no, let me think,' said the Eel. 'Yes, I think I know where to get it.'

'Then do so,' said Niccolò. 'Immediately.'

'No,' said Rodolfo. 'I absolutely forbid it.'

He had summoned Dethridge and Brother Sulien to the Embassy to meet Giuditta and the boys. But it wasn't till they were all together that the sculptor told them what it was all about. It was just the six of them in the blue salon; Giuditta had asked for Arianna and Silvia not to be included yet.

Nicholas was standing stubbornly in the middle of the room, his Dominican hood thrown back, revealing his unmistakeably di Chimici features. Luciano was looking at the floor. All he wanted at the moment was to have the decision taken out of his hands.

'Wait,' said Sulien. 'Do we know if this is even possible? What do you say, Doctor?'

'Yt has nevire bene assayed before,' said Dethridge. 'Any sich translatioune is perilous – bot two atte one tyme!'

'But we've both done it before,' said Nicholas. 'Doesn't that count? And if he doesn't do it, Luciano will surely die tomorrow.'

'There are other ways to save him,' said Rodolfo. 'I could contest the Grand Duke's right to challenge, someone else could offer to represent him – me for example – or we could smuggle him out of the city. Don't do this because you think you have no other choices, Luciano.'

When the Eel had gone, Niccolò sent for Gabassi again; the architect did not get much peace from the restless Grand Duke at the moment.

'Have you brought the sketches for my walkway?' asked his master as soon as the man got into the room.

'Yes, your Grace,' said the architect, rolling out his drawings on the table.

They showed an elegant roofed corridor zigzagging from the Palazzo Ducale across the top of the Guild offices and over the Ponte Nuovo to the Nucci palace.

'Excellent!' said Niccolò. 'I'd like you to start straightaway. My son Fabrizio and I can walk from here to the government seat or the other direction, above the noise and dirt and smells of the city. Quite right for people of our importance.'

'There may be a problem with smells from the shops on the bridge,' said Gabassi. 'You see that most of them are butchers or fishmongers.'

'Then we'll change the shops,' said Niccolò. 'I'll give orders moving all food shops out to the market. Then the silversmiths and gemstone workers, who lost so much in the flood, can move their workshops to the bridge. Any other problems?'

'No, my Lord,' said Gabassi. 'If your Grace will give me the funds and the authorisations I need, I can start building tomorrow.'

*

When Sky and Georgia met them later up at the friary, Nicholas looked morose and Luciano drawn and anxious. The others guessed that the Stravaganti had vetoed the plan and Georgia was relieved that the decision had been made. Brother Sandro greeted them in the cloister and dispelled some of the tension by asking Luciano straight out, 'Shouldn't you be practising for your duel?'

It jolted Luciano out of his torpor and sent him off back to the Embassy to find rapiers and some clothes of his own for Sky and Nicholas to wear; there was no way they could fight in robes.

'They said no, then?' Sky asked Nicholas.

'It was all the same stuff I've heard before – we don't know if it would work, too dangerous, not Luciano's only option,' said Nicholas. 'I'm sick of it. There's so little time left, and if we don't do it, Luciano is a dead duck tomorrow.'

'Don't say that,' said Georgia.

Sandro didn't ask about the forbidden option or who 'they' were who had said no. He felt a great respect for the Stravaganti, especially this startling-looking young woman. As far as he was concerned, if Sulien was one, then these time travellers were a good thing. And, as for Luciano, he held him in awe and some fear, since the friar had told him that this handsome young noble had died once and been reborn in Talia. Now he had guessed who 'Brother Benvenuto' really was, there were clearly great and frightening mysteries afoot, about which Sandro realised he wasn't qualified to talk.

But he understood Georgia's terror about the next day. Niccolò di Chimici was a fearsome opponent.

'Perhaps there is something that could put the Grand Duke off his guard?' he suggested tentatively, looking at Nicholas.

Nicholas looked at the little novice, light dawning.

'You're right!' he said. 'I think if my father saw me

and knew me, he might fall into a swoon or something. At least it would give Luciano the chance to disarm him. Thanks, Sandro.'

'We should all be there,' said Georgia. 'All the Stravaganti. Our circle failed at the weddings but we'd have only one person to protect this time. Surely seven of us could save the eighth?'

She was beginning to see some hope.

'I'll have to be there anyway,' said Sky. 'I'm one of his seconds. And Doctor Dethridge is going to be the other.'

'But how can Nick and I be there?' asked Georgia. 'Or the others?'

'I think you will find there will be quite a crowd of spectators,' said Sulien, joining them. 'Rumours are flying about the city that the Grand Duke is going to fight at dawn, and Giglians are not likely to pass up on such a spectacle.'

*

'Fight the Grand Duke?' said Silvia, when Rodolfo told her. 'What new devilry is this? You must stop it.'

'Luciano is determined to fight this duel,' said Rodolfo. 'I can't stop him or get him out of the city. But if we are all there we should be able to protect him.'

'Should?' said Silvia. 'Will that satisfy Arianna?'

'I think that Luciano and Arianna are not in each other's confidence at present,' said Rodolfo. 'They seem unhappy about more than the Grand Duke.'

'But that doesn't mean she wants Niccolò to kill him!' said Silvia.

Rodolfo sighed.

'I'll have one more try to persuade Luciano to leave the city,' he said. 'There's no need for Arianna to know anything about the duel yet.'

*

Barbara was feeling better. Her wound still hurt but Brother Sulien had promised to come and take the stitches out the following week and she could feel that the flesh was knitting together. She now had the novel experience of sitting up in bed, being waited on by her own mistress. The Duchessa was so mortified by what had happened that she brought her maid tempting morsels of food or fortifying drinks every hour.

'I can't just lie in bed doing nothing, my Lady,' said Barbara. 'Give me something to occupy my hands.'

'I'm sure that nothing is exactly what you should be doing,' said Arianna. 'Oh, if only I hadn't asked you to wear that hateful dress!'

'I was happy to wear it for your Grace. It made me feel like a real lady – it was so beautiful. What will happen to it now?'

'I should like to burn it,' said Arianna bitterly. 'But I can't do that because of its value. As well as the great tear where you were stabbed, I don't think the blood will ever come out of the brocade – the Embassy staff have tried. I suppose all the gems will have to be unpicked.'

'Then let me do that, at least,' said Barbara. 'That will not be taxing and, in spite of everything, I'd love to see it again.'

'Really?' said Arianna. It made her shudder to touch it and she hadn't even been the one wearing it. But she ordered the dress to be brought and Barbara bent over it assiduously with a tiny pair of silver scissors, snipping at the rows of embroidery that kept the stones in place. Each pearl or amethyst was put in a bowl as it was released and the pile grew steadily as the young women talked.

'It might be easier to clean when all the jewels and silk embroidery are off,' said Barbara. 'And the tear could be mended.'

'Well, if you will undertake the repair, you may have the dress if you want it,' said Arianna. 'It would make a fine wedding dress – if you have a sweetheart.'

Barbara blushed. 'I do have a young man who keeps asking me,' she said.

Arianna was surprised. 'Well, then, I promise to have some of these stones set for you into wedding jewellery,' she said. 'As a thank you for saving my life. And if you don't want this dress, you shall have another, at my expense.'

'Thank you, my Lady,' said the girl, quite happy to bear the scar of her wound in return for such a lavish gift. It made Arianna feel more ashamed.

'I shall miss you, Barbara,' she said, her eyes filling with tears. 'Who shall be my maid if you marry?'

'Oh, I don't want to leave you, my Lady,' cried Barbara. 'My young man is Marco, one of your Grace's footmen at the palazzo. We would both want to continue in your service, I'm sure.'

'Good,' said Arianna, blinking her tears away. 'How old are you, Barbara?'

'I am eighteen, your Grace – very late to marry, I

know,' said Barbara. 'But we have been saving.'

'You are less than a year older than I am,' said Arianna.

Barbara was horrified. 'Oh, your Grace, forgive me. I did not mean to insult you. It is different for nobility. Take no notice of my silly chatter.'

'That's all right, Barbara,' said Arianna. 'We do marry young in the lagoon. Two years ago, I would have expected it myself, when I lived on Torrone. Now, as you say, it is different. I have many duties to perform that are not compatible with romance.'

She fetched such a deep sigh that Barbara said, 'I am sure there is no need to worry about the young man.'

'What young man?' asked Arianna.

'Why, Cavaliere Luciano,' said Barbara. 'They say he has been having fencing lessons and may well defeat the Grand Duke.'

Arianna jumped to her feet, spilling bright jewels all over the floor.

'Defeat the Grand Duke? What are you talking about?'

*

Now that he had seen the red-headed man once, Rinaldo caught glimpses of him everywhere. But he never had a moment to think about where he knew him from. The Pope kept him constantly busy with errands between the Residence, the Via Larga, the Palazzo Ducale and the Nucci palace.

On one of these journeys he bumped into his old

servant Enrico. He was not someone that Rinaldo wanted to spend time with, but the man was friendly enough.

'How is your Excellency keeping?' he asked.

'I am that no more,' said Rinaldo. 'Can't you see I am a man of the cloth now?'

'Of course!' said Enrico. 'But how should I address your Lordship now?'

'Father will do,' said Rinaldo primly. 'I am only a priest. But the Pope's chaplain too,' he couldn't help adding.

'Oh yes, Uncle Ferdinando,' said Enrico with a leer. 'Not long till there's a Cardinal's hat in it, I shouldn't wonder.'

Rinaldo shuddered at the man's familiarity.

'It's amazing what you can get pardons for now, isn't it?' said Enrico conversationally. 'Kidnapping, murder. Confession and absolution are wonderful things.'

'What are you implying?' said Rinaldo. He had a feeling that this horrible little man might be trying to blackmail him.

'Implying?' said Enrico innocently. 'Nothing, Father. Just thinking of all the terrible things you have to listen to in the confessional. All the dreadful sinners you have to deal with. It must be a sore trial for a virtuous man.'

'I'm afraid I must bring this delightful encounter to an end,' said Rinaldo. 'I am taking a message from the Grand Duke to the Pope.'

'Maybe it's about tomorrow's duel,' said Enrico. 'You might want to come along to that. One of them will be in need of a priest by the end. And if it isn't the

Grand Duke, it will be a young man that you and I know rather well, if you get my meaning.'

He tapped the side of his nose and went on his way, whistling. Inside his jerkin was a phial of deadly poison bought from a certain monk from Volana. But even without knowing about that, Rinaldo was profoundly unsettled by their meeting.

*

'That's better,' said Nicholas. He and Sky had both pressed Luciano till all three of them were hot and panting. But Luciano had kept his defences up and even touched them lightly once or twice. He wasn't as good as Nicholas but he was better than Sky. Nicholas soon adapted to the heavier Talian rapier, which was what he used to use before his translation, but Sky still found it awkward and unwieldy. Luciano took comfort from the fact that he was a great deal younger and fitter than the Grand Duke.

'Let's stop for a bit,' said Sky.

They were in the kitchen yard at Saint-Mary-among-the-Vines, watched by Georgia, Sandro and Brother Dog. The little animal had got very excited when the boys first started fighting, but had calmed down a bit. He was still shivering in Sandro's arms, but had stopped barking.

'I can't believe you're going through with this,' Georgia said to Luciano, while the boys flopped on to the ground and Sandro went in search of some cold ale from Brother Tullio.

'Thanks for the vote of confidence,' said Luciano, breathing heavily, his dark curls wet with sweat. 'I thought I was doing rather well.'

'You are. But there's no reason to suppose the Grand Duke will fight fair.'

'Who will his seconds be?' asked Sky.

'One of them will be that man they call the Eel,' said Luciano. 'I know him of old. He was the one who kidnapped me in Bellezza. He was the one who kidnapped Cesare too, Georgia, and stole Merla.'

'A nasty piece of work,' said Nicholas. 'We need to watch him as closely as my father.'

*

The di Chimici princesses were assembled once more, in the Nucci palace. Francesca and Caterina were in attendance on their husbands, who were getting stronger with every hour. Bianca was visiting with her husband Alfonso. Lucia drifted through the empty rooms on the first floor in her black widow's weeds as if searching for something.

Princess Beatrice found her and brought her to the others.

'Come and live with me in Fortezza, Bice,' Lucia said impulsively, when she saw the other three couples. 'We can be old maids together.'

'We'll all come and visit you often,' said her sister Bianca. 'You won't be alone, I promise. We just have to get through this funeral of Carlo's today and then you can return with your mother and father to Fortezza. They will be a comfort to you.'

The thought of returning to her childhood home, husbandless, instead of living happily in Giglia with Carlo in the Via Larga, caused fresh tears to roll down

Lucia's cheeks. Much as she had dreaded leaving Fortezza for her strange new life, this ending was much worse. She was still in a state of shock from seeing her bridegroom murdered beside her just after their union had been blessed. That image haunted her dreams and so she had not slept properly for two nights.

'If there is anything I can do for you,' said Duke Alfonso, 'please tell me. Perhaps you would like to come to Volana with Bianca and me? My mother would look after you as tenderly as your own.'

'You are very kind,' said Lucia. 'But I think I will do best in my own city.'

Francesca sat holding Gaetano's uninjured hand. She pitied Lucia with all her heart, and not least because it was only providence that had saved her from the same fate. It could so easily have been Gaetano lying cold in the di Chimici chapel, waiting for his burial.

*

'I think I'll stravagate back early this afternoon,' said Nicholas. 'That is if you don't need any more practice, Luciano.'

'I'll be OK,' said Luciano. 'At least, I think I've done as much as I can. It's up to fate now – or the Goddess.'

Georgia was watching Nicholas closely. She slipped off the wall and signalled to Sky to follow her lead.

'I'll go back, too,' she said. 'I could do with a bit more sleep. And we'll all need early nights tomorrow if we're to be back here at dawn.'

'I'll walk with you to the city wall if you like,' said Sky. 'I'd like to see Merla again.'

'Can I come?' asked Sandro.

But Sulien came and called him into the pharmacy.

'You are a real friar with work to do, Brother Sandro. You cannot spend your days gadding about with Tino and Benvenuto, let alone with such an enchanting young woman as Georgia.'

While Sandro turned and trotted off obediently after Brother Sulien, Georgia suddenly flung her arms around Luciano.

'Take care,' she said, hugging him tightly.

He hugged her back.

'I'll be fine,' he said. But he looked pale and worried.

Nicholas went off to Sulien's cell to stravagate and Georgia walked through the cloister with Sky. She waited till they were out of the friary before voicing her fears.

'I don't trust Nick,' she said. 'I wouldn't put it past him to do something stupid. I want to get round to his house early and keep an eye on him.'

'Do you want me to come too?' asked Sky.

'Would you? I'd be happier if there were two of us. We'll need to watch him all day.'

'I'll stravagate back as soon as you've gone,' said Sky. 'And I'll ask him round to my flat tomorrow night.'

Georgia stopped outside the church.

'Listen,' she said. 'What's that music?'

There was a sound of muffled drums coming from beyond the Piazza della Cattedrale. A passer-by said,

'They are burying Prince Carlo.' Georgia and Sky stood still, their heads bowed for a few minutes.

Then they walked over the Ponte Nuovo. Gabassi the architect and a man Sky recognised as the Grand Duke's steward were arguing with a large butcher. They stopped to listen before heading towards the Nucci palace.

'A walkway across the river?' said Sky. 'And he doesn't want any bad smells as he walks along. Is there no limit to the man's arrogance?'

'He thinks the di Chimici are above the likes of ordinary people,' said Georgia. 'And he doesn't like it when he doesn't get what he wants. That's what this duel is all about, isn't it? He proposes to Arianna, she turns him down, so he wants to kill Luciano because he thinks he's his rival.'

'It's hard to believe it's going to happen here in the Nucci gardens in less than a day,' said Sky.

They skirted the gardens and turned off left down to where Merla waited with the Manoush in the little homestead. She sensed Georgia's approach and whinnied from far away, running up to the fence round the field. Sky caught his breath at the sight of the magnificent winged horse. If only there were time to get to know her.

Aurelio was whittling a recorder out of pearwood. He lifted his sightless eyes as they came up to the fence.

'This is Sky,' Georgia said. 'He is another Stravagante from my world.'

Aurelio bowed in Sky's direction, touching his breast and brow with both hands.

'You are troubled about something,' he said to

Georgia. 'What is wrong?'

'Luciano is going to fight a duel with the Grand Duke at dawn tomorrow,' she said. 'In the gardens of the Nucci palace. And I am afraid he will lose.'

Chapter 27

A Duel

Rodolfo had been so insistent that Luciano had agreed to talk to him again about the duel.

'You understand that you can't agree to this crazy plan of Falco's?' said the older Stravagante.

Luciano was silent.

'What is it, Luciano?' asked Rodolfo gently. 'Do you want to go home so badly? Do you not feel at home here in Talia with us? With Arianna?'

'She doesn't care about me,' said Luciano bitterly. 'She could have asked me to stay.'

'She refused the Duke's proposal,' said Rodolfo.

'But not for me,' said Luciano. 'For Bellezza. She cares more about her city than she does about me.'

'Do not throw your life recklessly away in this duel,' said Rodolfo, and he looked stern. 'I can get you out of the city. Promise me that you will not fight.'

'I can't promise,' said Luciano, moved by Rodolfo's concern. 'But I will think about it.'

*

At dawn the next day, many people converged on the Nucci gardens. The Grand Duke was last to arrive with his two seconds, Enrico and Gaetano, who had to lean on Francesca. Luciano was already there, with Doctor Dethridge and Sky. Georgia and Nicholas arrived at almost the same time; Nicholas had stayed at Sky's flat that night and stravagated soon after him.

Georgia was very relieved to see him; she had stuck to him all Sunday in their world until Sky took over and took him home. Now they mingled with the substantial crowd. Georgia saw Silvia standing near Rodolfo with Guido Parola. She scanned the gathering for a sight of Arianna but there were too many people present to see properly.

Sky was feeling very nervous about his role.

'Fyrste wee most assay to have the encountire annulled,' explained Doctor Dethridge. 'Wee most entire negotiatiounes with yonge Cayton and yondire villayne Henry.'

He means Gaetano and Enrico, thought Sky.

'Yf thatte fayles, thenne wee inspecte the weapouns to insure they are alike and notte tampered with. Yf that wee are contente, thenne the conteste most beginne.'

The four seconds approached and began to debate the issue of settling the quarrel without a fight.

All this time Luciano and the Grand Duke stood at some distance apart, not exchanging as much as a look. Luciano scanned the crowd for friends and saw a reassuring number of Stravaganti manoeuvring themselves into position so that they took up points on a circle. The first person he saw was Rodolfo, and he felt bad that he hadn't been able to take his advice. Sulien, Giuditta, Georgia, Nicholas – they were all there. He was surprised to see Gaetano as one of his father's seconds. That meant that three of the seconds were Luciano's friends, even though Gaetano could hardly take any action against his father.

Francesca was there to support her husband, Silvia could be located by the tall red-headed young man beside her and Luciano also caught a glimpse of the multi-coloured clothing of Raffaella the Manoush. It seemed as if almost everyone he knew in Giglia had come to support him. Almost. There was no sign of the slight masked figure he most wanted to see. Yet this duel was for her, at least as far as Luciano was concerned. He still didn't know exactly why the Grand Duke had challenged him. But with every pass he made with his foil, Luciano would be thinking about Arianna and venting the anger he had felt for a month, ever since the Duke's dinner party when Niccolò had announced his intention of marrying her.

Niccolò himself had a more complicated agenda – as always. He wanted to hurt the Duchessa, to punish her for continuing her mother's resistance to a di Chimici alliance and for slighting his offer. But this contest was also for Falco. He had wished a thousand times that he had put Luciano and his accomplice to death in Remora when his boy had died so mysteriously. It was only his grief and the befuddlement of his senses by witchcraft that had stopped him.

The witchcraft of Rodolfo. All the recent strife with the Nucci had deflected Niccolò from his other purpose: persecution of the Stravaganti. The Bellezzan Regent was one of that Brotherhood, he knew, and he suspected that Luciano was being trained in the same arts. This duel might flush out some more of them. The boy's seconds, for instance. That old man, he knew to be Luciano's father, or foster-father, but what about the young Moorish friar? The Eel had found no evidence to confirm that he was Brother Sulien's illegitimate son, so he was another potential Stravagante. Unlikely in a friar, and Niccolò owed Sulien thanks for his role after the Nucci attack and at the time of his own poisoning. Still, he was a friend of Luciano's, so a possible suspect. And there had been another young friar seen in their company. But there was no more time to wonder about him now, as the duel was about to begin.

Enrico refused to accept any peaceful settlement on his principal's behalf even though his own fellow second supported it. The Grand Duke was mortally offended, he said, that the Bellezzan had interfered with his suit to the Duchessa, poisoning – Enrico emphasised the word – her mind against him. He demanded full satisfaction.

Interfered with his suit? thought Luciano. So Arianna *did* say something about me when he proposed. Niccolò is jealous! It gave him fresh heart, but there was still no sign of Arianna in the crowd.

So they proceeded to the inspection of weapons. Enrico brought out the two rapiers in a long case, lined with black velvet. He offered Luciano first choice and the Bellezzan took the weapon further away from him, just in case his seconds had missed anything. He balanced it in his hand, took the tip and slightly bent it in a curve to test the blade; it was an elegant, even beautiful weapon. The Grand Duke took the other.

Sky swallowed. His mouth was dry. He felt that he would be making every pass and parrying every blow with Luciano. He didn't know how his friend could stand there so coolly, testing the rapier when, in a few moments, he would be fighting for his life. Neither weapon was bated and there were no face-guards or body padding; this was supposed to be a duel to the death.

There was a slight commotion in the crowd and the Duchessa of Bellezza appeared and stood beside a well-dressed middle-aged woman. Luciano met her violet eyes and made the slightest nod in her direction before taking up his guard. This is for you, he thought silently. If I get out of this alive, I'm going to tell you how I feel. He held his weapon in front of him as if making her a salute and with it a promise. The Grand Duke saw the gesture and followed his gaze to the masked figure in the crowd. His lip curled with disdain. So the lagoon slut was here to support her lover? Let her take him away in pieces or infected with a poison beyond cure!

He didn't press Luciano at first, letting the boy get over-confident. But it surprised Niccolò to see how good his opponent was. Nothing that would trouble the Grand Duke, but the Bellezzan would die valiantly.

Rinaldo di Chimici watched nervously. His uncle would win, of course, but Rinaldo, like everyone else, was caught up in the excitement of the contest. And there was a great deal of support for the underdog. He looked at the crowd. There was that red-headed fellow again – near the young Duchessa and an older woman, clearly his employer. Something about the association of the man with Bellezza made the necessary link in Rinaldo's brain and at that moment he knew who Guido Parola was.

Enrico was watching the young Duchessa too. The fight wouldn't get interesting for a while yet. She was a fetching little thing, he thought, sentimentally. It was a pity she was going to lose her inamorato – such eyes were not meant for tears. Perhaps she would recover one day and marry. But not the Grand Duke; he was much too old for her. Enrico allowed his mind to wander to his old love, his fiancée Giuliana, who had disappeared from Bellezza at the time of the old Duchessa's assassination. Would he ever find a woman to replace her? He still could not understand what had happened to her.

Rinaldo no longer had any attention to spare for the duel. Guido Parola owed him money; he had taken half his fee for assassinating the Duchessa, botched the job and disappeared. Now Rinaldo wondered if he could set Enrico on to him.

Luciano was beginning to sweat. He had been parrying as skilfully as he could but had never got close to touching the Grand Duke. The hilt of the rapier was getting slippery in his hand. He muffed the next blow and felt Niccolò's blade pierce his left shoulder. It was not a deep cut but the seconds halted the duel to attend to it. Both men were brought wine to drink while they rested.

Sky helped Dethridge clean and pad Luciano's wound with cotton strips. Rinaldo took the opportunity to approach Enrico.

'See that red-headed fellow over there?' he hissed. 'That's the man I paid to kill the Duchessa on the night of the Maddalena feast in Bellezza. I want you to catch him and make him give back what he owes me.'

Enrico didn't really want to be distracted now. This break gave him the opportunity he needed to smear the point of Niccolò's rapier with the poison he had with him. Rinaldo was standing between him and the onlookers, providing a perfect screen. And the other three seconds were all looking at Luciano.

'Funny he's with the new Duchessa now,' said Enrico, applying the poison. He knew Rinaldo wouldn't stop him – even if he was a priest now, he had no love for the boy who had fooled him in Bellezza.

'He's not with the Duchessa. He's a servant of that other woman – the good-looking middle-aged one,' said Rinaldo.

Enrico looked where he was pointing. And Rinaldo looked again.

'Yt is time to beginne agayne,' said Dethridge. 'Yonge Maister Lucian is fitte to fyghte.'

Enrico passed his master the poisoned blade, as Rinaldo gripped his arm.

'That's her!' he hissed. 'The Duchessa!'

'I know it is,' said Enrico. 'Now get back to the crowd. We have a duel to finish.'

'No,' said Rinaldo urgently. 'The old one!'

But he was pushed back among the other spectators and Luciano and Niccolò faced each other again.

The man's losing his mind, thought Enrico. How could the assassin be with the old Duchessa? I killed her myself. Lobbed a bomb at her in that crazy room of mirrors she had.

Nicholas didn't like the way the duel was going. Luciano's confidence had been weakened by the hit to his shoulder, even though the wound was not serious. Nicholas decided it was time to try Sandro's idea. He moved through the crowd until he was positioned where his father could see him, even though it meant breaking out of the circular formation with the other Stravaganti. Then he let his hood fall back.

Enrico was troubled by his conversation with Rinaldo and found it difficult to concentrate on the duel. Someone had died in the Glass Room, and if it hadn't been the old Duchessa, then who was it?

Suddenly, the Grand Duke sank to his knees, clutching his chest.

'Oh, Goddess save us!' muttered Enrico. 'Don't have a seizure now!'

He rushed to his master's side. Gaetano was raising his father and giving him more wine. 'Falco!' whispered Niccolò. 'I saw him, Gaetano. Over there!'

Enrico looked round but there was no one special to be seen in the crowd. Where the Grand Duke pointed was a young friar, one of Sulien's novices, with his face hooded.

But Prince Gaetano seemed disturbed. 'We should

stop the fight, Enrico,' he said.

'No, no,' said the Grand Duke, passing his hand over his face. 'It's nothing – a hallucination. Give me another mouthful of wine. I'll fight on.'

The Duchessa was pressing forwards to see what was going on.

'Is it over?' she called out. 'Does the Grand Duke concede?'

Sky was the second nearest to her. He shook his head. Arianna made to move forwards but the duel was about to resume. It was going to be dangerous if she got near the foils.

'Silvia,' he called. 'Guido! Keep her back.'

Silvia. That was the old Duchessa's name. Enrico saw the middle-aged woman and the assassin together restrain the young Duchessa. Rinaldo had been right. This was Silvia, the Duchessa of Bellezza.

Enrico lived in sixteenth-century Talia, so he had never seen a slow-motion sequence in a film. But that was just like what he was experiencing. If the old Duchessa of Bellezza was still alive, he thought again as he picked up the two foils, then who had died in the Glass Room that day when he had planted the explosive?

And then all of a sudden he knew exactly what had happened to his fiancée. If the old Duchessa was alive, she must have used a substitute. She had done it before. And the person she had used was Enrico's fiancée, Giuliana.

When Enrico passed the foils to the duellists, he made sure that Luciano got the poisoned one. It was the decision of a moment. As Enrico realised that he had killed his own fiancée, blown her into little pieces, a hatred like nothing he had ever experienced welled up inside him.

He would deal with Rinaldo later, and maybe the old Duchessa herself, for tricking him by using a double – but for now he wanted to kill the Grand Duke, the man who had ordered the assassination. If it hadn't been for him, Giuliana would be alive. Enrico's first instinct was to stab the man himself. But no, there was a perfect way to do it – they were in the middle of a duel, after all, one that the Grand Duke himself had rigged. It would be very satisfying to see Luciano kill him.

And if by any chance the Grand Duke managed to kill Luciano with the unpoisoned sword, well then Enrico would stab Niccolò himself and take the consequences.

The two duellists feinted, circling each other warily. The Grand Duke lunged, forcing Luciano backwards. Nicholas stepped forwards and pulled back his hood again. The Grand Duke faltered and Luciano struck. It was a light thrust but the point went in and his man was down.

The Duke's seconds went to him. 'You must stop it now,' said Gaetano to Enrico. 'Look at him. He's not fit to continue.'

The Grand Duke did indeed seem a lot worse than the strike warranted. Luciano had lowered his weapon, puzzled. Enrico took it from him. Brother Sulien came out of the crowd to offer his healing skills. But the Grand Duke was racked with spasms. In his agony he grabbed a red flowering bush in a pot by the path and was showered with crimson petals. It was obvious that Luciano's weapon had been poisoned. But both weapons had disappeared and the Grand Duke's second with them.

Niccolò di Chimici was dying in front of their eyes.

'Poison,' he said to Sulien, clutching his robes. 'I had one of the foils poisoned. They must have been switched.'

'What poison?' asked Sulien urgently. 'Tell me the name.'

But the Grand Duke shook his head slightly. 'I don't know,' he whispered. 'Enrico got it for me.'

'I can't help him,' said Sulien. 'If I had any of the Drinking Silver left . . . but I gave the last drops to Filippo Nucci.'

Nicholas pushed his way through the people clustered round the Grand Duke where he lay on the ground. 'Father,' he whispered, from within the folds of his hood. 'Forgive me.'

And those who were nearby thought it was the Grand Duke speaking, asking absolution of a priest.

Niccolò's eyes fluttered open. 'Bless you, my son,' he whispered.

And the onlookers thought the words were offered by the young friar to the dying man. At least that was the story that circulated in Giglia in days to come. That Niccolò di Chimici had died in a state of grace.

The Grand Duke's body was carried into the palazzo. Luciano stood stunned. Arianna ran to him as if to comfort him but stopped short of touching him. Dethridge took him in a bear hug. Sky was holding Nicholas back from going after the body and its followers. Georgia came running up to them and saw Luciano and Arianna gazing into each other's eyes. Her heart lurched. All was confusion.

'I killed him,' said Luciano stupidly.

'No,' said Nicholas, white-faced. 'I did.'

*

Prince Fabrizio was startled when servants burst into his room and knelt to him. It took some time for him to understand that they were addressing him as Grand Duke and that meant his father was dead. But Gaetano came in soon after, leaning on Francesca's arm, to confirm that Niccolò had indeed been killed in the duel. The two brothers, still weak from their own wounds, were taken by their wives to see Niccolò laid out on his high bed.

'I don't understand,' said Fabrizio. 'There is hardly any blood. How did he die? Could you not save him, Brother Sulien?'

'He told me that he had poisoned his foil and the weapons may have been switched,' said Sulien. 'But his man, Enrico, had disappeared, and the Grand Duke could not tell me what kind of poison had been used. He died before I could administer any remedy.'

Fabrizio bowed his head. It was only too likely that his father had sought to rig the duel and inadvertently brought about his own downfall. Was there to be no end to the disasters brought on his family? But now he must become its head and inherit his father's wealth and title. He would be not Duke Fabrizio the Second of Giglia, as he had imagined when he was a little boy, but Grand Duke Fabrizio the First of Tuschia.

The Pope entered the bedroom, summoned hastily from the Residence by Rinaldo. He approached the bed with his censer and intoned the first words of the prayer for the dying: 'Go, immortal soul . . .'

'Send to have all the bells tolled,' Grand Duke Fabrizio said to his brother Gaetano. 'The greatest of the di Chimici is dead.'

*

The Stravaganti were all at the friary, where Brother Tullio gave them all warm milk laced with brandy. Rodolfo had taken them there while Sulien attended the Grand Duke.

'I don't understand,' said Luciano again. 'I barely wounded him.'

'The foil was poisoned,' said Nicholas dully. 'That man Enrico must have switched them.'

'But why?' asked Sky. 'He was the Duke's right-hand man.'

'Perhaps he was a double agent,' said Georgia. 'Maybe he was in the pay of the Nucci?'

'He is a bad man,' said Sandro, who could not be kept out of the kitchen. 'I know he did murders.'

Rodolfo said, 'I think it was something Sky said that made Enrico swap the foils.'

They all stared at him.

'Me?' said Sky. 'What did I say?'

'I'm only guessing,' said Rodolfo. 'But I think he heard Sky call Silvia's name and then he realised that Arianna's mother hadn't been killed in the Glass Room.'

'You mean he was the one who planted the explosive?' asked Georgia.

'If he was, then he must have realised that he had killed his own fiancée,' said Rodolfo. 'That would have been enough to make him want revenge on the Grand Duke.'

'Will the new Grand Duke – Prince Fabrizio, I suppose – take some revenge on Luciano?' asked Georgia. All this stuff about the old Duchessa had rather gone over her head. The explosion in the Glass Room had happened before she had ever visited Talia.

'Let us say it would be a good idea for Luciano to leave the city soon,' said Rodolfo. 'Even though he was unaware of the Grand Duke's deceit and killed him in a fair fight.'

'But it wasn't a fair fight,' said Nicholas. 'I distracted him. Luciano might not have got him if I hadn't.'

'You weren't to know the foil was poisoned,' said Georgia. 'It wasn't your fault. You were just trying to save your friend.'

But it was as if Nicholas hadn't heard her.

The bells of the campanile in the Piazza della Cattedrale started to toll. Saint-Mary-among-the-Vines followed suit. Soon all the bells in the city had taken up the solemn note and Giglians knew their ruler was dead.

Sulien joined them and went straight to Nicholas. 'Come with me,' he said. 'You too, Sky, and Luciano.'

He took them into the church and set them on the maze, Sky leading the way. 'I'll go last,' said Sulien.

When Sky reached the middle he waited until the other three joined him. He hadn't really thought that Nicholas would walk it properly; he seemed so dazed and wretched. There was room in the centre for all of them to kneel and they did. It seemed hours before Sky was ready to step back out into the world.

Luciano followed him, slowly. Finally, Sulien helped Nicholas out, the boy leaning heavily on his arm.

'Now, listen,' said Sulien. 'You did not kill your father. Nor did Luciano. Or that wretch Enrico, come to that. Niccolò died by his own hand, as surely as if he had drunk that poison. There was nothing anyone could do to save him. He was your father and you loved him, but he was a man who killed his enemies and in the end that was what took his own life.'

He turned to Sky. 'I want you both to go back now. It will still be night in your world. I will give you both a sleeping draught, and when you wake up at home, look after Nicholas. He will need you. And Georgia. She must go too.'

Georgia opened her eyes in her own room; she was clutching the flying horse. It felt as if she had woken from an awful nightmare. Yet the person she used to care most about was unhurt. She could not get out of her head the sight of Luciano and Arianna staring into each other's eyes. But she realised she was more worried about Nicholas. Before she left Talia, she had arranged with Sky that she would come round to his flat in the night and ring once on his mobile. She would have to risk Rosalind hearing Sky let her in.

She dressed hastily in the dark and let herself quietly out of the house. The stars were out and the night was very still. As she walked through the dark streets of Islington, she remembered doing this once before, when she was making arrangements to stay in Talia for the Reman horse race. How simple it had been then! Scary, but easy. All she had had to do was stay on a horse for a minute and a half. Now she had no idea what to do, but Nicholas needed her.

Sky came to the door quickly and quietly and they passed through his flat and into his room. Nicholas lay on the bed fully dressed, his eyes open, but not focused. She sat beside him and took his hand.

'How are you?' she asked softly.

He turned his gaze on her and clung on to her hand.

'Let me go back,' he said.

In spite of how much he had grown up since then, he reminded Georgia of the boy he had been when he decided to leave his world.

She took the flying horse out of her pocket.

'Give me the quill,' she said gently.

Reluctantly, Nicholas drew it out of his jacket. Georgia took it from him and put it with the horse on Sky's mantelpiece, next to the blue glass bottle.

'You can't go back,' she said. She thought about the way Luciano had looked at Arianna after he had killed the Grand Duke, then she put her arms round Nicholas and took a deep breath. 'If you like, we'll destroy them both – both talismans. We have to live here, Nicholas. The other life is just a dream.'

The boy looked at her as if he were still half in Talia and scarcely knew who she was. She would have to try harder or she would lose him. He would go back somehow or would lose his mind in the attempt. And Georgia realised that she couldn't bear to be without him.

'Help me, Sky,' she said. 'We've got to make him see that his life is here.'

Sky was feeling only half-sane himself. He'd been

thinking about what Rodolfo had said. If he was right, then Sky had perhaps completed what he had been called to Talia to do. But it looked as if it had been to bring about Nicholas's father's death. How was he to console his friend?

'Nick,' he said quietly. 'I'm sorry. Really sorry about your father. And especially if it had something to do with me. I'm sorry about all the things we got wrong in Giglia – all the deaths and injuries. But Georgia's right. You belong here now, not in Talia.'

'I feel as if I don't belong anywhere,' said Nicholas dully.

'You belong with me, Nicholas,' said Georgia. Something shifted in her heart and she knew it was true. Nicholas was a real flesh and blood boy she could love. In fact she loved him already. Luciano was the dream, someone she had loved from afar. But she and Nicholas knew each other as they really were.

'I'm going to live here,' she said. 'I'm not going to go back to Talia again. There are some choices you can only make once. You can't go back to where you made a choice and then take the other one.'

Nicholas was looking at her intently now.

'I'm doing now what I should have done ages ago; I'm choosing you over Luciano. What do you choose?'

*

Paul Greaves whistled as he shaved. He wasn't going back to Devon until the afternoon and he was going to take Rosalind out to lunch. He hadn't been so happy for years. Of course it was early days; he had known her exactly a month. But already he felt they were meant to spend the rest of their lives together.

He frowned slightly at his reflection. What would Alice think about that idea? Or Sky? He realised it could make things awkward for them. But he brushed the thought aside. He liked Sky and hoped the feeling was mutual. It would be interesting to have a son, thought Paul. Then he smiled at himself, knowing he was letting his imagination run away with him.

Rosalind was making coffee in the kitchen when she noticed the time. She went and knocked on Sky's door.

'Wake up, sleepyheads,' she called. 'You'll be late for school.'

Sky came round the door very carefully, closing it behind him. He put his finger to his lips.

'Nick's not well,' he said. 'He's had a terrible night. I don't think he should go to school.'

'What's wrong?' asked Rosalind. 'Shall I go and talk to him?'

'No, Mum, he's sleeping. I'll ring Vicky.'

'But you have to go to school. I'll ring her, but I need to know what's wrong with him.'

Sky was saved by Paul coming out of the bathroom.

'Morning, Sky,' he said cheerfully. 'Mmm. That coffee smells good.'

'Better than my mother's,' said Rosalind. 'Well, look – you go and get showered, Sky, if you're going to get any breakfast.'

When he'd gone, Paul kissed her. 'You're looking particularly pretty this morning,' he said.

'Thank you,' she said, smiling. Then, 'Sky says Nicholas is sick and can't go to school this morning. But he wouldn't say what was wrong. I know Vicky's been very worried about him.'

They went into the kitchen. 'You don't think it could be drugs, do you?' said Rosalind, lowering her voice. 'I know they can get hold of them in school. But I'm sure Sky's never taken anything.'

'You're worrying about nothing,' said Paul. 'Nick's much too much of an athlete to mess around with drugs.'

'That's not logical,' said Rosalind. 'Athletes are always in the news for taking drugs.'

'Not that kind,' said Paul, smiling.

Georgia could hear them talking from where she stood behind Sky's door. Nick was at last in a deep sleep and it was safe to leave him. But she didn't know how she was going to get herself out of the flat and to school without being seen. She had left Maura a note saying she was going for an early run and might not see her before she went to work, so that end was sorted. But she hadn't reckoned on Paul being here for a leisurely breakfast with Rosalind. Only she was going to have to get out of Sky's room soon; she was busting for the loo.

Sky came back from the shower, damp and wrapped in a towel, so Georgia saw her chance. It was just her bad luck that the doorbell rang at that moment and Rosalind came out of the kitchen to answer it.

Sky and Georgia froze in the doorway. There was nothing they could think of as an explanation for why she was coming out of his room at that hour. In the end she just said, 'I'm sorry, Rosalind.' And bolted for the bathroom.

'Get dressed, Sky,' said Rosalind, more calmly than she felt. 'I must see who's at the door.'

It was the Warrior.

Georgia wondered whether to go straight to school. But she couldn't leave Sky to face the music on his own. She went into the kitchen and found Rosalind and Paul sitting with the man whose image stared from thousands of teenage bedroom walls. Sky's father.

'Who's this?' he said. Then, when Sky joined them, 'Oh, I see. You're taking after your old man at last.'

'No I'm not,' said Sky rudely. 'I'm nothing like you. Georgia's just a friend.'

'Call round for you early, did she?' asked the Warrior.

'They're both over the age of consent,' said Paul. 'They can do what they like.' But he didn't look very happy; he was disappointed in Sky.

'It's not what it looks like,' said Sky. 'I didn't spend the night with Georgia – not in the way you mean, anyway.'

'She spent it with me,' said Nicholas. He came into the kitchen, looking like a ghost.

The Warrior clapped his hands. 'Even better – a threesome!' he said.

'Will you stop being such a – sleazebag!' said Sky, furious.

Anything less like an orgy than the ghastly night they had passed was impossible to imagine. Georgia had held Nicholas in her arms while he had raved and wept and Sky had lain on the floor unable to sleep.

'I'm going out with Paul's daughter, Alice, if you must know,' he told his father.

'Coz-ee,' said the Warrior.

'I don't know exactly what has been going on,' said

Rosalind. 'But I really don't think it's any business of yours, Colin.'

'Colin?' said Georgia. She started to giggle. It was like finding out that P. Diddy was really called Sean.

Nicholas sat down suddenly. 'Can I have some coffee?' he asked. 'There's nothing going on,' he said as Rosalind poured him some. 'Nothing you'd understand, anyway, and nothing to do with sex. And it's over now – sorted.'

'That's all right then, isn't it?' said the Warrior. 'Everybody's happy. Look, Sky, I came to say goodbye. Me and Loretta are going back to the States. It's been nice meeting you.'

Sky couldn't answer. He felt hugely relieved that his father was going and wasn't insisting on being a part of his life.

'It's a bit awkward saying this in front of an audience,' said the Warrior. 'But if ever you want to come and visit, you know you're welcome. Just let me know and I'll send you a ticket. And I've told your mum I'll stump up for your university. She says you want to do sculpting or something.'

Sky looked at Rosalind in amazement. Then he felt rather rotten; his father could certainly afford it but he didn't have to. And he was holding out this peace offering in front of quite a roomful of people. Sky looked at Nick, who had just watched his own father die in agony.

He swallowed hard.

'Thanks,' he said. 'That's very good of you. I'll think about coming on that visit.'

Epilogue: *One More Wedding*

In the black and white church attached to the friary of Saint-Mary-among-the-Vines, Brother Sulien was performing a wedding ceremony. It was the day after the duel and there were not many guests – Brother Tino, Brother Sandro, Giuditta Miele and Doctor Dethridge were the only people gathered in the Lady Chapel when the principals and their two attendants arrived.

'This has to be the strangest wedding that ever was,' said Luciano.

'Stranger for me,' said Arianna, smiling at him through her white lace mask. 'They are my parents, after all.'

'And married already, don't forget,' said Luciano. 'What will Sulien do about that?'

'I'm sure he has thought of something,' said Arianna.

'Dearly beloved,' began Brother Sulien.

And married Rodolfo Rossi, Regent of Bellezza, to Silvia Bellini, a widow from Padavia. Sulien knew their history and knew how important it was to find a way for them to live together publicly. Signor Rossi would return from Giglia with a new wife, and if she looked rather like the first, well, Bellezzans knew that men often ran true to type. He was a great favourite with citizens, known as a fair man with a tragic personal history, and they would be happy for him.

The little party afterwards was a low-key affair, held in the refectory of the friary, with no di Chimici present. The city was officially in mourning for a period of thirty days, in honour of its Grand Duke. Giglia had suffered many devastating blows, with the Nucci slaughter followed by the flood and the fatal duel.

But the wet weather, followed by a period of intense sun, had brought on all the late spring flowers early and the city was filled with the scents of lily-of-the-valley, sweet peas and stocks. Silvia had carried a spray of early white roses, from a tree carefully nurtured by Brother Tullio over the kitchen door of the friary.

Two brightly dressed figures joined the company. They made obeisance to the bride and groom and then Aurelio raised the Duchessa's hand to his lips. 'I am honoured to make music for you and your parents,' he said.

Aurelio played his harp, accompanied by Raffaella on the recorder he had made. The first tune was achingly sad, more suited to a wake than a wedding, and the guests listened to it, remembering the dead of the last week. But then the music became lively and Rodolfo led Silvia into a dance.

'It will be odd for me to live in the Palazzo Ducale again,' she said to him.

'It will be bliss,' he said, smiling. 'Just think, we never had the chance to live together as man and wife and we have been together more than twenty years and have a grown-up daughter.'

'Don't,' said Silvia. 'You'll make me feel old.'

'You are as beautiful now as when I first met you,' said Rodolfo, tightening his hold on her. 'And this time all the world will know that we are married and nothing shall ever separate us again.'

There were few women at that party, but Dethridge led Giuditta on to the floor and Raffaella stopped playing to dance with Sky. She was vividly beautiful and danced with the flamboyance of her people, which rather embarrassed him.

The friars found it highly amusing that one of their novices should have such an exotic dancing partner, even though most of them knew by now that Sky was not a real friar, but an important visitor in disguise. The liveliness of the music caused even Brother Tullio to take to the floor. He grabbed Brother Sandro by both hands and whirled him round, Brother Dog barking excitedly as they twirled round the refectory.

'They look happy, don't they?' said Luciano.

'Sandro and Tullio?' asked Arianna.

'Rodolfo and Silvia, silly,' he said, smiling down at her.

'Is it wrong to be so happy after so many people

have died?' she asked. 'You and I have both killed someone and yet I feel better than I have for a long time.'

But before Luciano had time to answer, Gaetano burst into the refectory.

'I'm sorry,' he said. 'I don't want to break up the party, but Fabrizio has just issued his first arrest warrant. And it's for Luciano.'

*

Franco the apprentice was driving a cart out of the city gate that opened on the road to Bellezza. He had a flagon of wine at his feet and a pretty girl beside him on the box. The guards had orders to stop all those leaving the city and search their vehicles for any signs of the traitorous Cavaliere Luciano of Bellezza who had killed the Grand Duke by foul means.

'Good evening,' said Franco politely to the largest of them, a man he recognised. Franco was well known for his exploits within and without the walls of the city and had a night territory the size of a tomcat's.

'Ah, Franco,' said the guard. 'What might your business be on the road so late?'

'I am transporting a statue for my mistress, Maestra Miele,' said Franco honestly. 'It is the statue she made of the beautiful young Duchessa of Bellezza. Perhaps word of it has reached you? Another masterpiece.'

'Are you taking it to Bellezza?' asked the guard.

'Indeed,' said Franco. 'And you see I have found another little masterpiece to accompany me on the road.'

'A masterpiece of the street, certainly,' said the man, and his companions all joined in the coarse laughter. 'You won't mind if I take a look at the load?'

Franco jumped down and untied the canvas cover that had been roped over the cart. There was a massive packing case of light wood, packed in by blankets to stop it from being jolted.

'Big girl, that Duchessa,' joked one of the guards.

'Like the woman who made her,' said another. 'Did you ever see the size of her? Keep a whole company of us warm, that one would.'

Franco wanted to punch him on the nose; he adored Giuditta. But he kept quiet. He was a man on a mission and had no desire to cause trouble.

'I should get you to open her up,' said the guard Franco knew. There was a crowbar in the cart for when the statue reached its destination.

Franco sighed. 'You can't believe how long it took us to pack her up,' he said in the grumbling tones of apprentices the world over. 'Sacking, straw, more sacking. That's why I'm setting off so late. It took three hours to get the Duchessa in her box. Everything has to be done just so for Giuditta Miele.'

'Otherwise you're for it, I suppose?' said one of the guards.

'I wouldn't mind if she wanted to spank me,' said another.

More laughter. Franco had an idiotic grin fixed on his face.

'Oh well, let be,' said the chief guard. 'I trust you. Look at that face,' he told his men. 'Can't imagine an angel like that lying, can you?'

'Can't imagine an angel doing lots of things that

one gets up to,' said one of them, setting them off again.

Franco gritted his teeth behind his angelic smile.

'I appreciate it,' he said. 'It's a long way to Bellezza.'

At last the cart was through the gate and Franco was on his way.

Inside the wooden crate, Luciano sighed with relief. He had his arms round Arianna and, if she was cold and unresponsive, it was because she was only a statue.

*

After Gaetano had broken up the wedding party and the Bellezzans had all left, Sky had a long talk with Sulien before stravagating home. Georgia and Nicholas had been true to their new pact and not stravagated back to Giglia again. And Sky felt that his mission in the city was over. There was a sad autumnal feeling in the air, even though summer had not yet begun.

'My father turned up,' he said to Sulien, as they walked slowly round the Great Cloister.

The friar looked at him closely. 'And how do you find him?' he asked.

Sky shrugged. 'He's OK, I suppose. Generous with his money, anyway, trying to make up for lost time. But I don't know him. I feel I know you better than I do him.'

'But you have made a start,' said Sulien. 'Surely that is better than wondering about him?'

'He wants me to visit him in America, where he lives,' explained Sky. 'And I've said I'll go. It looks as if everything is going to be different from what I thought. My mother is getting together with my girlfriend's father and it looks as if I'll be able to study sculpture after all.'

'Then you will be an apprentice of Giuditta's, in a manner of speaking,' said Sulien.

'Maybe,' said Sky. 'But I won't be able to come here and do it properly. I think perhaps I should stop visiting Giglia. I've felt torn in half for too long. At first I had no father and now I seem to have acquired two.'

Brother Sulien put his arm round Sky's shoulder. 'There will always be a third here for you if you need one,' he said. 'You have done whatever was asked of you here and we should do whatever we can for you.'

In the school cafeteria four friends sat together. Sky was telling the others about the wedding and the party after it. Alice was enjoying it; this was much more the sort of thing she liked – not duels and murders.

'At least you got through one wedding in Talia without anyone getting stabbed then,' she said.

Sky had just been going to tell them about Gaetano and the news of Luciano's escape from the city hidden in Giuditta Miele's cart. Then he noticed that Georgia and Nicholas were holding hands under the table. He decided not to mention Luciano.

Sky turned to Alice. 'What do you think about your dad and my mum?'

'It's weird,' said Alice. 'Weird for us, I mean. But I think they make a great couple. She's nice, your mum.'

'Yes,' said Sky. 'She is, isn't she?'

'You're supposed to say – "he's nice, too", Sky,' said Alice.

'Well, he is,' said Sky. 'I like him. But it would be a bit peculiar having him as a stepdad.'

'Do you think it will come to that?' said Georgia, seeing that Alice was dumbstruck.

'What would that make you two?' asked Nicholas. In spite of all that had happened he was feeling light-headed with happiness. He had accepted his fate. And Georgia was holding his hand.

'Close relations,' said Sky.

'That doesn't sound so bad,' said Alice shakily. 'I think I could handle that.'

'I don't think it will happen till we've gone to university, anyway,' said Sky. 'I think they'll wait till then to make it easier on us.'

'Are you definitely going to take up your dad's offer, then?' asked Georgia.

'Yes,' said Sky. 'And I'm going to do part of my degree in California and live with him and Loretta for a year. He's offered to pay for that too and I think I owe him that much.'

'You won't be able to stravagate from there,' said Nicholas.

'Well, I've been thinking about that,' said Sky. 'And I think I'm going to give it up. Hang up my talisman and my friar's robes. I'd better concentrate on my exams if I want to get into university.'

At a staging post on the road between Giglia and

Bellezza, some very grand carriages were drawn up at an inn. The Duchessa of Bellezza, her father the Regent and his new wife, and their many bodyguards and servants were all being entertained by a flustered landlord. The young Duchessa was restless, casting many looks out of the window.

At last she heard the rattle of cartwheels.

'I am in need of a breath of air,' she said. 'I shall go and see how my cats are faring.' Taking only one guard, she stepped out into the night. She headed for the stables, where a weary Franco jumped down from the box and started to unharness the horses, who objected to the presence of the African cats in the stall next to them. Franco's young companion had been packed off back to Giglia at the last staging-post.

'Good evening, your Grace,' he said, bowing. 'You see that your statue follows you safely to Bellezza.'

'I am anxious to see if it is all right,' said Arianna.

'Certainly,' said Franco. He pulled back the canvas and pried open the crate with the crowbar, quite easily, for he had opened it a few times already on this journey and the lid was tacked only lightly into place.

The bodyguard's hand went to his sword when he saw a young man jump out, but the Duchessa laughed and Franco put out his hand to stop the guard drawing his weapon.

'Let us give them some time alone, my friend,' he said, taking the guard by the arm and leading him out of the stable. 'The Duchessa is in no danger from that one. He would give his life for her – and very nearly did.'

'Luciano!' said Arianna. 'I am so pleased to see you safe.'

He took her in his arms and kissed her. And, unlike the statue, she responded warmly.

'Your hair is full of straw,' she said, when they pulled apart.

'I am altogether unworthy of your elegant and beautiful Grace,' said Luciano, holding her at arm's length. 'Do take off your mask so I can see your expression.'

'My guard will run you through if he catches you looking at my face,' said Arianna, untying the mask.

'I don't think so,' said Luciano. 'I think it might be treason to kill a Duke.'

'But you're not a Duke,' said Arianna.

'I will be if you marry me,' said Luciano and kissed her again. He could see her expression clearly now. 'Won't I? Duke Luciano of Bellezza, Consort of the beautiful Duchessa?'

'Yes,' said Arianna. 'You would be.'

'Would?'

'If you asked me.'

'I'm asking.'

'And if I accepted.'

'Do you?'

'I do,' said Arianna. 'With all my heart.'

And she threw her mask away.

A Note on the di Chimici and the Medici

The history of the Medici is as tightly bound up with the city of Florence as that of the di Chimici is with Giglia. The Medici, or de' Medici to give them their proper Italian name, were a family which might have had an ancestor who was a doctor ('medico'). The six red balls on their family crest *might* represent pharmaceutical pills – or that might all be part of the family legend. What is certain is that, like the di Chimici, the Medici owed their fortune to banking.

The first Medici banker was Giovanni (1360–1429), roughly equivalent to the di Chimici ancestor Ferdinando. The Medici family benefited when King Edward III of England failed to pay back a gigantic loan to two other Florentine banking families, the Bardi and the Peruzzi. They never recovered. Cosimo the Elder (1389–1464), who married a Bardi, commissioned Brunelleschi (who built the church of San Lorenzo in Florence and the dome for the city's huge cathedral) to design a palace for him on the Via Larga, or broad street.

The plans were considered too grand and Cosimo switched to Michelozzo Michelozzi, whose palazzo (Medici-Riccardi) can still be visited on the Via Cavour (the modem name of the Via Larga). I stayed one block up the road from it when starting to write *City of Flowers*. It houses the fabulous Benozzo Gozzoli fresco of the journey of the Magi in its chapel, which is supposed to include portraits of prominent Medici family members.

Piero de' Medici (1416–1469), roughly equivalent to Fabrizio di Chimici, first Duke of Giglia, was best known for being the father of Lorenzo the Magnificent. He ruled for only five years, but his son Lorenzo (1449–1492), equivalent to Alfonso di Chimici, Niccolò's father, was in power for twenty-three years.

Lorenzo de' Medici, 'il magnifico', is the one that most people think of when they hear the name Medici. He was a great patron of the arts, a scholar, poet, philosopher and soldier, as well as a great womaniser, though a fond husband, a good friend and an implacable enemy.

I have bestowed the title of Duke much earlier in the di Chimici family, on Fabrizio (1425–1485). In fact it was Alessandro, the illegitimate son of Pope Clement VII, who first called himself Duke of Florence, in 1532. But the Medici then catch up, because Cosimo I, great-grandson of Lorenzo the Magnificent, had himself made Grand Duke in 1569, ten years before Niccolò di Chimici had the same idea.

Several Medici were Popes, like Ferdinando di Chimici, Lenient VI, the first being Leo X (Giovanni de' Medici, 1475–1521), Lorenzo's oldest son. Leo was as fond of eating and drinking as Ferdinando di Chimici, once serving a twenty-five course meal for six hundred guests.

As for enemies, the Medici had far more than the di Chimici! The Albizzi family, the Pitti, the Pazzi, the Strozzi . . . Florentine history is littered with them. The Pazzi conspiracy of 1478 was supposed to kill both Lorenzo and his brother Giuliano. The younger brother was indeed stabbed to death, during Easter Mass in the cathedral, but Lorenzo was only wounded. All the Pazzi were killed, imprisoned or exiled as Lorenzo avenged his brother.

It wasn't the first assassination attempt on a de' Medici. The Pitti had engineered one on Piero in 1466, as a result of which they lost the grand palace being built for them on the far side of Arno, which bears their name to this day. Brunelleschi was their first architect, but building stopped for a hundred years. The restless Grand Duke Cosimo moved from the Medici palace on the Via Larga to the Palazzo Vecchio in 1539 and into the Pitti Palace nine years later, though that technically belonged to his wife Eleonora of Toledo. Grand Duke Niccolò made the equivalent moves in a few weeks.

Although his grandfather Alfonso is closest in dates to Lorenzo the Magnificent, Gaetano resembles the flower of the Medici family closely in being charming but ugly, courteous, learned and a lover of the arts, as well as a fine horseman and swordsman. (He will make a much more faithful husband, however.)

But there is no historical equivalent to Falco. He was invented by me, inspired by Giuseppe Tomasi di Lampedusa's account of his solitary childhood wandering through the vast emptiness of his family's palaces, and by my two distant cousins, William and Henry, devoted brothers, one of whom badly damaged his leg (though, being a twenty-first-century young man, not with such disastrous consequences as Falco). All the rest of the di Chimici are complete inventions.

The dukes and princes of the di Chimici gave all their sons and daughters the honorary titles of Principe (prince) and Principessa (princess). They soon became princes and dukes in their own right anyway, as the di Chimici acquired power in more city-states of Talia (see Dramatis Personae).

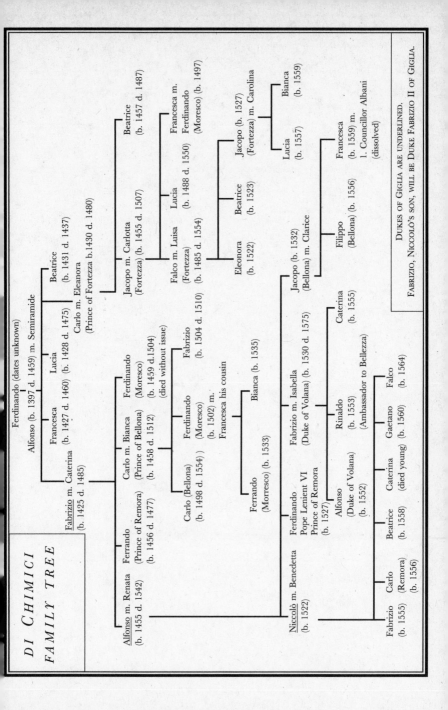

DI CHIMICI FAMILY TREE

Ferdinando (dates unknown)
Alfonso (b. 1397 d. 1459) m. Semiramide

Francesca (b. 1427 d. 1460)
Lucia (b. 1428 d. 1475)
Beatrice (b. 1431 d. 1437)

Fabrizio m. Caterina (b. 1425 d. 1485)
Carlo m. Eleanora (Prince of Fortezza b.1430 d. 1480)

Alfonso m. Renata (b. 1455 d. 1542)
Ferrando (Prince of Remora) (b. 1456 d. 1477)
Carlo m. Bianca (Prince of Bellona) (b. 1458 d. 1512)
Ferdinando (Moresco) (b. 1459 d.1504) (died without issue)

Beatrice (b. 1457 d. 1487)
Jacopo m. Carlotta (Fortezza) (b. 1455 d. 1507)
Francesca m. Ferdinando (Moresco) (b. 1497)
Lucia (b. 1488 d. 1550)
Falco m. Luisa (Fortezza) (b. 1485 d. 1554)
Eleonora (b. 1522)
Beatrice (b. 1523)
Jacopo (b. 1527) (Fortezza) m. Carolina
Lucia (b. 1557)
Bianca (b. 1559)

Ferdinando (Moresco) (b. 1502) m. Francesca his cousin
Fabrizio (b. 1504 d. 1510)
Bianca (b. 1535)
Ferdinando (Moresco) (b. 1498 d. 1554)
Carlo (Bellona) (b. 1498 d. 1554)
Ferrando (Morresco) (b. 1533)

Jacopo (b. 1532) (Bellona) m. Clarice
Filippo (Bellona) (b. 1556)
Francesca (b. 1559) m. 1. Councillor Albani (dissolved)

Alfonso (b. 1455 d. 1542)
Niccolò m. Benedetta (b. 1522)

Ferdinando Pope Lenient VI Prince of Remora (b. 1527)
Fabrizio m. Isabella (Duke of Volana) (b. 1530 d. 1575)
Alfonso (Duke of Volana) (b. 1552)
Rinaldo (b. 1553) (Ambassador to Bellezza)
Caterina (b. 1555)

Fabrizio (b. 1555)
Carlo (Remora) (b. 1556)
Beatrice (b. 1558)
Caterina (died young)
Gaetano (b. 1560)
Falco (b. 1564)

DUKES OF GIGLIA ARE UNDERLINED.
FABRIZIO, NICCOLÒ'S SON, WILL BE DUKE FABRIZIO II OF GIGLIA.

Dramatis Personae

 **Stravaganti**

William Dethridge, the Elizabethan who discovered the art of stravagation. Known in Talia as Guglielmo Crinamorte

Rodolfo Rossi, Regent of Bellezza

Luciano Crinamorte (formerly Lucien Mulholland), foster-son of William Dethridge and Leonora. First apprentice and then assistant to Rodolfo

Suliano Fabriano (Brother Sulien), pharmacist-friar at Saint-Mary-among-the-Vines

Giuditta Miele, sculptor in Giglia

Sky Meadows (Celestino Pascoli, or Brother Tino), sixth-former at Barnsbury Comprehensive

Georgia O'Grady, sixth-former at Barnsbury Comprehensive

Nicholas Duke (formerly Falco di Chimici), Year 10 student at Barnsbury Comprehensive

 **di Chimici**

Niccolò, Duke of Giglia

Fabrizio, Niccolò's eldest son

Carlo, Niccolò's second son

Gaetano, Niccolò's third son

Beatrice, Niccolò's daughter

Ferdinando (Pope Lenient VI), Prince of Remora

Rinaldo, the Pope's chaplain and nephew, formerly

Reman Ambassador to Bellezza
Alfonso, Duke of Volana, Rinaldo's older brother
Caterina of Volana, Rinaldo's younger sister, engaged
    to be married to Prince Fabrizio
Isabella, dowager Duchess of Volana, their mother
Jacopo, Prince of Fortezza
Princess Carolina, his wife
Lucia, their older daughter, engaged to be married to
    Prince Carlo
Bianca, their younger daughter, engaged to be married
    to Duke Alfonso of Volana
Francesca of Bellona, engaged to be married to Prince
    Gaetano

Nucci

Matteo Nucci, a rich wool merchant
Graziella, his wife
Camillo, their eldest son
Filippo, their second son
Davide, their youngest son
Anna and Lidia, their daughters

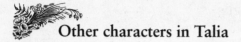

Other characters in Talia

Silvia Bellini, a wealthy 'widow' from Padavia
    (formerly Duchessa of Bellezza)
Guido Parola, her servant and bodyguard
Susanna, her maid

Arianna Rossi, Duchessa of Bellezza, daughter of
   Silvia and Rodolfo
Barbara, her maid
Paola Bellini, Arianna's grandmother, a lace-maker on
   the island of Burlesca
Enrico Poggi, chief spy of Duke Niccolò
Sandro, an orphan, working for Enrico
Franco, Giuditta Miele's senior apprentice
Brother Tullio, cook-friar at Saint-Mary-among-the-
   Vines
Gabassi, Duke Niccolò's architect
Aurelio Vivoide, a Manoush, a harpist
Raffaella Vivoide, a Manoush, his companion
Fratello, a mongrel dog, adopted by Sandro

Other characters in England

Rosalind Meadows, Sky's mother, an aromatherapist
Rainbow Warrior (aka Colin Peck), Sky's father
Gus Robinson, Rainbow Warrior's agent
Loretta, Rainbow Warrior's fourth wife
Gloria Peck, Rainbow Warrior's mother
Joyce Meadows, Rosalind's mother
Remedy, Sky's cat
Alice Greaves, Georgia's best friend
Paul Greaves, Alice's father
Jane Scott, Alice's mother, ex-wife of Paul Greaves
Laura, Rosalind's best friend, a House of Commons
   PA
Vicky Mulholland, Nicholas's foster-mother, a violin
   teacher

Don't miss any of the danger and intrigue in the celebrated

STRAVAGANZA

series!

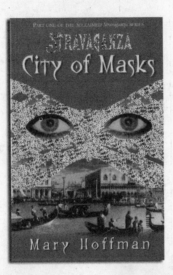

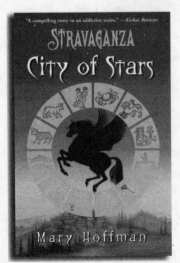

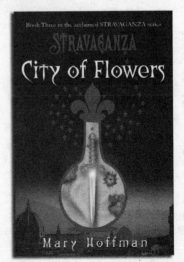

Check out

STRAVAGANZA

online!

WWW.STRAVAGANZA.CO.UK

- Download screensavers and send e-cards
- Create your own Bellezzan mask
- Read new stories by Mary Hoffman, found only on the Web site!
- Discover your Talian name
- Delve deeper into the world of Talia and the Stravaganti

A thrilling new adventure from the author
of the celebrated STRAVAGANZA series

Sixteen-year-old Silvano da Montacuto has wealth, good
looks and a new hawk. But when a man is murdered, Silvano
is accused of the crime. For his own protection, he is sent to a
Franciscan House, where he poses as a novice monk. But
murder seems to have followed Silvano, and soon several
more bodies turn up. . . .

Fans of Mary Hoffman's critically acclaimed Stravaganza
series won't be disappointed in the romance, intrigue and rich,
marvelous setting of Renaissance Italy.

Chapter One

Courtly Love

Silvano da Montacuto was not just young, handsome and rich. He was young, handsome, rich and in love. As he rode on a grey stallion along the main street of Perugia one evening in high summer, a hawk on his pommel and his hound pacing behind him, he could hardly have been happier.

Silvano was sixteen years old, slim and elegantly dressed, with a feather in his hat and a silver dagger in his belt – he was his mother's darling only son and his father's pride and joy. And he was on his way to the house of Angelica, his beloved.

But first to meet his best friend, Gervasio de' Oddini, to show him his new hawk, Celeste, and to ask his advice about how to pursue his courtship of Angelica.

'Like a hunter,' Gervasio was sure to say. 'Study your prey, learn her habits, accustom her to your presence by seeming harmless and kind. And then, when she is tame and off-guard, you pounce!'

'But I *am* harmless – at least I mean her no harm,' Silvano would say.

Gervasio would just smile. He was a year older than his friend and liked to play the world-weary older man, experienced with women, accomplished in the arts of courtly love as well as proficient in the skills of hunting, fighting and running up debts at the local inns.

The Eagle was where they were to meet this evening, their favourite inn near the main square of the city, the Platea

Magna. Silvano tied up his horse outside but took the hooded Celeste in on his wrist, Ettore the hound padding after them. The inn was an ideal place for a private conversation, full of loud-voiced drinkers and smoky with candles.

Silvano made out his friend through the gloom and threaded his way past wooden tables, stepping over outstretched legs. Gervasio was drinking with a man Silvano had never seen before, who slipped away silently as soon as he approached. Gervasio called for more wine and the two young men moved to a table in a quieter part of the room.

'Nice bird,' said Gervasio, admiring Celeste's barred breast feathers.

'From Bruges,' said Silvano casually, while bursting with pride. 'She was trained in Brabant, of course.'

'Of course,' said Gervasio ironically. His own hawk was a small Hobby, all his father could afford as his family were minor nobility and Gervasio was the sixth and youngest son.

Silvano was the only son and heir of the wealthy Baron Montacuto and his clothes, his horse and now his new peregrine all declared his status to the world. The friends spent a good ten minutes discussing the qualities of the falcon, who had been a birthday present, before getting on to the subject of the fair Angelica.

'If only a certain lady could be induced by soft words and compliments to bend to your will like Celeste,' said Gervasio, at last changing the subject to an area in which he did feel superior to his friend.

Silvano fetched a deep sigh in agreement. He was quite happy to discuss Angelica all night long but did not feel any confidence that she really knew of his existence. She was married to a wealthy sheep farmer, much older than her, who bought her fine dresses and jewels and perfumes but that was not the problem. In Silvano's eyes she was as much above him in beauty as he was above her in station and he could not believe she would ever look kindly on his devotion, even if she were free.

'Write her a poem,' suggested Gervasio, looking keenly at his friend. He was much more cynical than Silvano and couldn't see how a well-dressed and good-looking boy with money and a title could fail to impress a young woman married to a middle-aged farmer with a paunch and a wart at the side of his nose.

And there was no doubt that Silvano was good-looking. His light brown hair was cut so that it fell straight to just under his jaw and his eyes were a light silvery-grey with long dark lashes, both features inherited from his Belgian mother. The Baronessa Montacuto was delicate in face and form and what had been detrimental in her, causing her to lose three other sons and a brace of daughters before they drew breath, gave to her surviving boy a grace of movement and a fineness of feature that fitted his destiny perfectly.

He rode, fenced, hunted, sang like a dawn bird and could read Latin almost as well as a monk. But his future would not lie in the church. No, Silvano would be Baron Montacuto with a household of servants, the rents from substantial lands north of Perugia and a beautiful Baronessa to raise his brood of children. Only she would not be Angelica. The sheep-farmer's wife would be fat before she was twenty-five but Silvano would have moved on by then.

Gervasio's mouth curved as he thought of her ample charms. 'Write her a poem,' he said again. 'She'll be impressed.'

A faint pink flush had tinged Silvano's prominent cheekbones.

'You've done it already, haven't you?' laughed Gervasio. 'I knew it! Come on, let's hear it.'

Silvano dug into the purse at his belt and produced a piece of parchment, much scraped and criss-crossed with black ink.

He pretended not to be able to read his verse properly but actually he knew the words without the parchment:

> 'Twice wounded lies my bleeding heart
> And suffers still its secret pain.
> Amor himself shot the first dart
> My lady's eyes then aimed again.
>
> The god has left for heaven's gate
> Who now his work on earth has done
> For me to heal it is too late
> Unless to mercy she should come.
>
> One glance would mend the second scar
> Or could if it were soft and kind.
> One rose but thrown from out her bower.
> The first I'll bear till end of time.

'That's all there is so far,' said Silvano his cheeks now burning.

'That should do the trick,' said Gervasio, trying to keep a straight face.

'You really think she'll like it?'

'She will if you read it to her in your most pleading voice and flutter your long eyelashes at her. In fact,' said Gervasio, getting to his feet, 'Let's go and find her now and strike while the iron is hot.'

Angelica lived in the west of the city, near the Porta Trasimena, a short walk from the inn. The two young men walked past the vast bulk of the church of San Francesco, with its friary alongside it. It held a special horror for Gervasio who feared that he might one day be sent to live there as a friar, once his father had died and his brothers had shared out the patrimony. And he had no taste for poverty or obedience, let alone chastity.

Two young friars, in their dingy grey habits, walked barefoot out of the great church as they passed and Gervasio grimaced at the sight. He hurried Silvano along the road west.

*

Angelica sat at the window of her husband's townhouse feeling bored. Tommaso was off negotiating sheep prices in Tuscany but she refused to set foot in the old-fashioned stone farmhouse outside Gubbio, even when he was away. Buying the fashionable palazzo in the city had been part of their marriage-contract. Old Tommaso brought the wealth and substance to the match; Angelica the beauty. Her family were well aware that she had nothing else to offer: no name or breeding, no particular skills or accomplishments, just her perfectly oval face with the springy blond curls that framed it and her perfectly rounded limbs.

Tommaso wanted an heir; his first wife had been barren and he had waited patiently until she died. Angelica wanted a nice house, servants, and pretty clothes to wear. In her parents' home she had been little more than a servant herself and she had sworn not to have hands as coarse and red as her mother's. So the townhouse had been purchased and for the first year of her marriage Angelica had enjoyed buying furniture and hangings for it almost as much as she had revelled in the silks and lace and fur she could now wrap around her pampered body, according to the season.

But now she was bored. The expected – the bargained for – baby had not arrived. There had been the beginnings of one but it ended in pain and blood a few months into its life and Angelica had used that as an excuse to keep Tommaso out of her bed for many months. And she was beginning to wonder if all the pretty clothes in the world could make up for having a short fat middle-aged man for a husband.

Angelica glanced out of the window and immediately

turned pink with pleasure. There were two good-looking young men in the street below and she knew that one of them was in love with her.

Silvano looked up and saw her. She was dressed in a light blue gown with white muslin at the breast and she wore a double string of pearls round her throat. In his own throat his voice died and he knew that he could never recite his poem to her.

'You do it,' he hissed to Gervasio. 'You'll say it better than I will,' and he thrust the parchment into his friend's hand, turning away from the palazzo to hide his confusion.

*

'I won't, I won't, I won't!' said the girl, glaring at her brother. 'You can't make me!'

'I think you will find that I can,' said Bernardo. 'I am your brother and your guardian and, if I say you are to enter a convent, who will argue with me except yourself?'

Chiara was weeping with rage and fear. 'Then you will have to tie me up and take me there in a sack,' she spat. 'For no one will ever say I went there willingly!'

'If that is what I have to do, then I shall do it,' said Bernardo, quite unperturbed. 'There is no other choice. Father did not leave enough money for a decent dowry for you. The pittance that the Poor Clares are willing to accept as a donation would buy you no kind of husband. And you wouldn't want to be married off to a hideous old man, would you?'

Chiara stopped her raging for a moment. Could it really be that Bernardo was being kind and considerate in his way? But she knew his way of old and there had been little enough kindness in her life since their father had died six months ago. And not much before that.

'But why can't I stay here with you and Vanna?' she asked,

subsiding into sobs. 'It is my home and I could help you with the children.'

'We've been through all this before,' said Bernardo wearily. 'I can pay a servant girl to do that for far less than it would cost to keep you in meat and wine and decent clothing.'

'Then let me eat bread and drink ale and wear homespun!' cried Chiara. 'Only don't send me away.'

'You are being ridiculous,' snapped Bernardo. 'I am not selling you into slavery. Many girls like you enter religious houses and live devout and useful lives. Why should not you?'

'Because I am not without a family,' thought Chiara. 'And I don't have a vocation.' But she was too proud to beg for her brother to show her some affection. She had been starved of that since the death of their mother when she had been a little girl just losing her milk teeth. Their father had been like his son, a man not given to tender caresses or shows of emotion. Chiara wondered fleetingly how her sister-in-law Vanna could bear being married to such a cold fish.

But she pushed the thought down along with her own feelings of rejection. She had been silent for some minutes and the tears were drying on her face. Her future as a nun stretched drearily out in front of her, empty of adventure or romance and she felt deathly tired, as if she really had fought her brother physically and lost.

'I see you have no answer,' said Bernardo. 'That is settled then.'

He had won.

*

Silvano turned aside, biting his lip while Gervasio recited his verses to Angelica. They sounded banal now to his ears, and impossibly naïve, when said in Gervasio's light, slightly mocking voice, and yet he had filled them with all the passion in his heart while he was writing. Silvano couldn't wait to be properly grown up with a mistress of his own and a beard on his chin and some property to manage.

With his girlish features and slight body he was an easy target for his father's friends, who were all prosperous middle-aged men with chests like barrels and legs like tree trunks. Men of substance, who could drink all night and show no ill effects and get up at dawn to ride out hunting the next day. Yet Silvano was stronger than he looked and fearless and could wield the dagger he wore at his waist and a long sword when occasion arose. He just wished he could learn how to keep his feelings out of his face.

But what was this? Angelica was clapping her hands, her soft white hands, and laughing. She was saying that his poem was pretty. And now that he looked at her, he could see that she was picking a red flower from a pot on her balcony. True, it was a geranium and not a rose, which did not smell as sweet, but it sailed through the air gracefully enough, before being caught by Gervasio.

His friend handed it to Silvano straightaway, along with the parchment, indicating him as the poet. Did Angelica look a little disappointed? Silvano put the pungent flower in his hat and bowed to her with a flourish before putting the cap back on.

'Come away,' hissed Gervasio. 'We must leave now. That's the husband coming back.'

Tommaso was indeed toiling up the hill and Angelica's expression told the friends that she was surprised and displeased to see him in equal measure. She would have much preferred to spend the sunset hour flirting with two young men. Now she would have to organise dinner for her husband and listen to him grumbling about the price of sheep. And if she were unlucky, later than night he would come to her room and slobber over her, ruining her complexion with his stubbly face. She shuddered.

As the two friends strolled back down the hill, the farmer lifted his cap to them and they, in a gesture that he took quite rightly as irony lifted theirs to him with a flourish. Nobles didn't display much courtesy to farmers. Tommaso looked sharply at the flower in the younger man's hat and thought he caught a glimpse of a blue dress vanishing from the balcony of his house.

*

Sister Eufemia was in charge of the novices at the little convent in Giardinetto. It was a small community; in spite of what Bernardo had said to his sister, not many women entered the Order of the Poor Clares unless they had a real calling. True, there were new Houses being established all over Umbria and the rest of Italy, both for the Poor Clares and their brothers in the Order of Franciscans, but the community at Giardinetto had only twenty nuns and three novices. Chiara would be the fourth.

'This girl from Gubbio,' said the Abbess to Sister Eufemia. 'I doubt she has any real vocation.'

'Didn't the brother say she was a devout child, so racked with grief still for her dead father that she wanted to withdraw from the world?' asked Eufemia.

'I think the brother would have said anything to get her off his hands,' said the Abbess drily. 'But if we don't take her in, he'll find some other convent that will. And at least we can be kind to her. If she doesn't seem fitted to the religious life, she can be a lay sister. Perhaps she'll be useful in the pigment room?'

'Well, Sister Veronica could certainly do with the help,' said Eufemia. 'You'd think those painters in Assisi *eat* the colours we prepare for them – Sister Veronica simply can't keep up.'

'We must not complain about that, Sister Eufemia,' said

the Abbess, in a tone of mild reproof. 'It is all to the glory of the Blessed Saint Francis himself. It will be a wonder that brings many more pilgrims to Assisi when all the frescoes are finished.'

'True, Mother,' said Eufemia. 'Nothing is too good for the Saint, God rest his noble soul.' She crossed herself matter-of-factly as all the sisters did so many times a day they hardly noticed they were doing it. 'But you know the Brothers here have started their own pigment room? There will be work enough for both Houses before the Basilica is complete.'

The Abbess looked out of her window: she was the only person in the convent whose cell had one. The familiar outline of the friary just across the vegetable garden from the convent met her eye. Abbot Bonsignore had mentioned only recently that his House had agreed to take on production of pigments for the artists who swarmed over the Basilica being beautified in neighbouring Assisi. His new friar, Brother Anselmo, had the necessary skill and would be Colour Master. Abbess Elena had felt a momentary twinge of jealousy that her own House would no longer be the only local convent with a Colour Room; but, as she had just told Sister Eufemia, anything to the glory of Saint Francis could only be a blessing.

There was nowhere else in the whole of Italy where a Franciscan House and one of the Poor Clares sat so close together. Most Clares found it difficult to hear Mass the seven times a year they were bound to, but in Giardinetto, there was a friar free to come and celebrate whenever the sisters asked. And that friar was now Brother Anselmo.

The Friary was the older foundation but the sister House had grown up next door when two women had decided together to renounce worldly life and came to the Brothers for help. At first they lived in what was no more than an outhouse of the Friary and used the same church as the Brothers, taking turns to say the Office, so that the sisters were always half an hour later with their Hours.

But with time, more women wanted to join them and several had their own fortunes, which they used to build a proper convent and a small chapel of their own. In addition to their work on the land and with the poor people of the parish, they had specialised in the grinding of colours for the many artists who were flooding into Umbria from Tuscany, to decorate the many new churches being consecrated.

The present Abbess was the great-niece of one of the convent's founders and she ran a peaceful House. But in the few weeks since she had received the visit of Bernardo from Gubbio, she had felt uneasy. This was the first time she had agreed to take a girl without having met her first. The three existing novices were quiet and obedient; someone less so could disrupt the peace of the Poor Clares of Giardinetto.

*

Angelica lay wide awake and dry-eyed in the large bed, whose yellow silk hangings she had chosen so happily a few months earlier. Beside her, Tommaso snored with his mouth open.

'I cannot bear it,' she thought. 'Did God give me beauty just to waste it on a wild boar like that?'

She thought about the handsome young men and the poem, which she hadn't fully understood but which was full of the sort of pretty words she liked – flowers and wounds and love and sighs. Then she remembered what had just happened and a single fat tear trickled down her grazed cheek. It was like living in two different worlds and Angelica longed for a chance to escape from one to the other.

Mary Hoffman

Mary Hoffman lives in a big old converted barn in West Oxfordshire. Most of *City of Masks* was written in Mary's lovely study there, which is green and white, with French windows on to the garden, a silver mask on the notice board and a vase of peacock feathers in the fireplace.

City of Stars was encouraged by a terracotta tile of a flying horse, bought in Siena, and a shield featuring the ram of the Valdimontone district of that city, where the Palio horse race is held twice each summer.

For *City of Flowers*, Mary went to Florence for a month, then spent the next four months holed up in her study, sitting at the computer, putting on weight. She couldn't find a blue glass bottle just like the one on the cover, so had to make do with scent from Santa Maria Novella.

Mary goes to Italian literature classes each week in Oxford, produces four issues of the online children's book review magazine *Armadillo* every year, reads voraciously and plays with her Burmese cat, Kichri, a little red, who is her most devoted companion and has adapted well to life in the country (an Aga helps!).

www.stravaganza.co.uk
www.maryhoffman.co.uk
www.bloomsbury.com